THROUGH A FOREST OF LIGHT AND DARKNESS

A Year of Stories

Carrie Avery Moriarty

BLUE FORGE PRESS
Port Orchard, Washington

Through a Forest of Light and Darkness: A Year of Stories
Copyright 2019, 2022
by Carrie Avery Moriarty

First eBook Edition March 2021
First Print Edition March 2021
Second eBook Edition March 2022
Second Print Edition March 2022

Back cover image by Sebastian Unrau on Unsplash @sebastian_unrau
Cover and interior design by Brianne DiMarco.

ISBN 978-1-59092-622-2

For information about film, reprint or other subsidiary rights, contact: blueforgegroup@gmail.com

This is a work of fiction. Names, characters, locations, and all other story elements are the product of the authors' imaginations and are used fictiously. Any resemblance to actual persons, living or dead, or other elements in real life, is purely coincidental.

Blue Forge Press is the print division of the volunteer-run, federal 501(c)3 nonprofit company, Blue Legacy, founded in 1989 and dedicated to bringing light to the shadows and voice to the silence. We strive to empower storytellers across all walks of life with our four divisions: Blue Forge Press, Blue Forge Films, Blue Forge Gaming, and Blue Forge Records. Find out more at www.MyBlueLegacy.org

Blue Forge Press
7419 Ebbert Drive Southeast
Port Orchard, Washington 98367
blueforgepress@gmail.com
360-550-2071 ph.txt

For those who create,
whether in big or small ways,
may you find inspiration
in the ordinary and extraordinary.
Your Muse is your friend,
even if you have to fight with them.

TABLE OF CONTENTS

Through a Forest of Light and Darkness

A Year of Stories

Carrie Avery Moriarty

ROYALS

It's freezing," Tristyn said.

"It's always freezing," Erwin replied.

"Why do we have to be out here? No one will attack in this weather."

"The Queen has deemed us worthy of defending her land," Erwin said. "As if it were a privilege."

"Do you not consider it a privilege to guard her?"

Erwin looked at his partner, then around and whispered, "Nothing to do with the Queen is honorable. She is not as powerful as some say."

Tristyn was shocked. He'd known Erwin for only the few weeks he'd been with them, but he'd not heard him dissent since his arrival. The fact that he spoke it aloud was even more surprising. "Shh," he admonished.

"She isn't around," Erwin said.

"But the walls can hear you," Tristyn responded.

Erwin simply rolled his eyes, turning once again to look at the great forest beyond the castle walls. *No*, he thought. *She isn't nearly as powerful as she would like people to believe.*

"No, no, *no!*" the Queen shouted. Jocelyn ducked as the Queen threw a cup across the room. "Can't anyone do this right?" The dressmaker cringed and the chamber maid standing on the pedestal serving as the model trembled in fear.

Everyone knew the wrath of Queen Cecily could be felt as much as heard. Daughter of Tanis, great King of the Northlands and his consort, Divinity, Goddess of the Future, she wielded her power boldly, bowing down to no one. Rumored to have killed her father for his throne, she was feared by all who fell under her rule. Over the years she gobbled up land from lesser kings, adding to her power and wealth. None dared to stand against her.

"Perhaps a break is in order," Jocelyn said. "Give the couturier time to create something more appropriate for the occasion."

"Yes," the Queen said. "Fine, fine, whatever will get these imbeciles out of my presence."

Both the maid and the couturier nodded their thanks to Jocelyn as they hastily made their escape.

"Why do I allow them to remain?" the Queen pondered. "It is clear they are far beneath what is befitting my status."

"Because he created the purple gown," Jocelyn said. "Surely you remember it."

"Of course I remember," the Queen sighed, leaning back on the cushions where she lounged. "But surely there are others more capable. It seems Ioan has fallen behind on what is required for my court."

"I think he simply feels like whatever he does will not stack up to the original masterpiece," Jocelyn replied.

"Nothing will," the Queen said, sipping from another goblet.

"And that is why his creations are lacking inspiration," Jocelyn said. "He knows he can never live up to the first one, never recreate something as magnificent as that one piece was. Your desire for perfection has put the fear of the gods in him. How can he ever hope to please your high standards?"

The Queen glared at Jocelyn. True, she was her sister, but that is where the similarities ended. Cecily boasted light hair, pale skin, and crystalline eyes. Jocelyn was a near perfect opposite, with her black hair, deep, rich skin, and night dark eyes. Both had the height of their father and the slender build of their mother, but only Jocelyn kept the king's dark coloring.

The other thing Jocelyn had that Cecily lacked was patience and an even temper. Where Cecily exploded, Jocelyn soothed. Jocelyn was friendly to everyone she crossed paths with. Whether they were high born or a lowly stable boy, she greeted each with a smile and a kind word, something Cecily never understood.

"I'll call for a meal," Jocelyn said as she walked to the door. "Perhaps that will help with your mood."

"Make sure they bring something sweet," the Queen insisted.

"Welcome back to the warmth," Trahaearn said.

"And glad to be out of the frost," Tristyn replied.

Erwin simply made his way to the stone hearth to warm himself. While he enjoyed the camaraderie of his fellow warriors, he relished his time alone. Since he'd arrived there had been little need for the combat that they were all trained for, so Erwin simply spent his spare time reading. The others joked with him about it, but he knew that many secretly wished they had been taught. He'd contemplated helping some out with it but knew none would ask. It wasn't the warrior way to be knowledgeable in those sorts of things.

"What've you got there?" Tristyn asked when he'd made his way to the fire. "Some sort of frivolous musing?"

"Something like that," Erwin said.

"I honestly don't understand why you bother with those

things," Tristyn said as he sat next to his friend. "They'll get you nowhere in this life."

Erwin simply nodded, paying no mind to what his friend said. He knew more than most of the guard how important the history of the land was to his task.

"Ioan?" Jocelyn asked as she came into his room.

"Princess," he replied sweetly. "I wanted to thank you for assisting me in getting out of that situation."

"It was my pleasure," she replied. "How is Miribeth?"

"Shaken," Ioan replied. "She's not seen the Queen in this kind of mood before."

"You seem to be handling it well," Jocelyn said.

"She can't ruffle my feathers that easily," he replied. "Did you find what she was looking for in her dress? I am happy to recreate the purple gown, but I know she doesn't want to have the exact same thing this time."

"You are right," she said. "I think if you find something similar, with enough variance, you should be fine. What did you have in mind?"

"Come look at what I've drawn," he said as he made his way to a table near the window. "I was thinking of something like this."

Jocelyn looked down at the parchment with a sketch of what he had in mind and marveled at his talent. Not only could he create flowing beauty in fabric, but he had captured its likeness on the sheet.

"I cannot imagine her not loving this," she said in awe. "What colors were you thinking?"

"Her fondness for purple makes me hesitate," he said, moving to a counter across the room. "This, however, just came in from the southlands and I thought it might work well." He picked up a bolt of fabric that shimmered in the lamplight in hues of blue.

"It's magnificent," Jocelyn exclaimed. "I think she will

really enjoy the way it sparkles."

"I'd thought to add some jewels to the bodice for additional shine," he said, clearly pleased with her reaction.

"You know her very well," she said, smiling.

"You would look radiant in this fabric as well," he said.

"But my sister won't want to share it," was her reply. "I thank you, though, for the compliment."

"She has never liked sharing the spotlight," he replied. "Even when she was a tiny tot, she always wanted to be in the center of everything."

"That desire hasn't faded, either," Jocelyn laughed. "I should let you get back to your duties."

"A visit from you is always welcome," Ioan replied. "I'll have something to show her majesty by the end of tomorrow."

"I'll let her know," she said as she exited.

Making her way through the castle she found herself near the bastion of the rear wall. When her father was alive, he would often be found in this same place, discussing strategy and warfare with the men of his guard. While she didn't intend to discuss such things, she did enjoy time spent with men who worked hard to protect the people of the city.

"Your Grace," Trahaearn said, bowing low.

Trahaearn was head of the guard and known to her well. The other men in the room were quickly up and bowing upon hearing his proclamation.

"Stand up you fool," Jocelyn admonished. "I am not my sister. There's no need to placate me with such revelry."

"Not placating in your case," one of the men said.

Built sturdy with long legs and broad shoulders, the man commanded attention, and had he not spoken, Jocelyn would have noticed him anyway.

"I don't recognize you, sir," she said, hoping he would give her his name.

"And you shouldn't," he replied.

"Meaning?" she inquired.

"Twofold," he said. "I am new to the guard, just in the last month."

"And?"

"If you notice your guard you are not being protected as well as you should," he said.

"You'll have to forgive Erwin," Trahaearn said, glaring at the man. "He's new to the work of soldier."

"Only to your guard," Erwin replied, keeping his eyes locked on Jocelyn.

"Have you come to find our weakness?" Jocelyn asked.

Tilting his head Erwin asked, "Do you have one?"

"Every army has its weaknesses," Jocelyn replied. "Have you discovered ours?"

"We are the finest army in all the land," Trahaearn boasted.

"That we are," Jocelyn admitted, without taking her eyes off the newcomer. "But we still have areas that could use improvement."

Erwin nodded, a smirk gracing his lips.

"So," Jocelyn continued. "What say you? Have you found weaknesses within our guard?"

"Should that not be reported to the head of the guard rather than those of the royal family?" Erwin asked.

"Usually, yes," Jocelyn admitted. "However, I would not be the one he would tell. That luxury would fall to my sister, and she rarely listens to such *trivial* things."

"Even when they could mean her safety were in danger?"

"If what you've found puts her safety in danger," Jocelyn said, "then it should already be known to both Trahaearn and my sister, as well as me. Since I know nothing of the sort, and it appears the head of the guard is in the dark, you must not have found anything so urgent as to demand a report."

Bowing his head, Erwin said, "Nothing of grave need has arisen as of yet. I have seen things, however, that could do with some improvement."

Trahaearn began to bolster, but Jocelyn cut him off with a wave of her hand.

"Please," she said. "Won't you accompany me to a drawing room to discuss this further?"

Nodding his head, Erwin made to follow the princess. He didn't miss the expression on the face of the head of the guard and knew he'd have to deal with the repercussions later.

Jocelyn led the way inside the castle walls proper, moving with ease down the corridors until she came to a small room. She stepped inside, finally coming to stand in front of the large hearth on one wall. The fire inside was small, yet seemed to put out enough heat for the room to not be frigid. Following her lead, he stood next to the burning wood and waited for her to ask her questions.

"How long have you been here?"

It was not the question he expected, but answered it without reservation. "Six weeks tomorrow."

"And in that time you have not once been assigned to a post within." It wasn't a question, so Erwin held his tongue. "Is this why I have not sensed you?" she asked, looking him in the eye.

He smiled, a small thing, then answered. "My guess is that my shielding is much stronger than you have experienced, Your Grace."

"Stop with that," she said, brushing the words away with a hand. "Have you come to seek your place as the rightful heir to this land?"

"You're good," he said, relaxing. "Was it mere chance that you were in the guardhouse today? Or were you drawn because I was there?"

Jocelyn folded her arms across her chest and took in the

man who stood before her. True, she hadn't intended to seek out the guard, but whether she was drawn there by him or simple boredom was unknown to her. She didn't want to think she was drawn, as that would mean this man held more power over her than was acceptable. It also might mean that he was more dangerous as well.

"I often wander the castle," she conceded. "It's a large place, and my sister is sometimes difficult to be around."

"So I've heard," he said, that smile still playing on his lips.

"Are you here to remove Cecily from the throne?"

The question wasn't unexpected, but Erwin wasn't sure how to answer it. Instead he asked, "Does she need replacing?"

"Hmph," was all Jocelyn could manage in response. While her sister was good in many ways, her demanding nature and need for power could, and likely would, put all of them in danger at some point.

"That's not a no," Erwin said. "But I assume that if you were to say so, it may cause you some danger."

"My sister's reputation has preceded her," Jocelyn smirked.

"Have no fear," he said. "I have not come for the throne. My task is much more important."

"Did you see the dressmaker?" the Queen asked as Jocelyn returned later that afternoon.

"He is working on something that should be more to your liking," she replied. "I believe he should have something to you in the next day or two."

"Good," the Queen replied. "I would hate to have to replace him."

"Now, Cec," Jocelyn said. "You know full well you would never replace Ioan. He's too valuable."

"But sometimes he needs to know that I could," the Queen said. "What else have you been doing today?"

Jocelyn thought about her encounter with the soldier, but decided against telling her sister. "Just wandering the castle. Thought I might find a book to read in the library."

"You and your books," Cecily said. "Always wandering off in your mind. I just don't understand that."

"You like your real world and I like my fantasy," Jocelyn replied.

"Tell me about the guard," the Queen said.

It took Jocelyn a moment to realize what her sister had said. When it registered, she realized that she had been thinking about the man she spoke with earlier. Hoping to keep that meeting a secret she said, "The book I found was about a princess who hoped to overthrow her parents and take over the land for herself."

"So it was a book about me," the Queen said.

"That it was," Jocelyn said. Nothing did better to distract her sister than to talk about how great she was.

The discussion lasted most of the afternoon, Jocelyn recounting things that happened in their past as parts of the fictitious book she had read. By the time the evening meal was called she was exhausted.

"How long until the ball?" Cecily asked.

"Just over a week," Jocelyn replied.

"And is everything ready?" the Queen asked. "The dishes are planned, the decorations are being readied, the invitations have been sent?"

"Everything is on track," Jocelyn said. "The winter ball will be the grandest one you've hosted."

"Good," the Queen said. "We must remind everyone who is the most powerful in all the land."

"I am sure everyone is well aware of that," Jocelyn said.

"Joss," the Queen said. "What princes have been invited?"

"We can check the list in the morning," she replied. "Tonight, I need to sleep."

"Maybe we can find someone suitable to be my consort," the Queen said. "Do you think there is anyone worthy of my affections?"

"I'm not sure there is a man alive who could handle your power," Jocelyn said. "They will be lucky to be chosen, though."

"I believe it is time I start thinking about having a child," the Queen said. "Wouldn't it be grand to have a baby in the castle?"

"Are you prepared to go through the pregnancy?"

"Oh," the Queen said. "I can handle anything. I am the Queen, after all. Nothing is too difficult for me."

"Well, then," Jocelyn said. "We should begin looking for the proper father for your baby."

"Yes," the Queen answered. "That would be grand."

"You made quite the impression on the princess," Trahaearn said.

"How's that?" Erwin asked.

"She's asked that you accompany her to the ball," the head of the guard said. "Such an honor has never been bestowed upon one of the guard."

Erwin couldn't tell whether Trahaearn was pleased or annoyed with the request. "I shall endeavor to behave in a manner that would bring honor to you," he said.

"First," Trahaearn said. "You must go see the couturier. He will create something appropriate for you to wear to the occasion."

"Once my duties are complete," Erwin began. "I shall seek him out."

"You will go now," the head of the guard insisted. "Tristyn has taken over your duties for the day. When the royal family requests something, we fulfill their request immediately."

"As you wish," Erwin said and took his leave.

Everyone in the castle was busily prepared for the ball, with just three days left until the grand event. The guard was no different, ensuring their uniforms were in pristine order, their armor polished to a high reflective shine.

As he made his way through the halls of the castle, he listened with more than his ears to the essence of the building. While he couldn't detect anything specific from either the Queen or the princess, those around them told him all he needed to know. Those in the kitchen worried they wouldn't have enough ingredients for the inundation of hungry men and women set to come. Maids were hustling around, cleaning everything from chandeliers to chamber pots, ensuring nothing would look less than perfect when guests began to arrive.

Finally, he arrived at the couturier's chambers and was greeted by a young woman.

"This way," she said.

He followed her deeper into the room until she came to a stop. Erwin looked around at the grand gowns hanging on nearly every empty space available on the walls. When his eyes landed on the man in charge, he noticed he was being measured up.

"The guardsman, I presume," the man said.

"As requested," Erwin answered.

"Good, good," the couturier said to himself after his perusal of the man. "This way."

Following along, Erwin found himself in another room, this one full of mirrors and bolts of material for as far as he could see.

"If you please," the dressmaker said, indicating a stand in the middle of the room.

Unsure of what he meant, Erwin simply stared.

"Up!"

"Oh," Erwin said, clearly understanding that he should stand atop the box.

"Right, then," the dressmaker began. "Let's see what we have."

For the next hour the man fussed over Erwin, measuring things, holding swatches of fabric against his face, then discarding them. On and on it went, until finally there was a breakthrough.

"Perfect," the dressmaker said.

"Then we're done?" Erwin asked.

"Not hardly," the couturier replied. "That was for the color. Now, to sketch the suit."

With that, he sat down at a desk and began to sketch on some parchment. Shading and drawing, then crumpling the paper and tossing it into the fire. On and on it went for another good hour before he held up a sheet, eyed it against Erwin, who remained on the pedestal, and exclaimed, "Magnificent."

Erwin wasn't sure whether this meant he was finished or if the ordeal had a long way to go. He hoped it meant he was free to leave and return to the men of the guard, although he was likely to receive some grief from them.

"Off with you," the dressmaker said, making a shooing motion with his hand. "I'll call you back when I'm ready for the fitting."

Stepping from the platform, Erwin picked up his sword from where he'd lain it and exited the room. He quickly made his way back to the bastion and was not surprised to hear the jokes aimed his way.

"Where's the new dress, then?" one asked.

"Are you allowed back in with us rough gents?" quipped another.

"Shall I help you with your sword, son?" joked a third.

"That'll do," Trahaearn said, ushering Erwin to his office. Once there, with the door closed behind them, he asked, "What took so long?"

"That man is a perfectionist," Erwin replied. "Most of the time was spent finding the right fabric for the garments. Then it was to sketching, which he said I had to remain for. I was afraid he was going to have me there while he stitched the pieces together."

"I was hoping you'd found yourself with the princess," the

older man said. "That would have been a much nicer way to spend the day."

"Indeed, it would," Erwin agreed. "No sight of a single royal the entire time I was in the castle."

"No worry," the man said. "I've assigned you as the official guard of the princess for the ball. You are to wear your sword the entire time."

"How does the couturier feel about this addition to the wardrobe?" Erwin asked.

"He'll have to accept it," the head of the guard said. "The royal family's safety is the most important thing. If you must be there, you had better be ready to defend them, whether your sword matches your shoes or not."

"Oh, Ioan," the Queen cooed. "It looks marvelous. You really have done a marvelous job with this outfit."

"I am pleased it meets with your approval," the couturier said, bowing low.

"This is nearly as perfect as the purple gown," she said.

"It is beautiful," Jocelyn said.

"Would you care to see your gown?" Ioan asked.

"Oh," Jocelyn replied. "Do you have it done, yet?"

"It's just finished," he said.

"Why don't we wait," she replied. "I'll come down later this afternoon and see what you've created."

"Whatever suits you," he replied.

When he and the chamber maid left, Jocelyn turned to her sister.

"Have you looked over the names I gave you?" she asked.

"There are just so many," Cecily replied. "How am I supposed to narrow down my choices with just names?"

"I put them in the order of most power," Jocelyn said. "When they arrive, you can decide for yourself which one catches your fancy. Perhaps you will be able to narrow it down some if we discuss them."

"Yes, please," the Queen said with a wry smile. "Let's talk about their stunning attributes. I want to make sure my child has not only the most beautiful mother but a father who is at least passable where looks are concerned."

"Let's start at the top," Jocelyn said. "King Carasius, from the deep south region is very powerful."

"With a name like that," the Queen said, "he ought to be. What does he look like?"

And with that, the two women took the measure of each man on the list. They discussed not only their standing within the realm, but also the physical attributes each had. Having had conversations with everyone at the last several balls, Jocelyn was well versed in their knowledge and intellect as well, sharing with the Queen both the benefits and detriments of each suitor on the list.

Queen Cecily approved and removed men from the list based on each piece of information Jocelyn provided, and they finally pared the list down to a manageable handful of viable candidates. The test would be, which would the Queen choose as consort.

"None of them must know they are being considered for this enviable position," the Queen insisted.

"Of course not," Jocelyn replied. "We don't want to give any of them a false hope."

"I also don't want them trying to persuade me with more than what we have," the elder sister said. "There's no telling what these men would do if they knew they may end up in my bed."

"Isn't that the truth," Jocelyn agreed.

"Who is going to be your companion at the ball?" the Queen asked. "Or are you simply going to take one of the men I haven't chosen?"

"I've asked a member of the guard to accompany me," Jocelyn said.

"A lowly guard?" the Queen said. "You don't have to deprive yourself on my account."

"I didn't want to get in the way of any of those you may choose," Jocelyn said. Truth was, she was looking forward to having Erwin with her for this event. The men of the realm tended to get a bit grabby when the wine flowed as freely as it did. Having him there would keep the others in check.

"Well," the Queen said. "If you decide you need a more refined gentlemen, please feel free to choose someone from the list. As long as it isn't one that I've already picked."

"I think the guard will be fine," she said. She had peeked in while he was being fitted for his suit and was stunned at the ruggedly handsome figure he made. No, she would not be leaving him for one of the stuffy fools that tried to get on the good side of her sister. They were all false bravado, where Erwin was as real as they came; even if he did hold secrets she couldn't get at. That was the other reason she asked him to accompany her. She hoped to find out what he was hiding.

"Off to play make believe, then, are we?" Trystin asked.

"Simply acquiescing to the wishes of the royal family," Erwin returned.

"With the fancy duds to boot."

Erwin knew that some of the other men were jealous of his ability to mingle with the royals. What they didn't know, though, was that he had been mingling with royals his whole life. If the truth about who he was were known by the men of the guard, he would not have been welcomed nearly as easily as he was.

"It is what is required," Erwin replied.

"I suggest you be on your best behavior," Trystin said. "The Queen may decide she doesn't like you. I would hate to have to remove you from the ball."

"I'll endeavor to stay in her good graces," Erwin said as he finished fastening his sword.

Ioan had balked at the idea that his smooth lines would be ruined by such a monstrosity, but Erwin had assured him that it could not be left out. The statement that it was for the protection of the princess had finally made him see the need. Now, with the sword at his hip, and a dagger in each boot, Erwin was prepared to meet Princess Jocelyn.

"Stay on your toes," Trahaearn said. "Don't want you forgetting your place."

"I will do my best to represent the guard well," Erwin said.

"Just don't get in the line of fire when the Queen wants something," the older man said quietly.

"Thank you for the warning," the younger man replied.

"Don't drink too much, either," the head of the guard said.

"Erwin doesn't drink," Trystin quipped.

"I just don't drink to excess," Erwin replied. "Unlike some of you fools."

The comment was said in jest, and the men laughed at the joke. Erwin could feel their desire to be in his place. Most had known the princess for a while, and all who knew her felt she was much better suited to being head of the family rather than her sister. None, however, would make that statement aloud.

"I'm off, then," Erwin said as he left the men laughing.

Making his way from the bastion, he meandered through the halls toward the main area where the ball was to take place. The princess had asked that he meet her near the ballroom in the library where they first spoke. The closer to the room he got, the more unease he felt. Opening himself up without letting his guard down, he reached out to see where the oddity came from. He knew it would be a short while before most of the guests would arrive, but some were already on the property. He couldn't be sure, but there was definitely a foe among those who were there.

Slipping into the library he caught a flash of green. "Hello?" he called.

Princess Jocelyn turned then, and the sight was nearly more than he could bear. Her dark features set against the deep green of her gown drew him to her. Before he realized it, he was standing next to her.

"You look exquisite," he said.

"Thank you," she replied, a flush running up her cheeks. "You are not so bad on the eyes, yourself."

"Only because you cannot see yourself," he said.

She cast her eyes down, a move he'd never seen her do before. She was the brave, strong, honest sister. If it had been Cecily, he would have expected the move to be something she used to get attention, or to get what she wanted. Jocelyn wasn't like that, though. She didn't do anything simply for attention. No, this was a true reaction to what he'd said. It almost made him wish he could prevent her grief when his true intentions were revealed.

"Will you accompany me to the ball?" he asked formally, putting his arm out for her to grasp.

"It would be my pleasure," she replied with a small smile.

Walking from the library, they made their way toward the grand ballroom. Erwin could feel the danger the closer he got, but could not quite pinpoint where it was coming from.

Jocelyn let out a shudder and Erwin halted. They were still a few feet from the room, and no one had noticed them. He moved them into an alcove and asked, "Are you all right?"

"I'm not sure," she said. "Something feels...off."

Playing the role of guard, he let his hand fall to the hilt of his sword, moving in front of the princess as to guard her, knowing full well that the danger was not physical.

"I'm not fragile, you know," she admonished, pushing him aside.

25

"Never said you were," he replied, keeping her in his shadow. "I simply don't want to hear from Trahaearn that I failed in my duties."

With that, she laughed. It was a light sound, bubbling up and bursting forth, breaking the dark spell that had been over them.

"It's likely just my sister's mood," she said, encouraging him to return to their walk to the ball. "She'll have my head if I'm late and she has to entertain the lesser fools."

"We wouldn't want you to lose your head, now," he said with a smile.

"I certainly wouldn't," she laughed.

The darkness still hung in the air, but Erwin felt the power from his companion. She could definitely take care of herself should anything arise. Now he just needed to figure out where the threat was coming from, and whether he should allow it to do what he was sent to do instead.

"They're all fools," the Queen murmured in her sister's ear.

"None strike your fancy?" Jocelyn asked.

"King Dugal isn't bad," she said. "I just don't know if I can handle the beard."

"They all have beards," Jocelyn reminded.

"But his is just so..."

"Long?" Jocelyn offered.

"Scraggly," the Queen said, scrunching her nose up.

"Perhaps we can convince him to tame it," she said. "With the right incentive, men will do most anything."

"How do you propose we get him to tame his beard without guaranteeing him a spot in my bed?"

"Leave it to me," Jocelyn said.

She stood, and Erwin stood with her. She wasn't used to having a man be this attentive and she found she rather liked it.

"Shall I accompany you, your Grace?"

"No," Jocelyn said. "This is a woman's errand."

"As you wish," he said, retaking his seat. He watched her walk away from the table and down the steps to speak with one of the maids at the side.

"I need a favor," Jocelyn said.

"Anything for you," Elin said.

"I am tasking you with cleaning up King Dugal," the princess said.

"Beg your pardon?"

"His beard," Jocelyn said. "You need to get him to tame that monstrosity and look more presentable."

"Oh," the maid said. "I'm happy to do that."

"I knew you were the one to ask," Jocelyn said.

Erwin watched the exchange, and when the princess returned to his side he asked, "Everything all right?"

"Soon enough," she replied.

Erwin simply nodded. He watched the maid make her way around the room, filling wine glasses and fending off several advances by the older men with ease. She found herself next to a fit man dressed in fine clothes, even if they were bolder than most of the others in the room, save the royal sisters. He watched as the young woman bowed low next to the man, clearly giving him a view down her dress. When he reached up to grasp her arm she turned and slapped him, the report ringing through the room.

He could feel more than hear both the Queen and the princess hiding their amusement, and wondered what more was going on. The man stood and brought the girl flush against his body. She pulled back with a strength she shouldn't have and slugged him in the gut. Doubling over and returning to his seat, the man looked up toward the dais where the Queen merely smiled.

The young woman leaned over once again, only this time she placed her mouth next to the man's ear. Erwin wasn't sure what she said, but the man looked intrigued. She left the room and he followed shortly after.

"That's one way to get what you want," the Queen said.

"She is good," Jocelyn replied. "It's not the way I would have handled it, but she has her own resources."

While it appeared that Erwin was not listening, Jocelyn knew he heard the conversation. When the man reappeared, Erwin smiled slightly and turned to look at the women. Cecily paid him no mind, focused on the returning man. Jocelyn, however, looked him square in the eye.

"What do you see?" she whispered.

"He's been cleaned up," Erwin said.

"Anything else?"

"Has he sobered?"

"And?" she prodded.

Erwin thought a moment, then it dawned on him. "He's younger."

"Very good," Jocelyn said. "I wasn't sure you would notice."

"Most wouldn't," he replied. "I, however, am tasked with paying attention to the most minute details."

Jocelyn looked at him, taking in his countenance. "You don't seem surprised about the change," she said.

"The Queen has high standards," he said. "While the man is powerful, he wasn't quite up to what she expects at her side."

"What makes you think she wants him at her side?"

"Why else would you go to so much trouble?"

"Because he is at the palace," she said. "Those who are in our company should be expected to present themselves accordingly."

"If that were the case," he began, "most would be asked to leave or conform. I don't see you making that happen with anyone else. Therefore, I stand by my assumption that she is looking for a suiter to be at her side."

Jocelyn looked at the man with new eyes. "You are far more than simply a man of the guard."

It was a statement and Erwin felt no need to respond. Instead, he returned to his plate and took a bite. He knew the princess was watching him, looking for a tell that indicated who he was. He also knew that he could not let her know the real reason for his being here.

"Are you sure you want to walk with me back to the bastion?" Erwin asked at the end of the evening.

"I have some questions for Trahaearn," Jocelyn replied. "He's expecting me."

"Very well," he said.

They made their way through the castle in comfortable silence. Erwin had learned a great many things while he sat next to the royal family. Some of it useless, but other bits were far more than he could have hoped to discover by merely being part of the guard. While working with the men who kept the castle safe, he'd found a great many things that would be beneficial when the time came to act on his orders. This, however, allowed him to have the information in a much faster time frame, moving his timeline up greatly.

Opening the door to the passage leading to the bastion, Erwin paused as Jocelyn stepped through. They took the few steps in the frigid weather before he opened the door to the building itself.

"Your Grace," Trahaearn said when he saw her. The remainder of the guard who were in the area all stood and bowed low.

"Please," the princess said. "There is no need for such formality with me. I am not my sister."

The men continued to remain low until the head of the guard stood.

29

"As you wish," he said. "What brings you to our door?"

"I wish to speak with you," the princess said. "Privately."

Erwin took no offence to the words, simply made his way to the bunk where he slept and began removing the fine clothing he'd worn to the ball. He watched as the princess and the head of the guard stepped out the door, back into the cold.

"I'm rather disappointed in you," Trystin said.

"Why's that?" Erwin asked

"It's barely past midnight and already you're back in our company," the younger man replied. "I guess you weren't enough man for the princess."

"Do you know why she asked to speak with Trahaearn?"

"Likely to tell him to not have you back in the castle," the younger man laughed.

"How do you know it isn't to ask that I be assigned permanently to her guard?" Erwin countered.

"Not likely," Trystin said. "She has no need for a man to defend her in the castle."

"Really," Erwin said. "And how would you know this? Have you been assigned to her before?"

"It is well known that the princess, as well as the Queen, have a power they can use to defend themselves," the young man said. "There is no need for a mere mortal to assist them."

"I'm far from a mere mortal," Erwin said.

Trystin looked at his friend. He couldn't decide whether the older guard was simply being boastful, or if he were more than what he seemed.

"You're not as powerful as the Queen," Trystin finally decided. "None are that powerful."

"Then why does she have a guard at all?" Erwin asked.

"She likes to have us around," Trystan said. "It gives the appearance of normalcy."

"Not something she would need if she were as powerful as

you seem to think," Erwin said.

"You're like to get yourself drawn and quartered if you continue with these accusations," Trystin said just as the head of the guard came back in.

"Erwin," he called. "This way."

Erwin gathered his sword but left the rest of the garments he'd discarded where they lay. They stepped out the door and he noticed the princess was gone.

"The princess asked that I send you to her quarters," Trahaearn said.

"I shall go at once," Erwin replied.

"Do not," the older man began, then stopped. Gaining some composure, he continued. "It is absolutely imperative that you not cause the princess any grief. Treat her with the utmost respect and honor. Don't be vile or vulgar in her presence."

"Of course," Erwin said. "Did she say what she wanted of me?"

Trahaearn looked the younger man up and down, then said, "If you have to ask, perhaps you aren't as smart as she thinks."

"I would hate to assume," Erwin said. "She is the princess, after all, and should be treated as such."

"And you'll do well to remember that," Trahaearn said.

Erwin stood in the cold waiting for his superior to give him further instructions, but the man stood there, clearly pondering the ramifications of what was about to happen.

"Don't keep her waiting," he finally said when the younger man didn't move.

Wasting no time, Erwin returned to his bunk and gathered up his tunic, throwing it over his head before heading back out the door. He barely heard Trystin ask where he was going. There was no way he would answer that question. If Trahaearn wanted the men to know, he would inform them.

"Thank you for coming," the princess said as Erwin entered her quarters. "I am sure you have questions as to why I've asked that you come."

"When the princess summons," he said. "You answer without question."

"Just because you've come," she said. "It doesn't mean that you don't have some questions. But it is not for the reason I gave Trahaearn."

"He did not disclose your reasons with me," Erwin said. "Simply that I must come."

The princess turned and walked to the sitting area within her chambers. Erwin hesitated a moment before he followed. She stood before the fire, looking into the flames before she spoke.

"There is a danger coming," she said. "I can feel it."

"I will protect you," he said without thinking.

"But can you?" she asked as she turned.

He felt her gaze, felt the penetration of her thoughts. He yielded to her, allowing her to see within him the true nature of his being there. Her eyes widened when she realized why he was there.

"You've come to destroy us," she whispered. "And I've invited you in. How could I be so foolish."

"Princess," Erwin said as he stepped closer. "What do you know of the Boanzir?"

Jocelyn blinked. She had heard her father speak of the place, but had never been able to get more than the fact that they were allies from him.

"Are you from there?" she asked.

"More than that," he replied. He moved closer to her, standing right next to her so she had to crane her neck to see him. "I am the King of Boanzir."

"You were allied with my father," she said.

"I *am* allied with your father," Erwin corrected.

"My father died a decade ago," the princess said.

"Are you sure?" the King asked.

She looked at him confused. "I mourned him," she said. "The entire kingdom mourned his loss."

"Tell me about his death," he said as he guided her to the settee.

"My sister came to me," she began. "Told me he'd been killed in a freak hunting accident. That he'd been shot through with an arrow. She was distraught, like I'd never seen her before."

"What happened next?"

"The men who came back from the hunt were shaken," she continued. "Couldn't believe some of what they were saying. Some stating that a giant beast had slain him, others that it was an errant shot from one of the guard. None of the stories made sense to me at the time. I didn't think anything of it, though, because the medic who had been with them explained that the injury was so gruesome he wouldn't allow either of us to see his body, that he would be buried without a viewing to prevent us from having to suffer from the visual of his mangled vessel."

"So you never saw him," Erwin said. Jocelyn shook her head, even though it wasn't a question. "Which means you can't be sure that he was actually killed."

"Why would they lie to us?" she shouted. "Who would gain from this lie?"

"Your sister," Erwin said.

"No," Jocelyn retorted. "She adored our father. There is no way she would orchestrate such a fallacy as this."

"Not even to gain the throne?"

The question hit Jocelyn like a punch. Had her sister taken the throne without their father's death? Did she desire power so much that she would fake his death and send him elsewhere just to have her seat?

"Where has he been, then?" she asked.

33

"With us," the King said. "Safe and healthy, waiting for the right time to flex his power and regain his kingdom."

"But why wait so long?" she asked. "Surely he could have simply come back to the palace and taken his seat. Couldn't he?"

"Your sister's power is much more than he could overcome on his own," Erwin said. "The fact that I was able to come in as a guard without her being aware of my true nature is a testament to the fact that she has let the power she's gained go to her head. She thinks that no one would dare threaten her place."

"She comes to that conclusion through experience," Jocelyn said. "Several have tried to stand against her, only to be reduced to nothing. Most would rather give in that be exterminated."

"Then why is it that she has never attempted to go against my kingdom?"

"You are an ally," she said. "There is nothing to gain by threatening you."

"Or she knows that my power is greater than hers," he said. "Knows that if she were to attempt to go against me and mine, that we would not only withstand her charge, but push back with such a force that we would be the victor."

"How do I know you are telling the truth?"

"Your father told me to tell you that your rabbit's name was Sampson," he said.

Jocelyn blanched. She hadn't forgotten the sweet gift her father had given her the last time she saw him. While the rabbit was long gone, the memory of him still made her smile. Erwin saw that the statement had done what was intended, show proof that King Tanis was alive.

"Take me to him," she said.

"I'm afraid that I cannot do that," Erwin replied.

"Why not?"

"Your father wanted me to gain access," he explained. "Once I was able to determine your sister's power, I was to report back to him. At that time, we will devise a plan of attack."

"You plan to attack the palace?" she asked.

"Simply find a way to remove your sister," he explained. "We are hopeful that none of your countrymen will lose their life. It is the last thing King Tanis wants."

"How do you plan to remove her from power?" Jocelyn asked. "She'll not go willingly, and she's not likely to fall for any idle threat."

"I see you have your father's cunning intellect," he said with a smile.

"How would you go about removing her from power?" the princess asked.

"Get someone into her bed," he said coldly.

"King Dugal," Jocelyn seethed. "He is your puppet, isn't he?"

"Simply a willing participant," Erwin replied. "He was very willing to take on the task of bedding your sister. She is quite lovely, you know."

"You speak of it as if it is a conquest of battle," she said.

"Isn't it?"

"You men are all alike," she said as she stood and moved back to the fire. "Simply using women to get what you want, damn the consequences to the woman left in shambles from your little mind war."

"Are you saying your sister is that weak?" he asked. "Or were you speaking of your own heart?"

She turned on him, rage in her eyes. He could feel the power ebbing from her as she attempted to hold it in. "My heart is not at stake, here," she said.

"Neither is your sister's," he replied. "She is simply attempting to find a solution to her problem. That she is without an heir. She won't take a husband, either, as she is not willing to share her throne with anyone. Not even you."

"You do not know my sister," Jocelyn spat. "She is a good person."

Erwin laughed at that. "Since when has she ever been a good person?"

"Jest all you want," Jocelyn said. "You don't know her the way I do."

"Then tell me about her," he said. "Tell me why she is fit to sit on the throne, why she should rule this land, why I should willingly let her continue to amass power and lands."

"I..." the princess began, then stopped herself. He was right. There was no way she should be leading this country. Not just because their father lived, but also because she was not fit. She didn't have the best interests of the people in mind, simply what benefitted her most. Pinching the bridge of her nose to alleviate the headache that was coming on she finally said, "You're right."

"Will you help me?" Erwin asked.

She hadn't heard him stand, hadn't heard him move, but he was at her side. She looked up into his dark eyes and nodded.

"What do you mean, a holiday?" the Queen asked.

"Simply taking in the countryside," Jocelyn replied.

She'd told Erwin she'd help him. Now she had to leave without her sister knowing the reason.

"I'll be staying here," the Queen said. "No need for me to go traipsing through the woods in this weather. I'd rather be in bed with my new consort. I do have an heir to conceive, after all."

Jocelyn tried to hold her emotions in check, not give away the fact that King Dugal was not simply to be a consort. The Queen misinterpreted her silence, asking, "Do you not find my choice pleasing?"

"He would not have been my choice," the princess replied.

"No," Cecily said. "You prefer a lowly man to one born of high status."

"I simply choose to find a man who is worthy of my time," Jocelyn said. "My choice is not about an alliance, but rather one of the heart."

"And would that mean you're taking that guard with you?"

"Yes," Jocelyn said. Let her sister believe that she was off on a tryst with the man. Anything to keep her from knowing the real reason behind their trip.

"Well," the Queen said. "Let me know how he is."

Jocelyn hugged her sister, then made her way down the steps to the waiting carriage. She turned and waved before climbing in. Erwin was already inside and smiled when she sat across from him.

"Not willing to be by my side, yet?" he asked.

"My sister already has the wrong idea about this trip," she replied. "There's no need to give her more fuel for her imagination."

"I'm sure Dugal will keep her mind occupied," he said.

"Don't remind me," she said as the carriage jolted forward.

The ride through the region was slow going with the snow on the ground. Stopping each night to rest was a necessity, and Jocelyn enjoyed the experience of sleeping in their tents. It reminded her of her childhood. Now, however, she simply wanted the trip to be over and to see her father again.

"We're getting close," Erwin said after they'd been traveling nearly a week.

"How much farther?" Jocelyn asked.

"Just over that rise," he replied. "Should be entering the gates shortly after dark."

"Will my father meet us?"

"He's been keeping out of sight," the man said. "Without knowing who he could trust, he insisted that we keep his true identity a secret."

"What has he been doing this whole time?"

"Mostly working the land," Erwin said. "He's quite adept at farming. I would never have guessed he were a king had I not known."

"As much as my sister loves flowers," Jocelyn said. "She's never taken to the fields. Always demands that they be tended, but never seems to take an interest when the gardeners would discuss their work."

"And you?"

"Like my father," she said. "I love the outdoors. Give me good soil and the right temperatures and I can make nearly anything grow."

"Do you come by that from your father?" Erwin asked. "Or does your mother play some part in your abilities?"

"The earth work is my father," she replied. "But the ability to keep things alive when they shouldn't comes from the gifts my mother passed down."

"I see," he replied. "Your father is remarkable when it comes to his garden. Not only does he grow the foods we're used to, but he's been immensely helpful when it came time to decide what else we should grow. His ideas about grafting fruits together has been a big boon to our agriculture. The last couple of years he's increased our yield of crops to nearly double what they were before."

They continued to discuss farming and the role it played on their kingdoms. Jocelyn was remarkably well versed in the reasoning behind having a strong community of farmers. Their role in the kingdom was much greater than most realized, and Erwin was pleased that she was aware of the value it held. She would make a good ruler, if her sister could ever be unseated.

As anticipated, the carriage was rolling under the arch to the palace of Boanzir just after nightfall. Jocelyn was anxious to see her father, but Erwin had told her it would have to wait until morning. He didn't want anyone knowing he'd brought her in, either, so they opted to make the entrance less than royal. No one, save a very few close confidants, were aware that he had left the kingdom at all. Most believed he was on his annual retreat, studying with the monks in the mountains. Had they known their king was putting himself in harms way for another royal they would have been more than upset. His people loved him, which was why he felt the need to help King Tanis.

Seeing firsthand the way Queen Cecily treated her subjects was an eye opener. While his subjects felt they could call on him for their needs, the countrymen of the Northlands were fearful of their leader, often going without necessities in order to keep from disturbing her. The princess, on the other hand, was loved beyond measure. More than once he heard the men of the guard praise the younger sister, talking of her kindness and genuine interest when she spoke to one of them. How she took an interest in their lives, their families, and what was going on with them. She was the reason many continued to be steadfast to the crown. If it were left to Cecily, many would abandon their post and flee the kingdom.

"Welcome back," the head of his guard said. "Things went well, I presume."

"Better than expected," Erwin replied as he stepped from the carriage. Turning, he held a hand out and assisted Jocelyn from the coach. "I'd like to introduce you to Princess Jocelyn, younger sister to Queen Cecily."

Bowing low, the guard said, "Your Grace."

"Please stand," she said. "I don't need such formalities. It's a pleasure to meet you."

Standing, but giving a bow of his head the guard said, "As it is to meet you."

"Please have someone make up one of the guest quarters for the princess," Erwin said as they made their way into the castle. "Something close to mine, if that's all right?"

"Preferable," Jocelyn replied. "I don't need much, just a

place to rest for the night. Tomorrow will be busy, I'm sure."

"I'll have the cook bring up some supper for you both," the man said.

"Thank you, Steffan," Erwin replied.

They made their way through the back halls of the castle, climbing stairs to the third floor. When Erwin opened the door to a library, Jocelyn passed him and entered. She looked around and noted that the room boasted a large fireplace, comfortable chairs, and a chaise where one could lounge. All in all, the perfect room in her opinion.

"Please," Erwin said as he indicated the settee next to the fireplace. "I'll get us a fire going to warm us up."

"Do you mind?" Jocelyn asked, indicating the shelves full of books.

"Be my guest," he replied, then turned back to the task.

Jocelyn perused the bookshelves, running her fingers along the spines of the leather-bound tomes. Some were large, others tiny. Each holding universes within. She came to one that was rather worn and pulled it free.

"Boanzir," she read.

"It's full of our history," Erwin said. "From the founding of our kingdom through to my great grandfather's rule. The next volume is on the desk. That holds my grandfather's time through now."

"We don't have any historical documents," Jocelyn said. "Tragically, they were burned when my sister was small. My father said it was an accident, but I'm not so sure now."

"You think your sister did it intentionally," Erwin said.

Though it wasn't formed as a question, Jocelyn answered, "I do."

"And you still allowed her to take the throne when your father died?"

Jocelyn looked at him. What he'd asked wasn't said with

malice, but it was harsh. "She is the eldest," she said. "It was her place to take, not mine."

"Even if she wasn't fit to rule?"

"That is irrelevant," she insisted.

"Is it?" he asked. His tone wasn't one of condemnation, but it did hold concern. "The kingdom is only as good as it's leader," he continued. "Your sister, while gathering more land for the kingdom, is not a good leader. She is manipulative, selfish, and demanding in ways that are a detriment."

"But it is where she belongs," Jocelyn insisted.

"Not if you would make a better ruler," he replied. "She wants the power but doesn't think of what's best for the country. You would put the country above yourself, no matter the cost."

"Which is why she is ruling," she said.

"No," Erwin replied. "She's ruling because she said she should and you did nothing to stop her."

"How could I?"

"Simple," he said. "Take the throne away from her. You would have your country behind you, and it would be a simple transfer of power."

"You really don't know my sister," she said. "She will never give up the throne."

Erwin knew they could go round and round with this conversation and end up exactly where they were now. "Will you support your father's bid to regain his kingdom?"

"Of course," she said.

"Which means you want what is best for your country," he replied. "Proving my point, that you are the more fit ruler."

"It is irrelevant," she said. "Father is alive. He will return to the throne and Cecily will be removed."

"I'm afraid it isn't that simple."

The voice came from the doorway. Jocelyn turned, expecting to see the strong man her father was when he left.

Instead, she saw a man who had been broken down by the magic her sister had forced upon him. He was older, hunched over from the hard work he'd been forced to do the last ten years, and she saw that the spark that once was bright in his eyes had faded.

"Father," she said as she rushed to him.

"My sweet bean," he replied, calling her by a nickname he'd given when she was tiny.

"Why didn't you tell me you were alive?" she pleaded through tears.

"He couldn't," Erwin said.

Jocelyn turned to him and demanded, "You should have come to me."

"We didn't know who to trust," King Tanis said.

Looking at her father she asked, "Why didn't you trust me?"

"Let's sit," Erwin said, indicating the seats near the fire. It was burning well, now, and the heat was welcome after the cold they'd endured.

"Why did you wait so long?" Jocelyn asked when they'd gotten comfortable.

"The curse your sister placed on your father was extremely volatile," Erwin explained. "It wasn't as simple as telling you he was alive because he wasn't. Not really."

"So you did die," she said.

"In a manner of speaking, yes," Tanis replied.

"My brothers and I were on the hunt with your father," Erwin continued. "We were not near him when the magic was struck, but we saw and heard it. By the time we found him it was too late to do much of anything. He was shriveling rapidly, shrinking before our eyes."

"If they hadn't had a healer with them, I would not have survived at all," Tanis said. "They saved my life in that moment, but there was a long road ahead of me if I were to ever gain back any kind of strength."

"You brought him here," Jocelyn said. "To help him recuperate."

"And hoped to one day return him to his rightful place on the throne," Erwin agreed.

"Cecily has grown too strong," Tanis said. "She has not only gained lands, but has taken the magic from them as well."

"If we had been able," Erwin continued. "We would have unseated her immediately. Your father, however, was unable to stand against her. He would have failed, and she would have killed him outright. We couldn't let her know he was alive."

"Which meant we couldn't let you know," Tanis said. "I'm so sorry, bean. I would have come sooner, sent word, even, but it was too dangerous."

"So instead you send a spy," she said. "Someone to see whether Cecily was vulnerable."

"We had to assess her power," Erwin said.

"What do you get out of this?" Jocelyn asked.

"A better ally than I currently have," Erwin replied. "I also get to see the rightful king returned to his throne."

"Nothing more than political alliance and power," she said.

"I would hope that it would extend to you," he said. "Not just for political reasons."

"Am I to be a pawn in your business dealings?"

"You could never be a pawn, Jocelyn," Erwin said. "You are too powerful to be held down by someone else's rule. I'm surprised you withstood your sister's reign as it is."

"What is that supposed to mean?"

"There was a plot to kill you as well," Tanis said.

Jocelyn looked at her father, then back to Erwin, unsure whether to believe what they said.

"Cecily would never harm me," she said.

"Think about it," Erwin said. "She is in control of the

kingdom, has gathered power by the year, and the only one who could take that away from her is you."

"I would never do that," she said. "There is no reason for me to try to gain control of the kingdom."

"Which is why you have survived," Tanis said. "Make no mistake, I love your sister. She is the perfect replica of your mother in nearly every way."

"You never talk about mother," Jocelyn said.

"And we should," Tanis replied. "But that is a conversation for a later day. Now, I think we could all use some rest. Tomorrow is going to be demanding and I want to be prepared for all it will entail."

"What is happening tomorrow?" Jocelyn asked.

"Tomorrow," Erwin said. "We plan a war."

For nearly a month, King Tanis, King Erwin, and Princess Jocelyn, along with Erwin's army, plotted their overthrowing of Queen Cecily. It was not going to be easy, but they had something she didn't. They knew the war was coming.

"How have your letters been received?" Tanis asked one morning in early spring.

"The replies are such that it appears she believes my lies," Jocelyn said. "She is planning a ball in the next few weeks and asked that I return to help her."

"Will you?"

"If we think it is the best course of action to take, then that is what I will do," she replied.

"I believe you should return to the castle and help with the preparations," Erwin said. "It will give you an inside look at what her defenses are. That will help us immensely."

"I'm not a spy," she retorted.

"You are also not a puppet," King Tanis said.

"Make sure an invitation is sent to me," Erwin said.

"Why would she invite you?" Jocelyn asked. "You've never been invited to any of the other balls."

"Tell her you met him when you were traveling," Tanis said. "Let her think you've become smitten with him and that you simply want her opinion on him before you let the relationship go too far."

"I'll not lie to my sister," Jocelyn said.

"Does that mean you're not smitten with me?" Erwin asked.

Jocelyn looked at the man. True, they had spent many days together, talking well into the night about not only the upcoming war, but of how kingdoms should be run. She was taken with him, and not just for his handsome looks. He was intelligent, kind, and had proven himself more than a friend to her family. She could do much worse in finding a partner for her life. What she wasn't sure about, though, was whether she wanted to leave her father alone in the castle. Especially if her sister kept any of the powers she'd amassed.

"I see you thinking," he said. "Are you trying to find a polite way to tell me I'm not worthy of your affections? I already know that."

"I'm worried about leaving my father alone in the castle," she said.

"You know we'll be stripping your sister of her powers, right?" her father asked.

"She is stronger than you could possibly know," she said. "You have been away for a long time, father. What she is capable of is much worse than you can imagine."

"I think I have an idea," he said, and she realized that he knew first hand of her strengths.

"We have a good plan," Erwin said. "I think your returning to the Northlands is the best way to keep us knowledgeable of Cecily's movements. If you're gone too long, she may become suspicious."

"You really think she'll believe that I've falling for you?" she asked.

"I believe you can convince her that the sky is green and the grass is blue," he said.

"Then I shall leave tomorrow," she said. "It will take nearly a week to get home, and during that time I can come up with exactly the right words to give her."

"It's settled, then," King Tanus said. "We shall plan to attend the ball and bring the best gift this kingdom has seen."

"Its rightful heir on the throne once more," Erwin said.

"I've missed you so," Cecily said as Jocelyn arrived a week later.

"There is so much to tell you," Jocelyn replied as she stepped from the coach. "I've met someone," she said.

"Do tell," Cecily said, guiding her into the castle.

"It was the most ridiculous thing," Jocelyn continued once they'd made their way to a library.

"What is he like?"

Jocelyn told the tale they had created when they were planning her return. She'd explained that the guard had convinced her to go away with him. Once they were far enough from the kingdom, he'd changed, turned into an ogre bent on kidnapping her and ransoming her for control of the throne. When the King of Boanzir had come along, he'd slayed the ogre, setting the princess free. He took care of her, kept her safe, and allowed her to recover at her own pace within his castle.

Cecily, of course, was enraptured with the tale, completely taken in by this man's kindness. She insisted on inviting him to the ball, and the plan the three had created was in place. Jocelyn knew that her sister would try to take the King away from her, but she also knew there would be more than one king coming to the ball.

"Ioan must create a spectacular gown," Cecily said. "What is the King's favorite color?"

"I honestly don't know," Jocelyn confessed. "We never discussed anything of that nature."

"Well surely you saw what color he used in the castle," the elder sister said. "That would give a good indication as to what he prefers."

"There wasn't much color, truthfully," she replied. "It was definitely lacking in a woman's touch. Perhaps that is something we could offer him."

"I have something much more valuable to offer," the Queen replied.

Jocelyn knew what her sister had in mind and was nearly sickened by it. There was no way she would allow her sister to steal Erwin from her. It surprised her that she felt this way, like he was a possession she needed to guard. Had she really fallen for him during their time together?

"We should have Ioan create matching gowns," the Queen said.

"I wouldn't want to take any attention from you," Jocelyn replied. "You should have the best gown. I can simply wear something I've worn before."

"If you insist," Cecily said.

Her sister saw through the act and knew this was exactly what she was expected to do, bow down to her sister's power. After the evening meal, Jocelyn retired to her room, feigning a headache and exhaustion from her travels. Cecily, of course, let her go. The next few weeks were imperative for their plan to work. Jocelyn hoped she could play the part without suspicion until the time for the ball arrived. She would be glad when this charade was over.

"You look beautiful," Jocelyn said to her sister the evening of the ball.

"Don't I, though?" the Queen returned. "You are as pretty as ever."

It was a term Cecily used to put her sister down. Jocelyn never minded, but tonight she knew she looked stunning. She wore the same gown she'd worn when Erwin had escorted her to the ball, and she hoped he liked it as much tonight as he had then.

"When are we expecting the King of Boanzir?" the Queen asked.

"I believe he will be arriving a little late," the princess responded. "Apparently there was a mishap on the way, and they've had a delay."

"Then his entrance will be that much more spectacular," the Queen said.

Jocelyn held her tongue, knowing that the delay was needed to ensure that they were both in the ballroom when her father and King Erwin arrived. It wouldn't do to have the Queen be unseated if she wasn't in the room. They made their way to the ballroom, Jocelyn entering first so that the Queen could be announced with royal fanfare. It hadn't bothered the princess before, but now she saw it as grandstanding and knew that her sister simply did it to make a show.

Finding her seat on the dais, she slipped the tonic she'd been given into the Queens goblet. No one saw her do it, as they were all looking to the royal's entrance. Filling the cup with wine, she handed it to her sister with a smile. While not toxic, the liquid was to control her powers, make her mortal, at least for the time being. Once her father arrived, he would bind her powers with his own.

It was a surprise to learn that her father had magic within him. She'd always assumed he was mortal, and that all the power she and her sister held within them were from their mother. Tonight would be a defining moment in their land, one that would be talked about for years and years to come. She hoped it would be a pleasant retelling.

The royal guard announced that the King of Boanzir had

arrived and would soon be coming to the ballroom. Cecily primped herself up, taking in the last of the wine in her goblet, then turned to her sister.

"Do I look all right?" she asked.

"You look splendid," Jocelyn said. It was true, her sister was a beautiful woman. Too bad that beauty didn't penetrate the surface to the soul of the woman.

The herald called out the King's arrival and in walked Erwin, King Tanis at his right. Their true appearance had been shrouded in glamour, but Jocelyn knew it was them because she was immune to the glamour. Her sister, however, was taken in by Erwin's appearance. They'd been meticulous in designing his appearance so that it would be the most pleasing to her.

He walked to the dais and bowed low. "Your Majesty," he said. "It is an honor to be invited to your gala."

Cecily was completely under his spell. "It is a shame I haven't invited you before now," she said. "How I've missed the opportunity to spend time with such an honorable noble. Your kindness to my sister is deeply appreciated."

"It was no trouble at all," he said, bowing slightly to the princess. "She was in danger, and I wouldn't have that. I'm just happy I was able to protect her."

"Please," Cecily said. "Won't you join us on the dais?"

Again, Erwin bowed low, then he and King Tanis climbed the steps and settled themselves next to the Queen.

"We feast tonight in honor of our guests," the Queen said. "They've saved our beloved princess, and my dear sister, from a fate that none would desire."

The rest of the guests gave out a rousing cheer and the meal continued.

As the evening progressed, Jocelyn began to feel a darkness within the room, something she'd felt at the last ball. She'd dismissed it the last time after her conversation with King Erwin, but it was back, and definitely not coming from him. He caught her eye and she could see that he felt it, too.

Without warning, a dark cloud rose from the center of the room. Suddenly, the guard were around the dais and Erwin was next to her, shielding her from whatever may arise.

"Show yourself," the Queen shouted.

The fog gathered in the center of the room, and from the middle of it rose a being. Concealed in a cloak, the figure turned toward the dais. Eyes shone from under the hood and a voice that was deep and not quite real came from it.

"You are not the true ruler," it said. "You are an imposter. You do not belong."

It raised its arm, though they couldn't see any structure, simply more black fog oozing from the ends of the cloak.

"The King is here," it continued. "He sits amongst us all. He was never gone."

Jocelyn looked to her father, cloaked as he was in the glamour, and saw him smile.

"Beg for mercy, woman," the being said. "Though you do not deserve it."

"What are you going on about?" Cecily shouted.

She raised her hand to drive the being away, but it simply laughed.

"You are powerless," it said. "Stripped by those who know the truth."

Jocelyn saw true fear in her sister's eyes then. Never had she seen anything like what was manifesting in the middle of the room. The power it emitted could be felt, pushing against her body as it drifted closer.

"Why did you steal the throne?" it asked. "Because you sought the power you thought it held."

The answer didn't make sense to Jocelyn, but she didn't have time to think too long on it. The being was now atop the dais, floating along the table, though not truly there.

"The King of the Northlands is alive and well," it said.

"He's dead," Cecily screamed. "I killed him."

"You are not that powerful," the being laughed. "Always the petulant child, wanting what you couldn't have. Thinking you were greater than what you truly were. I thought you would have learned from your mistakes, but I was wrong."

"Divinity, stop."

Cecily looked at the man on the dais, confused.

"Tanis," the being said. "You should have controlled her better."

"Perhaps if you'd stuck around," he said. "She was more yours than mine."

"Who are you?" Cecily cried.

Allowing the glamour to fall away, King Tanis stood tall and proud. "Hello, daughter."

"Father?" Cecily whispered. "But, you're dead."

"Not nearly as much as you'd hoped," he replied.

Erwin watched as the King moved toward his eldest daughter, allowing the glamour to fall from himself at the same time.

"What did you hope to gain by killing me?" the King asked.

"I wouldn't," Cecily stammered.

"Silence," the being said. "Sit." As if forced, Cecily sat in a chair, but not on the throne. "Listen, child," the apparition said.

Suddenly, the smoke and fog faded and a tall, pale, beautiful woman stood where it was.

"Mother?" Cecily asked.

"You've been naughty," she replied.

"But," the elder sister stammered.

"You should have come back sooner. I've missed you."

The Goddess made her way to the throne, embracing her husband. "And I've missed you," she said.

"Whatever are we to do with our child?" he asked.

Divinity looked at her daughter and sighed. "She'll need to learn to be a better person," she said sadly.

"And we accomplish this how?" the King asked.

"By making her know what it is like to be powerless," the Goddess said.

"I've done that," the King replied.

"And removing the temptation from her grasp," the mother said. "She will learn to think of others before herself. It's a lesson she should have been taught much sooner."

"We have not done our duty," the King said. "For that, we have caused our subjects to pay."

"Then she will become one of them," Divinity said.

Jocelyn watched as her sister began to shake, both in fear and as a result of the magic that was being thrust upon her by their mother.

"Stop," she said.

Both the King and Goddess looked at their younger daughter.

"She won't survive," Jocelyn said. "It would kill her to become a peasant."

"What do you propose, daughter?" the mother asked.

"Simply strip her of power," she said. "That is punishment enough."

"You are kinder than I would have expected," Divinity said. "How is it that you don't hate your sister?"

"While she's not perfect," Jocelyn began, "she is still family. You love your family, no matter what. Whether I liked it or not, she kept me safe this last decade. She could have killed me or banished me, but she didn't. She kept me close and safe. For that, she deserves some credit."

Tanis looked at his younger daughter and smiled. "You are truly fit to rule this land," he said.

"Not until it is my time," she replied.

"Or until you find another land to rule," her mother said.

Jocelyn turned and looked at Erwin and smiled. Yes, she might just find another land that was better suited for her to rule. One where she could partner with someone who was as strong as her parents, and worthy of her affection.

Cecily stared as the others talked until she finally tried to escape.

"You are going nowhere," Divinity said. "I neglected my duties as a mother to you, and that is on me. From now on, you will do as you are told. You will learn kindness, compassion, and respect."

"But we will teach you in love," Tanis said as he took his wife's hand.

Late summer saw the wedding of King Erwin of Boanzir and Princess Jocelyn of the Northlands. It was attended by nearly everyone in the region. When they welcomed their first child, a son, he was named after Erwin's father, Caillin. Their second child, a daughter they named Eimile, was born two short years later. They grew to be kind, caring, and compassionate people, just like their parents.

Cecily never regained any of her powers, choosing a life of solitude in the castle without setting foot out of her room for the remainder of her life. Many speculated that she was kept as a prisoner, but Jocelyn knew it was her sister's own choosing.

King Tanis ruled the land with his wife, the Goddess, at his side. When his time in the world was coming to an end, he decreed that the lands should be ruled by Boanzir. Young Caillin began ruling the land at the age of twenty-one and continued to rule the way his parents and grandparents did, with kindness, compassion, and with the people of his lands best interest in mind.

Generation after generation followed in their footsteps.

Some tried to take control of the lands, but the lessons learned by the once-queen Cecily were stories that were handed down as a warning. None wanted a repeat of that time.

IMMUNITY

W ake up, love."

The voice was warm and sensuous, calling him from the depths of blackness, beckoning him from death.

"That's it," she coaxed. "Come back to me."

He inhaled sharply, drawing breath through a parched mouth. He was so thirsty, desperate for a quenching cup of cool water. Atop that, he was famished. Like he could eat for a week and still not be satiated.

"Open up," she said. "Open those beautiful blue eyes for me, love."

Blinking, he let his eyes adjust to the light in the room. It wasn't bright, but more than he wanted at the moment. Finally, he turned to see a woman who was more beautiful than any creature that ever existed. Raven dark hair, porcelain skin, lips like rubies, and eyes deep as the ocean.

"There they are," she said as she smiled. "Thought I might have lost you."

He worked his mouth, trying to convey his thirst, but couldn't make the words form.

"Up you go," she said, lifting him easily from prone to sitting. "Drink," she commanded.

Taking the goblet, he quenched his thirst with the thick liquid within, drinking it down so quickly he nearly choked, yet not able to consume it fast enough.

"Slow down, love," she said as she pulled the goblet from his lips. "There's more where that came from. Don't want you getting sick on your first taste."

Relinquishing the cup, he tried to speak, but had to swallow several times before he could form words.

"No rush," she said, laying a hand along the side of his face, caressing his cheek. "We have all the time in the world for questions. Rest now. I'll be back soon."

The words were like a spell, pressing him into the darkness once again. He let himself tumble into it, relinquishing the world around him.

"How is he?"

The voice was foreign and far off. He could feel more than hear the words, and that confused him some.

"Soon," the woman said. "Very soon."

Flashes and snippets of conversations flitted around him, yet he couldn't make sense of any of the words. Shrouded in darkness he felt safe, yet something teased the back of his mind saying he should flee. Nothing made sense, and still it was all comfortable and clear.

"That's it," she said.

Again he opened his eyes and saw the raven haired beauty.

"Drink."

She pressed the goblet to his lips and he was unable to resist quenching his parched throat.

"Well done, love," she said.

He tried once more to speak, but was unable to form words.

"Just a little more sleep," she said. "You should be good by tomorrow."

She pressed her lush lips to his and he drank her in, consuming her in that moment, with that intimate touch. He was hers to do with as she pleased, and he would not argue. Falling back on the pillows he was once again consumed by the darkness.

A deep, earthy smell consumed him as he took in a deep breath. Blinking, he opened his eyes to take in the room. Candles lined the walls, encased in sconces giving the room a warm feel. Satin sheets wrapped him, and his head rested on plush pillows. The walls were stone, but not masonry. Thick timber fitted with iron was set in the wall across from him, the only portal he could see.

Sitting, he felt a gnawing ache in his stomach. He looked around and saw a goblet on a table next to the bed. Lifting it, he took a sip, then gulped the remaining contents down swiftly. When he'd finished, he wiped his mouth with the back of his hand.

Slow blinks could not remove the clear truth from his mind. The deep red streak on the back of his hand made it clear what he'd consumed. His scream consumed him as he once again descended into darkness.

"Shh," her voice soothed. "You're safe."

He knew the voice, but couldn't place it. Then he remembered.

"No," he shouted.

"You're safe," she said again, using that soothing quality she had.

Pulling from her grasp, he opened his eyes, fear consuming him. He continued to retreat from her, even as she advanced on him.

"My love," she pleaded.

"No," he shouted once again. "Stay away. What are you?"

He saw the words hit her, taking her back a step. She was beautiful beyond comprehension, but he knew there was something evil within.

"You are mine," she whispered.

He felt the tug of some invisible force, felt as if he were being drawn to her, but he held fast in his position on the opposite side of the bed.

"What are you?" he asked again.

In a flash she was against him, pressing his larger frame against the rough wall, her body solid as steel.

"Your best dream and your worst nightmare," she said, then kissed him.

It wasn't the gentle kiss of a lover, but that of a dominant. She controlled it, pressing harder, forcing his lips to open, thrusting her tongue inside. He could taste her essence, a heady combination of flowers and blood. There was nothing he could do to stop her assault, no way to break the control she had over him. He was a slave to her wishes.

"Milady."

The voice broke the kiss and he was thankful. While she moved her head away, she kept him pinned where he stood.

"Decentius," she said.

"He can still break," Decentius said. "Take your time with him."

She stepped back, releasing him from her hold. He stood where he was, unsure whether moving or remaining still would be safer. When she walked across the room, he took in her generous curves draped in a deep red gown. She was barefoot, padding across the white tile in a silent saunter, swinging her hips provocatively. He couldn't help but enjoy the show she put on.

"I've been playing with humans longer than you've been alive," she said. "I know how fragile they can be. Besides," she continued, turning to look at the man against the wall. "I'm not sure if I'll bring him all the way. He's complicated, it seems."

"Shall I have him disposed of?" Decentius asked.

"I think I'll play with him a little longer," she replied. "Who knows. I might just turn him after all."

"My name is John Smith," he began. "I am twenty-nine years old and I live in Jamestown. I have two brothers, both younger than me. Their names are Jake and James. I was on vacation in London when something happened."

He stopped there. He wasn't sure why he was speaking these words out loud, just that he felt like he had to keep reminding himself who he was. It had been weeks since the encounter with the woman, the beautifully cruel woman who was keeping him as a hostage or a prisoner or something. Had his family looked for him? Were they still looking, or did they think he was dead? Would he ever see them again? These questions plagued him as the days wore on.

The door could not be opened from the inside. He'd tried so many times, but it simply wouldn't budge. He didn't know how long he'd been there, only that he'd not seen the woman since that one encounter.

Decentius brought him food, real food, every day. The goblet he remembered drinking from was nowhere in sight, now, but he knew he'd drunk blood. The terrifying thing was, he'd not only enjoyed drinking it, but craved it still. Bread, cheese, fruits, and water were what the man brought each day, that's all. No blood, thankfully. John wasn't sure he would be able to turn it down if he'd been given the choice. It had taken a couple of days for John to trust Decentius, but eventually they'd come to an agreement. John would stop trying to attack him each time he entered, and Decentius would tell him everything he was allowed when he came in.

Unfortunately, what Decentius was allowed to tell John was

a very small amount of information. They were still in London, they were in a castle that was not abandoned, but was also not occupied, and they were not allowed to go outside. When John had asked where the food came from, Decentius told him it was delivered daily by an "associate" of the family.

"Is she a—?" John had tried to ask early on.

"Don't ask that question," Decentius had interrupted him to say.

John didn't know whether that meant the man wouldn't answer it, or that he wouldn't be able to stop himself if it were asked. John knew the lore, the legends that had been passed down through time in the form of books, movies, and tall tales. What he didn't know, was whether any of that was factual. He had so many questions, things he needed to know in order to formulate a way to escape. And he would escape, whether it was alive or dead, he was not going to spend any more time than necessary in this place. It had been too long already.

"He won't succumb," Decentius said.

"I can convince him," Lilith replied.

"You are one of the most powerful," he said.

"Which is why I will bend him to my will," she replied.

"This one is different," he said. "Stronger somehow."

"He's human," she replied. "They are weak compared to us."

"No disrespect," he said, "but this one is different."

"How long have I lived?"

"Centuries," he replied.

"And how many have tried to resist me?"

"Hundreds."

"How many have succeeded?"

"None to date," Decentius said.

"Exactly," Lilith replied. "None. I am stronger because of

their attempts, too. Their resistance increased my strength. When I consumed them, they added to my power."

"Yet you have not been able to control him," he said.

"Do you doubt me?"

"I only wish to caution you," he said. "As I said, you are one of the most powerful."

"Exactly," she replied.

"But you knew this day would come," Decentius said. "Knew there was to be one who would withstand your powers."

"Legends do not interest me," she said.

"Yet this one seems to be more than mere myth," he replied.

She glared at him for a moment, then said, "I will win this battle."

John paced the room, exactly 74 steps from door to wall, the same across. Large compared to some cells, but still a confinement he didn't enjoy. He had to come up with a plan, a way to get into the good graces of the woman in command. He just didn't know how to do it. Decentius had been kind, bringing him food and water regularly. The man even brought him a few items of clothing and fresh towels and soap, along with a stack of books for him to read.

"When will she come back?" he asked.

"When she thinks you're ready," Decentius replied.

"Ready for what?" John asked.

"For her to complete the transformation," the other man said.

"She's planning to turn me into a..."

"Stop," Decentius interrupted him. "You must not speak that word."

"Why not?" John asked.

"Trust me," he replied. "It would not be good for you if you did."

"But she is planning to make me like her, right?" he asked.

"She will," Decentius replied. "Make no mistake, she is patient and strong. She will get what she wants."

"What does she want?"

"You," the man said.

"Why?"

"I'm not sure," the man confessed. "Something about you is different. It's like you call to a deeper level within her and she cannot resist."

"I don't understand what's so special about me," John said.

"Neither do I," Decentius replied. "But you've got something she wants."

"Are you sure?" Decentius asked.

"Do it," Lilith replied.

Decentius took the young woman to the room where John stayed. He unlocked the door and let her in, closing it behind her. He didn't go in the room.

"Hi," she said.

"Hello," John replied. "Are you one of them?"

"I don't know what you mean," the woman replied.

"Blood sucker," he began. "Night walker, vam—," he stopped himself before he finished the word. Something kept him from uttering it out loud.

"Are you high?" she asked.

"Not at all," he replied.

"You know those things don't exist, right?"

"I used to," he said. "Then I ended up here."

She cocked her head at him, taking him in fully. "I think you're high," she said.

John sighed and said, "Never mind. Just go."

"Go where?" she asked. "This is my room. Maybe you

should go."

"Your room?" he asked.

"Yeah," she replied, walking to the bed and jumping on. "And if you don't mind, I'd like to take a nap."

He blinked at her, unsure what to make of this new situation. This woman was around his age, if a few years younger, and looked completely different than either the other woman or Decentius.

"I can't really go anywhere," he said. "The door doesn't open from the inside."

"Nonsense," she said, getting up and walking to it. She twisted the knob and it opened without a problem. "There you go, all fixed."

Hesitantly he stepped to the door she held wide open. It only took a moment for him to make the decision that he should try to leave.

"Thanks," he said and stepped through the portal.

"Buh bye," she replied, then slammed the door behind him.

"Huh," he said as he looked at the door.

He looked around the hallway trying to figure out which way he should go. To the left it stretched into a darkness he couldn't see into, but to the right it was lit with the same candles that were in the room. It was clear that whoever had orchestrated this release wanted him to go to the right, and he'd never been one to follow instructions too well.

It didn't take long before he was completely blind, no light around him meant he couldn't see anything, not the floor, the walls, or anything that may be lurking in the dark. With his hand on the wall, he continued forward, stubborn as he was. The trip was slow going, him shuffling his feet along the floor to make sure he didn't stumble on anything that might be down there. He estimated he'd been walking down the hallway for about ten minutes when he heard them. It was soft at first, but it grew louder with every step he took, until finally he was able to make out a word.

"Help."

He continued along the hallway, listening carefully for any more voices, when his hand brushed from the stone walls onto a wooden door. Pressing his ear against it, he listened again. Nothing was moving in the room that he could hear.

"Where are you?" he asked aloud.

"Lost, little boy?"

The voice was just as sultry as he remembered. He pressed his body against the door, hoping that he couldn't be seen just as he couldn't see her.

"I asked you a question," she demanded.

He held his breath, hoping that she'd not be able to find him.

"So naïve," she said. "I can see you, even if you can't see me. Now, are you lost?"

Her hand caressed his cheek and he pulled away.

"Jumpy, aren't we?"

Candles flickered to light and he had to close his eyes to the intrusion.

"Now you can see me," she said.

Opening his eyes, he saw the beauty standing before him. Dressed in the same red satin she wore before, she appeared to have not changed at all, as if the time he'd spent alone in that room hadn't happened.

"Were you trying to run away?" she asked. "Or were you trying to find me?"

"Why are you holding me?" he asked.

"I'm not," she replied with a smile.

"Then show me the way out," he demanded.

"Find it yourself," she said, then turned and sauntered up the hallway from where he came.

He resisted the urge to follow her, instead walking further down the hallway. If there were someone who needed help, he should find them.

"Son of a bitch," he shouted.

He'd been walking for the better part of an hour, continuing down the hallway. Candles flickering to light as he approached, as if they were welcoming him in. He'd opened the door he first found, but it only held a small closet with not much in it, save a handful of pails and mops. The further he went, the thicker the air got, as if he were getting close to sea level and the ocean was just on the other side of the walls.

Now, though, he found himself at a dead end. A wall, just like the ones along the side, stood in front of him blocking his way. He'd pushed against it, thinking that perhaps it was an illusion or something, but it was as solid as the stone it was made from.

"Now what?" he asked himself.

With an exasperated sigh he turned and headed back the way he came.

When he first heard the screams, he wasn't sure what it was. The closer he got to the room he'd been living in, the clearer it became. Definitely screams of terror and pain. He wondered if it were the young woman he left in the room, or if someone else was screaming. Then they abruptly stopped, cut off mid scream.

He'd been running when he realized they were screams, but stopped short as soon as they halted. With a deep breath, he began to run toward where he thought the screams were coming from, not sure what he would do once he arrived.

The door to the room he'd been in was wide open, so he peered in. White tile awash with blood met his eyes, and the copper smell assaulted his sense of smell and taste. As he raised his eyes to the bed he saw her, head hanging off the edge of the

65

bed, throat clearly gorged, blood coloring her blonde hair a horrific shade of brownish red. He wouldn't have thought they'd leave this much blood in the room, but someone had obviously torn this poor girl's throat out.

"Oh."

He jumped at the quiet sound, turning to see the beauty behind him.

"You did this," he accused.

She looked at him, eyes wide, tears pooling in her lashes, and stuttered, "Never."

And John believed her. Unsure why, he could clearly tell she was shaken by the scene before them.

"Decentius!" she roared.

Nearly instantaneously, the man summoned was standing beside the woman.

"Oh, no," he said. "Not sweet Jane."

John heard the sadness in the other man's voice and wondered whether he was mistaken about them.

"Find them," the woman said, her voice steel. "Bring them to me in chains."

Without waiting for a response, she turned and stepped into the room, carefully stepping around the gore on the ground. She closed the door and John heard a lock thrown.

"Best leave her be for a while," Decentius said.

"Who did this?" John asked.

"Rogues," was all the other man said. "Come with me."

Decentius turned and began up the long hallway. John only hesitated a moment before following.

A flurry of activity began the moment they crested the stairs. John hadn't been anywhere in the castle but the room below and the hallway the other direction. He wasn't prepared for the grand scene he came upon. Men and women, all dressed casually, were at

Decentius' beck and call.

Orders were shouted in a language John didn't recognize, and everyone flew into action.

"We should have an answer soon," he said once everyone else had left with their assigned duties.

"What are they doing?" John asked.

"Hunting," Decentius replied.

John wasn't sure, but he thought he saw a cruel smile cross the other man's face. The sentiment was not lost on him, and he felt much the same. Whoever did this should be punished, and it should be painful. No one should go through what that woman did.

Minutes turned into hours which turned into days. Nearly a week after Jane was killed, the woman who he'd left in the room with her body crested the stairs. She looked heartbroken and exhausted.

"Well?" she asked Decentius.

"Three," he replied.

"The throne room," she responded, then turned on her heels and left.

"You'll want to watch this," Decentius said to John after the woman left. "Lilith does not hold back, not when her family is hurt."

They'd been sitting in the kitchen eating a small meal when she'd shown up. He'd stayed at the castle, even though it appeared he could have left if he wanted. Something made him remain. Whether it was the desire to see someone punished for the cruelty of Jane's death, or a devotion to the woman he now learned was called Lilith, he couldn't say.

Following Decentius, he stepped into a room and appeared to travel back in time. Before him was the splendor of the days he'd read about in fictional tales of King Arthur. White marble floors, columns, and walls surrounded a collection of people. At the front of the room was a dais with an actual throne, high points on the back, jewels encased in it, velvet cushions. Every splendor one could imagine.

Lilith stepped up and turned, planting herself on the throne. "Bring them in," she said.

John hadn't seen who had been brought to the castle, but knew they were not going to last long. The looks on the people gathered in the room were murderous, and he didn't blame them.

The commotion at the entrance to the room drew his attention and he had to blink several times to make sure what he was seeing was real. Chains around their necks, binding their front and rear legs, and muzzles on their snouts, were three creatures out of a nightmare. They had heads like wolves, but the bodies were more like a human, and he wondered if they were werewolves. He didn't dare ask, for fear of looking foolish. They certainly had the jaws to do the damage that had been done to the woman.

It took nearly a dozen men to drag the creatures to the throne, and once there, they were tethered to the columns at either side. They snarled and snapped at the men who handled the chains, but never once looked up at Lilith.

"Silence." Everyone, including the beasts, stood quiet. "You know what you're accused of," she said. "Defend yourself."

The creature on the left began to snarl, making guttural sounds and yips, nothing that made any sense to John.

"Then who?" Lilith asked.

More snarls and barks came, this time from one of the other beasts. Lilith listened intently, giving her full attention to the beast. John watched as what little color there was drained from Lilith's face.

"Find them," she said as she looked to the crowd. "Bring them to me, now."

Everyone in the room turned and looked at each other,

unsure what to do.

"Scatter," Decentius said, and the crowd disappeared.

John watched as the three beasts were unshackled and set free. They, too, vanished before his eyes. He was left with Decentius and Lilith and wasn't sure what he should do. He turned to the man at his side and what he saw sent chills down his spine. In the blink of an eye he was consumed by darkness.

He startled awake, blinking against the bright light. This wasn't the room he'd spent weeks in below the castle. No, this was a proper bedroom, with windows and everything. It was set up like every hotel room he'd ever stayed in.

"Excuse me," a voice said.

He turned and saw a woman standing just inside the door.

"Sorry to wake you," she continued. "I've been asked to bring you downstairs."

John assessed himself and found he was dressed, simply sleeping atop the bed. He cleared his throat. "Be right there."

Making his way to the restroom he did what needed doing, finishing quickly. He glanced at himself in the mirror and realized he had little color, looking much the way both Decentius and Lilith did.

He followed the woman down the hall, stepping slowly down the steps of the grand staircase. When they made the first floor, he took time to look around. He was either in a completely different building or a part of the castle he'd never seen. Following the woman, he tried to take in as much as he could. The walls were bare, no rugs on the hardwood beneath his feet, and he didn't see any furniture in the rooms they passed.

The woman stopped in front of a closed door and turned to him. "Right through there," she said, then walked away, back the way they'd come.

Hesitating only a moment, he stepped up to the door and

turned the knob.

"Come," she said.

He was drawn in by her command, walking to the chair next to the desk where she sat. She still wore the red dress, but her appearance was much more disheveled than it had been before.

"I need your help," she said, looking up at him, beseeching with her eyes.

He sat in the chair, then asked, "What do you want?"

"Someone is hunting my people," she said. "They came into my home and slaughtered my sister. You saw what they did to her. I cannot let them go unpunished."

She was right, he saw what they did to that poor girl. No one should suffer what she went through, even if they are monsters. "How can I help?" he asked.

"I can enhance your powers to find the truth," she said.

"My powers?" he asked, confused.

"Don't you know?"

"Know what?"

She shook her head and smiled sadly. "You were not brought here without consent," she said. "We invited you, asked you to join us. You took your time in answering. I insisted. I wouldn't have you joining us without all of the facts."

"I don't remember," he said.

"Unfortunately, that's the way the transformation works," she replied. "You lose some of your short-term memory."

"Then I haven't been a prisoner," he stated.

"I couldn't keep you if you truly wanted to go," she replied.

"What was with all the head games, then?" he asked.

"Those were what you designed," she said, pulling a folder from a drawer.

He opened it up and saw instructions in his own handwriting, saying things that they must do and things they shouldn't do in order to make sure he stayed.

70

"Why didn't you tell me?" he asked.

"You wouldn't have believed me if I did," she said.

"Then let's have this conversation again," he said. "Why did you want me to join you? Why am I here? And what can I do to help find the killers?"

"Same questions you asked last time," she said.

With the new, or old, depending on how you looked at it, information, John set out to the task at hand. He went to his apartment in Jamestown, pulling down some of the books he'd collected over the years on the subject. He'd never really thought about it as research, though. More like a passing interest in the subject.

Picking up his notebook, he flipped to the page where Lilith said he'd find the information she'd given him before he agreed to join them. Just as she said, it was all there. There were even drawings of the beasts he'd seen in the throne room. They weren't necessarily the enemy of Lilith and her children, more like a distant cousin. Some of the things he'd learned about them were correct, too, but most of it was pure fiction.

He had apparently spent weeks with Lilith going over the needs she had that he could help with. She was right, there were beings hunting her people. Problem was, they were hunting humans as well. They'd killed his brothers, which was why he probably blocked that out of his memory.

John had spent a week reviewing his notes. In doing so, the memories came flooding back. The sight of his brothers slaughtered in the basement of their family home. The long conversations with both Lilith and Decentius. The decision he'd made in order to find the beasts who were terrorizing not only his family, but the entire countryside.

It had started with livestock and was blamed on wolves in

the region. The first human victim the authorities were aware of was an older gentleman who had left a tavern and walked home. He'd been found along the side of the road the next morning, body mauled in a similar way to what he'd witnessed of Jane. It was blamed on wild animals and the man's intoxication. Then they started to increase in regularity. Adult men in good shape were turning up dead and the authorities didn't have an answer as to what was causing it.

He'd been interested in it from an investigative reporter perspective until his brothers became victims. At that point, the police stopped giving him information and he'd been forced to search it out by any means necessary. There had to be a solution, and it wasn't to blame it on the wolves.

"Do you have a plan?"

"I think so," John replied. "I'm going to set a trap."

"They won't fall for it," Lilith replied.

"If I make it convincing enough, they will," John said. "I plan to use myself as bait."

"You won't be able to stop them," she said. "And we'd lose your advantage."

"My advantage is exactly what is going to save me," he boasted.

"What do you mean?" she asked.

"I've been honing my skills," he said. "Working on a way to make myself appear vulnerable while maintaining my superior strength and speed."

"Some of my strongest warriors have not been able to stand up to them," she replied. "Many of my men have been slaughtered."

"No disrespect," John said. "But your men didn't have what I do."

"That may be true," she conceded. "My men, however, had years longer to build their strength. They were not young in their conversion."

"While I appreciate your concern," he said. "I am going to be fine."

"Just don't get over confident," she said. "I'd hate to lose you."

"There is one thing you can do for me," he said.

"Name it," she replied.

"I'd like to borrow some of your muscle," he said.

"Absolutely," she said. "How many men would you like?"

"I'd actually prefer children," he said. "Or young adults. I think I can use them in my plan as well."

"I'll have Decentius get you some," she said.

He began to build his plan, keeping Lilith informed along the way. After two weeks of deciding to help her, he put the final pieces into place. His plan would go into action tonight, and he was nearly giddy with anticipation.

Stepping from the bar, he stumbled his way along the sidewalk, tripping over his own feet. He retraced the route the first human victim took, hoping that he'd be attacked near where the other was. Working hard to keep his charade in place, he nearly toppled over an uneven piece of the walkway. That's when they arrived.

One helped him back to his feet while another stood next to him. Their breath was foul as they spoke to him.

"You good, man?" the one who'd helped him to his feet asked.

"'sall good," he replied, keeping his speech slow.

"Need a ride home?" the other asked.

"'sall good," he said again, attempting to move around them.

"We insist," the first one said, grabbing his arm.

"I'm good, 'sall good," he said again, feebly attempting to

brush them off.

It was all part of his plan, a way to get them to see him as vulnerable. They took the bait without hesitation and helped him walk to the gate to the cemetery where his backup held their ground, staying silent and invisible during this whole episode.

"Let's get you to sit down," the second one said. "At least until you're a bit steadier on your feet."

They helped him to sit on a bench next to the gate. He slumped down, nearly falling off the bench, working to keep the illusion of intoxication going. Sitting on either side of him, the beings kept him upright. Bobbing his head, he waited for the attack. When he was nearly out of patience, the first one leaned John's head back, exposing his neck to them both. Deciding he should react how the first man did, he pushed the arm of the one tipping his head feebly, unable to move it. When the second one bent his neck, John let out the signal.

With no noise, thirteen of Lilith's children were around them. They swooped in from every direction, and began to pull the men away. John worked with them as well, wresting the two to the ground. The desire wasn't to kill them, as there were only two and he knew this was just a small portion of the group behind the attacks, behind the murders. These two would be held and questioned to see if they could find the head of the organization.

It didn't take long for both beasts to be subdued. The others would take them back to Lilith for questioning while he went home to see what else he could learn from his books. This would not be the last fight, but he hoped they'd be able to get to the leader without having to go through all the subordinates.

"You have got to be kidding me," John said exasperated. "Both of them?"

"I'm afraid so," Lilith replied.

"What are we going to do?"

"We're going to have to find another way," she said.

"Fine," he said. "I'll come up with something."

The two beasts that John had helped capture had died before they got to Lilith's location. She didn't give details, just that neither of them had survived the trip. He wasn't sure what he was going to do now. The plan they'd put into place had been the best option. Now, he was forced to come up with some other way to try to find the head of the organization.

His phone buzzed, indicating a text had come in.

Meet me at the bar at 9pm. Don't tell Lilith.

He didn't recognize the number it came from, so texted back.

Who are you?

The phone pinged back indicating the message didn't go through. Either the sender had spoofed the number or had immediately disconnected it. He wasn't sure whether he should go or not, but decided that if this were a lead, he had to follow up on it. With only half an hour before the meeting was to take place, he had to hurry.

Nothing looked different at the bar than what he had encountered the night before, but John felt an oppression around him. As he walked toward the bar door, someone reached out and grabbed him, dragging him into the alley.

"Shh," she said.

John's eyes opened wide as he saw the young woman who had led him from the room to the office when he met with Lilith. She was clearly frightened, looking around for any danger that might crop up. The woman pulled him deeper into the shadows of the alley, far back from the street out front of the bar. He held his tongue, waiting for her to initiate conversation.

When the woman was satisfied that they were alone, she said, "They're using you."

Smiling, John said, "I volunteered."

"No," she said in a fierce whisper. "You're a weapon that Lilith has created to defeat her brother."

"What do you mean?"

"She isn't trying to find out who is killing people," she whispered. "She's using you to hunt down and kill her brother's family. She wants to rule the world, and if you kill her brother and his family it will open the door to her triumph. He's the only one who can stop her."

"I saw what they did to Jane," he insisted.

"You saw what she wanted you to see," the girl said. "Everything that happened in the castle was a well-orchestrated charade. Nothing is what it seems there."

"Then why do you stay?"

"I have no choice," she said.

"Stay with me," he said. "I'll keep you safe."

"You can't," she said. "Now go. I've been away too long."

Without another word she was just, gone. Almost as if she were never really there. John blinked a moment, then made his way back out of the alley. He wasn't sure what to do with this new information.

"I don't have another plan," he said.

"We need to figure out where the head of this group," Lilith insisted.

"And if we can't?"

"We have to!"

John had been having the same conversation with her for several days, always coming back to the need for her to find the head of this rogue group of beasts. He'd done some research on them, finding clear information on Lilith, but seeing nothing indicating she had a brother. The only reference he found was Gallu, and that was vague at best. The more research he did, the more it was clear that Lilith didn't have a brother. She did, however, likely have a son born from her connection to the archangel Samael. Nowhere, however, did he find anything with a name or more information on this son.

Days passed, and John still didn't have a new plan to find the head of this rogue family, nor a way to find Lilith's son or brother or whatever he was. He kept Lilith at bay with continued research and giving her information that he'd found, but she was quickly growing impatient.

Try as he might, he couldn't find anything that was helpful for his search. He wanted to talk to this other family head, find out if what the woman who'd come to him with the fact that Lilith had been the one to kill not only Jane, but likely his brothers as well. When the plain envelope with script writing on the front showed up under his door one day, he was skeptical. He opened it to find a poem written in flowing script.

I have the answers that you seek,
They are worth more than a simple peek,
Meet me when the moon does rise,
I'll give you your answer without surprise,
You'll find me where your deception started,
But you won't leave the area broken-hearted,
Truth is what you seek to find,
Come talk to me, I'm one of a kind.

While the poem was simple, the message was clear. He had either gained the attention of the head of the other family, or Lilith had somehow found out that he was searching for something she didn't want him to find. Either way, he knew that he had to go to the meeting. What he didn't know was whether he would survive the meeting.

"Haven't seen anyone, Mate," the bartender said.

"Thanks," John replied.

He'd gone to the bar, assuming the person who wanted to meet with him was going to be there. When he'd waited for nearly an hour, he figured the message was just a hoax. Exiting the bar, he made his way down the street toward his loft, walking past the bench where he'd sat when he fooled the beasts that were taken to Lilith. An uneasy feeling came over him, causing him to stumble and nearly fall. Once again, someone was there to help him to his feet.

"I'm glad you came," the man said.

John looked up to see a man whose beauty could only be surpassed by Lilith.

"Come with me," he said, guiding John down the street.

They walked nearly a block before the man diverted John into the cemetery. When they'd made their way to a mausoleum, the man opened the door and stepped in. John only hesitated a moment before following the man inside. Down the steps he went, following the light of a torch, until he reached the bottom of the long staircase.

"This way," the man said, turning to walk down the hall.

With no other option, John followed. It reminded him of the hallway he'd trekked down under the castle when he was a prisoner of Lilith. The more he thought about it, the more he realized that he had been a prisoner, no matter what she said. While this didn't feel like a completely free choice, it did feel less forced than what he'd experienced with Lilith and her group.

It didn't take long before they came to a large door set in the stone wall.

"I want you to be prepared before I open this door," the man said.

"What is in there?" John asked.

"My family," the man said. "The family that my mother is trying to destroy."

With that, the man opened the door and stepped in. John followed, unsure what he would find.

John hadn't expected to see families in the room. He expected to see much the same as he saw when he was in the castle. There were men and women of all ages, along with children from toddlers to teenagers. All of them were huddled in the space, wide eyed and fearful.

"You turn children?"

It was the first thing that came to his mind, and the man answered without hesitation.

"We never turn a child," he said. "These are the children born naturally to my family."

"But aren't you..."

"No," he said. "We are not like my mother. Some things are the same, but not much."

"Then how do you survive?"

"Follow me," he said, making his way through the crowd.

They all watched as John walked past. It was an uneasy feeling, but he didn't feel malice from them, simply curiosity. Reaching the other side of the large room, the man turned down another hall, walking up it to another door. John could feel the eyes of the people even after he turned the corner. The man opened the door and stepped in.

"Grace," he said.

John followed and saw the woman who had warned him about Lilith.

"What are you doing here?" he asked.

"You met my twin, Magda," the woman replied. "She is with Lilith. I am with Gabriel."

John looked at them in clear confusion.

"Sit," Gabriel said. "There is a lot to discuss."

For nearly two hours, John listened to the history of Lilith. The damage she'd caused in the beginning, the way she'd been thrown out of the garden, the threat she'd issued to God Almighty, and the havoc she'd wreaked since. Almost all of what Gabriel told him was not new information. What was new was the manner in which he heard it. First hand knowledge from events that Gabriel had witnessed were astonishing, and the vivid detail that he was able to recall was spectacular.

By the time Gabriel finished with his story and had brought John up to speed on what was currently happening, John knew he needed to take action. What he would do, however, was still unclear.

"She cannot be killed," Gabriel insisted.

"Why not?" John asked. "With as much pain and misery she's caused, I see no reason to let her live."

"Would you condemn the people out there to death?" Gabriel asked.

"Never," John replied. "But what do they have to do with Lilith?"

"If you kill my mother," Gabriel explained, "you kill us all."

"How?"

"We are all linked," Gabriel said. "I am her son, which makes all of my people her grandchildren. When you kill the creator of the family, the subordinate members also die. It's like when you cut the head off the snake."

"And because she's your mother," John said. "Then you would die, which would mean all of your people will die, too."

"My people and hers," he said. "All of this line would cease to exist. Trust me," he continued. "If there were a way for us to live and have her die, I would be a willing accomplice. Unfortunately, the way we are made means that when the top goes, so goes the rest."

"It's like cutting the family tree completely down,"

John said.

"Exactly," Gabriel confirmed.

"Then what can we do?"

"That's where Grace and Magda come in," he said.

"I don't understand," John admitted.

"Allow me," Grace said.

John had nearly forgotten that she was there, she was so quiet during their discussion.

"My sister and I are not what we appear," she said. "We came after Lilith, even after Gabriel was born. An emergency clause, if you will, created specifically for this purpose. Our only goal is to neutralize a threat of the magnitude like this."

"What are we talking about?" John asked.

"My kind is a much larger portion of society than you could ever imagine," Gabriel said.

"How so?"

"If Lilith dies," Gabriel began.

"Two thirds of the world's population would disappear," Grace finished.

"Two thirds?" John was shocked. Never in his wildest imagination did he think there were that many among them. "How do you hide? How is this not known?"

"Because we continue to change the lore," Gabriel said. "We used to be able to walk among you without you being aware. When the first fictional stories came out, we were pushed to change our way of life. Much of what you know is likely based on misinformation we've been able to put out to keep your kind unaware of our existence."

"But why hide?"

"Because humans are a fragile species," Grace answered.

"And fear runs you much more than you'd like to believe," Gabriel continued. "When we were first 'found,' humans assumed we were just a religious sect. As time passed, your kind saw that we were not growing old like you. They wanted what we had."

"That wasn't possible, though," Grace said. "You are too fragile to take on the attributes that Lilith's children possess."

"What happened?" John asked.

"We were forced to hide," Gabriel said. "Whether it meant moving frequently enough to keep suspicion to a minimum or literally hiding, we weren't able to continue the way we'd lived for centuries."

"Then," Grace intervened. "Someone decided that they would write a book. Tell everyone who we were, what we could do, and why we were a danger."

"Dracula?" John asked.

"That was one of the biggest," Gabriel said. "But it wasn't the first. Well before that we were outed as monsters, dangers to civilized society, and should be destroyed. Mother wanted to remove the human population from the planet."

"Then how would you survive?" John asked.

"Contrary to what you may have heard," Grace said. "They are not required to drink human blood."

"It's better," Gabriel said. "But she's right, not necessary."

"You're saying that we could all die and you'd be fine?"

"He doesn't know," Grace said, looking at Gabriel.

"Know what?"

"You're one of us," Gabriel said.

"I'm... what?" John didn't know what to say. He'd never thought he was one of them, even when he was captive with Lilith.

"Most people don't know they belong to us," Gabriel said. "You walk around without the knowledge that you are greater than the ordinary you think you are."

"But, how?"

"I am only half of what my mother is," Gabriel said. "The other half is my father."

When he didn't elaborate, John asked, "Who is

your father?"

"My father was an archangel who fell," he said. "While his fall was his fault in part, my mother's role was much larger. She seduced him, convinced him that she was still in the good graces of God, and that their union was chosen to be a greater part of the world."

"Their children were to rule a portion of the world," Grace continued. "At least that's what Lilith told him."

"By the time I was born," he said. "Mother had killed my father."

"She killed an angel?" John asked.

"They aren't as strong as her," Gabriel said. "It was brutal, and I was nearly lost in her fight. She used me as a weapon, though. Father tried to subdue mother instead of killing her, all to save me."

"If an archangel can't subdue your mother," John began. "What makes you think we can?"

"Because of me," Grace said.

"I still don't know why you are so important," John said.

Grace looked to Gabriel who gave her a subtle nod. When she looked back to John there was something different about her. He couldn't put his finger on it, but he knew there was a difference. Then she shifted. All at once she became pure light, so blinding that John had to close his eyes to her, covering them with his hands to ward off the pain from the light.

As quickly as she erupted, she was back to the small woman she'd been before.

"What are you?" he asked, pure shock in his voice.

"We're angels," she said. "My sister and I were created by God after Lilith killed Gabriel's father. We've all been given free will to choose our path, and most choose to follow."

"My father did not," Gabriel said.

"I thought you said Lilith seduced him," John said.

"Doesn't that count for anything?"

"If someone convinces you that driving over the speed limit, even just a little, is no big deal," Gabriel said. "When you get pulled over, do you use that excuse to get yourself out of a ticket?"

"No," John said.

"And so it is with this," Gabriel said. "He knew what was right and he chose to disobey, chose to go against what God had put into place as the rules."

"By doing so," Grace said. "He condemned an entire race. All of Lilith's children, whether they are hers by birth, by conversion, or by chance, are condemned."

"Then I am condemned, too," John said.

"In a way, yes," Gabriel said. "If we kill Lilith, you will die."

"Then what are we going to do?"

"Grace and Magda will take Lilith to the throne room of God," Gabriel said.

"What happens then?"

"God will judge her," Grace said. "And only her, without passing that judgement on to her children."

"What's to keep someone else from taking her place?" John asked. "I mean, if she can get to the point of being so corrupt that she is willing to kill her own child, what's to keep someone else with the same ideals from picking up where she left off?"

"You ask a very good question," Gabriel said. "The answer is nothing. We cannot assume that there won't be another to take her place at the head of that faction. What we can do, however, is put that person, and all who follow Lilith, on notice. Once she is gone, their protection is as well. If they choose to follow her path, we can end them, and their line, without any danger to us and ours."

"So this is a war," John said. "Supernatural as it may be, it's still a war. You believe you are right and she believes she is."

"Except she wants to kill us," Gabriel said. "We don't want

her family dead, we simply want her to be judged as we would want ourselves to be judged; on our own merit and not on those of someone we didn't have a choice being connected with."

"If that judgement leads to her death, then so be it," John said.

"It has been her choice," Grace said. "This began long before anyone else was involved. She has her own idea as to what is right."

"So do you," John said. "You are saying that what she wants and needs and does is wrong, but she sees it as right. It's like looking at a cup and one arguing there is a handle and another arguing that there isn't."

"Except the cup either does or does not have a handle," Gabriel said. "One of those people is wrong. Just because they can't see the handle doesn't mean that it doesn't exist."

"And just because you can see the handle doesn't mean the cup would be any less valuable without it."

"If I can see the handle," Gabriel said, "and you can't, I can turn the handle so you can see it. I've done this for my mother. I've shown her that there is a better way to be here, sharing this world with those who are not fully the same as us. She has not only refused to see the truth of it, but she's gone out of her way to destroy any evidence that that truth exists."

"We simply want her to acknowledge that her way is not the only way," Grace said.

"Which we've tried over and over and over," Gabriel said.

"So you're just going to take her to her execution, then," John said. "Without remorse, without thinking of those who may be hurt because of it."

"We're trying to make sure she doesn't hurt anyone else by her actions," Gabriel said. "Once God judges her, it will remove not only the protection her clan has from her, but also remove the lineage issue."

"I'm not sure what you mean," John said.

"Lilith is the head of our kind," Grace said. "If she is removed without causing a catastrophic failure down the line, then that risk is gone. The sins of the father or mother will no longer cause damage to their offspring."

"Wait," John said. "If she is taken out without it causing the rest of you to go the same way, then you could die and it would not kill your entire family?"

"Exactly," Gabriel said. "Once that happens, we can police our own without retribution falling on those who are not even aware of their connection to us."

"It's a big if, though," Grace said.

"How so?"

"God could choose to remove her entire line," she said. "Take her and all of her offspring from the planet."

"Then there's no difference as to whether we kill her or take her to God," John said.

"But there is," Gabriel said. "We have a chance to live if we take her to God. If we don't, we know we'll die."

"And God could spare her," Grace said.

"Spare her?"

"Let her live," Gabriel said.

"Would he take away her powers?" John asked. "Take away the lineage threat?"

"Maybe," Gabriel said. "We won't know until she gets there."

"Then this could be a fool's errand," John said. "It could do nothing but make her angrier than she already is. Give her even more reason to fight and kill you."

"It's a chance I'm willing to take," Gabriel said.

"Even if it means killing your entire family?" John asked. "Even if it means that you lose?"

"I will happily give up my life if it means that my family is safe," Gabriel said. "I'll give it up if it means that the few humans that are left are able to live in peace without the threat of my mother cursing them to a life they never even knew existed."

John looked at the other man. Everything about him said that the man was telling the truth. He just hoped he hadn't hitched his wagon to the wrong horse. "What do I need to do?" he asked.

"They said they'd only talk to Lilith," John said.

"Are you sure they have information?" Decentius asked.

"What they said seems to make sense," John replied. "I have a good feeling about what they are telling me. It hasn't been much, but what they've said seems to be exactly what she said she was looking for."

"I'll let her know and set up a meeting," Decentius said.

"Thank you," John relied, then hung up the phone.

"He bought it?" Gabriel asked.

"I believe so," John replied.

"Then all we have to do is wait," Grace said.

It didn't take long for John to hear back, and the meeting was set for midnight the next night. It barely gave them enough time to get everything into place, but they managed.

"And you're sure I'll be safe?" he asked again.

"Magda and I will protect all who are there," Grace said. "You are included in that group."

"As well as Lilith's people," Gabriel added.

"But..." John began.

"We have everything under control," Gabriel said. "If they attack, we will subdue them. We will not kill them. I won't be like my mother, killing anyone who opposes me."

"You have your father's soul," Grace said.

"I also have my mother's tenacity," he said. "I won't stop until she is dealt with."

"Even if it means your death?" John asked.

"No matter the outcome," Gabriel said. "I will not subject this world to her reign of terror any longer."

"Why now?" John asked. "I mean, you've been doing this for eons. Why did you decide to make your stand now?"

"You," Gabriel replied.

"I don't understand," John said. "What's so special about me?"

"There was always a chance that you would exist," he began. "Not you, specifically, but your abilities. Grace and Magda were the first to realize. They've been waiting until Lilith made her move. Once she did, they knew that the plan could be put into place."

"I still don't know what abilities I'm supposed to have," John said.

"You're resistant," Grace said.

"To what?"

"Our kind," Gabriel said. "My mother attempted to convert you. That's why you have some memory gaps and why she was feeding you blood. She thought her transformation worked, so she sent you out to find me and mine. If you could be converted, then you would be able to withstand our charms. She didn't count on you not knowing about what you could do."

"She also didn't know that we knew who you were," Grace said.

"Does she know Magda is like you?" John asked.

"My sister is very clever," Grace said. "She and I have the ability to project exactly what we need the other to see in order to persuade them to our desires."

"How do I know you haven't just convinced me to do what you want?"

"Because you can't be charmed," Gabriel said.

"I don't understand," John said.

"If I wanted to," Grace said. "I could convince anyone to jump from a cliff, step in front of a bus, or swallow bleach. There is nothing I could do to convince you to do that."

"Why not?"

"You are the one who can fix this world," Gabriel said. "My mother is already weaker because she took in some of your blood. She doesn't realize it, but that has made her vulnerable."

"And that vulnerability is what we needed in order to stop her," Grace said.

John thought about what they'd said. He had been weak when he first woke in the castle dungeon alone. The drinking of the blood had strengthened him some, but the regular food that Decentius brought did much more to build him back up. He knew that Lilith needed to be stopped, and what Gabriel and Grace had told him made sense. Still, he couldn't deny there was an inkling in the back of his brain that said something was amiss. Somehow, something more than what they were telling him was going on.

"I want to go with you," he said to Grace.

"And you will," she replied. "I need you to take me to Lilith."

"No," he said. "I want to go to the throne room of God. I want to see for myself that what you are saying is true."

"I'm not sure you'll survive," Gabriel said. "Even I am unable to go there."

"My life isn't worth anything if I simply take you at your word," he said. "I want to know that what I am contributing is for a worthy cause. That I'm not simply sending Lilith and her people to their death in a spat between family."

"You know that this will likely kill you," Grace said.

"Yes," he replied.

"As long as you know the chance you are taking," she said, "I am willing to take you along."

"Grace," Gabriel said. "He can't go with you."

"God has a way of surprising even us," she said. "Whether he lives or not is up to Him. All I can do is take him there."

"Thank you," John said.

"Don't thank me yet," she replied. "You know what they say; 'be careful what you wish for.'"

"Is she here?" Decentius asked.

"Is Lilith?"

John wasn't about to let Grace die if he could help it. She'd said that if Lilith didn't bring Magda, then she may not survive the interaction.

"Lilith is here," Decentius said.

"Who else did you bring with you?" John asked.

"Lilith demanded we bring her handmaid," the other man said.

"I suppose that's fine," John said. "Where are they?"

"Just inside," Decentius said.

They'd chosen an abandoned warehouse to do the meeting. Lilith must have arrived early in order to already be inside.

"Where's yours?" Decentius asked.

John turned to the van he'd driven up and opened the door. Grace stepped out and John was worried that Decentius would recognize her.

"Scraggly little thing, ain't she?" Decentius asked.

"But she knows things," John replied, thankful that whatever Grace was using to hide her true nature stood up to the other man.

She stood there, rubbing her fingers together in a rhythmic way, sending an eerie feeling over both men.

"Let's go," Decentius said and turned to enter the building.

John followed behind, with Grace on his heels. She continued the rhythmic rubbing of her fingers as they made their way through the building to a set of stairs. Grace started humming under her breath in time with her hands swishing sound as she rubbed them together.

"What's she doing?" Decentius asked.

"Dunno," John replied. "She's never done it before. Maybe she's nervous."

"Make her stop," Decentius said.

John turned to Grace, but she'd already stopped the noise. She continued to rub her hands together, but no noise came from them now. She also appeared to still be humming, but again it was silent.

As they made it to the top of the stairs, Decentius turned the corner and stepped up to a door.

"Ready?" he asked.

Grace nodded rapidly, still appearing to be a frail woman. Decentius opened the door and stepped inside. John went through next and saw Lilith sitting at a desk, Magda next to her. When Grace stepped into the room, Lilith stood.

"Thank you for helping," she said.

In that moment, Magda stood, sandwiching Lilith between her and her twin. John stepped back and was not surprised when both women burst into light. Covering his eyes, he heard Decentius scream, then heard a sizzling noise. He chanced a peek, keeping the twins light at his back. Where the other man stood, now only a pile of ash remained.

The light faded and John turned to see Lilith slack in the arms of the twins.

"Now we go," one of them said.

He couldn't tell who had spoken, as they now matched in fine white robes that fell to their feet. The one who spoke reached out a hand and he clasped it firmly. The room spun around him and his stomach dropped to his feet. As quickly as it started, John was planted on solid ground again, though he wasn't sure what he was standing on. No walls surrounded him, yet he felt somewhat confined. Before him was a wooden chair behind a battered desk. The chair was empty, but the twins didn't seem surprised.

"We wait," the one who held his hand said.

John barely had time to wonder how long they would wait when a man appeared in the chair.

"Ladies," he said. "What brings you to us?"

"Lilith," the previously silent one said.

The man at the desk stood abruptly, saying, "Why?"

"Gabriel requests a decision."

"Who's he?" the man asked.

"The immune one."

"One moment," the man said, then disappeared. John barely blinked and he was back. "This way," he said, turning to the wall.

Without realizing what was happening, John was suddenly in another room, this one much larger. He hadn't felt like he'd walked, nor had any time passed.

"Here," the man said to John, handing him a set of glasses.

Not knowing anything about where they were or what was going to be happening, he put the glasses on. Blinking in surprise he realized that there were hundreds of people surrounding him. They hadn't been there a moment before. He slid the glasses down his nose, and they disappeared. Pushing them back into place, he marveled at the crowd around him.

"Come," he heard, though he couldn't say whether it was aloud or in his head.

Before him was a large throne, a smaller one set to the right. The man sitting in the larger throne looked at him kindly, but he could feel the power rolling off him. Sitting to his right was a much younger man.

"Speak," the older man said, again inside John's head.

"We bring Lilith," one of the twins said. "Gabriel has asked for a decision."

"And the immune one?"

"Wanted to make sure we weren't simply taking Lilith to slaughter as she did for Gabriel's people," the twin who seemed to be the spokesperson said.

"Then he shall watch," the man said. "Bring her to me."

The twins moved forward, not walking, simply gliding. They approached the throne and set Lilith in front of it, then stepped back.

Looking at the woman he said, "My child."

Lilith jolted, as if shocked where she lay. John saw her eyes widen, fear rippled across her face, followed quickly by rage.

"You," she said glaring at him. "You did this to me. Why would you do this?"

"My child," the man said again.

"I am not yours," Lilith spat.

"I never left you," the man said.

"You threw me out," Lilith screeched. "Turned your back on me when I needed you most."

"You chose to walk away," the man said, now kneeling beside Lilith. "I was right there beside you, waiting for you to come back. All you had to do was ask."

"There were conditions to my coming back," she said.

John watched in amazement as the woman who he'd seen as so strong and confident crumbled to a sobbing child in front of this man, this God.

"I've always loved you," God said.

"But you wouldn't let me back unless I changed," she sobbed. "I couldn't be me if I wanted to come back."

"You could have been so much more," God said.

"It would have made me less," she replied. "I wouldn't be what I am. I wouldn't be me."

"Do you want to come back home?"

"Not if I can't be me," she said.

"Then the answer is no," God said. "If you wanted to come home, you would change. Since you don't want to change, you don't really want to come home."

"Come home," a man said. John wasn't sure where he came from, he was just suddenly next to her. "Please come back to me."

Lilith blinked, then turned her head away from the man. John waited, wondering what would happen next. Nothing moved in the big room, not the people, not Lilith, not even God. Everything was frozen in place. Then the quiet shattered with a thunder so loud John had to cover his ears and a flash so bright he had to close his eyes. In that moment, everything shifted.

"Welcome back," Grace said.

"What happened?" John asked.

"You were there," she replied. "You saw what happened."

"I mean after the thunder and lightning," John said, sitting up.

He was back in the office where he'd met with Gabriel and Grace before they'd gone to capture Lilith.

"You don't want to know," she said.

Gabriel came in just then. "You're awake," he said. "Good. Feeling better?"

"I'm not sure," John replied. "I feel like I've missed something."

"God gave you a choice," Grace said.

"I don't remember that," John said.

"That was part of the choice," she replied. "You saw everything that happened in the throne room. Everything Lilith went through before she was cast out for good."

"Then she's back here?" John asked.

"Never again," Gabriel said. "That was not what she chose."

"Who was the man who asked her to come back?" John asked.

"That was my father," Gabriel replied.

"But I thought he was dead," John said, clearly confused.

"Not exactly," Grace said. "God kept him safe."

"But he disobeyed..." John began.

"And then asked for forgiveness," Gabriel interrupted.

"Just like that," John said. "No harm, no foul?"

"Not quite," Gabriel said.

"God is more than generous with us all," Grace said. "We are given free will, the ability to make decisions for ourselves. Part of that is the ability to turn our backs on Him. He gives us a multitude of chances, but at some point, just like a parent with an errant child, He gives us the final chance. If we choose well, we are given forgiveness."

"And if not," John concluded. "We are thrown away."

"I think that's a bit harsh," Gabriel said.

"How so?" John asked.

"We are lost to God," he said. "We are not gone forever."

"But we're not given another chance," John said.

"That's true," Gabriel conceded. "It isn't easy for God to give us up, though. He mourns deeply, and those of us who have met him know that those wounds run deep."

"Then why does he give us the choice?" John asked.

"So we can live," Grace said.

"And live free," Gabriel continued.

"Until we have to face him," John said.

"That's why we have to tell the stories," Grace said. "We tell everyone we meet what will happen if they choose to disobey. Then it's up to them to decide."

"If God simply wanted obedient servants," Gabriel said, "he would have made us all drones."

"Which he didn't," Grace said. "Now you have to choose."

"Choose what?" John asked.

"Whether you will tell the story of Lilith and what

95

happened to her," Gabriel said.

"Or simply let it fall away and allow another to take her place," Grace said.

"But why me?"

"You cannot be bought," Gabriel said. "You are immune to the call of our kind."

"And you alone are the one who can tell the story the best," Grace concluded.

"How?"

Gabriel handed John his notebook, the one he'd written things down in from his meeting with Lilith. "Share your story," he said simply. "Share it with the world."

HUMANS 2.0

She bolted awake, gasping.

"It was only a dream," she said.

But she knew that wasn't true. Everything she'd seen, everything she'd heard, everything she'd done; none of it was going away. This was her new normal, and she had to learn to deal with it. Her hand went to her stomach, pressing flat against it. Inside was a life, tiny and unstructured, but still there, growing with each minute, slowly but surely becoming one of them.

Throwing the covers off, she rushed to the bathroom, losing all that was left from last nights meal in the toilet. She wiped her mouth with the back of her hand and moved to the sink, looking at herself in the mirror above, wondering whether the dark circles under her eyes would ever go away. There was only so much makeup could cover.

"Get it together, Mia," she told herself. "You can do this."

It was false bravado, but she had to do it. There really wasn't a choice. Pulling her shirt over her head, she dropped it on the floor. Her panties followed, and she stepped into the shower. The first rush of water was ice cold, but it warmed quickly. Ducking under the spray, she allowed the flow to wash away the last remnants of doubt. Somehow, someway, she would get through this and come out stronger on the other side.

"Feeling better?"

Mia rolled her eyes. "Like you care," she said.

"My job is to make sure you are comfortable throughout the duration of your pregnancy," Jack said. "If you are uncomfortable, or need anything, you need to let me know. I'm here to help."

"I'm fine," she said, walking into the kitchen.

"Breakfast is on the stove," Jack said. "If you want something else, let me know. I know pregnancy can cause foods you normally love to cause nausea. I'll fix whatever you want."

Mia looked at the scrambled eggs and wondered if they'd sit well. She pulled down a plate and went to dish them up. The smell overwhelmed her. Stepping back from the stove she shouted, "You're gonna have to let me have oatmeal."

"I'll get it going," Jack said as he entered the kitchen.

Mia passed him and took herself back to the table to sit and wait.

The Institute had assured her she would be well cared for and accommodated with a large payment upon completion of the study. She'd signed on the dotted line, so to speak, and was now part of what they called a revolution in the advancement of the human species. They gave her some information, explaining what to expect during the next three years, but some things they held back until she was signed up.

When her parents had died suddenly in a car accident, she'd put everything on hold to take care of the estate. They were not rich by any stretch of the imagination, but she hadn't realized how in debt her parents were. Because of this, it meant she couldn't return to school. She'd tried to find a traditional job, but without much training, and hardly any schooling, it was almost impossible to find anything that would allow her to keep the house.

That's when she met Rosie. The woman had walked into the coffee shop where Mia worked and ordered a mocha. Nothing fancy, just plain and simple. When she picked up her drink, she'd asked Mia if she was happy with her job. When Mia said she loved it, just wished it paid more, she'd offered her a place in the study. She'd explained that it would pay her for participating. There wouldn't be much to do, just be available at first. When Mia asked more questions, Rosie said she should come to the Institute.

After only a few months she'd not only been chosen but was the first to participate in the initial testing. Everything had been laid out for her, and she knew she would have a baby. They'd assured her she wouldn't have sex but would be inseminated. The procedure was very clinical, and she'd become pregnant with the first try.

Now she was into her second month and aside from the nausea, she had no other symptoms. The doctor said everything was going well, and she should expect to have a normal pregnancy and delivery. She'd also been assured that she would be able to have as much contact as she wanted with her child, which she was grateful for. She couldn't imagine not seeing her child after it was born.

Thirty women were in the initial trial, with five being chosen as host bodies for the procedures. Mia was the first to become pregnant, and the only one who was moving forward at this time. The other women who were still in the program remained at the Institute, though they were delayed in their continuation until Mia's pregnancy advanced further, which made her feel even more like an outcast.

"Today is ultrasound day," Jack said as he placed the oatmeal in front of Mia. "You'll get a chance to see the baby. Are you excited?"

"A little nervous," she admitted, taking a bite of her breakfast.

"Dr. Sanderson says we should be able to see some of the benefits from the program," Jack said as he sat with his own bowl.

"Why aren't you eating the eggs?" Mia asked.

"Didn't want the smell to bother you," Jack replied. "The other girls can eat them when they get up."

Housing at the Institute was similar to her dorm building at college. There were separate bedrooms, with private baths, and communal living and dining areas. Jack had his own room in the living space within the dorm facility as well, always preparing the meals and attending to any other issues that arose daily for the participants. He was a damn good cook, and Mia hated that she didn't feel like eating.

"Morning Mia," Claire said. "Morning Jack. Breakfast?"

Claire was not a morning person, and the Institute had put a firm rule on caffeine intake for participants, which meant that Claire, along with the other girls, couldn't have a morning cup of coffee. Mia didn't mind, but it was a near breaking point for Claire. She'd decided that tea would become her drink of choice in the morning, but was disappointed when it didn't give her the boost she was used to.

"Eggs are on the stove," Jack said. "If you're going to eat them, though, please do it in the kitchen."

"Why?" Claire asked.

"Mia's stomach can't take it," Jack said.

"It's fine," Mia countered. "I'm done, anyway."

Mia picked up her bowl and took it into the kitchen, running water over it and placing it into the dishwasher. She passed Claire on her way out, finding her way to her bedroom. She'd taken to writing in a journal daily, what she'd dreamt, what she was feeling, where things were going, and what she was worried about. The doctors had encouraged each of the women to journal as part of their stay, especially since they weren't allowed access to social media. This would be their way to remember what had happened while they were there.

"Mia," Jack called. "It's time for you to go."

"Coming," she replied, grabbing her jacket. She'd just have to journal after she returned from her appointment with the doctor.

"Urine sample first," the nurse said. "Then into the gown and across the hall to the exam room."

Mia took the little cup from the nurse and stepped into the bathroom. Even though she wasn't even a third of the way through, they were doing weekly testing on both urine and blood. She did her thing, changed into the gown, then sat across the hall and waited for Dr. Sanderson to come in. It was the same each week. He'd come in to discuss where things stood, how her numbers were within the blood and urine, then do the physical exam and leave.

"Good morning, Mia," Dr. Sanderson said as he came into the room. "I heard you weren't feeling well this morning."

"Just morning sickness," she replied. "Nothing unusual about that."

"You are right, there," he replied. "That is something I don't think we'll ever find a cure for."

"Too bad," she said. "You could make big money selling that cure."

There was a knock at the door, then it opened. The nurse came in with a portable ultrasound machine, moving it next to the exam table.

"We'll start with the ultrasound," the doctor said. "That will tell us most everything we need to know. Go ahead and lie back."

Mia did as she was told, resting her head on the pillow they'd placed at the top of the table. The nurse helped her get her feet into the stirrups, placing a blanket across her lower body. The doctor pushed her gown up above the blanket, exposing her abdomen. Squeezing the bottle of gel onto her stomach, he pulled the cord and wand from the machine, smoothing the gel around.

He flipped a couple of switches and the machine whirred to life, a black and white image coming up on the monitor that was attached to the cart.

"That's it," he said. "Let's see what we can see."

As he moved the instrument across her stomach, she saw grainy images flutter across the screen. Lines and squiggles that didn't make sense to her flashed back and forth. He pressed the end of the wand against her lower abdomen, shifting it side to side, trying, she assumed, to get a better view. That's when she saw it, held within a dark balloon. It was formed already, with a head and limbs and a body. Not much was there, but she could definitely see that it was a baby.

"Good," he said as he pressed a couple of buttons, causing the image to freeze on the screen. "Let's see what else we can find," he continued as he moved the wand around some more.

Just like with that first glimpse, she saw another balloon of darkness.

"Are there two?" she asked.

"At least," the doctor said, distracted by his chore.

"At least?" she asked.

The doctor looked at her then, seeing the panic in her eyes. "Don't worry," he said. "There shouldn't be more than four."

"Four?" Mia asked, clearly confused. "I thought it would just be one."

"Multiples were definitely expected," he said nonchalantly. "It was in the information you were given at the time you signed up."

"That was just a possibility," she said. "They didn't say it was almost certain."

"Don't worry," the doctor said. "You will be fine, and so will the babies. This is something we expected, especially for our first round of trials."

"How many do you see?" she asked reluctantly.

"I've just seen the two so far," he said. "Let's see if we see any more."

After about ten minutes the doctor was satisfied with the discovery of two additional babies, bringing her count to four, just as he'd said. She was given a clean bill of health and sent back to her dorm with some additional literature on what to expect in the next couple of months. Shaken, she'd ignored Jack and the other women when she came back, instead feigning nausea and closing herself in her room.

What have I gotten myself into? Four babies at once?

Mia didn't know whether to laugh or cry. She'd always wanted a big family, but this was a little more than she expected. She was barely twenty years old, and she had a whole lot of life ahead of her.

A knock sounded at the door.

"Mia?" Claire said.

Schooling her features, Mia replied, "Come in."

The door opened and Claire squeezed in, though Mia could see the other girls behind her.

"Jack said you had your ultrasound today," she said as she sat next to Mia on the bed.

"I did," Mia replied.

"Was there something wrong with the baby?"

"Wrong doesn't even cover it," Mia said, then realized that wasn't true. "The problem is there are four babies. They all look healthy, though."

"Four?" Claire asked. "Are you sure?"

"There could be multiples. That's what the info said."

"I was thinking twins," Claire replied.

"Me, too," Mia said.

"Four," Claire breathed out. "So, what does that mean, then? I mean, how is this going to work?"

"We watch for a while," Mia explained. "Make sure everything is okay with them all. Then we wait for them to get here."

"You're going to carry them all?"

Claire wasn't much older than Mia, which was why they connected right away. Unlike Mia, Claire's family was well off. Her problem was she didn't want to follow in their footsteps, do the college and career thing. She wanted to play and travel and experience life before she strapped herself down to a job.

"That's the plan," Mia said. "At least for now. I'll have ultrasounds weekly, in addition to the other testing they've been doing. Once I'm farther along, they'll start the genetic testing."

"Did they all look normal?" Claire asked. "I mean, we don't know what the father looks like, so I wondered if they did some sort of..."

It was a question the girls had discussed in the beginning, whether they would have human babies or some sort of hybrid with who knew what.

"They look like babies as far as I can tell," Mia said. "Look for yourself."

She pulled out the photos the doctor had printed showing each of the babies. Right now they were numbered, but in the next few weeks, they'd be labeled with letters for their size, A to D. She'd learn whether they were boys or girls and would be allowed to name them if she wanted, too. She hadn't decided if that was a good thing or not, though.

"Look at them," Claire crooned, then looked to Mia. "The other girls are worried about you," she said.

"Let's show them the pictures," Mia replied, standing. She hoped their excitement would help to distract her from the fears she was experiencing.

As the days went by, Mia began to experience less morning

sickness, thankfully. She did continue to grow, though, exponentially fast. It was as if her body had decided that because her mind knew there were four babies, she could accept the rapid growth of her abdomen. Sherry had conceived as well, so she wasn't the only one expecting now. It was nice to be able to share that spotlight, especially after being the only one for so long.

"How did you deal with the smells?" Sherry asked one evening.

"Totally faked it," Mia replied. "It got better the farther along I got, though."

"Well," Sherry said. "I can't wait to get to that point."

"I remember," Mia said.

With fall turning to winter, the women were allowed to write letters to their families. It had been hard for most of them, not being able to communicate with their loved ones for so long. Mia wasn't sure if she felt lucky to not have that worry, or sad because she couldn't share her news with anyone close to her.

Of course, the Institute insisted that the women not divulge any of the details about the study, including the fact that they would be having babies. Sherry had a hard time with it, knowing her mother was ill and may not survive the three years of the study. She really wanted her to know that she was going to become a grandmother.

"What traditions do you guys all have?" Claire asked as they sat around the living room talking one night.

"We always eat enchiladas," Gwen said.

"Why?" Claire asked.

"My mom's favorite dish," she replied. "She started making them when she was young and became quite the expert. Now, my dad won't let her skip. I'm gonna miss them, they're to die for."

"I don't think I'd be able to eat them," Sherry said. "Even the thought makes my stomach turn."

They all laughed at the face she made, and she joined

right in.

"This will be my first Christmas without my parents," Mia said.

"Oh," Claire said. "That's right. How are you holding up?"

Mia shrugged. "I guess I'll have new reasons to celebrate, soon," she said, rubbing her extended belly.

"What's the newest news?" Gwen asked.

"Tomorrow I find out whether they're boys or girls," Mia said. "The testing has been good so far. At least that's what the doctor is saying."

"Do you get new pictures tomorrow, too?" Sherry asked.

"I think I'm supposed to," she replied. "When is your first ultrasound?"

"I think it's in a couple of weeks," Sherry said. "I wonder if I've got four as well."

They all paused at that, wondering whether they would all be having small litters when their time came.

"Who's next?" Mia asked, seeing Sherry's worry.

"I think that's me," Amy said. "They said probably in the next week or so. They've been tracking my ovulation and are pretty sure that is when I'll be most fertile."

"Was it weird?" Claire asked.

"What?" Mia asked.

"The insemination process," Claire said. "I mean, it seems really weird."

"It's a little odd," Sherry said. "I mean, just think of a turkey baster full of baby-makers. That's what it's like."

"Eww," Gwen said. "That's just, eww."

"What did you expect?" Mia asked.

"Well," Gwen said. "I wasn't sure. I mean, okay, maybe that's what I expected, but it just seems eww."

"Not nearly as fun as the old-fashioned way," Amy said.

"Yeah," Claire agreed. "That's the best way."

They all burst into laughter as Jack chose that moment to come into the dorm.

"What?" he asked.

"Had to be here," Mia said, barely containing her laughter.

"And had to be a girl," Claire chimed in.

That sent the girls into another peal of laughter. Jack just turned around and walked out, shaking his head, which elicited even more laughter from the girls.

"This is going to be a little uncomfortable," Dr. Sanderson said. "I'm going to use the ultrasound to direct the needle. You should feel a pinch, but not much more. It's important that you be as still as possible for this procedure. If you shift, I may accidentally stick one of the babies."

"Okay," Mia said.

The procedure was explained to her last week, so she was prepared for the long needle the doctor produced. Still, it was unnerving to think that he was going to be sticking that into her stomach and into the sacks of each of the babies to get more genetic information from them. The other reason was that she had four babies. The doctor had explained that they needed to make sure that the babies' lungs were healthy and ready when it came time for them to be born. He said that test would be done later. Today's testing was for genetics only.

Throughout the pregnancy, she'd been receiving shots to boost not only the babies' growth, but her own stamina as well. The doctor told her that soon she would have to be on bed rest with monitors around the clock. When she'd asked why, he'd told her because of the number of babies, she would need to preserve her strength. To do that, she would have to only do what was necessary from about the twenty-week mark on. This would allow her body to use all of its energy to grow the babies.

She'd been so distracted by her thoughts that she hadn't

even felt the needle pokes, and didn't realize the procedure was finished until the doctor said, "Very good."

When she looked up, the nurse was reaching out to help her sit up. "That was easy," she said.

"Glad it didn't hurt," he said.

"When will you have results?" Mia asked.

"I should be able to tell you tomorrow what we know," he said.

"And whether they're boys or girls?"

"Yes," he said.

With that, he left the room.

"He's very happy with the results so far," the nurse said.

"I just wish he was a little more forthcoming with information," Mia said.

"It's all part of the study," the nurse replied. "Soon enough, we'll have more information."

"Do you know anything about the fathers?"

"I'm sorry," she replied. "They've only given me information on the mothers. How have you been feeling?"

"Tired," Mia answered honestly. "I also don't feel like eating. It's like I don't have enough room for food."

"That's normal," she said. "It's exponentially worse because you have more than one baby."

"Do they still look healthy?"

Mia realized she hadn't even watched the monitor when Dr. Sanderson did the testing. If she had, she would have seen the babies.

"They all look very healthy," the nurse said.

"Is every mother worried about the babies not being normal?" she asked.

"Every single one," the nurse said. "I've been doing this kind of nursing for years, and I don't think I've met a mother who wasn't concerned about her baby being normal."

"Did they have dreams?"

"What do you mean?"

"Like," Mia began. "Okay, this is going to sound weird, but I feel like my babies are eating me from the inside out. Like they're piranhas or something."

"That's a new one," the nurse laughed. "But odd dreams are normal. Let's get you up and dressed and back to the dorm where you can rest."

"I feel like that's all I've been doing," she said. "Sitting and sleeping and lounging around."

"And that's the way it's going to be from now on," the nurse said. "It's important that you take as many precautions as you can in order to give your babies the time they need to mature."

"I guess," Mia said as she let the nurse help her dress.

"So?" Sherry asked when Mia returned.

"It wasn't bad," Mia said, sitting on the couch.

"Really?" Claire asked.

"Yeah," Mia said. "My mind started wandering and before I knew it, he was all done."

"Do we have boys or girls?" Amy asked.

"Won't actually know until tomorrow," she said.

"Pictures?" Gwen asked.

"Next week," Mia said. "Apparently they can't do them the same time they do the amnio."

"I thought they were giving new pictures," Amy said.

"No pictures isn't even the worst part," Mia said. "In a week or two, they're going to put me on bed rest."

"Really?" Claire asked. "Why?"

"Apparently so my body can rest," she replied. "Not that I haven't been doing that already."

"Wasn't there some woman who had like half a dozen kids at once a couple of decades ago?" Gwen asked.

"Yeah," Claire said.

"I think I read that she had to lay with her head below her body to keep her babies in," Gwen said.

"Oh my gosh," Sherry said. "I don't think I can do this."

"I don't think it's gonna be that bad," Mia said, trying not only to convince Sherry, but herself as well.

"What if I have more than you?" Sherry asked.

"Dr. Sanderson didn't think there would be more than four," Mia said. "He said that was the most they expected."

"But what if they're wrong?" Sherry asked. "What if I've got a whole football team?"

"You're not gonna have that many," Claire said.

"What if they're not normal?" Sherry asked. "What if I've got mutants growing inside me? I mean, we don't know who the dad is. They could have put gorilla babies in me."

Sherry's voice kept pitching higher and higher the more agitated she got.

"Everything's gonna be fine," Amy tried, but Sherry wouldn't hear any of it, shouting, "They put monsters in us. They're gonna kill us."

It didn't take long before Jack came in, asking, "What's wrong?"

"You're trying to kill us," Sherry screamed, then lunged at him.

Jack put his hands up to fend her off, trying to catch her without getting hit. He managed to grab hold of her hands as she swung at him, twisting her around to hold her firm against him, effectively in a bear hug. She continued to thrash about, trying to free herself. The commotion drew one of the other men who worked with them into the living area. Between the two of them, they were able to subdue her just enough so she wouldn't hurt herself or anyone else. They finally got her settled enough to get her seated in a chair.

"We're not trying to kill you," Jack said, breathless.

"Do you know who the father is?" Sherry asked.

"No," he answered. "But I do know that your babies will be perfectly normal."

"You'll see tomorrow," Mia said. "The ultrasound will show you exactly what your babies look like. Do you remember how scared I was?" Sherry nodded, so Mia continued. "I thought the same thing, that they had put monsters in me. When I saw them, though, they were just babies."

"Did you dream they were trying to eat you from the inside?" Sherry asked.

"There are so many strange dreams, I couldn't tell you if that was one of them or not," Mia said.

"Cause that's what I dream," Sherry said.

"The nurse told me today that strange dreams are part of pregnancy," Mia confided. "Since we've had the other typical symptoms, we shouldn't expect to not have that."

Mia didn't want to share that she'd had the same dream, especially with how worked up Sherry was.

"Here you go," Dr. Sanderson said, handing an envelope to Mia.

She'd walked to the clinic to get her results and was thrilled that she'd been able to make it without having to stop and rest.

"This is going to have to be your last walk over, though," the doctor said.

"Why?" Mia asked.

"While the results were good," he said. "You are too far along to be taking any chances. We'll be coming to you for exams for a couple more months, then we'll move you to the clinic for monitoring until the babies are ready."

"Oh," Mia said. "Is it fine for me to walk back?"

"I'll call Jack to walk with you," he said. "This way he can help if you need to rest."

The doctor stepped into his office as Mia took a seat in the outer area. She held the envelope in her hand, unsure whether she wanted to open it or not. The results of her testing were in there, and she would soon find out if she was having boys, girls, or some combination.

"Jack's on his way," the doctor said as he stepped back out. "Did you want to go over the results while you wait?"

"Maybe," she said. "Is there anything bad?"

"Oh, no," he said. "On the contrary. Everything is going exactly as planned. Babies are doing really well with the continued dosages you've been getting. I also put pictures in there."

"Will I be able to understand the results?"

"I made sure to put them in non-medical language," the doctor said. "I know you girls are smart, but none of you have gone to medical school. Sometimes we doctors forget that what we know isn't the same as what our patients know."

"Thank you," Mia said.

Just then, Jack walked in. "Ready to go?" he asked.

"Or do you want to talk about the results?" the doctor asked.

"I think I'll look them over in my room," Mia decided.

"Then let's head on out," Jack said.

Mia stood, with help from both men, and they made their way back across the campus to her dorm. By the time they arrived, Mia was winded and needed to sit on the couch. Jack went to the kitchen and brought her a glass of water.

"Thank you," Mia said, drinking it down.

"You're back," Claire declared as she came in.

"I am," Mia replied.

"So?" Amy asked.

"I haven't looked at the results, yet," Mia said.

"Do you want to do that in private?" Sherry asked.

Mia looked at the other women. Each of them would be put

into this position at some point in the near future. Sherry was almost to the point of seeing her babies, Amy was supposed to be conceiving in the next couple of days, and the others were lining up right behind them. While Mia was private with most things, these women deserved to know what was in their future.

"Let's look together," she said, pulling the papers out of the envelope.

"I can't believe they're all girls," Claire said. "I thought you would be split half and half."

"Doesn't surprise me," Gwen replied.

"Why?" Mia asked.

"My guess," Gwen said. "They are using a method to make sure they are the gender they want. I mean, they are doing all of this testing, and giving you all of these boosters, it makes sense that they tailored the study so that they would get a specific gender when the time came."

"But why girls?" Amy asked.

"Because then they can reproduce, too," Gwen said.

They all looked at her like she'd grown another head.

"What do you mean?" Mia asked.

"The best way to get a new genetic makeup into the populous is to have girls," she said.

"I don't get it," Claire said.

"Because we get a HUGE part of our genetic makeup from our moms," Gwen said.

"I had no idea," Claire said. "So, do we get anything from our dads?"

"Oh, yeah," Gwen said. "Our gender is determined by our dad, along with a bunch of other things. I think they're using the self-propagating powers we have."

"The what?" Amy asked.

"Women can get pregnant without men," Gwen said. "It

doesn't happen very often, but it can. That's probably why they did so much testing on us when we signed up. We're probably good candidates for this."

"Then why didn't we become pregnant before?" Amy asked.

"And why did they do insemination?" Sherry asked.

"And how do you know all of this stuff?" Claire asked.

"Okay, let's answer these one at a time," Gwen said. "I know this stuff because it's what I studied in college. My major was genetics, but I couldn't finish because we ran out of money. That's why I signed up for this study. I figured if they chose me, I could get enough money to finish my studies.

"The reason we didn't get pregnant before," she continued, "is because it's really rare for that to happen. Some animals can do it, but most humans lack the complete ability. I think that's why they had to inseminate us, or, well, you guys. I'm not sure what method they're using."

"Turkey baster," Claire said, and they all laughed.

"I mean," Gwen continued. "They could be using semen from a male donor, or they could be using another method to cause us to self-propagate."

"Wait, they can do that?"

"There are several methods that work," Gwen said. "I didn't get too far into my studies, but I do know some things."

"You know a whole lot more than I do," Mia said.

"I think she knows more than most of us," Claire said.

"You now know most everything I know," Gwen said.

"Even if we can't understand it?" Amy asked.

"It's so complicated I don't really understand it all," Gwen said.

"Gotta pee," Mia said, trying to get up off the couch. It took Claire, Gwen, and Amy to help her get up. She rushed as fast as her body would let her to the bathroom, still barely making it in time.

"I can't wait to be done," she said when she came back out

of her room.

"How long?" Sherry asked.

"I'm at week nineteen," Mia said. "I'll be on bed rest here for a few more weeks, then they're moving me to the clinic."

"Did they say how long until the babies would be born?"

"Dr. Sanderson said I should make it to week thirty-two," Mia said. "They're already giving me the boosters to get the babies to grow faster. I just hope they stay in long enough."

It was a worry that the girls had discussed when they found out she was having so many babies, whether they would survive. Mia just had to hold out hope that she would be able to keep them inside long enough.

"We're gonna miss you," Claire said as Mia was getting ready to leave the dorm and head for the clinic.

"It's not like you can't come see me," she replied. "I'm just across the way. You'll know right where to find me, too."

"But it won't be the same," Amy said. "Who am I gonna ask about what's going on?"

"Sherry can tell you," Mia replied.

"Right," Amy said, rolling her eyes.

Sherry had been out of sorts since her emotional breakdown a couple of weeks earlier. She was only having two babies, so it wasn't as drastic as Mia. Still, there were times when the others wouldn't see her for days on end. When they'd try to engage her at meals, Sherry would simply answer with a nod of her head or a one-word response. Mia worried that she would break under the strains that were coming on daily with the pregnancy. There was nothing she could do about it, though. She just had to hold out hope that in the next few weeks she'd have a roommate at the clinic, both of them on bed rest waiting for the babies to arrive.

"Don't worry about us," Gwen said. "We'll keep Sherry in good spirits. Maybe I'll make some of my mom's enchiladas."

"Not if Jack has anything to say about it," Mia quipped.

"Or Dr. Sanderson for that matter," Claire said. "He's all about the healthy diet. I would kill for a donut right now."

"And a cup of coffee," Amy said.

"Ugh," Claire grunted. "Don't remind me. I miss coffee so much."

"Ready?" Jack said as he entered the room with a wheelchair.

"Seriously?" Mia whined.

"Doctor's orders," Jack said. "You aren't even supposed to be up on your feet."

"I had to pee," Mia said, knowing that was the only reason she was supposed to be up right now.

"You always have to pee," Jack said.

"It comes with the condition," Mia replied.

"Speaking of which," Amy said, turning to go to her own bathroom.

"Let's get going," Jack said.

Mia picked up her bag of books and sat in the chair and they headed out the door. It was a short walk across the campus to the clinic where she was taken into a room.

"Can I help you change?" the nurse asked.

"Do I have to wear the open-at-the-back hospital gown?" Mia asked.

"Not yet," the nurse said.

"I just realized," Mia began. "I don't know your name."

"Julie," the nurse said.

"Hi, Julie," Mia said.

"Hello," the nurse replied. "Now, let's get you into something a little less constricting."

She pulled out a short, full gown and helped Mia change while still sitting in the chair. Once they had the top done, she helped her up and she took off her pants and put on some loose shorts.

"These are nice," Mia said.

"Super comfortable," Julie replied. "And really easy to get into and out of. That's gonna be important in the next few weeks."

Once she was changed, Julie helped her onto the bed, placing pillows behind her head.

"You can only have these two pillows," Julie said. "And we're gonna raise your feet as well. We want to make sure that your heart doesn't have to work too hard to keep the blood moving. This will also give the babies a little more room."

"Am I gonna have to stand on my head?" Mia asked. Julie looked at her confused. "I heard about a mom who was having a bunch of babies and she had to lay with her feet up and her head down."

"We're going to get there eventually," Julie said. "Your feet will need to be above your head in order for your heart to have less strain. It won't be uncomfortable, though. We'll move you gradually."

"And I just get to lay here?"

"We've got some movies you can watch," Julie said. "And you brought plenty of books."

"But that's not gonna last three months," Mia complained.

"We can replenish your supply," Julie assured.

"I hope I don't die of boredom," Mia sighed.

"I'll be around during the day," Julie said. "And you can meet Kiki when she comes on later this evening."

"I didn't know there was more than one nurse," Mia confided.

"Dr. Sanderson didn't need another nurse until you got to the point where you had to be here," Julie confessed. "Now that you are, though, we will need someone to watch you overnight."

"Is she as nice as you?"

"She's super," Julie said. "I think you guys will get along

117

really well."

"How are we settling in?" Dr. Sanderson asked as he came into the room.

"We've got her changed and set up," Julie said.

"Are you feeling good about the move?" he asked.

"I guess," Mia said. "I'd love to stay with the other girls, but understand the need to be here."

"Good," he said. "Let's get you hooked up to the monitors."

With that, Julie stepped out and returned a moment later with a machine on a cart. She wheeled it up to the other side of the bed and began to plug lines into it.

"First," Dr. Sanderson said. "I'm going to need to see if I can tell where the girls are."

He gently pushed her top up, exposing her abdomen. His hands were warm as he moved them around her stomach, feeling each bump along the way.

"Perfect," he said once he'd finished. "Let's get baby A first."

He picked up a packet and opened it, pulling out circular stickers with snaps on the back of them. He placed one on her stomach, up near her ribcage. He moved around the rest of her abdomen, placing three additional stickers on her. With that complete, Julie handed him lines from the machine next to the bed. He snapped them onto each of the stickers.

"Let's see if we're good," he said to Julie.

She flipped the switch and Mia watched the screen come to life. It was larger than she expected, but then she saw why. Divided into fourths, each section showed the movement and heartbeat of each baby. This way they could monitor them all on one screen.

"I've got it recording," Julie said.

"Good," Dr. Sanderson replied. "I'm going to get an IV started," he said to Mia.

"For what?" she asked.

"We need to reduce your intake of food," he replied. "This way you will get all of the nutrients you and the babies need without putting a stressor on your internal organs."

"Will I get to eat at all?" she asked.

"Oh, yes," he said. "We'll start reducing your intake over time so it will be gradual. I still want you eating the whole time. There are only so many things we can get into your system through an IV."

"Good," Mia said. "I'd hate to give up eating."

"This will also help with the injections," the doctor said. "We can give you the treatment medications through the IV instead of subdermally. It will be a faster absorption and you'll need less as well."

"Hooray for small victories," Mia said.

"I love your positivity," the doctor said. "I'll be right back."

He left and Julie finished typing on the keyboard attached to the machine.

"I'm really getting excited," she said. "Are you?"

"I'll be glad when I don't feel like a beached whale," Mia said. "I'm also really glad I won't be getting shots every week anymore."

"Yeah," the nurse said. "That is one of the nice things about the IV. It'll cut down on a lot of things."

"Here we are," Dr. Sanderson said as he came back in. "I'll put it low enough that it won't interfere with your arm movements."

With that, he held his hand out. Mia placed her arm out and the doctor wrapped the rubber around her upper arm, tightening it to get the veins to show themselves. With a practiced hand, he placed the needle into her arm, catching the vein just right. He pulled the sleeve off the tube, then taped it down. Pulling a syringe out of his pocket, he flushed the IV, then capped it off.

"There we go," he said. "Perfect. I'll get the bags ready to go and we'll be on our way."

"Thanks for being so good at that," Mia said. "My mom always said she had shy veins."

"Yours are beautiful for this," he said. "It makes it much easier."

"Do you want to watch TV?" Julie asked after the doctor left.

"I think I'll nap," she replied.

"Good idea," Julie said. "You've got your call button and the remote is here as well. Should I put some of your books up here for you, too?"

"That would be nice," Mia said.

Julie picked up the bag Mia brought with her and placed it on the table next to the bed.

"I'll turn down the lights and let you rest," Julie said. "Just push the button if you need anything."

"Thanks," Mia replied through a yawn.

She hadn't realized how tired she was until the lights dimmed. Before she realized it, she was fast asleep, dreaming the strange dreams of pregnancy.

"They're looking better and better," Dr. Sanderson said.

"I can't believe how normal they look," Mia said.

"Why wouldn't they be normal?" the doctor asked.

"I just wasn't sure," Mia said. "We don't know much about the fathers, so I wasn't sure whether there was going to be anything odd about the babies."

"They're not mutants," the doctor said. "We've just given them some enhancement. They'll be stronger, smarter, and more resilient. They'll also have a better immune system to fend off disease."

"That's good," Mia replied.

"I think just a couple more weeks and we should be good to

deliver," he said, pulling the ultrasound wand from her stomach. "We'll do another amnio next week, just to make sure that their lungs are all good."

"I can't believe it's time already," Mia said.

"Aren't you ready?" the doctor asked.

"More than ready," she replied. "It will be nice to be able to sit upright again."

"This is the hardest part of the study," the doctor said.

"How's Sherry doing?" Mia asked as the doctor pulled her gown down over her stomach.

"She's doing well," the doctor said. "I think she was just worried with all that went on with you. Knowing she's only got two babies makes it easier for her."

"Who else is pregnant?"

"Amy lost her babies," the doctor said. "They simply weren't able to survive. Claire was just inseminated. We'll be confirming tomorrow."

"Can she come see me?"

"Absolutely," the doctor said. "I'll make sure she stops by after her appointment."

"Doctor," Julie said, peeking her head in.

The concern on her face made Mia's stomach drop.

"I'm coming," the doctor said. "You rest, now. We'll be seeing those pretty little faces in no time."

With that, he stepped out the door and closed it. Mia picked up the book she'd been reading, flipping it to the bookmark in the center. Try as she might, though, she couldn't concentrate. It had been this way for several weeks, though, so this was nothing new. Two more weeks, she could do this.

"You're doing just fine," Dr. Sanderson said.

"Just breathe," Julie said.

Mia had been fine waiting the two weeks, but her babies

had other thoughts. She'd felt twinges for a few days, but didn't pay any attention since the doctor and nurse both said it was normal. When the cramping became unbearable, though, she'd pressed the button. That set off a whirlwind of commotion, everyone she'd dealt with during her stay and more were suddenly crowding into her room, shoving things around, making room for equipment she couldn't identify.

"Can you feel this?" the doctor asked.

"I can't feel anything," Mia said. "And I can't breathe."

The panic was surging through her and she couldn't seem to remember how to breathe. One of the doctors put a mask on her face and she just wanted to shove it off.

"It's oxygen," he said. "It will help."

Gulping the gas, she slowly slipped into darkness.

"Hey there," Claire said.

Mia blinked in the darkness, barely able to make out her friend's shape.

"You really scared us," Claire said. "Are you feeling better?"

"My babies?" Mia asked.

"They're beautiful," Claire said. "You'll get to see them soon. Dr. Sanderson said they are perfect in every way."

Mia slipped back into the darkness, despite her desire to talk with her friend.

"I thought you'd like to meet baby A," Julie said as she came into the room.

Mia reached out instinctively, and the nurse handed over the bundle. Pushing the blanket aside, Mia stared down into the most perfect face she'd ever seen. The baby was pinker than Mia imagined, and had long lashes that lay across her cheeks. Mia ran her hand over the baby's head and felt the soft down of hair there. Tears welled in her eyes, slipping silently down her cheeks.

"Did you pick a name?" the nurse asked.

"Abigail," Mia said. "She's perfect."

"That she is," Dr. Sanderson said as he came in. "How are you feeling?"

"Fine," Mia said automatically.

"Mia," the doctor said.

She looked up at him then, seeing that he was truly interested in how she actually was.

With a deep breath, she said, "Besides being tired, I really am fine."

"No soreness at your incision?"

Mia looked down at her baby and smiled. "I don't have any pain."

"I'll need to check it," he said. "Julie, can you take the baby?"

Reluctantly, Mia handed her daughter over. Julie took the baby from the room as Dr. Sanderson looked at Mia's abdomen. He pushed a couple of places, but Mia couldn't feel any pain.

"When can I see my other babies?" she asked when the doctor was finished.

"I'll have Julie bring them in," he said. "I don't want you to overexert yourself, though. Only hold one at a time, and always have someone help you with them. You're going to be tender for a few weeks. We'll get you up and walking tomorrow and see how things go from there."

"Okay," Mia said. "Doctor," she began as he went to leave.

"Yes," he replied.

"Thank you," she said. "Thank you so much for giving me my babies. They're beautiful."

"It truly is my pleasure," he said. "I want to thank you for being part of this study. I truly believe that your children will be the future of our race."

With that he stepped out into the hall, shutting the door behind him. Mia smiled, truly happy for where she found herself.

"Oh my gosh," Claire exclaimed as she held Abigail in her arms. "She's just perfect."

"Isn't she?" Mia asked.

"I can't believe I have some inside me, too," Claire replied.

"Do you know how many?" Mia asked.

"Next week we'll find out," Claire said. "I hope there's only two, though."

"It was really hard with all four," Mia said.

She held Bridgette in her arms. Charlotte and Delilah were still in the nursery being cared for by the nursing staff.

"I feel so bad about Amy," Claire said, not taking her eyes off the baby in her arms.

"Me, too," Mia said. "Do they know what happened?"

"Amy said the doctor told her the babies weren't viable," Claire said.

"What does that even mean?" Mia asked.

Claire looked up at Mia, then said, "I don't know, and Amy won't talk about it."

"Has Sherry been doing better?"

"Yeah," Claire said. "She feels bad about Amy, too. She's been spending a lot of time in her room. Said she doesn't want to make Amy feel worse by being large around her."

"Julie said Sherry won't be put on bed rest as early as I was," Mia said.

"Probably because she's only got two babies," Claire replied. "She's not nearly as big as you were at this point."

"Yeah," Mia said. "I was as big as a house when I was twenty weeks."

"Ready to swap out?" Julie asked as she came into the room carrying one of the other babies. Kiki was right behind her carrying the other baby.

"Who's who?" Claire asked.

"I can tell," Mia said.

Julie handed the baby she was holding to Mia, who had shifted to place Abigail on her lap.

Pulling the blanket back she looked into the baby's face and said, "This is Delilah."

"How can you tell?" Claire asked.

"Not sure," Mia replied. "They all look the same, but they are all different, too."

"I'll take Bridgette," Julie said. "Then you can hold Charlotte."

Claire handed the baby she was holding over to the nurse, then took the one the other nurse was holding.

"I can't believe how big they are," she said.

"They are growing really fast," Kiki said. "Dr. Sanderson said that's something he expected, though."

"It's good, though," Julie said. "This means they will be stronger sooner than if they had not had the added genetics."

"Speaking of which," Mia said. "Has he said anything about how they seem?"

"I was just coming to talk with you about them," Dr. Sanderson said as he entered the room.

"I'll leave you two alone," Claire said standing with the baby.

"You can stay," Mia said. "Unless you don't think she should."

"If you're comfortable with me discussing this in front of her," the doctor said.

"Stay," Mia said. "You'll probably be getting this info soon anyway."

Claire returned to her seat, Charlotte sleeping in her arms.

"So," the doctor began. "You probably noticed that the babies are growing pretty fast."

"I did," Mia said. "I don't remember how fast babies grow,

though, so just figured it was my imagination."

"It's not," the doctor said. "Usually babies born this early would be kept in a neonatal ICU. Because of the enhanced genetics, their lungs were much more developed, even with the early delivery. They are also doing well on all of the tests that we would normally run on newborns, with scores well above that of a non-enhanced baby. What I'm really pleased with, however, is their ability to adjust to their environment."

"What do you mean?" Claire asked.

"They don't seem to be affected by the temperature, or anything else around them," the doctor said. "It seems they can handle most noises, rapid changes in temperature, and most other stressors we've put to the test."

"You're not hurting them, are you?" Mia asked, concern clear in her voice.

"Oh, no," Dr. Sanderson said. "Just light changes in the room, nothing drastic."

"Does this mean your study is a success?" Claire asked.

"Right now," the doctor said, "it appears that we are meeting and exceeding our expectations. This is good for the study, and also means that your babies will be strong and healthy as well."

"What happened to Amy's babies?" Mia asked.

The doctor seemed a bit surprised by the question, but schooled his features quickly. "Her babies did not survive past the first six weeks," he said. "We may not be able to use her in the study, unfortunately."

"Does this mean she won't be paid?" Claire asked.

"Absolutely not," the doctor replied. "Everyone who has made it to this point will be paid, whether they are able to continue or not."

"How is Sherry doing?" Mia asked. "I know she was having some issues before."

"She seems to be holding up pretty well," the doctor said. "We've added some counseling for both her and Amy as they move forward in the study. Hopefully, that will help her with the adjustments. I think finding out she was only carrying two babies helped her tremendously. It isn't as high risk as your pregnancy, Mia, but there are still risks we are watching. I think she will be joining you here in the next week or so."

"That will be good," Mia said.

"Now," the doctor said. "I'd like to check your incision once more before I go. Do you want me to come back after your visit?"

"If Claire doesn't mind, I don't," Mia said.

"Why don't I take Charlotte back to the nurses," Claire said. "That will give you the privacy for the exam, and I won't have to see the stitches."

"Okay," Mia said as Claire stood. "Why don't you take Abigail with you and leave Charlotte here, though."

"I can do that," she said.

With care, the babies were exchanged and Claire left the room. The doctor helped adjust the babies so he could get a look at Mia's incision, pushing the blankets down and the gown up.

"This is healing up very nicely," the doctor said once he'd done his exam. "How does it feel?"

"It's really not hurting at all," Mia said. "Which is surprising since I was sliced open just a couple of days ago."

"That has a lot to do with the additional injections you were receiving," the doctor explained. "I think that we'll continue the injections for the next couple of weeks, just to make sure your recovery goes well."

"Will I have to stay here the whole time?"

"I actually think you could go back to the dorm in the next couple of days," the doctor told her. "The babies are going to have to stay here for a few weeks, though, so it might be easier for you if you stay here."

"I'd rather stay with the babies," Mia said.

"I think that will be fine," the doctor said. "I'll let you rest, now."

"Thank you," she said. "Will you let Claire know she can come back in?"

"Sure," he replied, then left the room.

"Well?" Claire asked when she came back in. "What did he say?"

"That I'm healing nicely and should be able to come back in a couple of days," Mia replied.

"What about the babies?"

"They'll have to stay here for a couple more weeks," Mia said. "I'll be staying with them, too."

"Good," she said. "I don't know how we'd do with them at the dorm."

"Yeah," Mia said. "Not really sure how this is all going to work out, either."

"They sure are cute, though," she said, picking Charlotte up again.

"That they are," Mia said.

Within a month, Sherry had been put on bed rest for the duration of her pregnancy, Claire got the news that she was having three babies, and Mia had been released from the clinic. Her babies had grown so rapidly they were already exhibiting abilities that were far above their age. The doctor had said they would continue to grow exponentially faster over the first year.

Amy had been discharged from the study, which she had been fine with. The remaining women were on hold for insemination, as they did want to watch the first three sets of babies grow. It was decided that each new mom would be given a space of their own, with a bedroom for themselves, plus a couple of extra rooms for the babies. Dr. Sanderson had also brought in nannies for additional care of the babies, all of which had been screened and cleared for privacy concerns.

Sherry's girls were born four months after Mia's, going to the full thirty-six weeks that the doctor had hoped for. She'd named them Emily and Faith, moving along in the alphabet from Mia's four. Before the women knew it, their babies were well beyond where they should have been, doing things children much older were barely able to perform.

Gwen had become pregnant without being inseminated shortly after Sherry's babies were born. Dr. Sanderson didn't seem surprised, and began the process of adding the genetic code to her baby as well. She was only pregnant with one baby, and Dr. Sanderson attributed that to the fact that she had self-replicated.

By the time Claire was put on bed rest, two of Mia's girls, Charlotte and Delilah, were crawling. When Claire's three were born, Sherry's were crawling and Mia's were walking. Claire named her girls Grace, Hannah, and Isabelle, continuing the naming system they'd decided on. Dr. Sanderson didn't seem surprised by the children reaching milestones much faster than normal, and attributed it to the additional genetics he'd included. He'd decided that he would hold off on any additional pregnancies until after the first set of babies were more mature.

Gwen's pregnancy continued as normal, and when her baby was born, she named her Jordan. Her baby didn't advance nearly as rapidly as the first three sets of babies, but Dr. Sanderson said that might be because the baby didn't have the genetic additions prior to conception. He assured her that her baby was healthy and would grow naturally.

"How are you feeling?" Mia asked as Gwen sat next to her on the sofa.

The women had asked for a communal area where they could gather to talk about parenting and how their babies were growing. Dr. Sanderson had allowed it, saying that they would be better able to handle the multiple children easier if they were a community rather than individual families. After having spent nearly eighteen months together, it seemed right.

"I don't know how you guys do it," Gwen replied. "I'm exhausted all the time. And Jordan isn't nearly as active and mobile as yours."

"We have the benefit of them all being friends," Claire said.

"Don't forget about the nannies, too," Sherry added.

"But all Jordan does is eat, sleep, poop, and cry," Gwen said.

"That's normal," Claire said. "I think my nieces and nephews didn't do anything for the first six months at least. Our babies aren't normal. You have to remember that."

"But they all seem completely normal to me," Gwen said.

"Just growing at a much faster pace," Sherry said.

"Ladies," Jack said as he came into the room. "I hope you don't mind my disturbing you, but Dr. Sanderson asked that I come get you all."

The women looked at each other, unsure what this might be about.

"Did he say why?" Mia asked.

"I'm sorry," Jack said. "Just that I should ask you all to come to the clinic."

The women exchanged looks, then rose to follow Jack out the door. No one spoke as they made their way to the clinic.

"Oh, good," Julie said as they stepped inside. "Come on back. We've got some interesting things to show you."

Once again, the women exchanged looks, then followed the nurse back into the clinic.

"Ladies," Dr. Sanderson said. "I think it's about time for you to meet the designer of this study."

"I thought you were in charge of the study," Mia said.

"I am," he replied. "But I didn't create it. That honor falls on Martin."

With that, he opened the door to a large room where someone sat at a desk, his back to the door.

"Martin," Dr. Sanderson said. "Please meet the women in your study. The mothers to your children."

The chair swung around and a small man sat in it. "Hello, ladies," he said.

His voice was soft, almost feminine in nature. He stood and came around the desk, reaching out his hand. With arms longer than normal, the women looked at each other again, still trying to wrap their heads around this new twist in their situation.

"I'm Claire," the woman said, stepping forward and taking the small man's hand.

"Pleasure to finally meet you in person," Martin replied.

Each woman, in turn, introduced themselves and shook his hand. Once the formalities were finished, Martin said, "I would like to answer any questions you might have."

"Why didn't you introduce yourself before now?" Mia asked.

Smiling, Martin said, "I wanted to wait until I was sure that my design would work."

"And what, exactly, was your design?" Gwen asked.

"Please," Martin said, indicating the chairs in the room.

"I'll leave you to this, then," Dr. Sanderson said, exiting the room and closing the door behind him.

Once the women were seated, Martin sat in his own chair in the circle and began.

"I was born in the back of a bar," he began. "My mother didn't even know she was pregnant. She left me in the bathroom trash and never looked back. One of the waitresses heard me crying and came in to investigate. I was taken to the local hospital where one of the doctors noticed some anomalies about me. He tested me and found that I was not quite human."

"Not human?" Mia asked.

"Exactly," Martin said. "By the time I got to the hospital, I was already exhibiting signs that I was much older than a newborn. They confirmed with the bar that I was indeed born just hours earlier, due to the remnants of my birth left behind. The doctor began watching me closely and decided that he needed to do additional tests. Because of the results of those tests, and because Dr. Sanderson was very convincing, I was allowed to go home with him to be cared for outside the hospital. When he brought me in just months later, the staff couldn't believe I was the same baby.

"I grew to be the age equivalent of a toddler within six months," he continued. "By the time I reached the age of one, my body resembled that of a four-year-old. I grew exponentially fast, and by the time I was a two-year-old, I was conversing and able to understand vocabulary at a fourth-grade level. By age three, I was able to comprehend high school vocabulary, and by age four I was prepared to study doctorate education."

"Wow," Gwen said.

"Yeah," Mia agreed.

"What does this have to do with us?" Sherry asked.

"I think," Claire began, "that he is saying our babies are like him."

"Exactly," Martin said.

"As in your children?" Mia asked.

"Not exactly," Martin said.

"Then how?" Gwen asked.

"Dr. Sanderson was the doctor who first treated me," Martin continued. "He was able to find a gene that was altered in me pretty early on."

"Wait," Claire said. "How old are you?"

"I'm sixteen," he said.

"But you look like you're in your early forties," Sherry said.

"That is one of the things the gene seems to do," Martin said.

"Does this mean that our babies are going to grow old and die before us?" Sherry asked.

"We think we've been able to slow that part down," Martin said. "They are not growing nearly as fast as I did, and they seem to be slowing down the older they get."

"But what about Jordan?" Gwen asked. "She isn't growing as fast as the others."

"I think you are like my mother," Martin said. "She was able to conceive without a father."

"Then how are you a boy?" Gwen asked. "You should be female, not male."

"We haven't quite figured that part out," he said. "Needless to say, we were hoping that yours would be a boy as well. That would explain how I came to be."

"Sorry to disappoint you," she said.

"Not at all," Martin said. "We were relieved you were having a girl."

"But," Mia began.

"If she'd had a boy," Martin interrupted, "we would understand how my mother was able to conceive a boy without the benefit of a father's donation. Because she didn't, our assumption is that I do have a biological father."

"Then why did you mature so quickly?" Mia asked.

"We don't think my father is human," he said frankly.

The women looked at each other, not knowing who should ask the question everyone had on their mind. Finally, Mia asked, "What was your father?"

"While we can't be one hundred percent sure," Martin said. "We believe he was what is known as extra-terrestrial."

"Wait," Claire said. "Your dad's an alien?"

"He is definitely not of this world," Martin said.

"Have you met him?"

"No," Martin said. "Not that we haven't tried to find a way. It would make things much easier if we could discuss this with him."

"I bet," Gwen said.

"So, then," Claire said. "How are our babies like you if they aren't your children?"

"Like I said," Martin continued. "We were able to isolate a gene that had been altered within me. By using a technique of gene-splitting, we were able to separate what we wanted from other genes, then use a form of artificial insemination using spinal fluid to help you become pregnant."

"What about me?" Gwen asked.

"I think you spontaneously procreated," he said.

"Is Jordan going to be like the rest of the girls?"

"We're not sure, yet," he said. "We've taken some blood, and what we see is an altered state, but not to the point that the other girls are. While we are sure she is normal in most every way, she will not have the advanced growth the other girls have."

"When will our girls stop growing so fast?" Sherry asked.

"They are slowing down already," he said. "I believe that their growth rate will slow within the next few months. By the time they reach two they should be on track for regular growth."

"But they'll be older than other two-year-olds," Mia said.

"Mentally, they will be," Martin said. "For the most part, when they enter school, they will be on the high end academically, simply appearing smarter than the average kid."

"What happens after we leave the program?" Claire asked.

"That's what I wanted to talk to you about," Martin said. "While you are all free to leave at the end of the three years, I was hoping you would all be willing to stay on here. Raise your girls here where we can educate them and continue to monitor their growth."

"I think that would be fine," Mia said. "I don't really have any family, so staying here would be nice."

"I would love it if my mom got to see her granddaughters," Sherry said.

"How is she?" Martin asked.

"The last letter I got from my dad said the doctors called her a miracle," she said.

"I'm glad," he replied.

"Did you have anything to do with this?" Mia asked.

"I simply sent them something to try," he replied.

"You used my mom as a guinea pig?" Sherry shouted.

"No," Martin said. "I simply provided her with a medication that has shown a good return on other patients."

"I guess that means we're not the only study you have going on," Gwen said.

"My genes have proven to be helpful in many areas," he said. "I am simply putting what I have to good use where possible."

"What does that mean for our children?" Claire asked.

"It means that they will be the next generation of healthy humans," he said. "They will be resistant to diseases, just like me, as well as more intelligent than most humans, also like me. From the testing we will be able to do on them, the human race will move to a healthier, more balanced, and peaceful species."

"Peaceful?" Mia asked.

"Have you not noticed that your girls play with each other without argument?" he asked.

"I just thought it was because they were all so close in age."

"Even children of the same age tend to argue and fight," he said. "Especially siblings."

"True," Gwen said. "My brothers were always arguing, fighting, and pushing each other around."

"Is it part of their genetic makeup?" Sherry asked.

"We believe so," he said. "Dr. Sanderson and I were pretty sure that the babies would be more attuned to each other, but their connection and compassion for each other, as well as for each of you, is beyond what we could have hoped for."

"How will this help us now, though?" Claire asked.

"While it won't be an immediate change," Martin said. "Their ability to compromise and work out their problems without it coming to blows or shouts will show others that we can work together."

"Until they're cast aside because they're freaks," Sherry said.

"You probably haven't noticed," Martin said. "But each of you have changed while here."

"We know," Mia said. "We're now mothers, and have become like family to each other."

"It's more than that," he insisted. "The women who were not selected to have babies are altered as well. While they didn't stay at the Institute, they did stay in a relatively close area where we could monitor them and make the genetic adjustments. They have been receiving the same injections you did while you were pregnant. This has helped to boost their immune system as well as alter their genetic makeup."

"Wait," Mia said. "You've changed us, too?"

"Didn't you expect that?" he asked.

The women looked at each other and realized the truth. Over the last year, they have become more calm, willing to help each other out, and none of them have had to deal with even the smallest of colds.

"What happens next?" Gwen asked.

"Next," he said, "we put this into a larger control group. Our next phase has already begun with some men who have been willing to undergo treatment."

"What are you doing to them?" Sherry asked.

"Altering their aggression with some more calming traits," he said. "That trial began at the same time yours did, and the progress has been amazing. If you are all willing, we are wanting to see how they will co-exist with you."

"Like as neighbors?" Mia asked.

"More like an extended family," he said. "Dr. Sanderson is over at their dorm discussing this with them right now."

"So, they don't know about us," Gwen said.

"And they can't know about me," he said.

"Why not?" Claire asked.

"If they knew that I was not human," he said. "It would likely skew the results."

"We thought we were going to have mutant babies," Mia said.

"Why would you think that?"

"Our dreams were really pretty bizarre," she said. "Every one of us, with the exception of Gwen, had dreams that our babies were trying to eat us from the inside out."

"And our emotions were far worse than regular pregnant women," Sherry added.

"I'm sorry that happened," he said. "Honestly, though, most everything about your pregnancies were normal."

"When do we get to meet our neighbors?" Gwen asked.

"Let me check with Dr. Sanderson," he said, rising and moving to his desk.

He picked up the receiver on his phone and pushed a couple of buttons. The women couldn't hear him, but the call was short, and he returned quickly.

"They're ready whenever you are," he said.

The women exchanged a look then rose, almost simultaneously, to follow the small man out of the room. Making their way out of the clinic, they walked across the other side of the campus toward another building. It had been there all along, but they'd never paid it any mind, assuming it was an unused portion of the campus. Within minutes they were walking up to another door.

"Ladies," Dr. Sanderson said as he opened the door. "Come on in and meet your new family."

"How did we miss four pregnant women?" Micah asked.

"How did we miss five guys?" Mia countered.

"Truth," Johan said. "I guess we both missed things."

"I think they kept us on separate schedules to keep us apart," Gwen said.

They were all sitting in a conference room in the dorm the men had been staying in. Micah, Johan, Tom, Gavin, and Scott had been on the campus the entire time the women had, receiving injections and having testing done on them during this time as well.

"Where do you all come from?" Claire asked.

"We're all from the area except Johan," Scott said. "He came to the states for the study specifically, though."

"How did you find out about it?" Gwen asked.

"It was my doctor," Johan said. "He is a friend of Dr. Sanderson. When he found out about the study, he wanted to see if he could get some of his patients in as participants. I was the only one who passed the initial screening."

"So, what, you just flew here and started getting shots?" Sherry asked.

"Something like that," he replied.

"We all have similar backgrounds," Gavin said. "Mostly, we're just your average guy."

"How has it worked, then?" Gwen asked. "I mean, what kind of testing have you been going through? Besides the injections, are you getting any other alterations?"

"Geeze, Gwen," Sherry said. "Give them a little privacy."

"It's fine," Tom said. "It's pretty much just been hanging out. We're all doing online courses so we are using our time wisely. I have to say, it's been fascinating to see how much better we all are at school."

"It's true," Scott said. "I did not do well in school at all. But after starting this study, I have moved well past anything I thought I'd ever learn. I figured I'd end up a mechanic like my dad. Not that it's a bad thing, I just didn't see myself as an intellectual."

"We need mechanics just as much as any other profession," Mia said.

"Absolutely," Tom said.

"I think this will be good, though," Claire said. "Enhancing the race, I mean."

"Did you guys have another person in the study?" Scott asked.

"We did," Mia said.

"What happened to her?"

"She wasn't able to carry her babies," Gwen said. "Dr. Sanderson said she was discharged from this part of the study. I guess she went to the other group."

"Other group?" Tom asked.

"Martin told us that the women who were not chosen to carry babies were put into another control group where they received the gene therapy," Gwen said.

"I didn't know there was more than one study," Gavin said.

"You also didn't know there were women having babies at the Institute," Mia said. "But then again, we didn't know about you guys, either."

"Now that we know about each other," Johan said. "Maybe we should hang out."

"That would be fun," Claire said. "As long as you don't mind babies."

"I think we all love them," Gavin said.

"We're serious," Mia said.

"It's not exactly what I expected," Dr. Sanderson replied.

"You had to know this might happen," Gavin said.

"I knew," Martin said.

"You did?" Dr. Sanderson asked.

"It is the natural progression of life," Martin replied.

"Marriage?" Dr. Sanderson asked.

"We want it to be official," Gavin replied.

"How long have you two known each other?" Dr. Sanderson asked.

"I think you know that already," Mia said. "You introduced us last summer."

"But how well can you know each other in just a few months?"

"What else do we have to do?" Gavin asked. "There are nine of us, five guys and four girls. It's not like we have much else to keep us occupied."

"And neither of us have a family to go back to," Mia said.

"We want to spend the rest of our lives together," Gavin said.

Dr. Sanderson looked back and forth between them, realizing they were serious.

"Anyone else planning to get together?" he asked.

"It's only a matter of time," Martin said.

"What if you guys get pregnant?"

"Then we'll have the strongest, smartest, most beautiful baby in the world," Gavin said.

"But it will skew the study," Dr. Sanderson complained.

"It will actually make the study more viable," Martin said.

"Exactly," Mia replied. "You will get to see what happens when two subjects procreate."

"That sounds so clinical," Dr. Sanderson said.

"Well," Gavin replied. "It's better than saying when two people get busy making babies."

"You're sure?" Dr. Sanderson asked.

"We are," Mia replied. "I've never been more sure of anything in my life."

"And you?" the doctor asked Gavin.

"Absolutely," he replied.

"Then I guess it's settled," the doctor said. "We're gonna have a wedding."

It didn't take long before the remaining members of the study coupled up, all except Tom. But he seemed fine with it. He spent much of his time with Claire and Johan, and they seemed to make a pretty good team. Within two years the couples had welcomed three new babies to their families, with another on the way. Dr. Sanderson was pleased with the results, finding that the children born from these unions were on par with the ones conceived through the study itself.

Martin watched as his compound filled out with new families added from the other studies, pleased with how well the genetic alterations were taking hold. He hadn't expected the interest from the outside medical community, but once they heard about the health of the people within the compound, they started inquiring. Soon, half a dozen hospitals in the region were including the option of genetic alteration in their services.

A school was opened on campus, initially for the children of the study. Before long, though, members of the surrounding area were asking for permission to send their children. Initially, Dr. Sanderson and Martin wanted it to be exclusively for children in the study. With the influx of altered humans, though, it was opened to outside children as well, all of which had gone through gene therapy.

By the time Abigail, Bridgette, Charlotte, Delilah, Emily,

Faith, Grace, Hannah, Isabelle, and Jordan were ten, they were studying courses to get their doctorates. Martin was pleased with the advancement and decided that his work was finished at the Institute.

"Where will you go?" Dr. Sanderson asked.

"Back where I came from," Martin replied.

"I don't understand," the doctor said.

"Do you really think it was a coincidence that brought me to your hospital?" Martin asked.

"Of course," the doctor said. "You didn't exactly choose where to be born."

"But I did," the other man said. "And now I can go back home, knowing that my children will continue to repopulate this world, making it a much safer place to live."

The doctor stared in stunned silence, unsure what he was hearing.

"Don't worry," Martin said. "Within three generations, humans will have outgrown their childish ways. They will then be ready for integration into the larger community of the universe. Unfortunately, you won't live to see it. But have no fear. You are going to be remembered as the founder of this movement. You will be celebrated for eons to come."

THE EMBODIMENT OF ART

H ere we see the final submission to the collection," Hannah said. "Alexander was known for not only his artistic beauty with paint and clay, but he wrote beautifully as well. He titled this piece, 'My Beloved' in honor of his late wife, Beatrice, who preceded him in death shortly before he penned this piece. At twenty-nine, she was young, even for that time period. His son later collected all of his writings and transcribed them for publication, but kept each piece in its original format as well. You can find this collection, as well as prints of his paintings and copies of his sculptures in the gift shop on your way out of the museum."

Hannah had worked at the museum for a few years, and had always loved the collections they brought in. This one was extremely special to her, since she had studied Alexander Thornton in college, and fell in love with his work, particularly his writings. Her studies delved into his background and she found a lot of inconsistencies in what was readily available.

"We conclude our tour with this piece," she continued. "If any of you have any questions, please feel free to ask. Any of the museum staff can answer your questions. I want to thank you for visiting the Edison City Museum of Fine Arts today."

"Excuse me," a man said after the rest of her

group disbursed.

"Yes," Hannah replied. "How can I help you?"

"You seem to know quite a bit about this artist," he said.

"I do," she replied. "While all of the staff are given extensive information about each exhibit we offer, this one is close to my heart."

"I could tell," the man said. "I had some questions that may sound odd. Would you mind answering them?"

"Not at all," she said. "I'm happy to help." Hannah led the man away from the crowd, asking, "What did you want to know?"

"First," the man began, "I'd like to apologize for the bizarre nature of my questions."

"I'm sure I've heard them all," she laughed. It was true, too. There had been questions she'd had to answer with a straight face when all she wanted to do was look at the person and ask if they were out of their mind.

"My studies have led me to believe that Mr. Thornton may have killed his wife," he said. "I know that you may not have this information, but I wanted to see what you might know about it."

"Well," Hannah said. She had to be careful when she answered questions that were not part of the training she received from the Museum, especially when it went to the more off the wall things people wanted to know. This definitely fell into that category. After gathering her thoughts, Hannah said, "We do not have any information regarding the cause of death of Beatrice Thornton. There were many who speculated the same as you, that he had a hand in her death. No report or other evidence has ever been made available regarding it."

What Hannah didn't tell the man, what she couldn't tell any visitor, is that she had heard the same rumor, and that she had investigated it, even going so far as to visit his home, which was now a national landmark, to see what she could dig up there.

"I know there's nothing official," the man said. "But I also know that you probably know more than what you are allowed to share here."

"I'm not sure what you mean," she said.

"Just that you gave much more information than any of your colleagues during the tour," he said. "Some of the things you shared were well beyond the simple information given to tour guides. My guess is that you did some studies on this artist on your own."

Hannah looked at the man, unsure how to respond. Every employee at the museum was required to study the art they showed, given a week, sometimes more, to learn as much as they could about the artist and each piece they would have on display. While most of the other guides did a cursory review of the information given, she was of the mindset that the more you knew, the better you could inform.

"I'll admit that I do tend to dig pretty deep when we get a new artist," Hannah said. "It's just part of my nature. I like to learn, and this job gives me the opportunity to get to know some of the most amazing artist that ever lived."

"This exhibit has been up for two weeks," the man said. "My guess is you got the information it would be coming a month or two before. Even if I give you the benefit of the doubt, that is still only a maximum of three months you could have studied his work. With the number of pieces in this collection, there is no way you could be as knowledgeable about them as you are without a foreknowledge as to his art. So, I'll ask my question again. Did Alexander Thornton kill his wife, Beatrice?"

"I'm afraid I can't answer that," Hannah said. "My capacity of information on this artist is limited to what we were given when the exhibit became available for our museum. That is all the information I am allowed to share with our patrons."

She was giving him a hint, that she couldn't talk about it at the museum. Now, she just had to hope that he was curious enough to ask her to give him the information outside the scope of her duties.

"It's been very nice speaking with you," he said. "Perhaps we will bump into each other in the future. In the meantime," he continued. "If you are ever interested in a career outside this one, please contact me."

He handed her his business card, black with white lettering on it. Simple and classic.

"Thank you," she said. "I look forward to possibly meeting you in the future."

With that, the man walked away. Hannah flipped the card over and saw his name and number. She would definitely be giving Mr. Bradley Graham a call. Not only was she intrigued by what his interest in the Thornton exhibit was, but also in the man himself.

Bradley walked away from the Edison City Museum of Fine Arts with a lightness to his heart he hadn't felt in years. His research into Alexander Thornton had been thrust upon him by his father, and his grandfather before that. Four generations of Grahams had been investigating the man, trying to discover what truly killed his wife.

When Beatrice had first married Alexander, the family was thrilled. Thornton was well known, having been the curator of the museum in their home town of Charlotte, and a philanthropist in the community back in the mid nineteenth century. Shortly after their son was born, though, she had withdrawn from her family, and from the community at large. Her father and brothers had discussed their concerns with Alexander, who simply put them off, saying she was taking time to be a mother and would return to her societal duties in the near future.

She returned nearly a year after Edmund was born, but was not the same. Frail and demure, she did not resemble the woman who had been wed to Alexander just three years before. Shortly after that, she took ill and was bedridden. Refusing to allow her family to see her in such a condition, it took her father, Reuben, months to convince Alexander to go against her wishes. He brought their family doctor in to examine her and ensure that she was being treated well and not being held against her will.

The doctor confirmed that she was ill, but could not determine the cause. Beatrice had been outraged with her father's intrusion and withdrew even further, cutting the family off completely. Alexander had been kind, continuing to allow Edmund's grandparents to visit him. They watched him grow while their daughter stubbornly refused to see them.

Shortly before Edmund's second birthday, Alexander called Beatrice's family to the house, telling them the doctor did not expect her to survive the night, and they should come to pay their last respects. When they arrived, the doctor told them what to expect: a shell of the woman they knew. Reuben went into a rage, demanding that the doctor find out what had killed his beloved child. The doctor said he could not explain it, simply that she failed to thrive once her son was born, and died from the heartache that she could not have another child. This was the first the family heard of her inability to have more children, and they demanded Alexander tell them why they were not told before. He'd informed them it was their daughter's wishes to keep it a secret.

That was the basis of Reuben's quest to find the truth. He scoured Alexander's artwork looking for clues as to what had truly happened to his daughter. The only clues he could find were the fact that the artwork all seemed to revolve around her. Everything Alexander created was in some way associated with Beatrice. From the paintings to the sculptures to the written word, everything was about her. Slowly, Alexander drew away from the Graham family, finding them too difficult a reminder of his loss. His son, Edmond, was the only connection they had, and that tapered off as well.

By the time the boy was of age, he wanted nothing to do

with his mother's family. He blamed them for his mother's death, felt they had accelerated her demise and refused to even see them. This broke Reuben's heart. Year after year he tried to get in touch with Edmund, only to have his correspondence returned, unopened, with a note attached saying it was refused. Finally, Reuben gave up trying to connect, simply living with the information that was shared in the newspapers.

Passing the duties of finding the cause of Beatrice's death to her brother, Joseph, Reuben died a sorrow filled man, never truly knowing the reason behind his loss of not only his daughter, but a grandson as well. The task of finding the reason for Alexander's wife's death was passed down from generation to generation, always the eldest son taking the mantel of finding out the truth.

Now that it was his turn, Bradley had taken it upon himself to find every piece of art that Alexander Thornton created from the time he met his wife until his death thirty-seven years after her. While he'd been unable to acquire any of the pieces, he did take the time to visit each museum that held his work. Edison was the most recent, and he'd decided it would be the place he would find the answers his family had been searching for all this time.

"May I speak to Bradley Graham?" Hannah asked.

"Can I tell him who is calling, please?" the receptionist asked.

"My name is Hannah Collins," she said. "I met him yesterday at the Edison City Museum of Fine Arts."

"One moment, please," the other woman said.

Hannah twisted her hair with her finger while she listened to the music from the other end of the phone. She wasn't sure whether the man would remember her, or if he even meant that she should call him.

"Ms. Collins," a man's voice came over the phone.

Hannah was startled for a moment, but recovered quickly.

"Mr. Graham," she said. "I just wanted to see if you wanted to discuss the exhibit. I mean," she stuttered. "Well, you said you had some questions, and you thought that I might have some answers, but that I couldn't answer while I was at the museum and so I thought I'd just call you and see if you wanted to talk about it."

The words rushed out of her non-stop and she couldn't help but feel foolish for just blurting out so much.

"I'm sorry," she apologized. "I shouldn't have called. You probably were just being nice and didn't mean for me to call so I shouldn't have called at all. I'll let you get back to your work now and quit bothering you."

"Hannah," Bradley said.

"Um, yeah?" Hannah asked.

"I would love to meet with you," he said.

"Oh," she said.

"Are you available to meet for dinner this evening?" he asked. "Say around seven?"

"Um," she stammered. "Yeah, I think that's fine. I mean, yeah, that's fine."

"Great," he said. "I'll have a car pick you up."

"No," she said.

"Excuse me?"

"I mean," she stumbled. "Just that you don't have to send anyone. I can get to where ever we're going. Where are we going?"

"I'll have a car there at seven tonight," he said. "We'll have dinner at The Bayshore Club."

"I don't know if I have anything fancy enough for there," she said.

"I'll send something to you this afternoon," he said.

"I can't accept that," she said. "That just wouldn't be right."

"Consider it an early birthday present," he said.

"How do you know when my birthday is?"

"Ms. Collins," Bradley said. "It is my business to know things about my staff."

"Wait, what?" she asked.

"I am in the process of purchasing the museum where you work," he said.

"You are?" she asked. "I mean, I didn't know it was for sale."

"Everything is for sale, Hannah," he said. "I will see you this evening."

Before Hannah could answer, the call was disconnected. She realized that she didn't tell him what size dress she would need, nor where she lived. All of this was beginning to feel like she was stuck inside a book or movie.

Looking at the clock, she realized how late it was and decided she better get into the shower and get some things done, especially if she was going out to the Bayshore Club for dinner. She definitely needed to do some research on her date, too.

Bradley replaced the handset into its cradle and sighed. He hadn't intended to be so forward with Hannah, but there were two things he wanted from her. The first was any information she had on Alexander Thornton. That was the most important thing he needed. Selfishly, though, he wanted to get to know her. She had been impressive on the tour, pointing out things that he wasn't aware of, despite his extensive research on the man. While this had been a catalyst in asking her to dinner, he was well aware of his attraction to her. What he didn't know was how she would respond to his advances.

He pressed a button on his phone and said, "Stacey."

"Yes, sir," she responded through the intercom.

"I need you," he said.

"Coming," she replied and the door opened shortly after.

"I need you to get a dress appropriate for the Club and get

it sent to a Ms. Hannah Collins," he said.

"Do you have a size?"

"She's about your size," he said. "Perhaps a little taller."

"Color?"

"Emerald green," he said. "I'll need a matching tie as well."

"Reservation time?" she asked.

"Seven thirty," he replied.

"Yes, sir," she said then turned on her heels and walked out.

Stacey was perfect at her job: discreet, polite, and a bull dog when it came to giving out information. She was also extremely loyal to him. He paid her well above what the position should garner, but she was worth it, and then some.

Sighing, he returned to the task at hand, completing the merger documents for the acquisition of his newest property. While it wasn't a big money maker, the museum turned enough of a profit that it was worth the investment. Bradley had gained enough properties to afford him the luxury of owning things which made him happy, and this museum was one of those things.

His computer pinged and he looked up. It was a message from Stacey saying everything was taken care of for the evening. How she did things so quickly was beyond him, but he wouldn't look a gift horse in the mouth. No, he would accept what he'd been blessed with and use it to his advantage.

"The Bayshore Club?" Jenna asked.

"That's what he said," Hannah replied.

"Is he cute?"

Hannah had been sharing an apartment with Jenna for the three years she'd lived in Edison. Neither of them made enough to afford a place on their own, unless they were willing to live in the sketchy part of the city. They were as different as two people could be. Jenna preferred the night life and party atmosphere, while

Hannah liked the solitude of the museums and cultural centers the city boasted.

"Is that seriously all you are interested in?" Hannah asked.

"I'm just saying," Jenna said. "He's got to be rich to be able to take you to the Club. I just hope he's not one of those super rich guys who is uglier than a troll and hopes his money will buy him some action."

"Jenna!"

"What?"

"I can't believe you," Hannah said.

"Have you met me?"

It was their go-to question when one or the other did something so in-character that they couldn't believe the other was surprised. Hannah just rolled her eyes.

"Let's Google him," Jenna said. "I mean, you know what he looks like but I don't. Maybe he's not who he says he is and he's some crazy psycho who's just looking for a pretty girl to kidnap."

"Really?" Hannah asked. "That's what you come up with?"

"Happens all the time," Jenna replied. "Now, what's his name?"

Hannah gave Jenna the business card she received, then said, "I'm gonna take a shower. You figure out if he's a serial killer on your own."

Jenna grabbed the card and giggled. "I got you," she said, then pulled out her smart phone and went on the hunt for information. It was what she did best.

Hannah just rolled her eyes again and walked into her bathroom.

"I'm here to pick up Ms. Hannah Collins," the man said when Jenna opened the apartment door.

"Hannah," she shouted over her shoulder.

Hannah stepped out of her room, picking up her clutch from the kitchen table.

"You need me," Jenna said quietly as she passed her. "You just let me know."

"I'll be fine," Hannah said. "Good evening," she said to the man at the door.

"Good evening, Ms. Collins," he replied. "If you'll follow me."

He turned and walked back down the hall to the staircase at the end. Hannah followed, taking the stairs carefully in her heeled boots. While Jenna could probably run in her heels, Hannah preferred flats or tennis shoes to anything with a heel.

They stepped out of the building and she followed him to the awaiting town car. He opened the back door and she slid in. Once she was shut inside, he stepped around to the driver's side and climbed in. Starting the car, they were off for the short ride to the Club where he reversed his motions, coming around to let her out.

"Thank you," she said automatically.

"My pleasure," the man said.

She walked up to the door of the club where a doorman opened the portal. The inside was just as she had imagined, polished wood and marble accentuated the foyer.

"Your name?" the woman at the podium asked.

"Hannah," she replied. "Hannah Collins. I'm supposed to be meeting..."

"This way," the woman interrupted.

Hannah followed her through the dining room to the back where she saw her date sitting at a table sipping amber liquid from a glass. He stood when she arrived and pulled out her chair.

"Thank you," she said as she sat.

"I'm happy to see you again," he said. "Thank you for agreeing to have dinner with me."

"You're welcome," she replied.

"I took the liberty of ordering for us," he said. "I hope you don't mind."

"Um, okay," she said. She'd never had someone order her food for her and wasn't sure what to think of it.

"Would you like something to drink?" he asked her.

"Just water will be fine," she replied.

She fiddled with her hands in her lap, unsure whether she should begin the conversation or wait for him. Since she didn't really know what he wanted, she decided to wait. It didn't take long for a waiter to come by with salads for both of them.

"Thank you," she said.

The waiter nodded and left. She again waited for a signal from the man across from her, unsure whether she should begin eating or wait. This was so outside her comfort zone she didn't know what to do.

Bradley picked up his fork, gave her a nod, and said, "Enjoy."

Following suit, she also picked up her fork. The salad was full of spring greens and had a nice raspberry vinaigrette dressing. The flavors burst in her mouth with the first bite, and she audibly moaned her appreciation.

"Glad you like it," he said and she blushed to the roots of her hair. "Don't be embarrassed," he continued. "Nothing wrong with enjoying your meal."

This only made her blush more.

"Let's talk about Alexander Thornton," he said once the salads were nearly gone.

"What do you want to know?" she asked.

"First," he said. "I'd like to know how you know so much about him."

"I was an art history major in college," she replied. "I did my thesis work on him. It was a really fascinating study into the history of his work, and the life he lived. There were so many things I couldn't get answers to, though, and that was

really frustrating."

"How much do you know about his family?" Bradley asked.

"Besides his wife," she answered. "He had a son, Edmund. That's who gathered his collection and began the process of displaying it in museums. First it was displayed in the museum Alexander curated. Once that museum closed, the art was returned to his son for storage or to use as he saw fit. After that, though, it was taken out of circulation and thought to have been lost."

"Then how did it find its way to your museum?"

"That should be obvious," she replied. "It was found again. But we aren't the only one who displayed it after it was rediscovered. It spent time in several larger museums around the country, sort of a touring exhibit. When we were given the chance to acquire it, I pushed hard to make it happen."

"Because of your studies?"

"And because of its significance in the region," she replied. "Alexander Thornton was the most well-known artist to come out of the Carolinas, and it would be unfathomable to not have his work shown in his home state."

"What happens to it once the exhibit is over?" he asked.

"For someone who is buying a museum," she said. "You certainly don't know much about how they work."

"This is going to be my first museum," he replied. "Most of what I own are clubs, hotels, and restaurants."

"Then let me enlighten you," she said. "We do not own the pieces we display, for the most part. Primarily, we are an exhibition place where work is shown to the public. Most artists don't have enough space to show their own work, so we do host local artists as well. For the bigger shows, like the Thornton exhibit, we lease them from the owner, showing them within the guidelines they give us. I believe this is the way most museums work as well, though there are always exceptions."

"Seems like you know quite a bit about the industry," he

replied. "Perhaps I should hire you to take over the museum once the sale is final."

"And put Mrs. Lansing out of a job?" she asked. "I couldn't do that to her."

"I wasn't quite serious," he said. "I mean, you could do the job, no doubt, but I am not going to be making any staffing changes, at least for the time being. But I may want to have you work for me in some capacity. Would you be interested?"

"You don't even know me," she replied. "We just met a couple of days ago, and that was at my job where I was doing what I do."

"Which is why I think you would do well working for me," he replied. "Let's get back to the Thornton exhibit, though."

"Great," Hannah said, relieved that the conversation was going to move away from her. She hated being the center of attention, especially when it was in a conversation with an extremely handsome man.

"You said the pieces were lost, then found," he said. "Do you know where the art was between when it was 'lost' and when it was 'found' again?"

"There are actually several theories about that," she began. "The obvious first one is that the pieces were put into someone's attic at some point and forgotten."

"How long were they missing?" he asked.

"It is clear that they were displayed in the museum he curated for about a decade after his death," she said. "After that point, though, is where we move into suspicion as to what happened."

"What do you know as fact?" he asked.

"Well," she said. "The museum remained open for just over ten years after Alexander died. Without him to manage it, though, it became a money pit and they had to sell it. At that time, the pieces still in possession of the museum were given back to his son,

Edmund. He kept the collection out of circulation from any museum for the remainder of his life. His will deemed that they be offered for auction upon his death, since he had no family to pass them on to."

"That's where I lost track of the collection," Bradley said. "Who purchased them?"

"It was an anonymous bid that purchased them," she said. "They were shipped to New York where they disappeared. About twenty years ago, one of the pieces, the one titled 'My Starlight' showed up as a piece at the Met."

"What do you mean, showed up?"

"Just that," she said. "It arrived in an unmarked box with an index card indicating the artist and name of the piece, along with it's place of origin. The curator was stunned and tried desperately to find out where it came from."

"Obviously they did," he surmised.

"Actually, they didn't," she corrected. "The courier who brought the piece in said it was dropped off at their location with instructions to deliver it to the museum."

"Who dropped it off?"

"A taxi," she said. "When the company was asked about it, they were told it came from a hotel, which had no further information. They said that it was found in a storage closet on the premises with the note to deliver it to the museum, and the manner in which it was to be sent. There was also cash to pay for the delivery."

"Then where did they get the rest of the collection?" he asked.

"The same way," she replied. "Every month or so, another piece would be dropped off. Same information as to how it got there, from a different hotel each time. No one could piece together where the pieces were coming from."

"All of it going to the Met?"

"Each piece went to a different museum in the tri-state area," she explained. "It was a real mystery for the curators to figure out. Of course they talk, we're all in the same business. We share pieces regularly, and work together to make sure that each of our collections compliment without competing. After a year or so, the collection became rather large, with no one owning more than a couple of pieces. It was decided that the museums would work together to share this collection, gathering it all in one place to show the full scale of his work. It started at the Met, then moved around the tri-state area, followed by a tour of the country. When we were notified that it might be coming to the area, we pushed hard to be the ones to display it."

"Why is that?" he asked.

"Because this is where he was born," she said. "Alexander Thornton grew up in Edison, married here, raised his son here, and died here. He's buried in the cemetery on Water Street, next to his wife and child."

"I thought he was from Charlotte," Bradley said.

"His museum was in Charlotte," Hannah explained. "But he lived just outside of Edison. His house is a national landmark. I'm surprised you didn't know that."

"But he was originally from Charlotte," he said.

"Technically," she replied. "But he always said that Edison was his home."

"So," Bradley said. "What do you make of the rumors of his having something to do with his wife's death? I know you can't comment officially as a member of the staff of the museum, but my sense was you knew more than what you said the other day."

"Some of them are so ridiculous they're laughable," she said.

"Like the fact that he used parts of her in his art," Bradley agreed.

"Or that she was the true artist and he was jealous of her

work," she continued.

"That's the one that baffles me the most," he said. "It is obvious that he was the artist since many of the pieces from the collection came after her death."

"Unless you take the rumor that she didn't die when they say she did," Hannah said.

"That's a new one," he said.

"Really?" she asked.

"From what I know," he began, "she was buried and her family saw the body. They even had her examined."

"The research I read said her family didn't see her body," she replied. "What I learned was that he had his own doctor examine her and give the report to her family, but that he refused to let them see her after she passed away."

"I think we'll have to agree to disagree on this," he said.

"How do you know so much about it?" she asked.

"Let's just say I have more than a passing interest in his artwork," he said.

"Is that why you're buying the museum?" she asked. "Because, we don't own the artwork."

"I'm buying the museum because it is a good investment," he said. "My interest in the collection is personal, though."

"You're the one who is in negotiations to purchase it," she said. "I should have known."

"Why?" he asked.

"Your last name is Graham," she explained. "That was Beatrice's last name before she married Alexander. You're family, aren't you?"

"That I am," he confirmed. "Our family has been trying to gain access to the artwork in order to do some testing on it. We also believe that since Alexander had no other family, and his son never had children, it rightfully belongs to us."

"Why did your family not claim it upon Edmund's death?"

"Unfortunately," he said. "It was sold prior to our becoming aware of his death. Her brother, my great, great grandfather, was unaware that Edmund had died. He didn't find out until well after the collection and everything else in the house was sold. Nothing was left to her family."

"Who brokered the auction?" she asked. "I mean, did they even try to find family?"

"You know we're talking about the late 1800's, right?" he asked. "At that time, if there was a will, that was what happened to the property of the person who died. Since he had no children, there was no one to protest the will, and the artwork and everything else in the estate was auctioned off. My family wasn't even notified that it was taking place."

"Why not?" she asked. "I mean, it seems that in this small of a town, they would have known he died and could have asked about what was going to happen to everything."

"His will was very specific," he said. "His father's was as well."

"What do you mean?" she asked.

"It was specified in Alexander's will that everything was left to his son, Edmund," he said.

"That makes sense," she replied.

"There was also a stipulation that once Edmund passed away," he continued. "If he had no heir, then the property was to be sold at auction, and the Graham family was banned from purchasing any of it. It would be passed down generation to generation until no heir was alive, then it was to be sold."

"Banned?" she asked.

"Yep," he replied. "That's why no one knew it was for sale."

"Then how could an anonymous bidder purchase the collection?" she asked.

"My guess is that the person who purchased it was not anonymous," he replied. "They simply didn't want her family to know who it was."

"How did it get split up and sent to the museums, then?"

"It's been over a hundred years since the original sale," he said. "There was no provision in the will that stipulated it not be sold or sent elsewhere once the final heir let it go. Because of this, whoever purchased it originally was able to parcel it out and send it to the museums."

"Wait," she began. "It was originally sold in 1897 as a whole collection. After that, it disappeared for over a hundred years. It began showing up in 2000 or so. That's a long time for it to just be sitting in someone's garage or storage unit. Where did it go?"

"I don't know that that particular mystery will ever be solved," he said.

"If your family had known about the auction," she began. "Do you think they would have asked someone to bid for them? I mean, that would be a way for them to get the pieces without it faulting the will."

"The person who purchased it had to sign a guarantee that they would not be giving it to our family," he said. "Which means that whoever purchased it couldn't have been hired by my family because they would have had to lie on the paperwork in order to gain possession of the pieces."

"And you know they were purchased as a set," she said.

"By one entity," he confirmed. "Then, they simply vanished."

"If the will says that the person can't sell them to your family, how are you going to purchase them now?" she asked.

"They are not owned by the original purchaser," he replied. "The owners are the museums. By the time I am ready to purchase the collection, I will own your museum and will be able to properly show my ability to display and protect them."

"You've thought this through thoroughly, haven't you?"

"Very much so," he replied.

"So," she said. "How can I help?"

"I thought you'd never ask," he replied.

"Did you go back to school when I wasn't paying attention?" Jenna asked Hannah.

"No," Hannah replied. "It's for Bradley."

"It's Bradley now?" she asked. "Didn't know you were on a first name basis, yet."

"We've been working on this for five weeks," Hannah said. "We went to first names within the first week."

"Interesting," Jenna said.

"What's that supposed to mean?"

"Just that you've never given any guy a second glance before now," Jenna said. "Suddenly, some guy shows an interest in your favorite artist and you're all swoony."

"I'm not swoony," Hannah protested.

"You are," Jenna said. "You keep looking at your phone, wondering if you'll get a text or call or email from him. You're doing so much work after work that it's like you're studying for a doctorate. When I suggest we watch something or go out or do anything other than your research you snap at me and act like I'm trying to steal your favorite toy."

"That's not swoony," Hannah said. "That's moody, and it's because you're disrupting my flow."

"The only flow you've had is information overload from research," Jenna said. "You seriously need to take a break. There is more to life than art, you know."

"I am taking a break," Hannah said. "Tonight, Bradley and I are going out to dinner."

"But you'll be discussing Alexander Thornton," she retorted. "That does not constitute a break."

"We'll talk about other things," Hannah said.

"Will you be talking about going on a real date?"

"This is a real date," Hannah said.

"No," Jenna said. "A real date is where you go to a movie or to dinner or something. Not where you talk about work. That's not a date at all."

"But it's something we both love," Hannah protested.

"Even so," Jenna said. "You need to do something besides talk about that artist."

"The purchase is supposed to go through next week," Hannah said. "Once that's done, Bradley will be moving forward to purchase the collection from the various museums."

"Which will take another month of you doing nothing but research," Jenna said. "I need a girls night."

"Next week," Hannah said. "I promise. We'll go get manicures and pedicures and watch stupid movies."

"But I get to choose," she replied. "None of those foreign films you like so much. I want something with a sexy guy in it, preferably one who has his shirt off most of the time."

"You're ridiculous," Hannah laughed.

"Hey," Jenna replied. "You used to love those movies."

"I still do," she said. "I just think I'd rather have the real thing."

"Are you trying to tell me something about you and Bradley?"

"There are moments when I think he's interested," Hannah said. "But then things happen and it's just like I'm a business associate or something. It's sometimes like he doesn't see me as a woman."

"Maybe he doesn't see you as someone who is befitting his stature," Jenna said.

"Because I'm not rich?"

"Or because you are about to become an employee," Jenna replied.

"He doesn't act like that," Hannah said. "I mean, okay, maybe he does a little. But honestly, I think he sees me more as someone he works with instead of someone he could spend more time with."

"Then maybe it's time you made him take notice," Jenna said. "When do you guys meet next?"

"After tonight, we're supposed to meet on Tuesday," Hannah said. "Dinner to discuss the final pieces of the purchase."

"Then we need to make sure that he sees more than just a cog in his wheel of fortune," Jenna said. "I've got a plan."

"Why does that make me nervous?"

"Because my plans are awesome," Jenna said.

"Or because your plans sometimes fail miserably," Hannah replied.

"Not always," Jenna said with a blush.

"Just when they involve guys," Hannah said. "Do I need to remind you of Wilson?"

"Please don't say that name," Jenna cringed.

"Then don't set me up like you did that time," Hannah replied. "I don't think I could take another episode like that."

"No one wants that to happen," Jenna said. "Never again."

"We're signing early," Bradley said.

"Really?" Hannah asked. "When?"

"Tuesday," he replied.

"So, we're not going out, then," Hannah said dejectedly.

"We're going out," he replied. "It'll be a celebration, though."

"Wasn't it already going to be a celebration?" she asked.

"This just means it'll be official," he replied.

"Where are we going?"

"Have you ever been to Lincoln Center?"

"I don't exactly make the kind of money for that place," she replied.

"Then you're in for a treat," he said. "They have the best

blackened Cajun catfish."

"Sounds delicious," she replied.

"I'll pick you up at seven," he said. "Will you have enough time to get home and changed?"

"Tuesday is my day off, so it won't be a problem," she replied.

"Great," he said. "Wish I didn't have to cancel tonight, though. I was looking forward to seeing you."

"Work calls," she said. "I understand. I'll see you Tuesday."

"See you then," he replied.

The call disconnected and Hannah pulled it from her ear.

"Canceled?" Jenna asked.

"Until Tuesday," Hannah replied. "He's finalizing the sale early, though, so we're going to the Lincoln Center for dinner."

"What are you going to wear?"

Hannah's phone buzzed and she looked down, seeing a text from Bradley. *I'll send something over on Monday for you to wear.*

"That's apparently been taken care of," Hannah said, turning her phone to her roommate.

"He certainly likes to dress you," she said. "Isn't that kind of creepy?"

"I like it," Hannah replied. "Makes me feel like he pays attention to me."

"Or pays attention to how you make him look," Jenna said.

Hannah looked at her friend and said, "He doesn't treat me that way."

"Has he made you feel like anything more than an employee, though?"

"That's what I am," Hannah protested.

"But you want more," Jenna said.

"Of course I do," she replied. "That doesn't mean that I have to push it, though."

"Once this purchase goes through," Jenna began, "what's to keep him interested? I mean, you'll have done all the hard work. Where's the incentive to keep you around as more than just an employee?"

"That's not what this has ever been about," Hannah said.

"Be honest with me," Jenna said. "You want more than just a working relationship with him and you know it."

"It would be nice," she replied.

"Then we need to do something to make sure that once he's got the museum, he'll want to keep you around."

The determination in her friend's voice was a surprise to Hannah. She knew that her friend loved her like a sister, and would do anything for her. What she didn't get was why she was so set on Bradley being the one for her. She'd never been that interested in who she dated before.

"Love the red," Jenna said. "Did you know he was sending something in this color?"

"I wasn't sure what he was going to send," Hannah said honestly.

"But you got new heels," Jenna said.

"Black, patent leather," Hannah replied. "They'll go with anything."

"Fine," Jenna said. "But we've got to do something spectacular with your makeup."

"I like a classic, clean, fresh look," Hannah said.

"Not with that dress," Jenna replied. "That dress calls for dramatic, and that's just what we're going to give him. He sent the dress, you'll supply the pop."

"Just don't make me look like a French whore," Hannah protested.

"Have I ever?"

"Wilson," Hannah said, and Jenna cringed, saying, "Fine."

The next hour was spent with Jenna flitting and brushing and pressing and glossing and all other means of primping Hannah. By the time they were done, Hannah felt like she was wearing a pound and a half of cake on her face. When Jenna turned her to the mirror, though, she looked like a movie star.

"Now for the hair," Jenna said, pulling out a brush, comb, and all sorts of other paraphernalia. Hannah wasn't sure what her friend had in mind, so simply sat and let her play.

Another hour went by with pulling and combing and spraying and finally Jenna seemed satisfied.

"Perfect," she said and turned Hannah back to the mirror.

Hannah's jaw dropped open at what she saw. Staring back at her was a vision from the silver screen of yesteryear, as if she'd been dropped from a movie from the '50's.

"Wow," she said.

"I know, right?" Jenna replied.

"How?"

"Magic, my friend," she said. "Pure magic."

Jenna pulled the towel she'd draped across her friend's shoulders, uncovering the satin that hung off her shoulders.

"Shoes," she said and Hannah dutifully went in search of the new pieces, sliding her feet into them.

"Well?" she said hesitantly, doing a slow turn in front of her friend.

"You are a vision of beauty," Jenna said. "He's not gonna know what to do with himself."

"I don't care about that," Hannah replied. "I care whether he knows what to do with me."

"If he doesn't," Jenna said. "Then he doesn't deserve you."

Just then they heard a knock at the door.

"Showtime," Jenna said as she went to open it.

"Ms. Sanders," Bradley said.

"Mr. Graham," Jenna replied.

"Bradley," Hannah said as she came to the door, her black clutch in her hands.

"You look stunning," he said with a smile.

"You two have fun," Jenna said, nearly pushing Hannah out the door.

"Night," Hannah said just as her roommate gave her a wink and shut the door.

"May I?" Bradley asked, holding his arm out.

"Thank you," Hannah replied, taking it in her hand.

They made their way down the stairs to the lobby of her apartment building, stepping outside into the cool spring air. When he walked up to a silver Porsche she faltered. It wasn't that she didn't appreciate the beauty of his car. Oh no, she loved it. The problem was it was too much of a reminder of her brother. He was the black sheep of the family, always in trouble. One night he stole a car very similar to this one, went for a joy ride with friends, and found himself wound around a telephone pole. In an instant, she went from a big sister to an only child, and her parents were never the same.

"Is everything all right?" he asked.

"Just bad memories," she said.

Bradley opened the car door and ushered her inside. Hannah closed her eyes and took a deep breath. She hadn't realized how tense she was until the smell of the man she was heading to dinner with filled her senses. Somehow it had a calming effect on her, giving her a sense of peace.

"You sure you're all right?" he asked when he got in.

"Yeah," she said, smiling. "Let's go celebrate."

"Let's," he replied.

"Have I told you how beautiful you are?" Bradley asked.

"I think seven or eight times, now," Hannah replied.

"I'm sorry," he said.

"I don't mind at all," she replied. "It never gets old having someone tell you that."

"Then I'll say it again," he said. "You are absolutely stunning."

"Thank you," she replied.

"Did you enjoy your dinner?" he asked.

"It was delicious," she replied.

"Good," he said. "I thought you might want to take a drive by the waterfront."

"That would be nice," she said.

"If you're too tired, though," he began.

"No," she said. "I'd like that."

Bradley handed his valet ticket to the kid at the podium and they waited for him to bring around the car.

"What is your ultimate goal as far as your career?" he asked while they waited.

"I'd love to be the curator at a museum," she replied. "I know I can do it, I just have to find the right fit for myself. I don't want to leave Edison, but I'm afraid I won't be able to go much further until I venture into a larger city."

"Have you thought about my offer to work for me?"

"You haven't really given me a job description," she replied. "I don't even know what the job is. And you don't know whether I'm capable of handling the job."

"After watching the way you dove head first into the project I gave you," he began. "On top of what you already do, I think you have the right work ethic for my company. And I know how smart you are, simply by the information you've given me from the studies I needed."

"What is the job, exactly?" she asked.

"I'd like you to work for me as an assessor," he said. "I'm going to need someone to review and authenticate any pieces I might want to add to the Thornton collection. I don't know of anyone more qualified than you to take that on."

"Except you," she replied.

Just then the young man drove up in Bradley's car. Opening the passenger door, Bradley helped Hannah into the vehicle, closing the door behind her. He walked around the car, pressing a large bill into the kid's hand as he passed, then climbed into the driver's seat. They drove out of the parking area and made their way to the waterfront, neither talking on the short trip.

"I'm serious," he finally said. "I want you to come work for me."

"That isn't what I studied," she said quietly.

"But it is what you are good at," he countered.

They'd found a place to park in a lot that looked out over the bay. Bradley turned the car off and shifted in his seat to look at Hannah.

"When I took your tour in the museum," he began, "I knew you were the one I needed to help me with acquiring the Thornton pieces. It was my third tour at Edison, and my seventeenth overall."

"You've been following the exhibits?" she asked.

"Does that surprise you?" he countered.

"I guess not," she said.

"No museum held enough of the exhibit for me to see its extent," he continued. "I wanted to see which pieces were out and what was and was not being displayed from the collection I knew existed. My goal has always been to be able to collect the entirety of the collection in one place. While there are many pieces you have in your museum, there are so many more that haven't been displayed. That's why I wanted you to do the research. If I'm going to have the whole collection, I'm going to need to know what has been rediscovered.

"The number of tours I've taken have told me that he isn't as known as he should be," he continued. "It also showed me that you are one of the only people besides me who is aware of the scope of his work. I think if we work together, we should not only be able to procure the remaining pieces of his work, but also figure out exactly what happened to Beatrice. That is my ultimate goal."

"Wow," she said.

"I know it's a lot to take in," he replied. "Honestly, though, you are probably the smartest person I've met who has as much of a passion for this project as I do."

"What do you think we'll find once we have the full collection?" she asked.

"The truth," he said simply.

"Do you need an answer today?" she asked, unsure whether she really wanted to delve into this with him or not.

"I'd really like an answer within the next week," he said. "But I want you, so take as much time as you need to find a way to say yes to me."

Hannah blinked at him, unsure if he'd just said what she thought he did.

"I just realized what I said," he said, almost reading her thoughts. "I mean, I want you for the project."

"So you're not interested in me," she said. "Other than my mind."

"That's not what I meant," he said. "I'm very interested in you as the beautiful woman you are. There is no question about that. I just don't know whether we should be involved in a relationship if we're going to be working together."

"I understand," she said dejectedly.

"Oh, no," he said, suddenly embarrassed by what he's said. "Let me start again. Hannah, I'd love for you to come work for me. I would pay you a good salary and give you quite a bit of leeway within which to work. Additionally, I'd love to see you on a social level. I know it would be awkward with you working for me, so if I have to choose..."

He paused and she looked at him.

"Please don't make me choose," he whispered.

The vulnerability on his face was more than she could bare. The longing she saw in his eyes was something she'd always wished to see. Because he had asked her to work for him, she felt it would never happen. But here he was, asking for both.

"I really like the idea of working for you," she said and held up a hand to stave off his interruption. "I also really like the idea of dating you."

"Then you'll do both?" he asked.

Taking a deep breath, she nodded. The smile that broke on his face was the most beautiful thing she'd seen in ages.

"Don't ever feel like you can't tell me anything," he said. "I mean it. If something is bothering you, if you want to stop the dating, if you want to stop working for me, anything. Just tell me."

"I will," she replied.

Two Years Later

You're sure?" Hannah asked into the receiver. "In each sample?" she asked again "Thank you."

"Well?" Bradley asked.

They'd finally gotten almost all of the pieces they were aware of from the collection. Each had been tested for anything out of the ordinary, and the results had just come back.

"Traces of human DNA," she said.

"I knew it!" he shouted, then scooped her up in a hug. "You're a genius."

"That's only half the battle," she said as he set her down.

"I know," he replied. "But it's the biggest piece we've found to date."

"Mr. Graham," came the call from Stacey over

the intercom.

Bradley moved around the desk and picked up the receiver. "Yes?" he asked.

"I have a package for you," she replied.

"Bring it in," he said, then hung up the phone.

The door opened and Stacey stepped in holding a small box. Bradley took it from her and thanked her, then brought the box to the desk. He picked up the letter opener and sliced through the tape holding the box closed. Folding the flaps back, he reached into the packing peanuts and pulled out a smaller package.

"What is it?" Hannah asked.

"I'm not sure," he replied.

Pulling the tape from the smaller box he pressed the flaps back. Inside was a small bottle and a card. He handed the bottle to Hannah and opened the envelope, pulling the card out.

> *You have completed the collection. This final piece is what is left of Alexander and Beatrice Thornton. Please ensure that this is kept separate from the other pieces. Lock it in a safe, keep it in a bank, move it to another city. Whatever you do, do not take it near the rest of the collection. The risk is too high. You are now trusted with this secret, one which can never be told. They can never come back.*

"Is this real?" Hannah asked.

"Are you willing to risk finding out?" Bradley countered.

Hannah looked at the bottle in her hand, twisting it in the light. The dark liquid shimmered where it caught the glow and she shuddered, handing the bottle back to Bradley.

"I'll lock it up," he said, walking behind his desk.

He pushed a plant to the side and pressed on a panel in the wall which opened revealing a safe. Bradley pressed the buttons on the front and it popped open. He put the bottle back in the smaller box and placed it inside, closing the door and putting the wall back in place.

"Are you sure it's safe there?" she asked.

"It has to be," he replied.

"Maybe we should send some of the collection to another museum," she suggested.

"You're saying you believe the note," he said.

"My guess is you do, too," she replied. "Otherwise you wouldn't have put that bottle in the safe."

"I'll leave it there until I can get it tested," he said.

"The rest of the pieces are together at the lab," she said. "If you don't believe that card, why don't you take it to the lab now?"

"Why run the risk," he said.

"Then you do believe," she replied.

"What I know is that there are trace amounts of human DNA in the pieces at the lab," he began. "If this also has DNA, and it is my guess it does, then we do run the risk that the note is correct. We will have the rest of the results from the testing in the next week. By then, we'll know whether it is strictly Beatrice in the art, or whether Alexander put some of himself in it as well."

"If it's both of them," she began, "what will you do?"

"Either way, I need to reveal the truth," he said. "When I do, though, it will be a shock to the art world."

"I think that's an understatement," she said.

"Yeah," he replied. "Perhaps the understatement of the century."

"It's here," Bradley said.

"I'll be right there," Hannah replied.

The door to Bradley's office opened nearly immediately after he replaced the receiver on his phone.

"Let's see it," Hannah said.

Bradley sliced the envelope with his letter opener and slid

the sheaf of paper out.

"They couldn't condense it?" she asked.

"I wanted the full report," he replied.

"Please tell me they have a summary sheet," she said.

"Right here," he said pulling the top page off the stack. *Sequencing conclusion 1: Singular, male, not related to Graham sample.*

Bradley looked at Hannah who read the sheet over and over again.

"It's not her," she said.

"Definitely not her," Bradley replied.

"Then are we at square one?" she asked, looking at him.

"Let me look," he said, going back to the desk. He flipped through the pages to one that was marked with a flag. "Here's another results sheet."

"Why are there two?" she asked.

"Second sample," he replied walking over to her with the second page. *Sequencing conclusion 2: Singular, male, related to Thornton.*

"It's him?" she asked.

"Apparently," he replied, rereading the second page.

"Where did you get a Thornton sample?" she asked.

"From the last piece," he said.

"You had that tested?" she asked.

"I did," he replied. "It came back as blood from their son, Edmund."

"Then how is it related to Alexander only and not to your family?"

"I asked the same question," Bradley said.

"Well?" she asked when he didn't offer anything further.

"It seems that Beatrice never was able to bear a child," he said.

"But…"

"That's why she declined so rapidly," he said. "Edmund was the son of one of their servants."

"I thought..."

"Let me finish," he said. She waved him on, so he continued. "Beatrice found out right after their marriage that she was unable to bear children. She wanted a child, and wanted Alexander to have a child. They decided to have one of their servants, someone who looked enough like Beatrice that the family would be fooled, bear him a child. Since women were not seen as much during their pregnancy in that time it worked. When Edmund was born, they presented him as their own.

"Beatrice soon became insistent on having more," he continued. "When Alexander refused to have another with the servant, she went into a rage, attacking him. He defended himself, but she was injured in the process. The reason she died was because of that injury. Alexander threw himself into his art, focusing on it rather than his son. By the time Edmund was old enough to understand what had happened, he cut all ties with the Graham family. He blamed them for his father's state."

Hannah sat with her hand over her mouth, unsure what to make of the story she'd just heard. "How did you find all of this out?" she finally asked.

Bradley went to his desk and pulled out another stack of paper, this one very old looking. He handed it to her and she pulled the front page back and began to read. The more she read, the more she realized that Bradley was right.

"Where did you get this?" she asked.

"It came the day after the bottle," he said.

"Why didn't you tell me?" she asked.

"I wanted to authenticate it," he replied. "I didn't want to muddy the waters until I had all of the facts."

"This is so sad," she said. "It changes everything about his work."

"You are the one who knows his work best," he said. "I want you to write a book on it."

"What do you mean?" she asked.

"I have a vested interest in the story coming out," he said. "But the story is the important part. It needs to be written by an outside party."

"I'm hardly that anymore," she replied.

"But you are," he countered. "You and I may have a relationship, but you are not family. Everything you've told me has helped to find the truth. I know you can do this, and you deserve the credit."

"I didn't do anything," she said.

"Your desire to know everything helped push me to get to the bottom of it," he said. "Without you, this never would have seen the light."

"Where did this book come from?" she asked.

"I don't know who sent it," he said.

"Do we know it's authentic?" she asked.

"What is your gut telling you?" he countered.

She looked back at the book in her lap, the pages so old she feared they would rip if she weren't careful. Finally, she nodded and said, "It's real."

"And?" he coaxed.

"It needs to be shared," she finally conceded.

"Then you'll do it," he said.

"I'll need help," she said.

"My resources are at your disposal," he said.

She looked at him again, unsure whether to ask, but decided she needed to know. "Where does that leave us?"

"I'm not going anywhere," he said.

New Beginnings

What kind of storage space does it have?" Karen asked as they finished their tour of the upstairs.

She and her husband, Cliff, were looking for their first home, knowing they couldn't stay on base much longer. They hadn't told their family yet, but they were expecting a baby right after the first of the year, and that had given Cliff enough of an incentive to retire from the military. They'd been fortunate that his most recent station was near where they both grew up, so they were looking to settle down and raise their family in their home state.

"Storage space in these older homes is sometimes hard to find," the realtor said. "But this one has an attic on the third floor, easily accessible up these stairs."

The woman showed them to a door at the end of the hall.

"Can we go up?" Cliff asked.

"Absolutely," the realtor said as she opened the door. "You go ahead and explore. I'll wait downstairs for you when you're finished."

Leading the way, Cliff climbed the narrow set of wooden stairs. The sun came in through the dormers, filling the small space with a soft light. Looking around, he noticed a handful of boxes lining one wall, but the space was otherwise empty.

"It's perfect," Karen said as she stepped up behind her husband.

"You should be able to paint in here with the light no problem," he replied, smiling at his wife.

"May take some work to get it cleared out, though," she said, noting the boxes.

"Doesn't look like much," he replied. "Who knows. They may have this all gone by the time we move in."

"Does this mean you're sold on it?" she asked.

"Right neighborhood, right price, perfect amount of space," he began. "No reason to look any further. I think we found our dream home."

Grinning up at her husband, Karen said, "I love you."

"You, too, Bunny," Cliff said, kissing her on the lips. "Let's go tell the realtor."

"This is nice," Gayle said to her daughter. "But are you sure you can afford it?"

"Mom," Karen said. "We've been over this. Cliff has a job offer for as soon as he is discharged. That means he won't spend any time without work, which means we won't miss a paycheck, and we've got some bonus money coming with the new job. It's the perfect time for us to buy."

"I just wish you'd have let your dad look it over before you signed the paperwork," Gayle replied.

"They did just fine," Charles said, brushing his wife's concerns away. "It's a great house, Bunny," he said to his daughter. "I'm really proud of you."

"Thanks, dad," Karen replied.

"Fine," Gayle succumbed. "What's the first plan of attack?"

"Cleaning," Karen said. "The realtor said that no one has lived in the house for about three years. It's just been sitting here collecting dust. I've got cleaning stuff in the kitchen already, so let's get started."

"I'm going to go mow the yard," Charles said, excusing himself and getting to the task.

"He's always quick to find something else to do when the word 'cleaning' comes up," Gayle laughed.

"Cliff's the same way," Karen replied.

"So," Gayle began. "Why the sudden desire to settle? I thought he was going to be reenlisting."

"We're ready," was all Karen would say.

"They never cleared out the attic," Karen said.

"Wonder why," Cliff mused.

"I guess whoever owned the house didn't want any of that stuff," she replied.

"Did you go through it?" he asked.

"You know how mom is," she began. "Everything in each room has to be spotless before we can move on to the next. I'm surprised we got more than the downstairs cleaned, honestly."

"Is she coming to help again tomorrow?"

"She's got some kind of committee meeting tomorrow," Karen said. "I'll get the attic cleared out and swept so I can bring my painting stuff up. Maybe I'll even be inspired."

"Are you sure you're up for it?" he asked. "I mean, are you worn out from today?"

"I'm not a fragile doll, babe," Karen said. "My body will tell me when to take breaks."

"When do we get to tell them?"

"Let's announce at the housewarming," Karen replied. "That way we can celebrate two big things."

"Perfect," Cliff responded.

"But for now," Karen said. "I think I'm ready for bed."

"Thought you weren't worn out," Cliff said playfully.

"Hush," Karen replied with a smile.

"You need to see this," Karen said as she came downstairs, carrying a small box.

"What did you find?" Cliff asked.

"Look," she said, holding the box open.

"What are they?" he asked.

"I'm kind of afraid to touch them," she said, setting the box on the counter.

Cliff reached into the box, pulling out one of the small stuffed animals. "They're kinda cute," he said.

"We are not keeping them," she replied. "I am not letting our baby touch those things."

"Maybe we can donate them somewhere," he suggested.

"Fine," Karen replied. "Just as long as I don't have to look at them anymore. They're kinda creepy looking."

"It's just the dust," he said. "Once they're clean, they'll all be really cute."

Karen just shook her head.

"What else is up there?"

"Don't know," she replied. "This was the first box I opened."

"Maybe you'll find some antique that's worth a million

dollars and we'll be set."

"Wouldn't that be nice," she retorted.

"Need help?"

"Nah." Karen shook her head, then said. "You finish getting the wallpaper off this kitchen. I can't do the '70's look. It'll kill me."

"What will we do about the countertop?"

"I really don't care," she said. "Burn it to the ground?"

"I'll figure something out," he said.

"You always do," she smiled.

"Holler if you need me."

Karen kissed her husband and said, "I will always need you."

"Cliff!"

The shout startled him and he rushed up the stairs to the attic. Out of breath he panted, "You okay?"

Karen was staring into a box, hand over her mouth. When she turned to him, her face was streaked with tears.

"What is it, baby?"

She shook her head and clung to him, burying her face in his chest and sobbed.

"Hey," he cooed, rubbing her back. "What is it?"

She just kept hold of him tightly, shaking her head back and forth. Patting her back, he released her and walked over to the box she'd been peering into.

"Oh, baby," he said, seeing the small urn inside.

"It's just so sad," she hiccupped.

He pulled out a pamphlet that was laying beside the urn and turned it over. On the cover was the face of an infant with the words, 'In Loving Memory' below the picture. Flipping it open, he read the inscription about a child who was lost before their life ever got a chance to begin.

"Baby," he said, turning to his wife.

"I can't imagine losing our baby," she sobbed.

"We're going to be fine," he comforted. "This is from years ago. There is so much more that we know about caring for medical issues now."

"Why would they leave their baby here, though?" she asked.

"Let's see if we can find out who the parents are," he suggested. "Maybe we can return her to them."

Karen nodded, trying to dry the tears still staining her face.

"Are you sure it's her?" Karen asked.

"She's the only one I could find," Cliff responded.

It had been a week since she had discovered the small box with the pieces of a broken life. An urn with the ashes of an infant inside, the program from the funeral, and the wrist band from the hospital where the baby was born and died. Cliff had promised to try to find the family of the baby, and had finally come up with a name and address for the mother listed on the paper.

"What do I say to her?" Karen asked.

"That you know how much it would mean if someone cared enough to return your baby to you in the same circumstances," Cliff suggested.

Taking a deep breath, Karen finally said, "Okay. I'm ready."

Holding his wife's hand, Cliff walked through the automatic door to the nursing home he'd found.

"Can I help you?" the receptionist asked.

"We're here to visit someone," he said.

"Great," the receptionist said. "Sign in here."

"We're not family," he said. "We've never met her, and we aren't sure where she is."

"What's her name?"

"Dorothy Sparks," Karen said.

A look of sadness came over the receptionist's face as she said, "Mrs. Sparks doesn't get any visitors."

"Well," Cliff began. "We'd like to see her, if it would be all right."

"I think she would like that," the receptionist said. "If you'll sign in here, she's in room 302. You can take the elevator there to the third floor."

Karen put their names down on the sign in sheet, then they pressed the button to call the elevator.

"You're sure you want to do this?" Cliff asked once they were inside.

"I have to," Karen responded.

They took the rest of the ride in silence until the bell chimed that they'd reached the third floor. Stepping out, they saw a caregiver waiting. "Can you tell us where we can find Mrs. Sparks?" Cliff asked.

"Are you family?" the caregiver asked.

"No," Karen said. "But we have something that belongs to her. We purchased her old house and it was left behind. We think she'd want it back."

"She's just down this hall," the caregiver instructed. "First door on the right."

"Thank you," Cliff said.

"You're welcome."

They took the few steps down the hall and came to the door marked 302. The name plate next to it showed two spaces for names, but only one was filled. "Ready?" Cliff asked.

Karen took a deep breath, then nodded. They stepped into the room, walking past the empty bed near the door to the one closer to the window.

"Mrs. Sparks?" Karen asked. The woman in the chair didn't respond. Stepping closer, she tried again. "Mrs. Sparks?"

She was small, fragile almost, with white hair done up in a bun on the top of her head and a light pink robe covering a floral night gown. When she turned, her eyes held no light, only a sadness that seemed to be soul deep.

"Are you Mrs. Dorothy Sparks?" Cliff asked.

The woman nodded, but was clearly confused as to who they were.

"We bought your house. The one on Fir Street."

No real response came from the woman, she simply stared at the intruders.

"We found something that might be yours," Cliff explained.

Karen pulled the small box out of her bag and opened it. She brought out the paper with the baby's picture on it and handed it to her husband.

"Is this your daughter?" he asked, showing the paper to the woman.

A single tear broke from her eye, trailing down her cheek. She blinked and more fell as she turned to Karen.

"We thought you might want her back," she said, pulling out the urn.

Reaching a frail hand out, the woman grasped the urn. Karen helped her bring it to her lap, not wanting any of the ashes to spill, nor the vessel to break. Once it was in the woman's lap, Karen let go. Tears rushed down the woman's face as she gently ran her hand across the urn. Unable to stop her own tears, Karen placed her hand on the older woman's shoulder. Looking up, eyes bright with tears, a smile crossed the woman's face.

"Thank you," she whispered, her voice barely audible.

"Welcome back," Charlotte said.

"Thanks," Karen replied. "Is she doing well today?"

"She has been getting better and better," the receptionist said. "I think your visits are really helping her. The staff has noticed as well."

"I'm just glad I can help," Karen replied.

"When are you due?"

"Three weeks," she replied. "I feel like a whale."

"But you're glowing like an angel," the receptionist said.

Smiling, Karen made her way to the elevator, riding it up to the third floor. Stepping out, she walked to the room she'd been visiting for months.

"Karen," Dorothy said. "You are absolutely beautiful."

"Thank you, Mrs. Sparks," Karen returned.

"So?"

"Here you go," Karen said as she handed over an envelope.

Flipping the top open, the older woman pulled out the card inside. Looking at the younger woman, she opened the card.

"Look at that," she exclaimed.

"Wonders of modern technology," Karen said as she sat in the chair next to the older woman.

"I can't believe this," the woman said, running her fingers across the image. "It's almost as if you can see her."

"Three-dimensional imagery at its finest," Karen laughed.

"Oh, what I wouldn't give to have had this back when I was young," the older woman said.

"I wanted you to be the first one to know," Karen said, growing serious.

"What's that, dear?"

"We've decided to name our baby Evelyn," she said.

The older woman looked at Karen. "Why?" she squeaked out.

"Because she brought us to you," Karen said, tears threatening to spill. "We're naming her Evelyn Dorothy."

The older woman brought her hand to her mouth, tears spilling down her own cheeks.

"Now don't you cry," Karen said, tears falling from her own eyes. "We'll both be a mess."

"I don't know what to say," Dorothy nearly sobbed.

"We'd like to know if we can have her call you grandma."

"Oh," the older woman said. "I'd like that so much. I really would."

She reached her hand out and Karen took it, holding it tightly in both of hers. "I'm just so glad that little house is going to actually hear the pitter patter of small feet."

"Maybe we can bring you over," Karen suggested. "Let you see what we've done?"

"I don't get around too well," Dorothy offered.

"Cliff is strong," Karen argued. "He can carry you if need be."

"Oh, stop," Dorothy chided.

"We really want you to be part of our lives," Karen admitted. "We feel like you've given us so much, it's the least we can do."

"Well, maybe," the other woman said.

"Then it's settled," Karen said.

"Here," Dorothy said, offering the card back to Karen.

"That's yours to keep," Karen said.

Dorothy pulled the card to her chest and smiled.

"I've got a doctor's appointment, otherwise I'd stay longer."

"No fuss," Dorothy said. "You just stop back by when you get the chance."

"I will," Karen said as she hugged the older woman.

"She's perfect," Cliff said, holding his daughter.

"She really is," Karen agreed.

"Knock, knock," Gayle said as she came into the room.

"Mom," Karen said, reaching out.

Gayle came into the room with a small bag, handing it to her daughter as she embraced her. "Dad and I thought we'd get something for the little one."

"You've done so much already," Karen said.

"We couldn't resist," she said.

Karen pulled the tissue from the bag and gasped. "You found her," she whispered as she pulled a battered stuffed rabbit from the bag.

"We've been saving her for the baby," Gayle replied.

"Ready for visitors?" Charles said as he stepped to the door.

"Daddy," Karen said.

"I've brought someone who wanted to see the baby," he

said, stepping aside.

"I hope you don't mind," Dorothy said.

"Come in," Karen said through tears. "Come meet Evelyn."

The older woman made her way slowly to the bedside and sat in the chair Gayle offered her.

"Grandma Dorothy," Cliff said, placing his daughter into her arms. "Meet Evelyn Dorothy."

Taking the baby, Dorothy peered into her eyes. "Aren't you just perfect," she cooed.

Karen looked at her husband and smiled. 'Thank you' she mouthed. He nodded, confirming that bringing the previous owner of their house into their family was the right thing to do.

UNHAPPY ENDINGS

Content Warning: Suicide

W hat do you mean it's not here?" Shelly asked.

"Just what I said," Richard replied. "It's not here."

"Did you look?"

Richard looked at her, eyebrows raised. "No," he barked. "I walked in, and when it didn't jump into my hands, I had to assume it wasn't here."

The sarcasm in his voice set her off.

"Never mind," she muttered. "I'll look myself."

"Why do you never believe me?"

Not answering, Shelly began moving papers and folders around the desk, looking in each one. After her thorough search, she concluded, "It's not here."

"Just like I told you," Richard said.

"So," she began. "Where is it?"

"I think I would have it in my hands if I knew that," he said.

"Where did you have it last?"

"At my desk," he said. "Which is why I was looking for it there. I wonder if Karen picked it up and filed it."

"Why would she file it?"

"Because it's her job," Richard said walking out the door.

"It's her job to take things from your desk and file them?" Shelly asked, following him out the door.

"Karen," Richard said as he got to her desk.

"What can I do for you, boss?"

"Have you seen the Mackenzie documents?"

"They were on your desk this morning," she replied. "I knew you were working on that project today, so I left them there."

"Well," Shelly said. "They seem to have grown legs and wandered off."

"Oh dear," Karen replied. "Let me check with Mark."

Picking up the receiver on her phone, she pressed a couple of buttons, then waited.

"Yeah," she said into the receiver. "Have you seen Mackenzie?" She paused, then asked, "Can you check your desk?" Another pause. "I'll wait." Placing her hand over the mouthpiece she said, "He's checking his desk."

"Obviously," Shelly muttered.

Richard gave her a glare, then patiently waited for the answer.

"Great," Karen said. "Bring it on up."

"Why did he have it?" Shelly asked once the phone was back on its cradle.

"We can ask him when he gets here," Karen responded.

"We'll be in my office," Richard replied, gripping his sister's arm and nearly dragging her into the office, closing the door behind them.

"Why aren't you waiting out there?" she barked. "Don't your employees know to leave things where they are?"

"Shelly," Richard said sternly. "I trust my employees. They were hired because of their professionalism and work ethic. I do not need you coming in here and thinking you can read them the riot act because you perceive some kind of injustice."

"I never," she sputtered.

"Exactly," he responded. "This is why the firm was left to me, not you. I have the business degree. I have the smarts to run the company the way Dad and Granddad wanted it run. It is my responsibility to make sure that things run smoothly for everyone, clients and employees alike. Until the board sees fit to remove me from my position, you need to trust that I know what is best and that I will work to make sure that things run smoothly."

"Why are you so bossy?"

"I'm not bossy," he corrected. "I am firm with my convictions, something Dad couldn't bring himself to be where you were concerned. He always let you get away with things you shouldn't have, and it's left you with less coping skills and not nearly enough common sense as you should have by this age."

"Seriously, Richard," she tried. "Why can't you just let me be part of the company? It's my legacy just as much as it is yours."

"And I'll make sure the legacy is still around," he said.

Just then, a knock sounded on his door. Opening it, he saw Karen, Mackenzie file in hand.

"Here you go, boss," she said.

"Thank you, Karen," he said. "And thank Mark, too."

Everyone at the firm knew that Shelly Draper was not in charge, even though she liked to throw her name around to get attention. Newer employees were warned that she was to be respected, but anything she demanded needed to be run by her brother prior to any work actually being done on the project.

"My pleasure," she replied, closing the door.

"Let me have it," Shelly said, reaching for the file.

"Sit," Richard barked.

"I'm not a dog," Shelly retorted.

"No," Richard said. "They are much better behaved than you. Now sit and we'll talk about it."

"Sometimes I just hate you," she mumbled, but complied

with her brother's wish and sat in one of the chairs next to his desk.

Walking behind the desk, he sat, opening the file on top of the stack of others that were there. Shelly bounced in her seat, impatience obvious in her demeanor.

"Looks like Mark was doing the work I planned to get to after lunch today," he said.

"Why is he doing it when it isn't his job?"

"It actually is his job," Richard said. "Sometimes, however, I pick up any slack that might happen because of someone else's work load. This was one of those times. Turned out he didn't need my help after all."

"So," she hedged, leaning forward. "What is happening?"

Richard held up his finger as he reviewed the top page in the file. He then clicked on his keyboard a few times to pull up the electronic file. A few mouse clicks later he turned to his sister.

"We got it," he said.

"Yeah," she shouted, jumping from her chair. "I'm so excited. When do I get to hold it?"

"Shelly," he said sternly. "Sit."

"Still not a dog," she replied, but complied again with his instructions.

"While we have claimed the art," he began, "it doesn't mean we'll have it here tomorrow. It takes time for these things to go through the proper channels. It has to be brought to the country, make it through customs, be authenticated, and after all of that is done, then it will be shipped to the warehouse. Once it's there, a final inspection will be done. After that, it will be available for us to display it as we have already discussed. You are not going to get to hold it."

"It's a stupid vase," she gruffed. "Why can't we just have it at the house?"

"Because it is worth half a million dollars," Richard replied.

"So," Shelly said.

"So," he replied. "It will be kept in a safe place where it will not come to any harm. This vase is several hundred years old. It's not like one you can buy on a shelf at some store. It's a treasure that needs to be properly displayed."

"But it's pretty," she complained. "And I want to be able to look at it any time I'm sad. It cheers me up."

"You're just going to have to find something a little less expensive to do that," he said.

"Are you going to commission replicas to sell?"

"We just got the go ahead to make the purchase," he said. "I haven't had a chance to discuss anything with my team. Until that happens, no decisions can be made."

"I think you should make sure there are replicas," she said. "Then, anyone who is sad can buy one and have it at their home to make them happy."

"I'll take that request under advisement," he said. "Now, can I get back to my actual job? There are other things that I need to take care of."

"Okay," she replied. "See you when you get home."

She walked out the door, leaving it open on her exit. Richard sighed once he knew she was well out of earshot. He loved his sister dearly, but she was such a high maintenance person he couldn't handle being around her for long periods of time. Karen walked in a few minutes after Shelly left, closing the door behind her.

"You are a saint," she said. "I don't know how you deal with her on a daily basis. She is exhausting."

"Hey," he replied.

"I know," she said. "She's family, so you just have to put up with it."

"Thank you for running the file down," he said.

"It's my job," she replied. "So?"

"We got it," he smiled. "Now I just have to get through all the hoops to get it here. She wants replicas to be available."

"You told her you can't do that, right?"

"I told her I'd check with my team," he replied.

"But, Richard," Karen said.

"I know," he replied. "I just had to get her out of here. Even I have my limits as to how much I can take of her. She would have probably gone into full meltdown mode if I'd told her no."

"As long as you don't make me tell her," Karen replied.

"I'll tell her something," he said.

"Mark said he'd be ready whenever you were done," she said.

"I'll head down there now," he replied.

"Hey," Richard said at Mark's doorway.

Mark looked up from his computer and pushed his glasses up on top of his head.

"You alone?" he whispered.

"Yeah," Richard said as he came into the room. "She left after I told her we got it."

"I don't know how you do it," Mark said.

"What?"

"Put up with her crazy," Mark replied.

"I guess I'm just used to it," Richard said.

"I don't think I could ever get used to that," Mark laughed.

"What are our next steps?" Richard asked, steering the conversation back to business.

"The letters are ready for your approval," Mark replied. "Once you've reviewed them, I'll get them printed and sent out. Should only take a week or so to get the answers we need. After that, it's just a matter of waiting on the government. We all know how quickly they move on these types of things."

"Yes," Richard replied. "What's your next project?"

"This was the last one," Mark said.

"What do you mean?"

"You remember I'm moving, right?"

"Oh, yeah," Richard said. "I completely forgot about that. Where are you going, again?"

"I'm going back to Montana," Mark replied. "Dad isn't doing well, and mom wants me to come home and take over the business for him."

"You will be sorely missed," Richard remarked. "But I really do wish you well on this new chapter."

"Thanks," Mark replied.

"I'll let you get back to it," Richard said, walking out the door.

"Shelly called," Karen said as Richard made it back to his office.

"She just left," Richard said.

"Oh, I know," Karen said.

"What did she want?"

"Apparently she wants to go to Brazil and look at something someone discovered down there," Karen said without expression.

Richard sighed, running a hand across his face. "Why does she do this to me?"

"You're asking the wrong person," Karen replied.

"I don't think anyone has the answer," Richard said, then stepped into his office.

Sitting at his desk, he pulled up his sister's favorite website for searches on new finds in Brazil. At the top of the list was a portion of an urn. The notes indicated that it was from far before the Portuguese came to the country, but it couldn't be confirmed at this point. Of course his sister would want to get that. She was all about things that predated the western influence in South America, and this was no different.

His phone buzzed and he picked up the handset. "Yes," he said.

"She's on line one," Karen said.

"I'll take it," he replied, then pressed the button for the line. "Hello, Shelly," he said.

"Did Karen tell you I called?"

"Yes," he replied. "I am looking at what I think you are interested in."

"The urn?" she asked.

"That's what I figured," he sighed.

"It could hold the key," she bubbled.

"Or it could just be another thing you set your mind on."

"Can I go?"

"Are you seriously asking me this?"

"I want to go," she begged.

"You know I can't let you," he argued.

"But it could be exactly what I need," she replied.

"Until I see more information on it," he began, "I'm not going to put any time into it."

"I'll do it all," she offered.

"You can't," he replied.

"Why?" she asked. "Because I'm too dumb? Or because I'm crazy?"

"Shelly," Richard sighed. "We have been over this with every piece you've found. I can't allow you to travel alone, and I can't afford to have a team go with you. We will have to wait and see what new information they come up with before we make any plans as to whether or not to get it."

"It's the key," she demanded. "I can feel it in my soul."

"Shelly," he barked. "Just stop. I have a business to run, and that requires all of my time. I cannot give you any more time to follow these foolish notions you have of finding a cure. You need to learn to live with it."

"You just don't understand," she shouted back. "You don't have to live like I do. No one tells you when to get up or when to go to bed. They don't make you take stupid pills every day that do nothing but drown your creativity. I can't even decide what I want to eat because of it. I want freedom. I want to really live. And you're just determined to keep me locked up. I bet if you could get away with it, you would lock me in a dungeon and throw away the key. You'd leave me to rot in the dark."

Richard pinched the bridge of his nose, trying to hold back his anger.

"Shelly," he began. "I love you. You're my sister. You are the only part of my family that's left. I know you don't mean to be horrible, but you need to understand that everything I do is for your own good."

"You hate me," she shouted, then disconnected the call.

Sighing, he placed the receiver back in its cradle. "That woman is going to be the death of me," he muttered.

"I'm home," Richard called as he came into the house.

The silence around him was deafening.

"Hello?" he called.

Still nothing.

He placed his briefcase on the credenza in the entry and made his way to the kitchen. Surely someone was here. Usually he could smell dinner when he walked in, but the house felt cold and empty as he made his way through it.

Stepping into the kitchen he grabbed his stomach, one hand going over his mouth. Nothing prepared him for the sight he was met with. On the floor was their cook, Julia. Her throat was slit all the way across, blood pooling around her head. Her eyes stared in horror at the ceiling. Next to her was Gloria, the housekeeper. She was in the same state, throat sliced all the way across, a puddle of blood under her as well.

"Shelly," he shouted, racing from the room and back the way he came. He took the steps to the second level two at a time, bounding up the stairs as fast as he could. Racing down the hall, he ripped open his sister's door and stopped cold.

"Oh, Shelly," he sobbed as he saw her on the bed.

Stepping up next to it, he looked down into the peaceful face of his sister. If he didn't know better, he'd think she was just resting. But her eyes were wide, her lips blue, and a faint trace of blood had dribbled from the corner of her mouth. In her hand she held an empty pill bottle. He picked it up and turned the bottle, reading the label.

On the night stand he saw a nearly empty bottle of whiskey and a bloody butcher knife. He closed his eyes, swallowing back the bile that rose in his throat. He placed the pill bottle next to the whiskey, turned, and left the room.

"I understand this must be difficult for you," the detective said.

"I just can't believe she did all of this," Richard replied.

It hadn't taken long for the police to arrive after he'd made the call. First to arrive were uniformed officers, followed by detectives, and finally the county coroner. He'd explained the situation when he'd called 911, telling the agent that no one would be able to be saved. He'd told the story so many times he'd lost count.

"It seems like she was having some issues," the detective offered.

"She's mentally unstable," Richard replied.

"Was she on any other medication?"

"I've got a list of her medications in the book," he said. "She had more than mental health issues. There were also physical issues she had going on."

"If you can get me a list of her doctors," the detective began.

"I have a notebook that has all of the information in it," Richard said. "It has her providers, list of medications, last visit notes, and everything about her conditions."

"What conditions did she have?"

"She contracted polio when she was a child," he explained.

"Didn't she get vaccinated?"

"Unfortunately, her body had a tendency to refuse vaccines," Richard began. "She could get the dosage and within a week, no trace of it would be found in her system. We went to Nigeria on a safari when we were little and she contracted it there."

"I didn't even think it was around anymore," the detective said.

"It's pretty much gone," Richard replied. "There are very few places where it is still around, and we happened to go to one of them."

"You said she had mental health issues," the officer suggested.

"She was schizophrenic," Richard said. "She was on medication for it, but her dosage had recently changed. It's in the book."

"Can you get the book?"

"Sure." Richard stood and walked to his office. Reaching up onto the shelf, he pulled down the black notebook where all of Shelly's medical information was kept. He turned and handed it to the officer.

"Do you mind if we hold onto this for a while?"

"That's fine," Richard said.

"I think this is all I need for now," the detective said. "Here's my card, if you think of anything else."

"Thank you," he replied. "I know this can't be easy for you, either."

"Death is never easy," the detective said. "Whether it's for the family or for those who have to investigate it."

"I appreciate you're being so kind," Richard said.

"We'll be in touch," the detective said, then walked out of the office.

Richard could still hear the rest of the authorities mulling around the house, finishing up their tasks. When someone knocked on the office door, he raised his eyes to look at the man.

"We're all done," he said. "Once the coroner has completed the autopsies, you will be informed of the results."

"Thank you," Richard replied.

"I'm sorry for your loss," the man said, then turned and left.

Richard heard the front door close, then held his breath, listening to the lack of sound. Breathing out heavily, he stood from the desk to assess what was left to accomplish. He did not relish the cleanup that awaited him.

Three days later

I'm so sorry for your loss," the man said.

It was the hundredth time Richard had heard the phrase that day. But it was to be expected. He'd opted to have the funeral open to the public, and apparently Shelly had quite a few friends around town. Hundreds had come out for the service, and they were all filing out now. Soon, he would be left without any distractions.

"How are you holding up?" Karen asked.

"I'll survive," he replied.

"If you need anything," she said.

"Thanks," he responded.

The two women his sister had killed had been buried at their family's request, and Richard had paid for everything, including a generous severance package that did nothing to ease his guilt over their deaths. What he wanted to do was rewind time and see the warning signs that must have been there. He should have known his sister was dangerous, should have been able to prevent the tragedy. But that wasn't something he could control.

He'd decided to have the open ceremony at the funeral home, but had not invited anyone to the burial at the cemetery. That, he wanted to do on his own. Once he made it there, he climbed from his car and walked to the open grave. His sister's body had arrived and was placed in the contraption that would lower her into the ground.

"Why did you do it?" he asked the box.

Of course he didn't get a response. He was left with only questions and no answers. He would never know the reasoning behind what his sister had done. The coroner had confirmed that she'd overdosed on the medication shortly after the other women had been killed. They had been struck on the head, then their throats had been cut while they were unconscious. It was swift and seemingly painless for them, mercifully.

Shelly hadn't suffered, either. She'd taken several of the pills, combined with the whisky she'd used to swallow them, and had simply fallen asleep and never woke up. They had determined it happened shortly after she got home from her trip to his office that morning, just after the phone call in which she accused him of not caring about her. Nothing could have saved any of the women, and Richard had to simply live with that fact.

COMPANIONS

I can't believe you bought one," Blaine said.

"Why not?" Grayson asked.

"Just not something I would expect," Blaine replied. "You don't strike me as the type to jump onto this type of bandwagon."

"It's not a bandwagon," Grayson responded. "Never before have we had the opportunity to have a companion without the messiness of the human element."

"But it's so foreign," Blaine said. "I mean, a robot?"

"Artificial intelligence," the other man corrected. "She will have her own mind, her own ideas, and will be able to make cognitive decisions on her own."

"Can she defy you?"

"Of course she can," Grayson said. "She is her own person."

"I'm gonna stick to real women," Blaine said. "I just don't think I could handle a robot in bed."

"It's not about the sex," the other man explained. "It's about someone to spend time with, to have meals with, to share ideas and hopes and dreams with. It's about friendship."

"Still," Blaine interjected. "You're what, 38? That seems a bit young to be giving up on the human race for those kinds of things."

"I'm not giving up," Grayson argued. "I'm just taking a

break. I need to after Sydney."

"That was a whole basketful of crazy," Blaine offered.

"She just had some issues she needed to work out," Grayson explained. "Nothing wrong with needing space. Nothing wrong with not knowing for sure what you want, either."

"But the way it went down?"

"True," Grayson conceded. "It could have been handled much more tactfully. But there's no undoing the past."

"So," Blaine said. "When does she arrive?"

"Because I picked a basic model," Grayson began, "it should only take a couple of weeks."

"Basic model?" Blaine asked. "Why didn't you go all out? Get all the bells and whistles? It's not like you can't afford it."

"I don't need anything fancy," Grayson said. "She'll have everything I need."

"Do they name them at the factory?"

"You're allowed to pick a name," Grayson explained. "Or they can send them without one, and you can determine the name after you get to know them."

"So, which did you choose?"

"I named her Ivy," he said. "It's simple enough, but not so plain. I think it will suit her well."

"Well," Blaine concluded. "I guess it's your choice. I just hope you're happy with the results."

"I'm sure I will be," Grayson replied.

Twelve Years Later

Y ou ready?" Ivy called.

"Just about," Grayson replied.

"Hurry up," she said. "I don't want to be late."

Grayson stepped from the bathroom and caught her looking

out the window. Walking up behind her, he wrapped his arms around her waist.

"Grayson," she laughed, swatting his hands away.

"I know," he said. "I just wanted to hold you for a minute."

"We're going to be late," she admonished.

"I know," he replied, letting her go. "You look lovely."

Her cheeks blushed and she turned her head away. "You're too sweet," she said.

"I'm honest," he said. "I don't think I could be happier than I am right now."

Smiling, she pushed to her toes and kissed him.

"What was that for?"

"Just because," she shrugged.

He smiled back, staring at her beautiful face.

"Gray," she whispered. "We have to go."

He closed his eyes and took a deep breath, then opened them and said, "Okay, let's go."

The went out of their condo and rode the elevator to the lobby.

"Your car is here," Fife, the doorman, said.

"Thank you," Grayson replied.

They stepped out into the sunlight, pulling glasses over their eyes to avoid the danger it posed to them. Walking to the car, he opened the back door and allowed her to slide in. He then walked to the other side and got in himself.

"All ready?" Chaz, their driver, asked.

"Yes," Grayson replied.

With that, the car pulled from the curb and entered traffic. It didn't take long for them to arrive at the gallery. Chaz pulled into the line of cars waiting to unload their passengers, and waited for their turn. When they stopped at the edge of the red carpet, one of the men waiting opened Ivy's door. Grayson popped out of his own, rounded the car and offered his hand to help her stand.

"Welcome to The Gap," the man said. "Follow the carpet and they will ask for your code when you get to the door."

"Thank you," Grayson said.

Placing his hand on the small of Ivy's back, he guided her through the throng of people gathered on the carpet. There were celebrities and cameras and everything you would expect at this type of gala. Thankfully, he was not known by sight, so could slip through without having to deal with the hubbub of it all.

"Code, please," the young woman at the door said. Grayson held out his phone and she scanned it. "Welcome in," she said once the code registered.

"Thank you," he said.

They entered the large room filled with people dressed in their finest. Making their way to the bar that was set up to one side of the room, Grayson ordered drinks for the two of them, handing Ivy's to her once it was prepared.

"Where to first?" Ivy asked after taking a sip of her cocktail.

"Blaine said he'd meet us at the top of the stairs," Grayson said.

"Perfect," she replied.

The walk to the staircase was stalled by the number of people who were already in the gallery. It took a few minutes for them to make their way through, but once at the bottom of the stairs, their path cleared.

"Grayson," Blaine shouted from the top of the stairs. "So glad you could make it."

"Wouldn't miss it for the world," he replied.

"Ivy," Blaine said. "You look lovely as ever."

"Thank you, Blaine," she replied. "You clean up pretty well yourself."

"Have you seen anything?" he asked.

"We just got here," Grayson replied.

"Then let me show you the best," Blaine said, turning to go

back up the stairs.

Grayson and Ivy followed him up, excited to see what their friend had to show them. They crested the stairs and turned right, keeping up with Blaine, but just barely.

"It's in here," he said, ducking into a small alcove set back from the main gallery.

Grayson walked in first, then heard Ivy gasp. Pulling her into his chest, he glared at his friend. "What is the meaning of this?" he growled.

Blaine looked at his longtime friend, confusion clear on his face. "What's wrong?" he asked.

"What's wrong?" Grayson barked. "What's wrong is that you have taken something beautiful, something I love very much, and made a gross..." he stopped, feeling Ivy shaking in his arms.

"I'm sorry," Blaine said. "I thought you, of all people, would understand."

"It's macabre," Grayson said. Ivy clung to his chest, shaking with sobs. "Why would you invite us to this?"

"Ivy," Blaine said, reaching out to her.

"No," Grayson said, putting himself between his friend and his lover. "You don't get to touch her."

"I wanted people to see the reality," Blaine explained.

"The reality of someone being flayed open?" Grayson asked. "The reality that is a murder?"

"That's not what this is," Blaine offered. "This is to show everyone that they aren't the same as us. They never will be."

"And yet here she stands," Grayson said. "Right in front of you. Beside me for over a decade. You've been over to our home. We've been nothing but kind to you, and this is how you repay us? You tear open the very fabric of what it means to be alive and strip it from not just Ivy, but all the others out there who are like her."

"But she's not alive," Blaine pleaded. "She never has been."

"She has more life in her than you do," Grayson said. "She's shown more compassion, more grace, and more dignity than you ever will. Especially after this."

With that, he turned and steered Ivy from the room, guiding her back to the steps. They walked down without turning back to the pleading from Blaine.

"Leaving so soon?" the doorman asked.

"We never should have come," Grayson barked as he held Ivy in his arms. He pulled out his phone and sent a message to Chaz asking him to bring the car back and pick them up. The response was immediate, so he moved them toward the pickup area.

They reached the space allocated for returning cars at the same time Chaz arrived, so didn't have to wait. Grayson opened the door and helped Ivy in, then went around and climbed in himself.

"Something wrong?" Chaz asked once the doors were closed.

"Just take us home," Grayson said, drawing Ivy back against him. She continued to cry softly for the short ride home.

They made their way into the building and up the elevator, finally reaching their condo.

"Would you like a bath?" Grayson asked her.

She simply shook her head and walked to the bedroom. He followed her and watched as she climbed into the bed, not bothering to change, simply sliding her heels from her feet. Grayson was at a loss as to what to do to help her. He was struggling with what he'd seen, but this had to have been torture for her.

"I'll let you sleep," he said, then quietly closed the door.

He found himself in his den, so poured a glass of whiskey, then sat at his desk. He turned on his monitor and booted his system up. Once it was running, he navigated to the gallery's website to see if there were any indications that the exhibit had been mentioned, but found nothing other than Blaine's name. He opened a message to send to the curator. They needed to know that what they were exhibiting was not acceptable. The message was short, simply saying he was disappointed they had allowed such a horrible display and asked that they have it removed immediately.

Downing what was left of his whiskey, he got up and poured another glass. Sitting back at his desk, he opened his message app and began to write to Blaine. They'd known each other for years, and Grayson had never suspected his friend was capable of such disregard for others. Sending the message, he planned to close down, but received a response immediately.

> *I'm sorry you were disturbed by my piece. I never intended for it to be an attack on you or Ivy. It's simply showing everyone that these companions aren't all that they seem.*

Grayson growled at the response and swallowed the rest of his whiskey. He wanted to reply, send some scathing rebuttal, but knew it would fall on deaf ears, so he left it.

When he went back to his bedroom, he noticed that Ivy was no longer in the bed. Walking to the bathroom, he found her sitting on the floor, sobbing.

"Baby," he cooed. "Let me help you."

"I'm not enough," she sputtered. "I'm not human, so I'll never be enough. I'm just a machine."

"That's not true," Grayson said. "You're so much more than just a machine. You are beautiful and kind and compassionate. I was lost until you came. Because of you, I have purpose in my life again. You have done that for me."

"You saw that," she waved her hand indicating the past and what was at the gallery. "You know what's inside me. It's all wires and filaments and steel rods. There's no heart, no soul. I'm nothing but a machine."

"Some people may see you that way," Grayson began.

"Most people do," she sobbed. "And now, because of his... his... whatever," she waved again. "Now, that's all anyone will see when they look at me."

"I will never see that," Grayson whispered, not trusting his voice to be louder. "The only thing I see when I look at you is the love you have given me. The times you've shared with me, learning and growing and becoming such an amazing person."

"But I'm not," she insisted. "I never will be a person. At least in the eyes of some."

"True," he agreed. "But they don't matter. Who is the most important human to you?"

"You are," she replied.

"Well," he said. "I think you're perfect, and I wouldn't want you to be human at all. All of the things that make you who you are, are what I fell in love with. That is what really matters. If Blaine can't see your importance, then that's his loss. If someone else thinks you're less than because you were manufactured rather than born, then it's their struggle to deal with. You are perfect in every way I could have ever wanted. I wouldn't change you for the world."

Ivy smiled at that, and Grayson reached over to wipe the tears from her cheeks.

"Thank you," she whispered.

"There is nothing to thank me for," he replied. "I am just telling you how I feel and what I know. Just the truth, as I've always promised you."

He helped her up from the floor, then walked with her back to their bed.

"Do you think we'll ever get rights?" she asked.

"What do you mean?" he asked.

"Like you have," she said. "The right to make our own decisions and such."

"Eventually people will realize that you are more than just a collection of circuits," he said. "Until then, just come to me and I'll remind you how perfect you are."

She pressed to her toes and kissed him deeply. "Thank you," she said.

"Always," he replied.

Six Months Later

I'll get it," Ivy called as she walked to their front door.

"Hi, Ivy," Blaine said when she opened the door.

"Blaine," she said. "How are you?"

"I'm miserable," he confessed. "I've done a lot of soul searching over the last few months and I wanted to apologize."

"For what?" she asked.

"Come on, now," he said.

Grayson walked up behind Ivy and demanded, "What brings you to our door, Blaine?"

"I've come to apologize," he said again. "I honestly didn't think it was that big of a deal."

"And you've learned otherwise?" Grayson asked.

"Can I come in?" he asked.

"Of course," Ivy said, but Grayson said, "I'm not sure."

"Grayson," Ivy insisted. "He's your friend. He's our friend."

"No," Blaine said. "I understand. I did come to say I was sorry, to both of you."

"Why the change?" Grayson asked, still blocking the doorway so that Blaine could not come in.

"You," he said, looking right at Ivy. "Your reaction to my..."

"Your art piece," Ivy offered.

"I hate to even call it that," he said. "But yes. Your reaction to it was not what I expected. Never in a million years would I want to do something to make you uncomfortable, let alone cause you

213

such grief."

"Did you take it down?" Grayson asked.

"I did," he said. "That very night. I hadn't expected your reaction, Ivy. I thought you would see it as an intriguing piece showing what's on the inside."

"But it's not all that's inside of her," Grayson said.

"I know," Blaine said. "I didn't know you would see it as Grayson explained. It never even crossed my mind."

"So," Ivy said. "Why did you do it?"

"I thought I could convince people that you were simply a machine," he said. "That the collection of parts was what you were."

"And?" Grayson asked.

"And I was wrong," Blaine said.

"What changed your mind?" Ivy asked.

"You," he said pointedly. "The fact that you saw it as, well, as murder. That I had taken someone apart and displayed their parts. My concept was that I could show the benefits of what was inside."

"But you were missing the most important part," Grayson said.

"I know that now," Blaine said. "You showed me not only that I was wrong in believing that you, and those like you, are simply a collection of computer parts. You have emotions, feelings, and should be valued as a part of society. You are important, and we need you around."

"How could you have doubted that?" Grayson asked.

"I shouldn't have," Blaine replied. "Watching you over these last several years has shown me the importance of the companion program. You were a mess after Sydney. I thought you were crazy to buy a companion, and told you so. Now, though, I think it was probably the best thing you ever did."

"I've never been happier," Grayson said.

"The only problem is," Blaine began.

"No," Grayson demanded.

"Hear me out," Blaine pleaded. Grayson nodded, so he continued. "If everyone chooses companions over human partners, we will cease to exist."

"Companions aren't for everyone," Ivy said. "We are available if you are unable to have a relationship with another human. I am part of the early waves, and babies are still being born. We are not wanting to take over, we simply want to be here for you."

"If I wanted to have a child," Grayson added. "I could have chosen several ways to make that happen."

"But not with Ivy," Blaine argued.

"True," Grayson agreed. "There are options, though. It's been over fifteen years since the first models came out. In that time, science has advanced at an enormous rate. I wouldn't be surprised if a new model came out with the ability to reproduce."

"Never," Ivy said.

"Never say never," Grayson replied.

"I know things you don't," she said.

"Like what?" Blaine asked.

"The fact that companions will never replace the true human experience," she explained. "We are meant to add to, but not replace, real relationships."

"Are you saying what we have isn't real?"

"At any point," she began, "you could decide that you wanted to go back to having a relationship with a human. In doing so, you would give up your control of me and I would return to the factory. Once there, I would be given the option of being 'cleaned' and repurposed for another human, or I could remain in tact and have the experience of a past for someone who wanted that."

"So, like a breakup?" Blaine asked.

"Exactly," she said. "When you and Sydney went your separate ways, you didn't have any control over where she went from here. She was free to choose. I am offered that same option."

"What happens when he dies?" Blaine asked.

"I return to the factory with the same options," she said.

"But what if I want you to have what I had?" Grayson asked. "If I want you to remain in our home?"

"Until we are afforded the same rights as humans," Ivy said, "we will not have that as an option. We are simply the property of the human. Once they have gone, we revert to being owned by the company who built us."

"What if Grayson wanted you to be given to someone else?" Blaine asked. "Like, if he wanted me to have you once he was gone."

"It doesn't work like that," she said.

"If you were his wife," Blaine began.

"I would be human," she interrupted. "And as such, would be afforded many more rights than what I have now."

"So," Blaine began. "A couple hundred years ago, a woman was considered property of her father or brothers or uncles. They didn't have any rights to choose their future. Before that, people who didn't look the same were treated as property as well. Now, we are doing the same thing to you and your kind?"

"It is the way things go," she said.

"Then we should change it," he said. "How can we change this?"

"It's an uphill battle," Grayson said. "One we've been working on fighting for half a year."

"You have?"

"Your display made me realize that Ivy deserves the same rights as you and I," Grayson said. "Since that time, I have been trying to find a way to get laws passed to give companions more rights."

"My piece pushed that?"

"If someone could purchase a companion and slaughter it,"

Grayson said. "And if they could do it without any repercussions, that wasn't acceptable. If something happens to Ivy, like someone injures her or rapes her or kills her, there is nothing we can do to that person. The only thing we can do is file a claim against them for damage to property. It's as if they hit my car or stole my microwave."

"Really?" Blaine asked.

"You did it," Ivy said.

"That was a manufacturing error," he said.

"She was still a person," Grayson said.

"She didn't run," he said. "There was no spark, no activity, nothing."

"She just died," Ivy said. "At some point, she was going to be a companion. She would have had the same experiences as me. But she didn't live. That didn't give you the right to rip her body apart for display."

Looking between Ivy and Grayson, Blaine realized they were right.

"How can I help?" he finally asked.

"We'd like to use your piece," Ivy said.

"As an example," Grayson clarified.

"Fine," Blaine said. "I will do whatever it takes to make sure that you are not treated as property."

"I appreciate that," she said, reaching out and hugging him. It took him a minute to react, but then he hugged her back.

"Welcome to the fight," Grayson said, reaching out and shaking his hand. "It's a long road, but I think it will be worth it."

EMERGENCE

I don't understand," he said.

"Come with me and I'll show you," she replied.

"Show me?"

"Just trust me," she implored.

He did trust her. From the moment he placed his hands upon her, she was the only thing that mattered. What she was saying, however, was madness.

"Ready?" she asked.

"Yes," he replied, though he wasn't sure what to expect.

"I promise, it'll be worth it," she said, then let go of his hand.

He could hear her moving away from him slightly, then he was blinded. Not like he was on a daily basis, but a brightness he'd never experienced caused him to shut his eyes and hold his hands over them.

"What is that?" he cried.

"Come with me," she said, grabbing his arm.

He followed her without question, riding in her wake, unable to experience anything around him. Then he began to hear things he'd never heard before. His life had been filled with the sounds of small creatures digging, insects buzzing, and other people breathing and talking in hushed tones. Here, however, he heard sounds he'd never experienced.

Gradually, his eyes became somewhat accustomed to the brightness surrounding him. Blinking, he removed his hand and experienced something new. Color, texture, movement.

"Isn't it amazing?" she asked.

He turned to her voice, and for the first time actually saw Layla. Oh, he'd 'seen' her before, with his hands. But this was a whole new experience, one he simply couldn't describe.

"Where are we?"

"The surface," she beamed.

"Surface," he gasped.

"It's perfectly safe," she said, releasing his hand. "Come and smell this."

He followed her, unable to resist her urging. She picked something from a clump and brought it to his nose. He inhaled and was assaulted with a sweetness he was unaccustomed to.

"I think it's a rose," she said. "That's what Sam said."

"Sam?" he questioned.

"Here he comes," she said, then shouted, "Over here."

Jacob followed her line of sight and saw someone walking toward them. Having never seen any of the others, he was unsure whether this person was larger or smaller than those underground. All he knew was the man was taller than him, and appeared to have more body mass.

"Layla," he said, giving her a hug. "You brought a friend."

"This is Jacob," she said.

"Pleasure to meet you," the man said. "Welcome to the surface."

"Are you sure we're safe up here?" he asked.

"It is perfectly safe," the man said. "But you should stay in the shade until your skin becomes accustomed to the sun."

Jacob looked at Layla, completely confused by what the

man was saying.

"You see how parts of the ground are darker than others?" she asked.

He looked at her, still confused. She was using words that had no meaning to him.

She sighed and looked to the other man. "Was I this confused when I first came up?"

"Yes," the man answered. "But you adapted quickly. Each of you will have a different time table when you come up. Some may adapt more quickly, like you did. Others may take a little longer."

"Each of us?" Jacob asked. "You mean more are coming to the surface?"

It seemed impossible that anyone, let alone everyone, would want to chance coming to the surface. The dangers they had been warned about were sure to be up here. It was the reason they'd retreated hundreds of years ago.

"Some may choose to stay below," Layla explained. "But I want to live on the surface full time."

"That will come," Sam said. "But you need to do it gradually. Remember what I said about exposure."

"Where did you come from?" Jacob asked the man.

"Underground, same as you," the man said. "Well, I didn't come from underground. I was born on the surface."

"Your parents came from underground?"

"And their parents before them," the man said. "My family retreated about the same time as you. By the stories, it was about six hundred years ago. The great war made surface living nearly impossible for everyone."

"Why come back, then?" Jacob asked.

"We're explorers by nature," Sam said. "We like to find things out, see what's on the other side of the wall. It isn't in our nature to hide forever."

"But we weren't hiding," Jacob insisted. "We were staying safe."

"I know," Sam replied. "But it's safe to come back up."

"How can it be?"

"Look around," Layla said. "Trees are growing, plants and animals are thriving. It is just like the stories that we've been told for years. It is the way it was."

"Which means it will end up the way it was, too," Jacob insisted.

"Not necessarily," Sam said. "As long as we remember what happened, and what caused it, we can make this place safe for everyone."

Jacob began to scratch his arm, leaving deep lines on his pale skin.

"I think he's probably had enough," Sam said to Layla.

"Oh, no," she replied. "Come on. We have to go back underground."

She grabbed Jacob's arm and pulled him back where they came from, shoving him through the door before she followed.

"What's happening?" he asked, still clawing at his arms.

"You've never been exposed to the sun," she explained. "It can cause your skin to burn if you aren't careful."

"Why have you done this to me?"

"Because we need to return to the surface," she said. "If we don't, we'll die down here."

"We've lived here for a long time, Layla," he explained. "We haven't died, yet. I don't think we'll die any time soon, either."

"Jacob," she insisted, placing her hands on either side of his face. "We were not created to live underground. We belong up top."

"I'm not sure that's true anymore," he said. "What does your father think about all of this?"

At the mention of her father, Layla sucked in a breath.

"That's what I thought," Jacob said. "You haven't told him, have you?"

"He doesn't understand," she said. "He isn't curious at all."

"Because he knows it's not safe up there," Jacob explained.

"But it is," she insisted. "You saw for yourself. Sam has lived up top for his whole life and he's perfectly fine."

"You don't know he's telling the truth," he cautioned. "He could be trying to get to our supplies."

"Why would he want what we have?" she asked. "He has everything he could ever need up there. More than what we have, that's for sure."

"Have you seen his supply collection?"

"Yes," she insisted. "I've been going up daily for a couple of months now. I can stay in the sun for almost an hour, and the shade for several hours. Didn't you notice that our skin wasn't the same color?"

"The stories from the old days say that there were many different shades of skin before the fall," he argued. "Who's to say that your skin wouldn't naturally be darker than mine?"

"It wasn't," she said. "I don't think anyone who is here has dark skin anymore."

"What makes you say that?"

"Something Sam explained to me," she said.

"And you're going to take it at face value?"

"I actually checked it out," she said. "He has books from before the fall. They explain how the skin of people who were exposed to the sun became darker."

"I don't understand," he said. "What are books?"

"You know how we share stories from long ago?" she asked.

"Yes," he replied.

"Well," she began, "these are those kind of things, only they are put on a surface where you can read them. There are markings on these surfaces, and each marking makes a sound, and when you collect the sounds together, they make words. I've been learning how to use them, and Sam says that I am a natural."

"But what does that have to do with our skin?"

"One of the books I read talked about our bodies," she said. "It explains how our systems work inside and how our skin on the outside was used to protect us. Because we've been down below for so many years, our skin hasn't had to protect us from the sun, so it's changed. Now it's lighter, because it doesn't need mela...I don't remember what it's called, but it's in our skin, and we don't need as much of it now because we don't need its protection."

"I think you're talking too fast," he said. "There's something that used to be in our skin that isn't anymore? And when it was there, we could be on the surface and not have to worry about the sun."

"They still had to worry," she said. "It depended on what kind of skin you had."

"Isn't skin all the same?"

"No," she said. "Some of us have darker skin with more of that mela-whatever in it. Others don't have as much. The mela-whatever helps to protect the skin, but it isn't always safe. They still had to think about the sun and how long they were in it."

"If we stay down here, it doesn't burn," he said. "I don't know why you would want to go up there and risk it."

"Because it's beautiful," she said. "Didn't you see the colors? The textures? All of the animals and the flowers and the sky? It's breathtaking."

"But we have everything we need down here," he tried. "There isn't anything they have up there that we can't find down here."

"Jacob," she said. "You know I love you with all of my heart, but I just don't understand your hesitancy. Why don't you want to go to the surface and live there?"

"Because it's not safe," he insisted. "You saw what

happened when I went up there. My skin burned. It still hurts, even though we've been back underground for a while."

"You'll be able to stay above ground longer and longer each time," she said. "The more you go up, the more time you'll be able to spend. It won't be long until your skin will darken like mine. Then you can stay up there for a long time."

"I can't," he said. "I just can't do it. It's not safe, and you'll never convince me it is."

"You're saying that if I decide to move to the surface, you won't go with me?"

The hurt was clear in her voice. She wanted him to come with her, but she was going to go, even if he didn't.

"I don't want you to go," he begged.

"But I can't stay," she replied.

Neither one of them spoke. Both knew the other's mind was made up. She wanted to convince him, but nothing she said was working.

"I will miss you," she finally said, then moved away.

Jacob didn't know how long he stayed there, simply thinking about what she'd shared with him. His curiosity was telling him to follow her up, but the logical side of him knew it wasn't the right thing to do.

Two months later

Jacob," Frank said. "Where is Layla?"

He couldn't betray her secret, but he didn't want to lie to her father.

"She said she was going exploring," he finally said.

"I know that," the older man said. "Do you know where?"

Jacob could either tell the truth and out Layla's trips to the surface, or lie and hope the older man couldn't hear it in his voice.

"I can't tell you," he finally said. While it was the truth, it wasn't what Frank wanted to hear.

"You are her partner," he said. "I am her father. You are beholden to me, too."

"She is my first responsibility," Jacob insisted. "I owe you thanks for allowing us to be together, but I am not responsible for telling you everything we share between us."

Jacob could hear the anger in the older man's breathing, but Frank didn't express it in words. Finally, the older man moved away and Jacob was left feeling proud, yet a true disappointment. Seeking Layla out, he found her in their space.

"I need to tell you something," she said when Jacob arrived.

He could hear fear in her voice, something he hadn't ever heard before. He went to her, wrapping her in his arms, and asked, "What is it?"

"I am to have a child," she said.

Jacob's heart filled with joy. "When will the babe be here?" he asked.

"In about six months," she replied. "I want to have it on the surface."

"No," Jacob insisted. "I won't let you."

"You can't stop me," she said. "It's my choice, and I want this child to know the beauty of the world above ground."

"How will you survive?" he asked.

"The same way Sam and his people do," she explained. "By working the land. I want you to come with me."

"I can't," he said.

"You can," she replied. "I talked with Sam and he and his family are going to help us build a house where you and I can be out of the sun for long periods of time, gradually giving our skin time to build up resistance to the sun."

"But how will the baby survive?"

"Jacob," she said, caressing his cheek. "Babies were born

above ground for hundreds of thousands of years. When we moved underground, we became more fragile. This is why we have such a hard time with babies surviving. We are meant to be on the surface."

"I'm worried," he confessed. "What if something happens?"

"Nothing is going to happen," she assured. "And if it does, we will deal with it. Something could happen whether we are underground or on the surface."

"Some things can only happen on the surface," he insisted.

"Come with me tonight," she said. "I want you to be able to spend more time on the surface. We can do this at night and not risk the burn from the sun."

"Can we tell your father?" he asked.

"I don't want anyone to know," she said. "Least of all him. He doesn't want to return to the surface, doesn't want our people to have the freedom that would allow."

"What do you mean?"

"You didn't grow up with him," she said. "Every day I heard him telling the other men that they needed to ensure that we were unaware of the changes above ground. He knew it was safe to return, but didn't want to lose control of the people. If he let us go up, he wouldn't be able to contain us. We would have the freedom to move away, make our own decisions, do our own thing."

"He wouldn't do that," Jacob insisted.

"He's been doing it for years," she replied. "I remember asking him about it when I was younger. He scolded me for saying such sacrilegious things, saying that the surface is what killed my mother. This is why he can't know."

"Why didn't you tell me this before?" he asked.

"I didn't want you to think less of him," she replied. "He does want to help our people, but he wants to do it his own way. Going to the surface isn't what he wants, and he doesn't think it is best for us. Now that I've been up there, though, I know it is."

"Have you told anyone else about going to the surface?"

"Just Kara," she said. "She has been going with me, and plans to move up there soon as well."

"What does Michael have to say about it?"

"I don't know," she said. "We haven't talked about that, yet."

"Layla," Kara whispered.

"What is it?" Layla replied, concerned with the fear in her friend's voice.

"We have to go now," the other woman said. "Michael is going to tell your father."

"What?" Layla nearly shouted.

"He thinks we're being coerced by the surface people," she said. "I grabbed what I could, but we have to go, now."

"Jacob," Layla said. "Are you coming?"

"Yes," he said. "My place is with you."

Layla sighed in relief, then said, "Grab the bag by the door. It's all we will need."

Doing as she asked, Jacob picked up the bag he found near the door. Even though they had no light, he could sense things without his eyes. It was a skill that they had improved during their time underground. It took them only minutes to make their way to the place where Layla had first brought him to the surface.

"Where do you think you're going?" Frank asked.

"Father," Layla said. "I am an adult. You cannot tell me where to go."

"I am the leader of our people," he insisted. "You will mind me, and the other leaders, or you will pay the consequences."

Before he knew what he was doing, Jacob rushed toward the older man, knocking him off his feet.

"Go now," he shouted to Layla and Kara.

He could hear them moving toward the door, then was blinded by the light coming through it. He released his hold on the older man and moved toward the light, hoping he would be able to get out before Frank could recover. The loud clang of the door shutting behind him made his heart sink. Because he hadn't shielded his eyes, he couldn't see anything around him. Finally, soft hands grabbed his and pulled him away from where he was standing.

"Come on," Layla shouted. "We have to get away from the door."

Following without seeing, Jacob tripped and struggled over the uneven ground beneath his feet. Underground he knew what the floor felt like, where the roots where, what tripping hazards lay in the way. Up here, though, he was not only blind from the light, but also unfamiliar with the land he walked on.

"Over here," he heard Sam shout. "Let's get you out of the sun."

It didn't take long and Jacob found himself feeling cooler, the light dimmer. Blinking, he opened his eyes and saw a structure. Wooden walls held up the high ceiling.

"You good?" Sam asked him.

"I think so," he replied. "What is this place?"

"This is the barn," Sam said. "It'll be safe for you to stay here until the sun sets. Then you can come outside and see the land. We've been working to build houses for those who might want to come to the surface, and have one ready if you are going to stay."

Jacob looked at Layla and smiled. "We can't really go back," he shrugged. "So I guess we're stuck up here."

"How are you guys doing?" Sam asked.

They had been working at night and had learned to tend the land. It was tough, but Jacob, Layla, and Kara were all getting stronger with the manual labor they were doing.

"I didn't realize it would be this much work,"

Jacob confessed.

"My grandparents say it is much different than when they were below," Sam agreed.

"When did they come up?"

"My father was very young," Sam said. "Still a child, really. Several families decided to escape the underground. The man in control of the area they lived in was becoming more and more violent. It wasn't safe for them to stay, so they did the only thing they could do."

"Weren't they afraid of what they'd find on the surface?"

"Anything was better than living where they were," he said. "The danger was very real there, and the surface only held mystery. My grandfather had heard some had tried to go to the surface about fifty years earlier, but they were never heard from again. No one knew whether they survived or perished."

"That's still a big risk," Jacob said.

"But completely worth it," Sam replied. "Turns out the people who came up before had found others on the surface who helped them to adapt. Some have been here for almost a hundred years."

"That long?"

"I've met the great-grandchildren of some who were the first to come to the surface," he replied. "They've also told us of some who never went underground."

"How did they survive?"

"Many continued to live on the surface after the great war," Sam explained. "They didn't have anywhere to go, so had to ride out the storms. It wasn't easy, and they lost many in their tribe. But after a while, things began to get better. Three generations after the fall, they were back to living much as they had before, minus all of the technology."

"That's fascinating," Jacob replied. "To think we could have been living on the surface for hundreds of years instead of below."

"Not sure it would have been doable," Sam confessed. "Back then we couldn't agree on anything. It's what caused the great wars to begin with. Having been separated for so long, though, might not work in our favor either. There are some who stayed on the surface who resent those of us who sought shelter, calling us the descendants of cowards."

"That seems harsh," Jacob said. "What we were told was it wasn't safe to remain. That's why we went underground."

"I think it is just a matter of learning to understand each other," Sam said. "Most are fine with us returning, at least in the small numbers so far. When more begin to emerge, though, things might become difficult."

"Staying below may soon become impossible," Jacob said.

"What do you mean?"

"Layla's father was unhappy that she wanted to return to the surface," Jacob began. "She told me he's known it was possible for years, but has refused to allow anyone from our tribe to come up. When Layla brought me up the first time, I was terrified. I think others would be, too. But if what she told me is true, her father may make it unbearable to stay."

"Then we better continue to work on creating more shelters for your families," Sam said. "Those who stayed taught us so much. We need to continue teaching those who decide to come up as well. And we do that by learning."

"It is a process I've been enjoying," Jacob confessed. "Although my body has not enjoyed it nearly as much as my mind."

"Give it time," Sam said. "Before long, you will be able to do things you never thought possible."

"That's already happened," Jacob laughed. "Beginning with being on the surface itself."

"Are you sure?" Jacob asked.

"Everything she's told me fits," Sam replied.

"I don't want to give Layla false hope, but..." Jacob left the sentence unfinished.

"I think we'll have a gathering," Sam decided. "We can invite her to come, then Layla can make her own determination."

"As long as she doesn't upset her," Jacob said. "If it is false, it would crush her."

"But if it's true?" Sam asked.

"Nothing could be better," Jacob said.

"Perfect," Sam said. "I'll ask Penny to get things set up."

"I'll tell Layla that we are helping," Jacob said. "So she doesn't have to feel like she hasn't contributed. She already feels that way as it is, with her limits because of the babe."

"How close is she?"

"Should be within a month," Jacob said.

"Should we wait?"

"No," Jacob replied. "Either way, I think it would be good for this to happen before the wee one arrives."

"As long as it isn't going to be too taxing on her," Sam said.

"If it's true, she will be thrilled," Jacob said.

"I just hope it is," Sam replied.

"Hello, Layla," a woman said.

"I'm sorry," Layla replied. "I don't think we've met, yet. I'm new to the surface, and have met so many new people I have lost track."

"We haven't been introduced," the woman said.

"Layla," Jacob said, coming up to the women. "I'm glad I found you."

"I'm not hard to spot," she replied. "I'm nearly as big as the barn."

"You are beautiful," the woman said.

"Thank you," Layla replied. "I'm sorry, I don't know your name. This is my partner, Jacob."

"Truly a pleasure," the woman said. "My name is Grace."

"That was my mother's name," Layla said.

"Pleasure to meet you, Grace," Jacob said.

"I'm glad my daughter found someone strong to help her escape," Grace said to Jacob.

"She is the strong one," Jacob replied.

"Did you just say daughter?" Layla asked.

"Yes," Grace said. "I believe you are my daughter."

"But my father said my mother was dead," Layla gasped.

"To him, I was," Grace replied. "When I left the underground, he told me I was never allowed to return. I tried to bring you with me, but he would not hear of it."

"But why didn't you stay, then?"

"I couldn't live under his rule any longer," she said. "Even then, he was beginning to show his need for control over all of us. He never wanted to come up to the surface, even when we'd talked to people who had been here. I begged him to let me bring you up, but he wouldn't hear it. He demanded I leave as soon as he found out I was planning to sneak away with you."

"Why would he do that?"

"Because some men need control," she said. "I have been waiting for you to discover the escape hatch. I knew you were smart, and I planted seeds in your memories, telling you stories of the surface, making sure you knew that it was safe to come up. I'm just glad you made it out before your baby got here."

Layla ran her hand across her stomach, soothing the child that was active inside.

"I only asked father one time about the surface," Layla recalled. "He told me it was too dangerous, that some had tried to come up, only to return sick. That's what he told me about you. You came to the surface and never returned. He said he couldn't risk anyone coming to search for you, even though he wanted desperately to find you. He never let me talk about it again."

233

"But you found a way," she said.

"Kara's family had talked about coming to the surface," Layla explained. "Her father told her repeatedly that she was not to discuss it with anyone. When we became friends, her father was worried that she would tell me and I would tell father. I asked her to come with me first, so she told me about her family's plan."

"Did they make it up?"

"Kara came with us," Jacob explained. "We don't know what happened to her family."

"She's thinking of going back down to find them," Layla confided.

"Doesn't she know how dangerous that can be?"

"She doesn't care," Layla said. "Her little brother is down there, and she is worried about him, as well as her parents."

"Then we need to send a group with her," Grace said.

"What do you mean?" Jacob asked.

"There have been talks in some of the communities up here," Grace said. "Many of those on the surface left loved ones below. Some know their family will not share in their desire to be surface dwellers, but others know that it is just a matter of time before their families join them."

"When are you planning to go?" Jacob asked. "I'll go with you."

"Sam has been working with the leaders of the other communities to set it up," Grace said. "That's how I heard about you. When he was talking with our leaders, asking if we had loved ones below that we thought might want to come to the surface, I asked about the hatch."

"Why did you leave the area?" Layla whispered.

"I didn't want to see your father again," Grace said.

"What do you mean?" Jacob asked.

"He probably never told you he came to the surface," Grace said. Layla shook her head, and Grace continued. "At first it was nearly every night, but it tapered off gradually. I last saw him twelve years ago. He begged me to return to the bunker, said that I was being selfish staying above ground. I told him that he was the selfish one, not wanting you to grow up in the fresh air of the surface. That last time, he said if I didn't return with him, that I would never see you again."

"And you thought the surface was more important than me?"

"No, darling," Grace said, shushing her daughter. "I begged him again to let me keep you up here. To let you grow up in the wilds of the surface where you had room to run and jump and play. He refused, telling me that I would never see you again, that I was dead to him and he would tell you that I had died because I came to the surface."

"You said to keep her up here," Jacob said. "Did she come to the surface before?"

"Not the first few times I came," Grace explained. "But when I was sure it was safe, I brought her up with me. Oh, how you loved to run in the grass of the meadow. You danced and sang and carried on with such a joy. When I finally decided to leave, I told your father what my plan was. He had his friends escort me to the hatch and throw me out. You sobbed so much, begging him to let you go with me. How you wanted to see the world. He simply held you back and had his men lock the hatch."

"I remember," Layla said. "I remember it like it was a dream. The sunshine and the flowers. How easy it was for me to breathe up here. When father held me back, I think something shut the memories out, like they broke that part of me. Finding the hatch was like opening a piece of my past."

"And now you can live it for real," Grace said. "You and your family."

"You have to rescue her," Layla sobbed.

"We're going tonight," Sam replied.

"I won't leave her there," Jacob insisted.

"I told her not to go alone," Layla continued. "But she insisted she could handle it."

"Why didn't you tell us as soon as she left?" Grace asked.

"She made me promise," Layla said. "Told me to wait two days before I said anything. She knew you would go searching for her."

"They won't hurt her," Jacob said.

"You don't know that," Layla insisted. "Father has become more and more paranoid about anyone who talks about the surface. When we left, he was alone. But if he'd had time, he would have gathered his men to keep us underground."

"He wasn't that bad when I left," Grace said.

"Times have changed him," Layla said. "More and more he's talked about hunters on the surface. People who remained after the wars becoming mutants and eating those who ventured above ground."

"What kind of weapons does he have?" Sam asked.

"I don't know," Layla replied. "There's never been a need for anything underground, so I don't think he has anything."

"Weapons were forbidden," Jacob asserted. "Even the council members were barred from having anything that could cause harm to another."

"Just because it wasn't allowed doesn't mean they don't have something," Sam said.

"I think the most you'll find are some bladed weapons," Grace said. "Your biggest disadvantage will be the darkness. Living underground built up our other senses, so you should plan to take a light source. Just know that if it goes out, you'll be in more danger than them."

"I can lead them," Jacob said. "I know my way around down there and can act as a guide in the dark. Once we find Kara, we can escape without them even knowing we were there. If we use a light source, they'll know we're there and we won't get far."

"You know she's going to be kept in confines," Layla said.

"Exactly," Jacob said. "That gives us the advantage. We know where she will be and can get in and out without being found."

"With the guard?"

"Michael will be there," Jacob said. "I can reason with him."

"He's on my father's side," Layla said.

"But he loves Kara," Jacob insisted. "Love can make you do some pretty crazy things."

"Promise me you'll be careful," Layla said.

"It will be highest on my list," Jacob replied. "Now," he continued, turning to Sam. "Let's get a plan of action in place."

"Stay close," Sam insisted. "Jacob is our guide. He knows where we need to go. Be quiet and follow along. Watch your footing so you don't stumble. You'll be blind down there, but we'll be fine."

After the decision to rescue Kara was made, Sam had asked for volunteers to go on the mission. Five men agreed to go, and they'd spent the day laying out their plan. Jacob had drawn a rough map of what the tunnels were like and which way they would go to get to Kara. Now was the time to put their plan in action.

"I love you," Layla said, hugging her partner. "Be smart and come back to me."

"I'll do my best," Jacob returned. "Ready?" he asked the group of men.

Grace held her daughter as the men grabbed the rope they were using to stay together in the dark. Jacob had worn a cloth across his eyes most of the day to return his vision to what it was before he'd emerged. He hoped it would be enough. With a deep breath he nodded. Philip, one of the men who would be waiting just inside the entrance opened the hatch and stepped inside. He helped Jacob through, then let the others come in to follow. Once the last man was through the portal, he shut it tight.

"And now we wait," Grace said.

"Slow your breathing," Jacob hissed.

The men behind him were so loud, he was sure the entirety of the community could hear them coming. Being thrust back into the dark, he found he easily adapted to the environment he'd grown up in. He didn't need his eyes to see where he needed to go, that was ingrained in his mind. Each curve and dip brought him closer to the confines and closer to his return to his partner.

"Finally," a man said. "I was wondering when my replacement would get here. What took you so long?"

Jacob recognized David's voice in the dark. Why they'd left such a young man in charge at the confines surprised him, so he deepened his voice and replied, hoping to fool the younger man.

"Just overslept," he said.

"I know how that goes," the younger man said. "She's been quiet the whole time. Shouldn't be any trouble."

"No problem," Jacob said.

Jacob heard the younger man leave without noticing the others with him. That would likely get him in trouble, but for now he was thankful for the guard's youth.

"Kara," he said once a sufficient amount of time had passed.

"Jacob?"

"It's me," he said.

"Layla told you," she said. "I didn't want you to risk yourself."

"I've brought help," he said.

"Now?" Sam asked.

"Yes," Jacob said.

The room flooded with light, even though it was a small match. Eyes adjusting quickly, the men worked to free Kara from her cell.

"We need to get Michael," she said.

"He didn't want to come," Jacob insisted. "He's the one who told Frank we were leaving."

"They've disciplined him for allowing me to go," she said. "He won't survive if we don't take him with us now."

"Are you sure?" Sam asked her.

"As sure as I've ever been," she replied.

"Then lead the way," he said, dousing the light and plunging them once again into darkness.

"Michael, please," Kara begged.

"I won't go to the surface," he insisted.

"They'll kill you," she sobbed.

"You know she's right," Jacob said.

"I've done nothing wrong," Michael countered.

"Then why did they punish you?" Kara asked.

"Discipline is mandatory in order to ensure we are safe," Michael repeated the motto they'd been taught from birth.

"Do you hear yourself?" Jacob asked. "There is a bounty of supplies on the surface. We want for nothing. Are you telling me you'd rather survive on scraps and roots and bugs?"

"We do just fine down here," Michael countered, but they could hear the doubt in his voice.

"Michael," Kara said, placing her hands on his cheeks. "I love you. I want you to live a life full of everything that is beautiful, but you can't do that trapped beneath the surface."

"Jacob," Sam said.

"Michael," Jacob said. "We need a decision. Are you going to stay here and face near certain death, or are you willing to risk just a little bit and find a life that is beyond fulfilling on the surface?"

"Please, Michael," Kara begged again.

They could all feel the tension filling the space.

"You're sure it's safe?" Michael finally asked.

"Much safer than staying down here," Jacob said.

"Okay," he finally said. "I'm trusting you, Jacob."

"You won't be disappointed," he returned.

"Let's go," Sam said.

"How long have they been gone?" Layla asked.

"They'll be fine," Grace comforted.

Philip opened the hatch and the men tumbled out, blinking even though it was night and the light wasn't too bright. Layla waited in anticipation of seeing her partner emerge. Finally, everyone was out of the door, and Philip stepped out and shut it.

"Where's Jacob?" she asked Sam.

"He's fine," Sam insisted.

"He should be with you," Layla replied. "Why did you leave him there?"

"He and Michael are getting our families," Kara said.

"Why didn't the rest of you stay behind?"

"Michael insisted," Sam said. "Since they are both from below, they felt they would be the best to rescue the remaining members of both Kara's and Michael's family."

"You were a team," Layla insisted. "All in together, and all out together. That was the plan."

"We're going back," Sam said. "Just need to get a few more supplies."

"Going back?" Grace asked. "For what?"

"Layla was right," Sam began. "Her father has changed over the last few months. He's become even more demanding on the community. Michael told us what they did to him, even though he alerted them to your leaving."

"It was horrible," Kara said. "No one is safe down there."

"The plan is to give everyone the opportunity to come up," Sam said.

"Will they come?" Grace asked.

"Michael and Jacob are planning on getting their families out," Sam said. "Once they have them to the door, they will rescue as many others as possible. This is why we are getting supplies to go back."

"What are you going to do?"

"Light the underworld," Sam said.

While they talked, the rest of the team had gotten sticks to use as torches. They wrapped some cloth smeared with pitch around the ends. Once they were done, they brought them over, preparing to return underground.

"We're ready," Philip said.

"Bring him home," Layla said to Sam.

"Let's go," Sam said, giving Layla a reassuring smile. "We've got a community to liberate."

"Stop," Frank shouted.

"No," Jacob returned. "You've held us in captivity for far too long. It's time we all saw the light of day and lived a life of freedom."

"Charles," Frank called. "Are you going to let your son get away with this?"

"I'd actually like to find out for myself," Charles replied.

The noise had drawn many in the community to the area near the hatch, and the murmurs were building with many wondering whether what Jacob had said was true. Three loud raps sounded on the hatch, and the group grew quiet.

"I'm going to open it," Jacob said. "There will be light, but it will be minimal. It is night on the surface, so we won't have to deal with the sun. If you want to come, you are all welcome. If you'd like to remain, that is your choice."

With his speech finished, he turned to the hatch and twisted the wheel, unlocking it. It opened and flooded the area with the soft blue light of night. The gasp was nearly deafening as the community as a whole saw for the first time.

"Jacob," Sam said, holding a torch above his head.

"I've got some friends I'd like you to meet," he replied, then stepped back to allow the first of the group to set foot on the surface.

"Welcome," Grace said. "We're happy to see you."

Blinking, men, women, and children stepped through the hatch into the night air, many taking deep breaths of the fresh air that surrounded them. Children stumbled and giggled as they felt the grass beneath their feet for the first time. An owl hooted nearby, and a young woman gasped in fear.

"It's safe," Layla said, holding the woman's hand. "That's a bird. They won't harm you."

The woman blinked and smiled at Layla.

"Come on," Layla said to the group. "Let's find you something to eat."

"Tonight, you'll stay in the barn," Sam said. "Tomorrow we'll show you around and help you get acclimated."

"Come back," Frank shouted from the opening.

"Frank," Grace said. "You need to let them choose. I know you want them to be safe, but that can be provided for them up here, now. Won't you come join us?"

Frank looked at her and blinked.

"Please, father," Layla said. "I want you to be happy."

"I'm staying down here," he said firmly.

"The door is always open," Grace said. "Come up when you're ready."

With that final statement, she turned and began the walk to

the barn. Layla watched her father as he silently begged her with his eyes to stay with him.

"I love you, daddy," she said. "But I belong up here, now."

She waited a few minutes longer, then watched as he reached out and pulled the hatch closed. The clank of the locking mechanism broke her heart, knowing that her father would not come up with them.

"He might come around," Jacob said as he hugged his partner.

"I hope so," she said before turning with him to follow the others from their community toward the barn.

Epilogue
25 years later

"Granny," Francis said. "What's that?"

The child was pointing to a rusting hunk of metal in the middle of the field.

"That's where we emerged," Layla said. "Back before your daddy was born, we lived underground."

"Why?"

"That is a very good question," she said. "A very long time ago, the people in charge of the government couldn't agree on much of anything. They had some terrible weapons which were unleashed on the world. Our kind scrambled to find someplace safe to live, and underground shelters where the best option we had."

"Why didn't they just talk?" Francis asked. "It's much better to find a way to get along by talking."

Ruffling the child's blonde hair, Layla laughed. "Grown ups aren't nearly as smart as you, my sweet child."

"Are we going to have to live underground?"

"I certainly hope not," Layla said. "It was not a fun place to be. I'm much happier up here on the surface where I can see the sun, smell the flowers, and look at your beautiful face."

"I don't want to live underground," Francis said.

"Then you need to make sure you know how to solve conflicts," Layla said.

AMARI

This is it," Kevin said. "The most beautiful place in the world."

"It is pretty," Jessie said. "But I'm not sure it's the most beautiful."

"Seriously?" Kevin scoffed. "Where have you been where the natural beauty was better than this?"

"I dunno," she replied. "I mean, there have to be some amazing places all around the world that you haven't seen, right?"

"Sure," he replied.

"So, then," she continued. "It could be that you just haven't seen the most beautiful place."

"I suppose," he said. "But of all the places I've been to, this one is spectacular."

"I'll give you that," she agreed.

"Let's go down," he suggested.

They took the trail that sloped down to the lake, simply enjoying the surroundings. With it being early, they could hear the call of the birds through the trees, the chatter of chipmunks racing around the undergrowth, and the hum of insects collecting nectar from the flowers on the edges of the trail. Within minutes, they found themselves in a meadow that sloped gently toward the lake.

"You're sure we can eat here?" she asked.

"I do it all the time," he replied. "As long as we take out what we brought in, we're good."

"It's just that most parks ask that you stay on the marked paths and not venture into areas like this," she said.

"Do you see any signs indicating we can't use the meadow as a picnic area?"

Jessie looked around, not seeing really much of any life. Shrugging, she said, "I guess we're good."

"Like I said," he began. "I do this all the time."

He spread the blanket out on the grass, then set the basket on one corner.

"Sit," he said, patting the blanket next to himself.

Jessie complied, sitting down and taking the sandwich he offered her. Biting into it, she savored the flavors of marmalade and peanut butter as they blended together.

"When we're done, we can swim," he said.

"Thought you weren't supposed to swim for half an hour after eating," she said.

"We can wade in, though," he said. "Take some of the heat out of ourselves. Get a little of that mountain refreshment from the water."

Jessie had to admit, even if it was just to herself, that this was a pretty romantic trip he'd planned. While she didn't know him well, they'd shared a few dates and found themselves to be fairly compatible. Maybe this would last.

"Have some lemonade," he said, offering her a glass.

She sipped it, but it didn't taste quite right.

"What's in this?" she asked.

"Special recipe," he said. "I make it myself. It's got lavender and mint in it. You're probably tasting the mint, since that's the strongest flavor."

"It's not bad, but definitely different," she said, taking another sip.

"Glad you like it," he said. "I've got plenty if you want more."

They spent the next few minutes in companionable silence as they ate their lunch.

"Ready for that dip in the lake?" Kevin asked.

"I'm actually thinking a nap in the sun might be nice," Jessie suggested.

"You rest," he said. "I'm going to check the water and see what it's like."

The screams woke her. She bolted up, looking around. Blinking, she got her bearings, remembering the hike up to the lake, the lunch, and the nap. It was silent, now. She looked around for Kevin, but didn't see him anywhere. Then she remembered the lake. He'd said he was going to go take a dip, so she decided to head down there and see if she could see him.

As she rose, she realized that not only had the screaming stopped, but there were no other sounds, either. Looking back and forth, she watched the landscape to see if she could see any movement. The stillness was eerie and unsettling. Slowly, she moved toward the lake, hoping to catch something, anything to ease the fear that was swiftly rising within her.

The lake was like glass. No wind blew. Nothing made a sound around her. Everything was still. Looking into the water, she could see that there were fish under the surface, but they were frozen in place.

"Help," she shouted, hearing her voice echo back from the mountains around her. Other than that, she was met with silence.

Backing away from the lake, she moved to where she had been sleeping and picked up her phone. Pressing the button to bring it to life, she was met with a black screen. Shaking it and pressing every button she could, using the fingerprint scanner to try to get some reaction from it did nothing. Fear began to grip her as she tried to find Kevin's phone. When she did, she had the same result, simply a black screen.

"Help," she called again, only to be met with nothing but the echo of her own voice once again.

Her breathing was rapid and she could feel her heart pounding in her chest, but still nothing around her moved. She tried the phones again, hoping desperately to get a reaction from either of them so she could call for help, but they remained void of life.

"This has to be a dream," she muttered, trying to reassure herself. "This can't be real."

Panic was building in her as she grabbed her things, along with Kevin's car keys, and practically ran toward the trail that would lead her back to the car. There hadn't been many people on the trail when they first arrived, so she wasn't expecting to see anyone on the way back, either. As she rounded a bend in the trail, she froze. There, in the middle of the trail, frozen like the landscape around her, was a mountain lion. Jessie held still, sure the creature would smell her and turn to attack. She waited several long minutes, but the lion never moved.

Carefully, she eased closer to the beast, not wanting to have whatever spell had befallen the world to release its hold and put her in perilous danger. Once past the creature, she quickly ran down the trail toward the parking lot.

Jessie halted abruptly as she stepped from the trailhead. The lot where they'd parked was empty. Not only was Kevin's car gone, but the other few that had been there when they'd arrived were also missing.

"Help," she called again, hoping for some response. Again she was met with only silence.

Pulling the keys from her pocket, she pressed the lock button on the fob. What she hoped to accomplish with this was unclear, but she heard the distinct horn sound, albeit muffled. Pressing it again, she tried to distinguish where the sound was coming from. Muffled, yet audible, she determined the car must be close. Stepping into the lot, she pressed the button again, moving closer to where they'd parked. It sounded as if the car was still there, just hidden by something. Standing in front of the stall where they parked, she again used the fob to confirm the car was there. Sure enough, she heard the honk of the horn. She also heard muffled voices, but couldn't figure out where they were coming from.

Closing her eyes, she focused hard on the sound. Slowly she began to make out individual voices, but still couldn't clearly determine what they were saying. Focusing harder, she picked up one from the others. It was Kevin, she was sure.

"Kevin," she shouted, hoping to break through whatever was keeping her in this frozen landscape.

"I heard her," she heard him say.

"Where is she?" another voice asked.

"Jessie," he called.

"I'm here," she shouted. "I can't see you, though."

"Jess," he shouted again.

"Kevin," she shouted.

Silence once again enveloped her.

"Kevin," she screamed as sobs began to take her over.

She knew something was wrong, but couldn't figure out how she got to where she was, nor how to fix the problem. Never in her life had she been so scared. She crumpled to the ground, overcome with the emotions of it all.

"I swear I heard her," Kevin said to the officer.

"I know," the officer replied.

"Where is she?" Kevin pleaded.

"We'll find her," the officer said.

"Argh," Kevin grumbled in frustration.

Just then, another officer approached with a woman Kevin could only describe as eclectic. Her hair was wild around her head, with a swath of colored fabric holding it back from her face. The top she wore was full of swirls and swoops of purples and pinks and reds. Her skirt had stripes in every color imaginable. While the colors and patterns clashed, they somehow looked perfect on the woman.

"Shhh," she said as she came up to them. "Let me listen to the ethers."

Kevin looked to the officer he'd been working with, questioning with his eyes.

"Gwen," the officer said to the woman.

"Rick," she replied. "You know this is needed. You can't deny it, now."

"I'm not sure this is the time," Rick said.

"The sooner I can connect with the other side," Gwen began, "the better chance I have of bringing her back."

"Where is she?" Kevin asked.

"She's halfway," Gwen said, as if that explained everything.

"Halfway to where?"

"Gwen believes that there are alternate planes of existence," Rick explained. "Halfway is just one of them."

"Halfway is between the worlds, Rick," Gwen chastised. "It's between planes. Not in or on any one in particular. If we can get her back before she goes the rest of the way, we can save her."

"And if we can't?" Kevin asked.

"Then she'll have to survive in the other plane," Gwen explained.

"Help me," Kevin begged.

"Sir," Rick said.

"No," Kevin barked. "If there's a chance that she's right, I want to do everything I can to get her back."

Rick just threw his hands up with an exasperated sigh and walked away.

"What do you have that she might also have with her?" Gwen asked.

"I think she has my keys," Kevin said, holding his bunch out to the woman.

"Why do you think she has these?"

"I heard the car honk," he explained. When she looked at him in confusion, he continued. "Just a few minutes ago I heard the horn, like when you press the lock button on the fob."

"Can you show me?"

Kevin pulled the keys back to himself and pressed the fob, eliciting the intended horn reaction.

"Did you hear or feel anything else?"

"I swear I heard her yelling," he said. "I heard her call my name. When I responded, I think I heard it several more times."

"How long ago?"

"Just before you came up," he said.

"May I?" she asked, holding out her hand.

He dropped the keys into her palm, unsure exactly what to expect from her. She closed her eyes, then wrapped her fingers around the keys, squeezing them tightly. Kevin held his breath, hoping against hope that this strange woman would somehow find Jessie.

Gwen's eyes popped open and she shot a look at Kevin.

"Name," she said.

"Jessie," Kevin responded, then thought she meant him, so he added, "I'm Kevin."

The woman nodded, then closed her eyes again. He watched her mutter under her breath, unable to make out any of the words she said. For several long minutes they were silent around the strange woman as she spoke incantations while squeezing his keys.

Just when he began to wonder whether anything was

actually happening, the woman opened her eyes wide. The white of them startled Kevin and he took a step back. She looked around as if she could see something other than what was there.

"Hello," she whispered.

Kevin waited, unsettled by the demeanor of the woman, yet strangely intrigued by what she was doing, wondering whether there really were other planes of existence.

"He does want you back," the woman said.

He was again struck by the oddity that was going on around him.

"Believe," the woman crooned. "You have to believe if you want to come back."

Holding his breath, Kevin wondered what Jessie was saying to the woman in that alternate plane they seemed to share.

"Please come back," he whispered, hoping somehow that it would convince Jessie that she was wanted.

An audible 'pop' sounded around him and he felt his ears ring and became unsteady on his feet, falling back against his car. He blinked a couple of times, then realized that he'd fallen to the ground and his car was missing. Looking around, he saw the woman, her eyes clear and focused on something behind him. Turning, he saw Jessie standing there, fists on her hips, glaring at him.

"What did you do?" she accused. "How did you get here?"

"I...I don't know," he stammered, clearly confused at the current situation.

"You believed," Gwen said, looking at Jessie.

"I didn't want him here," Jessie replied. "Why would I want to stay here?"

"Focus," Gwen said, still staring at the other woman.

Jessie closed her eyes after one more glare at Kevin.

"Focus and chant," Gwen assured.

Once again, Kevin was left watching a woman mutter under

her breath in some other language. What Jessie said made no sense to him, so he sat still, waiting. Time slowed as his heart beat pulsed in his ears. It was eerily silent in whatever plane he found himself. Minutes passed with nothing but the muttering of the woman he'd fallen for punctuating the quiet around him. Then, without warning, he was thrust back to the plane he was used to, sprawled across the ground next to his car, Jessie standing at the end of the trailhead, and Gwen smiling smugly, a look of triumph on her face.

"What the hell?" Rick shouted, breaking the hush that had fallen all around them. "Where did she come from?"

"I told you," Gwen boasted. "I brought her back from halfway. Maybe next time you'll believe me."

"Kevin," Jessie said as she rushed to him.

"Jessie," Kevin replied, sitting up. "Are you okay?"

"What happened?" she asked.

"I'm not sure," he replied.

"Can I check you out?" a medic asked.

"Umm," Jessie stammered. "I guess. Kevin needs help, too."

"Yep," the other man said. "Let's get both of you to the aid car and see what's going on."

With help, Kevin stood, then both he and Jessie made their way through the crowd of people standing around them.

"Up you go," the medic said as he helped first Jessie, then Kevin into the back of the ambulance. "Just need to see what's going on with you before I can safely let you go on your way."

"You're sure?" Kevin asked for what seemed like the hundredth time.

"Yes," Jessie said. "I want to spend the rest of my life with you."

"And you don't think it's weird?"

"Everything about that day was weird," she returned.

"Nothing can compare to finding yourself in the same place, but having everything different."

"Nothing could prepare me for you disappearing on me," he replied. "I'm just glad Gwen was there to help."

"Where did she come from, anyway?"

"I have no idea," Kevin confessed. "She came up with one of the cops that were there. The officer I had been dealing with seemed to know her, though."

"It was strange when she appeared," Jessie said after a time. "I thought I was losing my mind, at first. Then, when I got to the parking lot and nothing was there, I was afraid I was dead. It wasn't until I heard your voice that I began to believe that this might not be the end of me."

"When you were gone," Kevin began. "I didn't know where you went. You were napping, then I turned around and you were just not there."

"I heard screaming," she confessed. "That's what woke me up. Nothing was moving where I was, either. It was really terrifying."

"I can only imagine," he said. "I'm just glad I found you."

"Me, too," she agreed.

"And they don't suspect?" Rick asked Gwen.

"They are completely oblivious to the facts," she returned. "To them, they were lost in the alternate plane, then brought back to the one they vanished from."

"Good," he said. "We have needed new blood for a while. They'll be perfect as a life source for Amari."

"Yes," Gwen agreed. "I'm just thankful we are offered the opportunity to hunt for him."

"So long as we are still able to move between planes," Rick began, "we will continue to be of value to Amari. That, in and of itself, is a notion to be proud of."

"When will they be reaped?"

"Not until they procreate," he said. "Their child will then be transferred back to the other plane to continue our work there."

THRUVITH

W hat do you think?" Gayle asked.

"Ummm..." Nicole murmured.

"You hate it," Gayle said. "I knew it was too much."

"No," Nicole said. "It's just not what I expected."

"Not what you expected?" Gayle asked. "It's a freaking wedding dress. White, lace, sparkles, what else is there?"

"But it isn't you," Nicole said. "You don't do things in any traditional way at all. I expected something much less..."

"Normal?" Gayle offered.

"Well, yeah," Nicole agreed.

"Jack wanted traditional," Gayle explained.

"He knows you, right?" Nicole asked in jest.

"Apparently his parents aren't super excited about us getting married," Gayle whispered.

"I thought they liked you," Nicole argued.

"For a girlfriend," Gayle said. "But his dad told him I wasn't wife material."

"He actually said that?"

"Not to me," Gayle said staring at herself in the three mirrors surrounding her in the dress shop.

"But he told Jack that," Nicole surmised.

"Am I making a mistake?"

For the first time ever, Nicole saw a crack in her best friend's shell. Gayle was the strongest person she'd ever met. Her mom died when she was two, and her dad followed when she was sixteen. Because he'd been sick, they'd done up the paperwork so that she would be emancipated upon his death. The life insurance policy was enough to pay off the house she grew up in, and pay for college. She'd met Jack freshman year, and they'd been inseparable since. At 23 she was well educated, working a great job with an amazing company, and had more than enough to keep herself comfortable.

"Gayle," Nicole said. "Jack is perfect for you. And you're perfect for him. His parents shouldn't have a say in whether you two get married, you're both adults."

"But they mean a lot to him," Gayle whispered. "I don't want to make him choose."

"Okay," Nicole said. "How did he say it?"

"Say what?"

"That his dad didn't think you were wife material," Nicole clarified.

"I don't understand," Gayle said.

"Was it in a way that was more like, 'I can't believe he said this,'" Nicole explained. "Or was it more like, 'I hadn't thought of that' kind of way?"

"I don't know," Gayle said.

"This calls for more than what we can do right here," Nicole said. "Let's get you out of that dress and go somewhere to eat. This is a serious conversation that I can't do with you standing there looking all Cinderella like."

Nicole shooed her hands, ushering her friend back to the dressing rooms to change from the ruffles and lace she was wearing. Once she was back in her regular clothes, they made their way down the block to a café. They were seated and ordered, and then Nicole picked up the conversation again.

"Tell me exactly what he said," Nicole began. "And how he said it. I need to know if I need to get out the big guns and go after him, or if we can figure this out without any bloodshed."

Gayle sighed and dropped her head into her hands, then said, "I don't remember."

"Where were you?"

"Umm..." Gayle muttered. "I think we were in the shower."

"Okay," Nicole began. "First of all, there should be no talking in the shower. That should be all moans of ecstasy."

"Lord help me," Gayle mumbled.

"And second," Nicole continued. "If he's thinking about anything but pleasing you while you two are in the shower, then there's more than just his dad's argument to consider. I mean, y'all should just be getting freaky in there. No thinking."

Gayle laughed a little, letting a breath out, then said, "It wasn't like that."

"Why not?"

"Because it was this morning and he was getting ready to go golfing with the guys and I was getting ready to meet you," Gayle explained.

"But you were in the shower," Nicole said, as if it explained everything.

"You are incorrigible," Gayle laughed.

Just then, the waitress brought their salads, and conversation lulled.

"Okay," Nicole said after finishing a bite. "You're in the shower. Not getting freaky," she added with a roll of her eyes. "And he says, 'dad thinks you're not wife material.' Am I getting this right?"

"Yeah, I guess," Gayle surmised.

"And you said..." she left the sentence hanging, waiting for her friend to fill in the rest.

259

"Nothing," Gayle replied.

"Nothing," Nicole sputtered, eyes wide. "The dude you're getting married to tells you his dad doesn't think you add up and you say nothing?"

"I mean," Gayle muttered.

"No," Nicole argued. "You should have said it was a good thing you weren't marrying his dad. I mean, who says something like that?"

"I don't think he meant it like that," Gayle mumbled.

"Tonight, you find out," Nicole replied. "You ask him point blank if he regrets asking you to marry him. Ask him if making his parents happy is more important than making you happy. Tell him that you're fine walking away if he isn't in it for you."

"But I'm not fine walking away," Gayle argued.

"Even if he's willing to put his parent's happiness ahead of yours?"

Gayle sighed and put her head back in her hands.

"Hey, now," Nicole began. "I know you want to marry him. I know you love him with your whole self. But you've got to look at the long term. If he's quoting his dad saying you don't measure up, what's next? You don't cook like his mom? You don't do the laundry right? You should stay home and raise kids instead of continuing in your career?"

"Stop," Gayle whispered.

"I'm worried about you," Nicole said.

Gayle looked up, tears pooling in her lower lashes.

"It's already started," Nicole guessed.

Gayle nodded.

"Oh, honey," Nicole cooed. "What can I do?"

Gayle blinked and the tears tumbled out as she sobbed, "I don't know."

"He said that?" Ben asked.

"Yeah," Nicole replied. "And that's not all."

"Why do I get the feeling I'm gonna have to save Jack's ass?"

"If he keeps this up," Nicole began, "he better hope you can save him."

"Tell me," Ben insisted.

Nicole gave a blow by blow of the conversation she'd had at lunch earlier with Gayle. By the time she'd finished, Ben was just shaking his head.

"I'll talk some sense into him," he said.

"As best man," Nicole said. "It's kinda your job. If he wants one of those Stepford wives, he better find someone else."

"I just don't know why he didn't mention any of this today," Ben said. "He acted like nothing was wrong and everything was smooth sailing."

"You do realize how oblivious he is, right?"

"For some things, sure," Ben countered. "But this is kind of a big deal. I mean, we're just a couple of months out from the big day. He better get his shit straight."

"You better help him out with that," Nicole retorted.

"Oh, trust me," Ben said. "I will. Gayle is like a sister to you, which makes her family to me. No one messes with family."

"This is why I love you so much," Nicole said, hugging Ben. "You fix everything."

"What's up?" Jack said as he picked up the call.

"We need to talk," Ben said without preamble.

"I know that tone," Jack laughed. "What did I do now?"

"You, me, Riley's Coffee Shop," Ben replied.

"This is serious," Jack said, his humor now gone.

"As a heart attack," Ben replied.

"I'll be there in fifteen," Jack said.

"You're buying," Ben informed.

"I didn't know what you wanted," Jack said when Ben walked in.

"I'll order," he replied.

"Here," Jack said, holding out his credit card.

Ben took it, ordered his coffee, then sat with Jack to wait for it to be done.

"What did I do?" Jack asked after his friend picked up his drink.

"Gayle's not wife material?" Ben asked.

"Who told you that?" Jack accused.

"Apparently your dad told you," Ben insisted. "Then you had the nerve to tell Gayle."

"It's not what you think," Jack argued.

"Then enlighten me," Ben offered.

"My parents are of a very traditional mindset," Jack began. "They think that a woman should keep herself pure until marriage. That they should be requested of their father, and that they should not, under any circumstances, live with their husband until after the wedding day."

"So," Ben interrupted. "Because you two live together, she's not really good enough to be your wife?"

"She would have been," Jack mumbled.

"But," Ben said, leaving the word hanging.

Jack took a deep breath, then let it out. "She doesn't have a father to ask permission to marry. Because of this," he continued, "she likely is of loose morals and has played me to take her in as my wife because she's not capable of managing on her own." The way he said the last, it was clear that he was quoting someone.

"I'm sorry, what?"

"I know," Jack agreed. "It's ridiculous to think that Gayle is anything less than a perfectly capable woman who can do anything she puts her mind to."

"You know she is," Ben said.

"Absolutely," Jack confirmed. "She's probably the more stable person in the relationship. They just see her as this orphan who didn't grow up in a traditional family, didn't have family dinners and family holidays and everything else that I had. It's ridiculous, but they are kind of insisting that we do a prenup and everything, just so she won't take advantage of me."

"They do know she's got more money than you, right?"

"No," Jack said. "They would think she got it through ill-gotten means."

"Her dad was smart," Ben argued. "He started a fund for her before she was born, took the money he got from her mom's life insurance policy and put it in her name. He also made sure that he had sufficient insurance, just in case something happened to him, which it did. She owns the house you guys live in," Ben continued. "Has a job that pays way more than you, and has so many investments that you could probably be a kept man and never have to work a day in your life. What is their problem?"

"Exactly that," Jack said. "They feel like she is taking advantage of me."

"How does that even make sense?"

"It doesn't," Jack said.

"You need to talk to them," Ben insisted. "And I'd do it today, before Gayle gets cold feet and pulls out of the engagement before you even get to the alter."

"How do I do that?"

"You tell them to go shove their ideals down the sink," Ben barked. "Tell them that she makes you happy and that you couldn't imagine your life without her. Besides, they aren't the ones marrying her, you are, and your happiness is more important than their approval."

Jack sat there, hand over his mouth, obviously trying to not to say something.

"What?" Ben snapped.

"There's something else," Jack said.

"Well?"

"It's complicated," Jack said.

"Then uncomplicate it," Ben insisted. "Look, you love Gayle, right?" Jack nodded, so Ben continued. "And you want to spend the rest of your life with her." Another nod. "So, either put up or shut up," he concluded.

"It's not that easy," Jack said.

"Why not?" Ben asked. "Are you some kind of spy or something?"

Jack looked at Ben, eyes wide, and Ben said, "Oh my god, you are."

"It's not like that," Jack insisted.

"Then tell me," Ben pushed.

"You're gonna think I'm crazy," Jack said.

"I already do," Ben laughed.

Jack closed his eyes, took a deep breath, then opened them again.

"I come from a place called Thruvith," Jack said.

"And that's where, exactly?"

"Time and space fold," Jack began.

"Are you trying to tell me you're an alien?" Ben scoffed. "Cause I'm not buying that."

"In the general sense, yes," Jack explained. "But it's not like what you're thinking."

"Then what am I thinking?" Ben asked.

"Little green men and flying saucers," Jack suggested.

"And that's not you, right?"

"Exactly," Jack said. "I come from Earth."

"You said you didn't," Ben argued.

"Not this Earth," Jack corrected. "The Earth I come from

shares this space with your Earth. You know those old science fiction movies that talked about alternate universes?"

"So you're saying you're from another universe?"

"Pretty much," Jack confirmed.

"Do I have an evil twin in your universe or something?"

"It doesn't work like that," Jack explained. "That would make it a parallel universe, where one different choice could change the course of someone's history. This is another world that holds the same space, but has its own history not connected in any way to this one."

"Then how did you get here?"

"That's a little more complicated," Jack said.

"You've brought me this far," Ben said. "Let's go the whole nuthouse way."

"This isn't the time or place," Jack said. "I need to go talk to Gayle. Explain things to her before I explain them to you."

"So," Ben began. "You're gonna tell her you're an alien and your dad wants you to marry someone from your own planet?"

"Something like that," Jack said.

"Good luck with that," Ben laughed. "She's way more cynical than I am. I mean, I don't even know if I'm convinced. You better up your game if you want to convince her."

"I think I've got it covered," Jack laughed.

"Just don't pull off your face," Ben jested. "Nobody wants to see that."

"Gotcha," Jack joked. "No face removal to confirm alien status."

With that, he walked out the door, leaving Ben to contemplate all he'd learned about his friend in the last half hour or so.

"Jeez, Jack," Gayle said, hand to her chest as Jack came around the end of the couch. "You scared the crap out of me."

"Sorry," Jack replied. "Can we talk?"

"That doesn't sound good," Gayle replied.

"It's good," he said.

"Okay," she said.

Gayle paused the show she had going on the television and turned to Jack who sat on the other end of the couch.

"I'm not crazy," he began.

"Never thought you were," she replied.

"You might," he said. "After I tell you what I have to tell you."

"Now I'm scared," she whispered.

Jack reached out and grabbed her hand, pulling her closer to him. She scooted down the couch until she was sitting right next to him.

"I love you," he said.

"I love you, too," she replied cautiously.

"Okay," he said, then blew out a breath. "I come from Thruvith."

"I don't know where that is," she said.

"You wouldn't," he replied. "I need you to trust me."

Gayle nodded, though her stomach churned. She did trust him. That's why she'd agreed to marry him, why they decided to move in together.

"My planet is in the same space as Earth," he began. "It's just in an alternate universe. We didn't intend to come here, it just sort of happened. Now that we're here, though, we can't get back. My parents have tried, trust me, but there just doesn't seem to be a slip to go back through."

"But you're human, right?"

"Kind of," he said. She looked at him, clearly confused. "It's pretty much the same as human. There are some differences between our worlds, but physiologically it's pretty similar."

"So," she began. "Are there two of you here?"

"No," he replied. "And there isn't another one of me on Thruvith, either."

"That's good, I guess," she said.

"It is," he agreed.

"Is that why your dad doesn't want you to marry me?"

"That's part of it," he said, stroking the back of her hand with his thumb. "The other part is that he's not sure whether we can have kids or not."

"Why wouldn't we be able to?"

"While we're pretty much the same," he said. "There are some differences. Dad's afraid we won't be able to have a baby, and if we do, it'll have major issues with it, biologically."

"That could happen if you were from here, too," she said. "He's a doctor. You'd think he knew that."

"He does," Jack said. "But it would be the first time someone from my planet and someone from Earth had a baby. It really is an unknown outcome, and he's just worried that we won't be able to handle it."

"Then we don't have kids," she said.

"But you want them," he argued.

"I do," she replied. "But I want you more than I want kids. And we can always adopt. There are a ton of kids out there in the system that don't have a home and need one. We can be the home for those kids."

Jack pulled her into a hug, kissing the top of her head.

"This is one of the things I love about you most," he murmured against her head. "You always find a solution."

"I'm not saying that I don't want to try to have a baby with you, though," she said, pulling back to look Jack in the eye. "We can try and see what happens, right?"

"Absolutely," he said, kissing her tenderly.

"I can't believe you got this one," Nicole said as she helped Gayle dress.

"Jack and I decided that we weren't gonna let his parents dictate our lives," Gayle responded. "That included my wedding dress."

"But black?"

"With red accents," Gayle insisted. "It's better than that god-awful thing I first tried on."

"Oh, yeah," Nicole agreed. "I don't think anyone would look good in that monstrosity."

"That's for damn sure," Gayle agreed.

"But why black?"

"It's traditional," she said.

Nicole looked utterly confused.

"Ask Ben about where Jack comes from," Gayle said.

"He's not from Chicago?"

"Not even close," Gayle laughed. "Now give me my flowers and let's get this show on the road."

Nicole laughed at her friend, handed her the bouquet, and walked out of the small room they had used for dressing.

"Rayna," Gayle called.

"Mama," the little girl said.

"Whatcha doing?"

"Playing space invaders," the girl replied.

"Well, play nice," the mother said, rocking the baby in her arms.

As they'd planned, Jack and Gayle fostered, then adopted shortly after their wedding, taking in a set of twins whose parents had been killed in a fire, with no other family to take them in. The girls were three when they got them. It took time for them to feel safe, so Jack decided to stay home with them to give them a stable home life. Before long, they brought in another child, this time a teenager. He was a struggle in the beginning, but once he realized that the boundaries they'd put in place were to help him, he settled down and excelled in everything. He graduated high school and was now at college doing remarkably well.

Their third wedding anniversary saw them expecting a baby of their own. Both were nervous, unsure whether this little one would have issues or would come out normal. They were both thrilled to welcome a beautiful baby girl with dark hair like her mother and gray eyes like her father. Two years after Rayna was born, they welcomed Jack Jr., or JJ as they called him. Again, nothing abnormal about him was found, either.

Now, she held Willow, a baby that had been abandoned on the steps of a local church, left in the middle of the night with nothing but a light blanket to ward off the cool evening air. Because of their willingness to take in 'difficult' children, the state asked them to take her in since she'd shown some abnormalities their doctors couldn't explain. They asked Jack's father to check her out, and it turned out she was also from Thruvith, and they were the perfect people to raise her.

Finding Willow was also a way to figure out how to get back to Thruvith if they wanted to. Jack's parents wanted to see their home world again, but didn't want to leave the grandchildren, so found a way to keep the slip open to go between worlds easily. Every time they came back to Earth, they brought stories of what was happening on the other planet, as well as some much-needed technology. Thruvith was much farther advanced than Earth in that department, but there were things Earth had excelled at that Thruvith could learn from.

With the back and forth, they helped advance both worlds, giving each a new perspective on what it meant to be human, whether that was from one side of the slip or the other.

Jack and Gayle's home became a place where lost children found a safe space to thrive, and they never stopped taking kids in until their age made it too tough to handle the little ones. Even so, their kids followed in their footsteps, caring for the kids who were left behind, forgotten, or simply misunderstood. It was a legacy both felt proud of.

Eventually, when they were both old and looking at the end of their lives, Jack asked Gayle if she wanted to go through the slip and visit Thruvith.

"Are you sure we should go?" Gayle asked him.

"We don't have to," Jack said.

"I think I'd like to see your home world," she said.

"I'd love to show it to you," he replied.

Holding hands, they slid through the space between worlds and stepped onto Thruvith, Gayle for the first time, and Jack for the first time in decades.

"It's beautiful," she said, looking around in wonder.

"I'm glad you like it," Jack replied.

FATES

There is something immensely beautiful in letting go. Whether it's giving up on a dream that will never come to fruition, saying good bye to a loved one when they've lived a long and fulfilling life, or walking away from drama in most any form. It's the latter that I find myself in right now. I knew I shouldn't have gotten involved, but it seemed so perfect. That should have been my first clue. Nothing in this life is perfect. I suppose I should start at the beginning, otherwise none of the rest of this story will make sense.

"Good morning, class," Mr. Richards said. "Hopefully you had a nice rest over break and are ready to jump right back into our studies. We only have a few more weeks of the quarter left before we have finals, and I want you all to be prepared."

We'd been studying the fates and their multiple genesis, focusing highly on the Greek version, Moirai. It was monotonous at best, and right now I just wanted to be done with it. Couldn't we all just read the Iliad and call it good?

"I've paired you up," the professor continued, and an audible groan rippled through the students. "I know you like to choose your own partners, but I wanted to make sure that each student had someone they could rely on to be at the same level of skill as themselves. If you have a true conflict with who I've matched you with, please come see me after class and we can discuss it."

With that, he turned the projector on with the list of students in the class, showing who we would be paired up with for the final project. I searched the list looking for my name, only to see it next to someone I'd never met. This could either be a fantastic partner, or someone I would come to loath by the end of it.

"Please take a minute to meet your partners," the professor said. "I want you to exchange contact information so you will not have an excuse as to why you weren't able to work together."

I stood, turned toward the classroom, and looked around. My friend Kathy was looking at me with horror in her eyes. I hadn't seen who she was paired up with, so took a quick look at the list. Of course she would be stuck with James. The guy was stupid smart, but about as fun as a turd in a swimming pool. Poor Kathy.

"Are you Izzy?" a young man asked me.

"You must be Sean," I replied.

"I am," he said with a smirk.

"You're not gonna screw me on this project, are you?"

"As long as you don't screw around, we'll be fine," he replied.

"I don't screw around with my homework," I stated flatly. "I'm a 4.0 student and intend to keep my average there."

"Good," he replied.

"Great," I said.

We exchanged contact info and decided who would be doing what with respect to the project. Our task was simple, explain the Fates, describe how they worked within mythology, and come to a conclusion as to whether we agreed or disagreed with the idea that they were still around. I already knew the answer to the final question, whether they still existed. It would be interesting to see whether my partner agreed with me.

After class, Kathy caught up to me.

"Your partner is cute," she whispered as we found our way down the hall.

"I guess," I replied. "Didn't really look at him."

"Trade ya?"

"Not a chance," I laughed. "I'm sorry you're stuck with James, but it's your own fault. If you weren't so smart, you'd be stuck with someone like Brent."

"Ugh," she said, rolling her eyes. "Can you imagine trying to do the report and having him just go, 'but I thought they were sexy babes like in that animated film.'"

"I don't envy the person who ended up stuck with him," I said.

"So," she offered after we'd been walking a while. "What's he like?"

"Who?"

"Sean," she said. "Duh."

"Oh," I replied. "I guess he's fine. I mean, we didn't really talk much."

"I am definitely going to need all the details after your first get together," she said. "I expect detailed descriptions of everything you do."

"You mean like, 'we looked information up on the internet,' and the like?" I asked.

"There better be more than research going on with you two," she said. "Like, there better be sparks and sex and—"

"Whoa," I said, stopping her mid-sentence. "There will be no sex."

"You're no fun," she laughed. "I'd totally take advantage of

273

the forced communication and closeness."

"I'm not you," I said. "I have no need for a boyfriend right now."

"Who said anything about him being your boyfriend?"

"You are incorrigible," I said.

"Details," she said, then grabbed my arm.

The rest of the day went along boringly as usual, and on the way to our off-campus apartment, we stopped at the Frosty Freeze for shakes. I know, shakes in the middle of winter seems odd, but it was comfort food for us. Every time we had a big assignment given to us, we stopped and picked up a shake to ease the burden we felt. Today was no different. I know a lot of the college kids would have stopped at a bar, but Kathy and I were mild mannered, boring, very responsible people. Besides, nothing at a bar could beat a salted caramel shake from the Frosty Freeze.

Kathy grabbed my arm and stopped me short as soon as we walked in the door.

"He's here," she whispered.

"Who?"

"Sean," she insisted. "Go talk to him."

"What for?" I asked as I began to walk toward the counter.

"Because he's cute," she said. "And he's your partner, and you need to talk about the project, and…"

"Stop," I said, and did just that, jolting her as well. "Are you twelve?"

She looked at me, completely baffled.

"You're acting like we're in junior high and he's a cute boy I've got a crush on," I explained. "We're twenty-one, in college, and it's an assignment for philosophy. We've already had a conversation about it, and we have each other's contact info so we can keep in touch. There is nothing to talk about."

"But he's cute," she insisted.

"You are the most ridiculous person I know," I laughed. "I need a shake."

With that, I walked away from her and up to the counter to order my treat. She followed quickly and made her own order. When our shakes were ready, we walked to the dining area. Whether it was fate or something else, the only table available was the one right next to Sean.

"Hey," Kathy said as we sat down.

Sean looked up from his book and smiled.

"I thought I was the only one who did shakes in the winter," he said. "It appears I am in good company, though."

"It's our customary treat when we get a big assignment," I said. "Reminds us of the simple times before finals and the like."

"I hear ya," he replied.

"So," Kathy began, but I glared at her. "Um..." she stammered.

I rolled my eyes and asked, "What flavor?"

"The best flavor," he smiled. "Salted caramel."

"Me, too," I laughed.

"Must be fate," he said.

There it was. That word again. I don't know if it was just because we were studying them, or if there was something more going on, but it seemed like things were aligning, coming together, as if they were all planned by some unseen force.

"We good to meet on Thursday?" he asked.

"I've put it in my phone," I said. "Library, right?"

"Why don't you meet at the apartment?" Kathy suggested, and I stomped on her foot under the table. "Ouch," she cried, then glared daggers at me.

"It has to be the library," he said. "I don't think we can check out some of the books I'd like to use as references, so we'll have to do the research there."

"I'll bring my laptop so we can make notes," I said. "Unless you want to do that part."

"I'm good with you doing that part," he said. "We can work together, but if you want to house it on your laptop, that works well."

"Perfect," I said, then took a sip of my shake. "Ugh," I said, pulling my mouth off the straw. "I think I got yours, Kath."

"Mine's right," she said, taking a sip of her own.

"Be right back," I said, then got up and walked back up to the counter. "You gave me a strawberry shake," I said to the worker.

"That's what you ordered," she insisted.

"I only ever order salted caramel," I replied.

"I'll have to charge you for a new one," she said.

"I don't think so," I replied. "I ordered a salted caramel, not strawberry. The fault is on you, not me."

"I'll have to ask my manager," she said, clearly annoyed with the whole process.

She walked away from the counter to the back and I stood waiting for them to make me a new shake.

"Can I help you?" an older woman asked.

"I ordered a salted caramel shake, but got a strawberry," I said.

"Do you have your receipt?"

"She never gave me one," I said, indicating the worker.

The older woman looked to the younger one, then said, "I'd be happy to make you a new shake. We pride ourselves on making sure our customers are happy."

She then turned around and began the process of making my shake. I turned to watch Kathy and saw her rapidly whispering to Sean, looking at me the whole time. What was she saying to him? Probably something completely inappropriate that I would have try to explain away when I talked with him later.

"Here you go," the manager said, handing me my newly made shake.

"Thanks," I replied, and took a drink. "Perfect," I said after taking a drink to make sure they got it right. I went back to where my friend was sitting.

"What?" she asked when I sat down.

"I didn't ask anything," I replied. "Do I need to know something?"

"Your friend was just letting me know how well you liked working on projects at your apartment," he said, holding in a laugh, but barely.

"I'm sure she was," I replied with a smirk of my own.

"How she would be willing to let us have the whole place to ourselves," he continued. "In case there were things we needed to work on in private."

"I see," I replied. "I'm sure she let you know that there would be times she would need the place to work on her project with her partner, James, too."

"She didn't mention that," Sean replied, catching on to where I was going with my line of thinking. "I'll be sure to let him know she is fine with him coming over to your place to work the long hours needed for this project."

Kathy's face was priceless as she sat there, open mouth, watching me make her little plan to get me alone with Sean backfire.

"In fact," I continued. "Maybe they'd like to have the apartment for the rest of the week. You know, to get the project done quickly."

The elbow to my ribs was painful, but totally worth it to see her on the receiving end of the shenanigans she often pulled.

"I'll shoot him a text right now," Sean said, pulling out his phone. "Let him know we're here making plans for the week. That way he can meet us and know exactly what to expect."

"No," Kathy said in shock. "Please don't," she begged.

"Relax," he laughed. "I don't even know who he is."

The relief in Kathy's face was obvious.

"Anyway," Sean said. "I'll see you Thursday."

"And in class," Kathy added.

"Of course," he replied.

"Have a nice night," I said, then watched him walk out the door.

"I see you checking out his ass," Kathy said once he was out the door.

"Whatever," I replied.

"That's what you're wearing?" Kathy asked as I tied my sneakers to head out to meet Sean at the library.

"What's wrong with it?"

"It's not very sexy," she said.

"We're studying," I said. "I have no need for sexy. We've had this conversation."

"You are absolutely no fun at all," she complained.

"Look," I said. "I know you think I need to have a guy in my life, that I'm somehow missing out on something without a boyfriend, but I'm actually doing really well without having the distraction of another person to deal with. You're about all I can handle in that category."

"Are you calling me high maintenance?" she asked, and I almost felt bad for saying it.

"I know you mean well," I offered. "I just sometimes wish you didn't push so hard."

"But you're lonely," she said.

"Not in the least," I replied.

"You're not?"

"Nope," I said.

"I don't get it," she replied.

"Look," I began. "I know you like to have a guy fawning all over you, but that's not me. We've known each other too long for you to not know that I don't need a man to make me whole. I am who I am, and if a guy wants to be a partner with me, that's great. Otherwise, there's no need."

"But..." she began, but I put my hand up.

"Nope," I said. "I'm out to meet another student to work on a project. That's all it is. See you when I get back."

With that, I walked out the door and headed to the library. When I walked in, I saw Sean sitting over where we had talked about meeting. He already had a couple of old looking books open on the table.

"Hey," he said when I sat down.

"Hey, yourself," I replied.

"I thought I would go ahead and grab these," he said, indicating the books. "Figured it would give us a jump start on the project."

"I did get some information from a couple of online sources," I said, pulling out my laptop.

"Not Wiki, right?" he eyed me suspiciously.

"Definitely not," I laughed.

"Good," he replied. "I figured you were smart enough to know that."

"Thanks," I replied.

"So," he said, indicating one of the old books in front of him. "I found this, but wanted to see what you thought of it before we put it into the final report."

He turned the book and pushed it across the table. I looked

at the picture in the book, then read the description next to it.

"That's pretty much the information I got," I said. "Guess the older books aren't necessarily better resources."

"True," he said. "But look at this."

He pushed another book across the table to me. This one looked even older than the first one.

"They let you handle this one?" I asked, concerned that we shouldn't be actually reading it.

"This one is mine," he said and I looked at him.

"You have books this old?"

"And older," he said. "It's a hobby of mine."

"What?" I asked. "Books, or the Fates?"

"Both," he said. "Read that paragraph there," he suggested, pointing to one about half way down the page he had the book opened to.

I read the words, but was completely baffled as to what they meant. I looked up to him to ask, but noticed that there was something off about him.

"You okay?" I asked.

"What?" he asked, shaking himself. "Sorry. Just got lost in thought."

"You were..." I didn't know how to describe what I'd seen. It wasn't like he was glowing, but then again, it was.

"Sorry," he said, shaking his head.

"What was that?" I asked, unsure of exactly what had just happened.

"What was what?" he countered.

"Forget it," I said, not sure whether it was worth trying to figure out or not. "What does this mean?" I asked, trying to get back on topic.

"Let me see," he offered, pulling the book back across the table. "Oh," he said, after reading the paragraph he had indicated before. "The Greek words and the Latin words aren't the same thing," he said. "But you already knew that, right?"

"Sort of," I said. "What I don't get is why they couldn't figure out what they had wrong."

"It's not so much that they got it wrong as they didn't get it quite right," he said.

The authority of his words gave them more weight than you would think they had. It was as if he knew more than just what the books said.

"What do you mean?" I asked, hoping he'd explain why he came to the conclusion he did.

"Well," he began. "They're both right, in that they both have a portion of the mythology correct. The Fates do portion out to each of us what we should have when we are born. They also allot us things as we gain merit. Does that make sense?"

"I guess," I offered. "But it feels like you know more than just what's written here. Like you somehow have inside knowledge of what's being said."

He stared at me as if I'd grown a second head, and it was really uncomfortable. Then the feeling went away and it was as if I was meant to spend the rest of my life with him. I closed my eyes and shook my head. Maybe Kathy's words were getting to me. Like I was seeing what she wanted me to see all along.

"Hey," he said, reaching out and grabbing my hand. "You okay?"

The shock I felt when his skin touched mine made me pull my hand away.

"Izzy," I heard, but it wasn't Sean who said it. I looked around, but didn't see anyone else near us.

"You okay?" Sean asked again, and I looked at him.

"Did you hear that?" I asked.

"What?" he asked.

281

"I thought I heard someone else say my name," I said.

"I didn't hear anything," he said, pulling his hand back across the table.

When I looked at him it was as if I'd slapped him. Something was definitely off with him.

"I've gotta go," he said and gathered his books up.

"But we're not done," I objected, but he was packing up and moving away from the table.

"I'll email you," he said and was gone before I could protest.

"That was strange," I mumbled and began to pack my stuff up as well.

I stood up to leave and nearly ran right into a man who was standing next to the table.

"Are you Izzy?" he asked, and his voice was velvet, caressing without really touching me.

I blinked, unsure why this man was talking to me. I'd never seen him before, and trust me, I'd remember. He was tall, dark, and handsome, just like the saying. Somehow, I found my voice and said, "I'm Izzy."

"Don't trust Sean," he said, and the power from his words sunk into me physically.

"Why not?" I asked.

"He's not who he seems," was all the man said, then he turned to walk away.

"Wait," I called and he turned back to me. "Who are you?"

"Hector," he said, then walked away.

"What is going on?" I asked no one in particular.

I walked back to my apartment and Kathy was there, waiting for an update.

"So?" she prompted.

I dropped my bag on the couch and flopped down next to it.

"I have no idea what's going on," I said without preamble.

"Color me confused," she replied, sitting next to me.

"I met Sean," I said. "We got started on our project, then he just bolted."

"What did you say?"

"Really?" I asked. "You assume it's something I said that caused him to run off?"

"You made it pretty clear that you were not at all interested in him in any fashion other than as a partner for your project," she said.

"Why does that matter?" I asked.

"Because he's super cute," she said. "And sometimes you just need to go there."

"That's the thing," I argued. "We were doing fine. Going over some books about the subject, chatting about things. Then I heard someone say my name and he got all butt hurt and packed up to leave."

"Who said your name?" she asked, completely enthralled in my retelling of my day.

"I guess it was Hector," I said.

"Who's Hector?" she asked, drawing the question out.

"I have no idea," I said. Apparently, that wasn't a sufficient answer because she simply stared at me, waiting for more. "He was there when I went to leave," I explained. "I ran right into him."

"Is he cute?"

"No," I said, and her face fell. "He's like a god. Carved out of marble. Chiseled with precision. Molded with care. Fashioned in perfect harmony with all that is good and right in the world."

"So," she laughed. "Just some dude."

I laughed with her, then said, "He was there, told me not to trust Sean, and was gone. It was the weirdest thing."

283

"He told you not to trust Sean?" she asked.

"Yeah," I said.

"Did he say why?"

"Nope," I replied. "Just said not to trust him. With the way he acted, though, I guess that's not a bad suggestion."

"Damn," she said. "And I was hoping he'd be the one to thaw out your frigid temperament."

"Please," I replied. "I am not frigid."

"Seriously?" The look she gave me clearly said she knew me all too well.

"Okay," I admitted. "Maybe I am a little chill. But come one, have you not seen the horror stories from college campuses? Every other day there's some story or another about women getting raped, fraternities causing issues, and nothing good ever comes from those stories."

"But he's adorable," she insisted.

"And not to be trusted," I replied. "I gotta see if I can get this project done. I doubt I'll get any help from Sean, now. How's yours going?"

"Don't make me talk about it," she said. "It's horrible."

"James is that bad, huh?"

"Worse," she retorted. "I just don't wanna."

"Sorry, kid," I said. "Grin and bear it."

"Still sure you don't want to trade partners?"

"Maybe I should have," I replied, then headed to my room.

"Miss Reese," Mr. Richards said as I walked into the class the next day.

"Yes?"

"I need to pair you up with someone else," he said.

"What's wrong with Sean?" I asked.

"He sent his project in without your input and has left the campus," he said.

"So," I began. "I'm just supposed to start over?"

"It was my understanding that you had already begun your work with Sean," he said. "I am sure that Hector can get up to speed quickly."

"Hector?"

"Izzy," the man from the day before said and I nearly jumped out of my boots.

"Where did you come from?"

My heart raced as I saw the man from the day before standing right beside me.

"I just walked in," he said with a wink. "Thank you, Professor, for finding a new partner for me."

"Hold on," I said. "How do I know this guy is going to be up to my level of work?"

"Trust me," the professor said. "Hector is very intelligent, and he will make a great partner."

The rest of the class was filing in, so I went to a seat with Hector in tow.

"You better not screw this class up for me," I whispered.

"Don't worry," he smirked.

Kathy came in just then and sat down on the other side of me.

"Who's the hottie?" she whispered in my ear.

"My new partner," I muttered. "Hector."

"THE Hector?"

"One and the same," I replied.

"Where's Sean?" she asked after a look around the room.

"No clue," I replied. "Apparently he turned his final paper in without my help and skipped town."

"This thing is due on Monday," she said.

"Trust me," I said. "I know."

"Class," Mr. Richards said. "We're just about at the end of the quarter. Hopefully you all have completed, or nearly completed your final assignment with your partners. If not," he continued, "I suggest you spend the weekend with your partner getting the finishing touches on them. Presentations will happen beginning on Monday."

"Presentations?" I asked.

"Yes," the professor replied. "It was in the syllabus, clearly spelled out. Two people work on the paper, then it is presented for the class to determine which conclusion is correct. Your argument needs to be compelling enough to convince those who have the opposite view as you to change their mind."

I turned to see Hector looking at me with a glint I didn't really find comforting in his eye. This was going to be a long weekend. By the time we finished class, I was more than a little concerned about my grade in this class. I knew what I wanted to say, but the trick was going to be making sure this new dude was of the same mind. Honestly, I wasn't sure myself any longer.

"Izzy," Hector said as he caught up to us after class.

"Yeah," I replied.

"We should meet," he said. "Maybe go over what you've got so far on the project."

"You thinking of just letting me do the whole thing?" I asked, not at all concerned with the annoyance in my voice.

"Look," he said, grabbing my arm. "I know you kind of got thrown into this thing, but I intend to hold up my end of the project. I am actually pretty knowledgeable when it comes to this subject."

Kathy nudged my arm with her shoulder and I glared at her. I knew she wanted me to invite Mr. Tall, Dark, and Handsome to the apartment, but I'd just met him, and I wasn't sure I wanted to trust him completely.

"Library at five," I finally said.

"They close at five," he replied. "Guess we'll have to meet somewhere else."

There was that glint again. Something about it set me on edge, like it was a feral look rather than something sexy. It was like he was too pretty to be real.

"You can come to our place," Kathy offered, then rattled off our address.

"Kathy," I seethed.

"What?" she feigned innocence.

"I'll see you at five," Hector said, then walked away.

"What are you doing?" I barked.

"You're right," she swooned. "He is gorgeous."

"Wipe the drool up and talk to me," I said. "You just invited a complete stranger to our apartment. Without checking with me first. Did you ever think I had a reason I didn't invite guys over?"

"But you're not gay," she said, confused.

"That's not what I'm talking about," I said. "I'm talking about common safety. Think before you act, and before you speak."

"You are so paranoid," she said.

"Just because I'm paranoid, doesn't mean someone's not out to get me," I retorted, then stormed off, leaving her standing in the hallway utterly confused.

"Where are you going?" I asked Kathy as I was gathering the books I had on the Fates later that night.

"Out," she replied. "Figured you didn't want me around."

"Look," I said. "Don't be butt hurt about this. I just like my space to be my space. I don't really like to share it with anyone."

"So I'm no one, then," she mumbled.

287

"That's not what I mean," I tried. "I know you think he's cute. You're right. But just because he's good looking doesn't mean he's to be trusted. Have you not seen the guys they catch doing crap to women? They're all really good looking. How do you think they get away with it?"

"You think the worst of everyone," she said. "No one is good enough. No one can compare to your ideal man."

"There is no ideal man," I replied.

"Obviously," she replied. "Look at Hector. He's the perfect specimen. Sean was pretty good, too. You were just too busy trying to be unattached that you couldn't see it."

"I know you mean well," I said. "I just don't have time for romance right now."

"When will you? When you're forty? Fifty? A hundred?"

"I have a long life ahead of me," I tried.

"But you don't know that for sure," she said. "You know what happened to Carol, right?"

"Come on," I said.

"No," she interrupted. "I'm serious. She was all about making sure she was ready for what life had in store for her until she ended up with cancer. Then, she tried to live her whole life at once."

"I know," I replied, wiping tears from my eyes. "But I don't have cancer."

"You don't know that," she replied. "Carol didn't know until it was too late. I don't want you to miss out."

"If I promise to go out with you after finals," I offered. "Will that get you off my back now?"

"Only if you promise to bring Hector with you," she smiled.

I laughed. "I'll ask him," I promised.

"Good," she said. "Cause he's here."

With that, she opened the door and let him in. Before she

stepped out, she eyed me seriously and bobbed her eyebrows up and down, nodding her head. It didn't take much to realize what she was meaning.

"Hey," he said after she closed the door.

"Hey yourself," I replied. "I guess we better get to it."

"About that," he said, and I turned and looked at him.

"What?" I asked.

"I actually have a whole thing done," he replied, pulling out a tablet. "I'll show you and you can see if it's enough, or if you want to add anything."

"It was supposed to be a partnership," I replied, taking the tablet he offered.

"I lost my partner same as you," he said. "I was pretty much carrying her, though, so had done most of the work already."

Powering the tablet up, I turned it so he could enter the password. "Here," he said, taking it from me. He input his password, then swiped around and found whatever it was he was looking for. "This is what I've got so far." He handed the tablet back to me.

I looked at his work and was impressed. He had everything I wanted to put into it, and then some. After I read through his information, I was confused by his conclusion.

"You believe they still exist?" I asked.

"Don't you?"

"Well," I said, then thought about it. Hadn't everything that had happened in the last week or so proven that there was some sort of other worldly force at work here?

"You didn't come to the same conclusion?" he asked.

"Nope," I replied. "But you make a really good argument."

"Why don't you think they exist?"

"You really want to know?"

"That's why I asked," he said, and his smile was charming.

"All my life," I began. "Nothing has ever been easy. I've worked for everything I got, especially when it comes to school. My brains gave me the chance to get a college education, even though my parents were willing to pay. The scholarship made it much easier on them. I always wanted to be a teacher, so college was necessary."

"A teacher, huh?" he asked.

"Elementary school," I said. "I figure if I get to kids early, then maybe I can give them a good foundation to build on."

"That's a really noble goal," he said, and seemed honestly impressed.

"I think so," I said.

"Then I really hate what I have to do," he said.

"Sean?"

"Izzy," he said.

"Where am I?"

"Izzy," Hector said.

"Wait," I said. "What's going on?"

"You have to choose," Sean said.

"Choose what?" I asked. "I don't know what's going on."

"You died," Hector said.

"I did?" I asked. "When?"

"Long before you thought you did," Sean said.

"Hold on," I said, walking backwards away from the two men. "Where are we?"

"Nowhere," Hector said.

"And everywhere," Sean added.

"You guys aren't making sense," I said, still struggling to figure out where I was.

"It's like this," Hector began.

"Don't explain it to her," Sean argued. "She has to choose without knowing."

"How is that fair?" Hector asked.

"All's fair in love and war," Sean said.

With that, both men morphed into something that was obviously not human. They began to charge at each other, teeth gnashing, swords appearing from thin air, and a high-pitched scream that nearly burst my eardrums. I continued to back away from the fight, hoping this was nothing more than a nightmare. Except I knew it wasn't.

"Izzy."

It was just barely audible, but I somehow knew the voice.

"Kathy?" I asked.

"Come with me," she said, and I saw her just beyond the two brawling beasts.

Skirting around the edge of the room we were in, I made my way to her and she pulled me through a door that hadn't been there before.

"Where did you come from?" I asked.

"Come with me," she insisted again.

"No."

It was so loud that I had to pull my hand from my friend's and plug my ears.

"I was trying to help," Kathy said. I couldn't see who she was talking to, though.

"She must choose," the voice said.

"What is going on?" I asked.

Suddenly, I was sitting on my couch in my empty apartment. I looked around, confused about what had happened.

"Kathy?" I called.

"Hey," she said, coming out of her room. "You ready?"

"For what?" I asked, unsure of what had just happened.

"Class," she said. "It's finals week. You get to do your Fates presentation today."

"With who?"

"By yourself," she laughed. "You did do it, right?"

"Umm," I stammered, unsure exactly what was going on.

"Here," she said, handing me a steaming mug. "Coffee. You obviously need it more than me."

"Okay," I said, taking a sip.

"Now," she said. "Let's go so we're not late."

She picked up her backpack and held mine out to me. I grabbed it as I stood up and slung it over my shoulder. As we walked to class, Kathy rambled on about something she saw on a show she's been watching lately. Something about a missing treasure on a cursed island or something like that. Honestly, I had no idea what she was talking about. I was still trying to wrap my head around whatever it was that happened to me.

"Miss Reese," Mr. Richards said as we walked into class.

"Yes?" I asked, feeling that déjà vu feeling I didn't particularly like.

"You ready?"

"Absolutely," I feigned confidence I didn't have.

"Good," he said. "Go ahead and get set up."

"You got this," Kathy said as she gave me a side hug and went to find a seat.

I opened my laptop and hooked it up to the AV system, pulling up the project I didn't remember finishing. As the rest of the students filled in the seats, I began to worry that I wouldn't be able to pull this off.

"Class," Mr. Richards said as the door closed behind the last student. "Please give your attention to Miss Reese. Once her presentation is over, you will have a chance to ask questions."

Just like that, all eyes were on me, and I could feel moisture gathering in the small of my back.

"Right," I began. "The Fates have been discussed for as long as time has been kept," I began, and somehow my presentation just flowed.

By the time I got to the end, the students were riveted to their seats, eyes trained on me, taking in everything I said.

"When I started this project," I concluded. "I was sure that the answer to the question of whether the Fates were real, and whether they were still around, was unequivocally no. After the research I did, and the people I talked to, I believe that the answer is, without a doubt, yes."

"Thank you, Miss Reese," Mr. Richards said. "Do we have any questions?"

A hand rose at the back of the class, and Mr. Richards nodded, indicating the student should ask their question. The man that rose took my breath away.

"Which did you choose?" he asked, and I couldn't help but smile.

"Sean," I said. "It was always going to be Sean."

DREAM

That was amazing," the man with the conductor said.

"Thank you," Christie replied. "I'm glad you liked it."

"We'll let you know as soon as we've made a decision," the conductor said.

"Thank you," Christie said. "I hope to hear from you soon."

With that, she placed her violin into its case and snapped it closed, dropped her music into her satchel, picked them up and walked off the stage. Ever since she was a child, she'd always dreamed of performing on stage, playing her own music for everyone to hear. While this wasn't going to be for that, it was a step in the right direction.

She'd been gaining respect within the music community, and this audition was for a steady paying gig. Those were so few and far between that she had almost given up hope in getting in with this particular orchestral group. Oh, sure, she'd had the paid gigs, quartets for weddings and other events of that sort, but this was for a spot with the big guys. Richard Bowman was one of the most prominent conductors in the area, and the fact that they even had an opening for her to audition for was a miracle in and of itself. Now, she just had to hope her piece was sufficient to get her in the door.

As she walked the few blocks to the subway entrance, she thought back over the audition. She'd been in key, on tempo, and had performed flawlessly, even if she was sweating like a whore in church. No, she couldn't look at the negatives, she had to stay focused on the positive part of her performance. The other man in the audience had seemed impressed with her piece, even if Mr. Bowman wasn't forthcoming with his opinion.

"Breathe," she told herself as she bounced down the stairs to the station.

"Spare change," an old man that sat at the bottom of the steps said, holding out a paper cup that looked as if it were ready to fall apart at any given moment.

Christie reached in her coat pocket and pulled out the two quarters she'd stuffed in there earlier, knowing he'd be there. "Here you go," she said, dropping them into his cup. She knew it wasn't much, knew it was likely going to go to booze of some sort or another, but she just felt like giving today.

She slid her Metro Card and went through the turnstile to get to her train. It would be there shortly, so she pulled out her phone and opened it up. Pulling up her social media, she posted a status about the audition, saying she felt it went well, and asking for positive vibes to be sent her way. Hearing the train coming, she locked her phone and stuck it in her pocket, and waited to get on.

The trip home was just as boring as it always was, and she stepped off the train to go up the stairs to the street, walking just a few blocks to her brownstone. Keying into the building, she stopped at the mailboxes and checked for anything. Unfortunately, the only things in there were bills. The city was getting expensive, and her job at the bistro was not going to get her where she needed to be. If she got this position, though, things would turn around quickly.

Walking up the stairs, she keyed into her apartment, closing and locking the door behind her. Taking a deep breath, she dropped the mail into the basket on her kitchen counter that doubled as a breakfast bar and walked to the closet in the corner. The one room space was sparsely filled, just a full-sized bed against the wall with the window, a small chest of drawers at the end, a night stand with her lamp and alarm clock on it, and the stools at the bar. She barely had enough space to turn around in it, but it was hers. She put her violin into the closet and stepped into the bathroom to splash her face.

She stripped from her performance black dress and hung it up in the closet, pulling out jeans and a shirt to replace it with. Once she was dressed, she went to the kitchenette to put the kettle on the little two burner stove. Tea was always a way to get through the waiting process, and this was one of those times. It wasn't as if she expected to hear anything today, but she needed the relaxation the chamomile tea offered. She got everything ready to wait for the water to boil, and went to her bed.

Her laptop was still sitting on the top, so she opened it to see what other opportunities she might find in the city. Spring was usually the time when she could bet on gigs becoming available, and her small group of four that played together often was always on the lookout for something. When she pulled up the internet browser, she saw she had an email waiting. Clicking to that tab, she opened it.

Ms. Butler:

Thank you for your time today. We appreciate your interest in our ensemble. There are still several additional applicants, so will not be able to make a decision until we have heard them all. You will be informed if you are chosen to fill the position we have open.

Sincerely;
Richard Bowman, Esq.

297

Her kettle began to whistle, so she closed the email with a sigh. She knew it was too much to hope for an answer that quick, but seeing the email lifted her heart just enough for it to plummet when she read the contents. Flipping the stove off, she picked up the kettle and poured the water into the pot for her tea to steep like her grandmother had shown her, then went back to the bed to look for other openings. Hopefully, there would be some folks looking for music for their events in the upcoming months.

"You still haven't heard?"

It had been a week, and she'd planned this lunch with Darci to hopefully celebrate her getting the position she'd auditioned for.

"Just the formal response thanking me for the audition," Christie said. "I guess I didn't get it."

"They don't know what they're missing," Darci said as she took a sip of her ice tea.

Christie laughed at the grimace she made. Being from the south, nothing Darci drank up here was sweet enough.

"There's always next time," Christie said, though she knew the next time could be a long time coming.

"Who is that?" Darci asked, looking over Christie's shoulder, nearly swooning in her seat.

Christie turned around to see the man who had been at the audition last week. Not the conductor, but the one who had said her music was beautiful.

"That's one of the guys from the audition," Christie said, then turned back around. "Wonder what he's doing here."

"Looks like he likes what he sees," Darci whispered behind her glass. "He's coming this way."

"Ms. Butler, right?" he asked as he stepped up to their table.

"Right," Christie replied. "I'm sorry," she apologized. "I don't remember your name."

298

"Not surprised," he said. "Charles Ward, assistant to Richard Bowman, at your service."

"So," Darci began. "When are you going to tell Christie that she got the job?"

"Darci," Christie seethed.

"That's quite all right," Charles laughed. "We haven't made a firm decision, yet. But you are at the top of the list."

"I am?"

Christie was shocked. She knew she was good, but to be at the top of the list for a position within Richard Bowman's orchestra was more than she ever dreamed.

"Yes," he said. "Trust me when I tell you that if it was me, the decision would have been made the moment you finished your piece."

"Told you," Darci said, smacking Christie's hand.

"You're serious?" Christie asked, still not believing what he had said.

"Look," he said as he sat. "I've been in the business for quite some time. Been working with Dick for nearly ten years. When I tell you you're good, believe me."

Christie just stared at the man, dumbfounded.

"I shouldn't have barged in on your lunch," he began.

"Please stay," Darci said. "I'm sure Christie won't mind."

Christie looked at her friend, then at the man who was watching her. "Stay," she finally said.

"If you're sure," he replied.

"She's sure," Darci said.

"What can I get you?" the waitress asked when she came back to the table.

"Just coffee," he replied.

"Cream?"

"No thanks," he said. After the waitress walked away, he asked, "Have you been in New York long?"

"I went to Columbia," Christie began. "It was a lot of work, but I fell in love with the city and decided to never go home."

"Your hometown's loss is our gain," he replied. "When were you at Columbia?"

"I graduated a couple of years ago," she explained. "It's been a struggle making ends meet, but I'm hopeful that I get this position and will be able to move from the starving artist role to something a little more permanent."

"Do you have an agent?" he asked. "I mean, someone helping you find places to play?"

"I don't have the money for that," she replied.

"She's just using her good looks, charm, and amazing talent," Darci threw in.

"Darci," Christie seethed.

"What?" her friend replied. "It's true. You're gorgeous, funny as hell, and ridiculously talented. You could compete with anyone out there. I'm surprised it's taken this long for you to get noticed."

"So am I," Charles said.

Christie looked at him, dumbfounded.

"She's right," he added. "You have the kind of talent that comes along once in a great while. I honestly don't know what's taking Richard so long to snatch you up. If he doesn't, he's nuts."

"You really think so?"

"Absolutely," he replied. "If he doesn't bring you in, I will find you a place. There's no reason you shouldn't be with the biggest orchestras in the city. You really do have that much talent."

"Told you," Darci said.

Christie sat there, stunned. She knew she was pretty good, but to hear this man who just met her and only heard her play one piece say she was great was more than she could handle.

"Here you go," the waitress said as she set a cup of coffee in front of Charles.

"Thanks," he replied, then added a packet of sugar in the raw to his cup.

Stirring it, he watched Christie struggle with the truth, that she was a remarkable musician who just hadn't caught her break. Yet. His phone began to buzz in his shirt pocket, so he pulled it out.

"Speak of the devil," he said before answering. "Mr. Bowman. How can I help you?"

Christie sat in silence as she watched the man sitting next to her. His eyes widened, then he smiled like the cat that ate the canary.

"I am actually sitting next to her right now," he said. "I'd be happy to tell her in person."

A couple more moments, with him giving the affirmative "uh-hu" before he hung up.

"Well?" Darci prodded.

"Welcome to the Bowman orchestra, Ms. Butler," he said with a smile.

"I got it?"

"Like you should have a long time ago," he replied.

"Oh my god," Darci said. "You got it!"

"I got it," Christie mumbled. "I really and truly got it."

Tears started rolling down her cheeks as she looked at her friend, then at the man who had given her the best news she'd received since the acceptance letter from the college came.

"Hey," Charles said. "Are you all right?"

"I can't believe I got it," she stuttered.

"Cupcakes all around," Darci shouted, then got to her feet to go get the confections she mentioned.

Christie had her hand to her mouth, holding back the sobs that were threatening to break free. She had truly made her dream come true. She was going to be playing with one of the best orchestras in the country. Her daddy would be so proud. The thought of him missing this milestone in her life by just a few months pushed her over the edge and a sob finally found its way out.

"Hey," Charles said, unsure what was wrong with her. "Here," he said, offering her his handkerchief. She took it and proceeded to wipe her eyes, but it did little good. Her tears were falling too fast for her to gather then in the small cloth in her hand. Charles opened his arms and she leaned in from the side, putting her head onto his shoulder and let the tears fall.

"What happened?" Darci asked when she came back to the table.

"Don't know," Charles replied. "It just started."

It took a couple of minutes, but Christie was finally able to pull herself together and pulled away from Charles.

"I'm so sorry," she sniffled.

"It's quite all right," he replied. "Are you..."

He left the question hanging, unsure exactly what he wanted to know.

"Yeah," she sniffed again, then wiped her eyes with the only dry spot on the handkerchief. She then looked at it and realized that it was a very nice cloth, monogramed with his initials. "Oh god," she said. "I've ruined your handkerchief." When she looked at him, she saw she'd smeared her makeup onto his shirt as well. "And your shirt," she said with a hitch.

"It'll wash," he assured.

"No," she said, pulling another napkin. "I got mascara on it. It's waterproof. It'll never come out."

"I can buy another one," he said. She looked up at him confused. "Seriously," he offered. "I just want to make sure you're okay."

All Christie could do was nod, her throat growing tight again with emotions.

"An official email will be sent out," Charles said. "I'm really glad I got to tell you in person, though."

"I've got her," Darci said, seeing the worry in his face. "Don't worry. She's thrilled, I promise."

Charles looked to Christie again, and she nodded. "If you're sure," he said, clearly waiting for a response from Christie, not her friend.

"I am," she squeaked out, trying to smile.

"Then I'll see you at rehearsal," he said, standing with his coffee and making his way back to the front of the café.

Once he was far enough away, Darci scooted closer to Christie and whispered, "He is super cute. You should totally go for him."

Christie slapped her friend's hand and laughed, finally able to get past the knot in her throat.

"You are something else," she said.

"I am," her friend replied. "It's an acquired taste, but once you get it, you can't give it up."

The both of them laughed again, easing the tension that had come upon Christie. She'd done it. Honestly and truly, she had made it to the big time.

"You need to cut back that much?"

"I know it's short notice," Christie said to her boss. "I just got this position in the Bowman Orchestra. The only days I don't have rehearsal or performances are Mondays and Thursdays."

"Does this mean you'll be leaving us?" her boss asked.

"Not yet," she replied. "I want to keep this until I know for sure that the orchestra will work out. That, and I have to make sure I can make ends meet."

"Well," her boss began. "I'd hate to lose you. But I am so thrilled for you, at the same time."

"I can't tell you how thrilled I am," she said as she put her apron on.

"When do I need to change the schedule?"

"They said rehearsals start in two weeks, so that gives you a little time," she replied.

"I should probably get your autograph now," her boss said. "So I can say I knew you when..."

"Very funny," Christie replied. "I'll still be by to get coffee every chance I get."

"I'll hold you to that," he replied. "Now, get to work."

The order was issued with a smile, and Christie knew it was all in fun. As she worked, she wondered if this was the beginning of the end of normalcy for her. What would it be like when she was recognizable? Would people hound her every time she went to the grocery store? Maybe she wouldn't even be able to come here and see her friends. But she was getting ahead of herself. She was still the same girl who came to New York to follow her dreams.

"Americano," the man at the register said.

"Room for cream?" Christie asked before she looked up. "Oh, hey," she said, recognizing Mr. Ward, the assistant to Mr. Bowman.

"I didn't recognize you," he said. "No cream, but thanks."

"Absolutely," she replied, ringing up his order and placing the sticker on the cup, handing it off to her barista. She told him the price and he offered her his card. Sliding it through the reader, she asked, "Receipt?"

"Not today," he said. "You're all ready to start next week?"

"I thought it was two weeks," Christie said, confused.

"We begin rehearsals on Tuesday," he said. "Did you not get the email?"

"I did," she said. "I'll have to read it again to make sure I have the dates correct."

"I would hate for you to miss the first rehearsal and be cut," he offered. "You're far too good to be left on the sidelines."

"Thank you for letting me know," she said.

With that, he walked away from the register to wait for his order to be ready. By the time she got her first break, her boss had already left. She pulled out her phone and pulled up her email. Sure enough, she was supposed to start next week, not the week after. She sent a quick text to her boss, apologizing for the mistake, then went back to work.

When her shift was over, she hung her apron on the hook in the back room, picked up her purse to slide over her shoulder, then made her way back up front.

"See ya," she called to one of her coworkers.

"Have fun," Penny replied.

Walking the couple of blocks to the train, she was lost in herself, humming a tune she made up as she went along. Down the stairs, swipe the Metro Card, through the turnstile, and wait for the train. It was a daily thing, something she didn't even have to think about, she'd been doing it so long. She hopped on the train and stood next to the door, knowing her stop was just a few down the way.

"Ms. Butler?"

She looked up from her phone to see Mr. Ward stepping into the car.

"Hello," she said, scooting over to give him room.

"I wonder whether we've ridden the same train for days and never seen each other," he pondered.

"Definitely could have," she replied.

"Even in this big city," he began, "it's still a small world."

"That it is," she said. "So," she began after a pause. "Going home?"

"I am," he replied. "You?"

"Same," she said.

They rode in comfortable silence for a while before Christie's stop was coming up

"This is me," she said as the train slowed.

"Me, too," he replied.

"Shall we walk together?"

"Sure," he said. "At least until we have to separate."

Up the stairs to street level, the turned the same direction. They made small talk about their mutual love of music, and discussed their history in getting to where they were. His predecessor had died suddenly just two years earlier, and Richard had given him the position because of how well liked he was by the members of the orchestra. It hadn't been his intention to be second to the top, but the position was growing on him.

"This is me," she said as they came upon her building.

"No way," he replied.

"Wait," she halted. "You live here, too?"

"Next door," he said, pointing to the brownstone building next to Christie's.

"Well isn't that fun," she said.

"I knew someone musical lived in this building," he said. "I've heard you playing. Always wondered whether it was a recording or live, but when I heard the same piece being worked on, I knew it was a musician."

"Why didn't you come over?"

"And say what?" he asked.

"Oh," she colored. "Guess that would probably have been a bit awkward, huh."

"Probably," he laughed.

"Did you want to come up?" she offered.

"Nah," he said. "Gotta finish up some work. I'll see you next week."

"Unless we end up on the train together," she laughed.

"True," he replied. "Have a good evening."

"You, too," she said, then keyed her way into the building.

Once she was inside, she grabbed her mail, what little there was, then bounced up the stairs to her studio. Pulling her phone out, she dialed her friend.

"What's up, buttercup?" Darci answered.

"You'll never guess who lives next door," Christie blurted out.

"The Pope?" Darci laughed.

"No," Christie said. "I'm serious."

"I have no idea," Darci said.

"Charles Ward," Christie said as if that made all the sense in the world.

"Who's that?"

"The dude who we ran into at the café," she replied.

"The hot dude?" Darci asked. "The one you're going to hook up with?"

"I'm not going to hook up with him," Christie said.

"You should," Darci offered.

"He's kinda my boss, now," Christie said. "That's usually frowned upon in polite society."

"Doesn't mean it doesn't happen," Darci countered. "Actually…"

"Not gonna happen," Christie interrupted.

"Seriously," Darci said. "I have to live my life vicariously through you. I can't do that if you're not gonna bang some sexy guys."

"You could go out," she countered. "You know, find a guy. Go on a date and get yourself laid."

"You gonna watch Robbie?"

"Not on your life," Christie said. "Your kid is too wild for me."

"He's a little angel," Darci cooed.

"When he's sleeping," Christie laughed.

"Speaking of," Darci said and Christie could hear the little boy in the background calling for his mama.

"I'll let you go," she said.

"Think about what I said," Darci said. "I expect details."

With a laugh, the call ended.

"That girl is gonna get me in trouble one of these days," Christie said to her empty studio.

She dropped her backpack onto her bed, then pulled out her violin and began to learn the music she'd received for the upcoming week.

"What do you think?" Charles asked Richard after the first week of rehearsals.

"She's good," Richard replied.

"I told you," he said. "Are you going to move her up?"

"I can't do that to the guys who've been here longer," Richard explained. "It wouldn't be fair to them."

"So she loses out when she's better than them," Charles began. "Just because they got here first? It isn't her fault."

"Let's do this run and see how things turn out," Richard offered. "I know she's good and will do well. I just can't upset the whole apple cart at this point."

"If you don't," Charles said. "She's likely to be poached."

"That's what I'm worried about," Richard confessed. "If anyone else sees how good she is, they're likely to offer her more than I can. If I were her, I'd jump at the opportunity."

"So do something about it," Charles said.

"Give it another week," Richard said. "Then we'll reevaluate."

"How's it going?" Darci asked.

It had been two weeks since she'd started rehearsals, and Christie was loving every minute.

"I'm better than some of the chairs ahead of me," she confessed.

"Are they moving you up?"

"I doubt it," Christie sighed. "It's seriously an old boys club thing in this industry. Because I'm the new kid on the block, I get the back of the bus."

"That's stupid," Darci complained.

"It is what it is," she said.

"It shouldn't be," Darci said.

They sat and drank their coffee in the little shop they'd been meeting in for years. It was their home away from home, close enough to the theatres, yet still close enough to where Darci worked for them to grab a quick visit between their shifts.

"Ms. Butler," Charles said as he came up to the two of them.

"Mr. Ward," she replied. "What brings you in?"

"I wanted to tell you," he began, then looked at Darci.

"Oh," Christie said. "This is my best friend. You might as well tell me in front of her, cause I'm gonna tell her anyway. That way it'll cut out the middle man."

Charles laughed, then sat in one of the vacant chairs. "I don't know if you're aware, but I've noticed some other composers have been in attendance at our rehearsals."

"Really?" Christie asked. "I didn't know they were open to the public."

"They're not," Charles explained. "But composers are connected. They know when there's fresh blood, and they like to come in and check out the competition."

"And Mr. Bowman is okay with this?"

"Not really," Charles said. "But he doesn't really have a choice. If the theatre owner is willing to allow another composer to come in, the one who is in residence doesn't get to say no."

"What does that mean for Christie?" Darci asked.

"That there have been people talking," Charles said. "And they are saying that they like what they see."

Christie looked at her friend, then back at Charles. "What

does that actually mean?" she asked.

"That what I feared would happen is likely to," he said.

"You mean she's being fired?" Darci asked.

"On the contrary," he said. "You're going to be poached."

"Poached?" she asked. "What does that mean?"

"Someone is going to put you in the first chair," he said. Christie looked at him, baffled.

"That's good, right?" Darci asked.

"That's very good," Charles replied, still watching Christie.

"First chair?" Christie whispered, blinking.

The smile that spread across Charles' face was enough to make it clear that he was not kidding, but was honestly thrilled to be the one to tell her the good news.

"That means you're not gonna be her boss anymore?" Darci asked, and Christie looked at her with daggers, knowing just what her friend was thinking.

"Unfortunately," Charles said. "I feel like I've been witnessing the birth of a new star. You're going to be talked about for years to come. You know that, right?"

Christie blinked at him, still stunned with what she was hearing. She'd always been told she was good, but to be taken from the back of one orchestra and placed in the first chair was something completely different.

"Here," Charles said, handing here a business card. "I really want to keep in touch with you. Let me know how things go."

"I haven't changed orchestras, yet," she said, eyes wide.

"Expect to get an email or call soon," he replied.

Just then, her phone pinged with an incoming email.

"Told you," he smiled. "Call me. We can go to dinner some time and talk about what it's like at the top."

As he walked away, Christie opened the email on her phone. She read, then reread it several times, her mouth falling open with each line. She looked at her friend and said, "He's right."

"About?"

"Look," she said, turning her phone around so her friend could read the email.

"Oh my god," Darci said, looking between her friend and the phone. "They're gonna pay you that much?"

"I get to do solos," Christie said. "And they want me to start right away."

"Email them back," Darci said. "Don't let this opportunity pass you by."

Before she had a chance to respond, her phone pinged another incoming email, and then another, and another. She looked up at Darci and smiled.

"I think I'll have several to choose from," she said.

"Let's look," Darci replied.

They spent the next hour pouring over seven different offers for positions in orchestras from all around New York. She even had a couple from Europe come in.

"How am I supposed to choose?" she asked when she felt like they'd all come in.

"I know someone who could help you," Darci said, holding the business card Charles had left on the table out.

"I couldn't ask him," Christie said.

"Why not?"

"It would be unethical."

"Since when?" Darci chided. "He offered to help, wanted you to stay in touch. Here's your chance to kill two birds with one stone."

"You really think he'll help?"

Darci looked at her friend. "Do you really need to ask me that?"

Christie sighed, then picked up the card and dialed his number.

"Hello?"

"It's Christie," she said. "Christie Butler?"

"Hello," Charles replied and she could hear the smile in his voice.

"I have a problem," she said.

"How can I help?"

"There are too many offers," she said.

"That's a good problem to have," he laughed. "What do you say to dinner tonight?"

"Um," she hedged.

Darci looked at her and she mouthed that he wanted her to go to dinner. Nodding, Darci pushed her friend to say yes.

"Strictly professional," he said hearing the hesitancy in her voice.

"I'll buy," she insisted.

"Or you could come over and I could cook" he suggested.

"I can't ask you to do that and help me," she argued.

"What if I insist?"

"I guess I can't refuse," she replied.

"Good," he said. "So, why don't you plan to come over in say, half an hour?"

"You'll be ready by then?"

"I'm ready now," he replied.

"But," Christie began.

"Look," he said. "When I talked with you in the café, I knew you were going to be getting offers for most of the afternoon. Richard told me he'd been approached by several conductors and head hunters. It was only a matter of time before you were overwhelmed. I stopped on the way home and picked up some stuff to cook. Bring your friend," he offered. "There's plenty to go around."

"Oh," she said, stunned.

"Say you'll come?"

"I guess it would be rude to refuse," she replied.

"And your friend?"

"Let me ask," she said, turning to Darci. "Dinner with Mr. Ward?"

"Not on your life," Darci replied. "This is all you and him."

"I guess she has something she is doing," Christie said into the receiver.

"Maybe next time," he said. "I'll text you my address so you have it. You already know how to get here, so it should be fine. See you soon."

"See you soon," she echoed, then disconnected the call.

"I want details tomorrow," Darci said.

"Shut up," Christie laughed. "It's professional. Nothing more."

"But it doesn't have to be," she replied. "Take the plunge, jump in with both feet."

"He's helping me with my career," Christie said. "I don't want to lose him because I push something that isn't there."

"Babe," Darci began. "I saw how he looked at you the first time I met him. He wants you. Trust me. I know that look."

"We'll see," was all Christie could say.

They left the café and headed to the subway. Bidding her friend farewell, she got on her train and rode it to her stop. She pulled up the text when she was close to her building and saw that he did, indeed, live right next door. She climbed the steps and pressed the button for his apartment.

"Hello," she heard his disembodied voice.

"It's Christie," she said.

She heard the buzz and the click of the door. Pulling it open, she stepped inside. Taking the stairs to the left, she climbed the first flight, then walked around to take another. On the third floor, she looked at the numbers on the apartments, determining which way they were going, then turned left and walked a couple of doors down until she saw 3B. Raising her hand to knock, she gasped as the door opened.

"Hey," he said. "Sorry, didn't mean to scare you."

"How did you know I was here?"

"I didn't," he replied. "Just wanted to have the door open when you got here. You're faster than I thought."

"Years of doing stairs," she laughed.

He held the door open, allowing her entrance to his apartment.

"You have so much space," she said as she looked around.

"It's one of the nicer ones in this building," he replied. "Can I take your coat?"

"Sure." She slipped it off and handed it over. "Smells good."

"Hope you like pasta," he said.

"More than you know," she laughed.

"It's just about done," he said, stepping into the kitchen. "Make yourself at home."

"What can I do to help?"

"Oh, no," he said. "You're a guest. My mother would skin me alive if I allowed you to help."

"Alrighty then," she said, walking toward the windows on the back of the living space. "Great view," she said as she looked out over the city.

"It's even better at night," he said. "The lights of the city are spectacular."

"I bet," she said.

"Wine?" he asked.

"Oh, no," she said. "I'm good with water, thanks."

"Sure thing," he said. "Whenever you're ready."

Christie turned around and walked back to the table set near the kitchen. He had a much larger apartment than she did, with actual divided spaces for each room, even with how cozy it was.

"What offer has you most intrigued?" he asked after they'd

begun their meal.

"They're all so different," she replied. "This is really good, by the way."

"Thanks," he said. "My grandmother taught me to cook, insisting that it would be a good thing to use to catch a girl."

"She was right," Christie said. "You'll have to tell her."

"Back to you," he said. "How many offers did you get?"

"I think there are ten total," she said. "I'll pull up my emails after dinner."

"Are they all from here?"

"Four or five from New York," she began. "There are a couple from out in California, then a few from Europe. It's a little overwhelming, honestly."

"Well," he said after a few more bites. "I can tell you who to stay away from here. The California ones will be harder to know, and those in Europe, unless they're really big ones, I will be of no help."

"You never did tell me how you ended up here," she said. "What's your story?"

"I grew up in the middle of nowhere," he began. "My mom loved music, and always wanted to be in a big band. Growing up, she watched those shows on the TV, dreaming of sitting behind one of the podiums, playing beautiful music. Unfortunately," he laughed. "She couldn't carry a tune in a bucket."

Christie laughed. "That was my dad," she said. "Tone deaf doesn't even begin to describe it."

"I know what you mean," he agreed. "Dad was a professor at the local university. One day when we were visiting with him, I found my way to a piano and started plunking away. Apparently I was pretty good, because a crowd started to form, and everyone watched in amazement as I fiddled around with a song I'd only heard on the radio."

"Sounds like me," she said.

"I bet," he agreed. "Needless to say, there was no doubt I had a natural talent. My parents cultivated it and pushed me to pursue music. It paid my way through college and found me moving to New York before I realized what was happening. I was grabbed by Richard as an assistant with finding new talent, because he said, 'it takes someone with great talent to recognize it in someone else.' That's one of the reasons I was so shocked it took him so long to offer the spot to you."

"Why did it take that long?"

"He said he wanted me to be sure," Charles said. "He knew, though. He also knew that you wouldn't be with us long once word got out."

"About that," she said, wiping her mouth. "How did word get out? I mean, I know that conductors talk, but it seemed like this went really fast."

"With New York, everything is fast," he said.

"It does seem that way," she agreed.

"Let's look at your offers," he said.

For the next two hours, Christie showed him the emails that she'd received, and Charles told her which ones to stay away from and which ones were good options.

"I just wish I didn't have to choose," she said, frustrated.

"But you do," he said. "What do you say I make a few calls and see if I can find out anything?"

"You've been more than kind," she said. "I couldn't ask you to do that."

"Why not?" he asked. She didn't have an answer for him. "Look," he continued. "I like you. You're a good person with a smart head on your shoulders. You're beautiful and talented beyond anything that should be legal. I can't just watch you go out there and end up in a horrible situation. I'd feel responsible."

"How would you be responsible?" she asked.

"Because I'm the reason people know about you," he

confessed. "I asked Richard if it would be all right if we invited a couple of other conductors in to listen to you after your audition. He was hesitant, but saw exactly what I saw. Raw, pure, tremendous talent. He knew it would just be a matter of time before you were poached outright. This way, he could have a hand in trying to find the best fit for you."

"I'm afraid I don't understand," she said.

"Like I said," he said. "New York moves fast."

She sat there, looking at the man next to her, completely confused.

"Tell me what to do," she whispered.

Charles reached out and held her hand. "Sleep on it," he said. "Give yourself at least one day to bask in all that is the wonder of being so wanted that people are fighting over you. Then," he continued, "sit down with someone you trust and go over what they've offered, and what I've told you. Do some research, see what there is out there about the ones you want most, and make a decision."

"You make it sound so simple," she said.

"It is," he replied. "If all else fails, tack them up on the wall and throw a dart."

She laughed, then said, "Thank you. Not just for this, but for dinner and for being so nice."

"I like you," he said. "Now, go home and sleep on it. The decision doesn't have to be made today, or even this week. Give yourself time."

Standing, she thanked him once again, then made her way out the door. She walked down the steps, out of the building, and down the block to her own place. Keying her way in, she bypassed the mailboxes and made the climb to her studio. Once there, she checked the time, and decided she'd call Darci in the morning. Yawning, she undressed and climbed into bed, plugging her phone in so it would be ready to go when she got up. Tonight, she would dream of all the possibilities, and tomorrow she would make a decision.

Christie's phone began blaring before it was even light out, and she rolled over to peer at it. Darci. Of course it was her.

"Hello," she mumbled as she answered.

"About time," Darci said. "You didn't call last night, Christie. I was worried."

"It was late when I got home," she said. "I didn't want to wake you up. Unlike you, who has no problem calling when normal people are sleeping."

"So," Darci prompted, waiting to hear the details of the night before.

"We talked," Christie said, yawning. "And he gave me some great insight into some of the offers. He also told me to talk to someone I trust. I guess that's you."

"Those aren't the details I was hoping for," Darci sighed. "Did you kiss? More?"

"Good lord," Christie mumbled. "No. It was a dinner with a colleague. Nothing more."

"You're boring," she replied. "Seriously, he isn't your boss anymore, so you should go for it."

"He did tell me he liked me," Christie said.

"Woah," Darci said. "Liked you as in *liked* you?"

"I guess," she replied.

"And that didn't give you incentive to kiss him?"

"It was dinner," Christie argued. "We talked about work."

"Which doesn't involve you two together anymore," Darci interjected.

"It's too early for this conversation," Christie yawned again. "Can I call you when I've had more sleep?"

"Fine," Darci said. "But if you're not gonna kiss him, then you are doing it wrong."

"Good night, Darci," Christie said.

"Night," Darci replied.

Christie disconnected the call, then saw that she had more emails. Deciding that she really couldn't sleep anyway, she pulled the app up on her phone. Blinking, she counted the unread emails. More offers had come in, ranging all across the US, Europe, and even Asia. She just stared at them, unsure what to even do. Deciding she needed more help, she sent a text to Charles, hoping she didn't wake him, but also wanting his help with this. She didn't wait long before she got a reply saying he was awake and she could call if she wanted. Booting up her laptop, she stepped into the bathroom to take care of business before getting on a call. When she came out, her phone was ringing. She looked at the screen and saw it was him, so she answered.

"Sorry," she said by way of an answer. "Had to powder my nose."

"It's all good," he replied. "How many more did you get?"

"I lost count after about a dozen," she said.

His low whistle was the reply.

"This isn't fair," she said. "There are a lot of other talented people out there. Why am I getting all these offers?"

"Word is out," he said. "I say pick from one of the first ones you got. Unless there's something that really catches your eye in one of the new ones."

"Maybe I should just stay where I am," she sighed.

"And give up on this amazing opportunity?"

She sighed, then said, "I guess you're right."

"I know I am," he replied. "Do you want me to do anything?"

"Make the decision for me?" she asked.

"I can't do that," he replied.

"Sure you could," she insisted. "Then I wouldn't have to make the decision myself. You have no idea how bad I am at decision making."

"Tell you what," he began. "You let the offers sit, no answering any of them. And we will meet with Richard on Thursday. It's not a rehearsal day, so he'll be available to talk. You can show him every offer you have and ask him his opinion. That way you'll get the best guidance anyone could. He knows almost every conductor in the states, and some of those who are in Europe. Can you do that?"

"Thank you," she said. "You have no idea how helpful that is. It makes it seem possible, now."

"Happy to help," he replied. "Rest. We'll talk again in a couple of days."

Christie hung up the phone and looked at it again. Three more emails had come in while she was talking to Charles. How was she ever going to decide?

The days flew past, offers piling up one on top of the other, until Christie couldn't keep track of who was who, which offer had multiple requests, and where all the offers were from.

"Hey," Darci said as she sat down next to her friend.

"Hey, you," Christie replied.

"Today's the day?"

"Yep," she said. "I'm meeting Charles here and then we're going to see Richard."

"You think you'll stay in New York?"

"I'd like to," she said. "It'll depend on what is the best option for me, though."

"Christie," Charles said as he came in. "Darci."

"Hey," Darci said. "Don't steer my girl wrong."

"I wouldn't think of it," he replied. "You ready?" he asked Christie.

"I guess," she replied.

"Break a leg," Darci said.

"That's only when you're actually performing," Christie laughed.

"Whatever," she replied. "Don't forget us little people when you're world famous."

They left the café and walked down the street.

"Did you figure out which ones you like best?" he asked as they got closer to the theatre.

"I couldn't figure it out," she said. "I really would like to stay in New York, though, and there are several offers from orchestras here in the city."

"We'll be sure to let Richard know," he said.

They stepped into the theatre and made their way to the office area. Knocking on the door to the conductor's office, they heard him call for them to come in. When they walked in, he wasn't alone.

"I'm sorry," Charles said. "I thought we were scheduled to meet."

"Come in," Richard replied, standing. "I'd like to introduce you to Margaret Schofield."

"Hello," the woman said. "It is truly a pleasure to meet you. I hope you don't mind me barging in on your meeting, but I wanted to offer you a position face to face."

"Okay," Christie said, shaking the woman's hand.

"It's a little unorthodox," Richard said, sitting down and indicating the others should follow suit. "I was to give you some guidance on what offer might be best for you, and here I have another to show you."

"It really is my fault," the other woman said. "I insisted he invite me when I found out you were meeting with him."

Christie sat with her hands in her lap, twisting her fingers around each other, more nervous than she'd ever been in her life.

"Margaret has an offer that you haven't yet seen," Richard said.

"And one I hope you will consider seriously," she added.

With that, she began to lay out an offer that was not only a good fit for Christie musically, but it was more money than any of the other offers she'd seen. Add to that, the opportunity for her to travel not just around the states, but abroad as well.

"It will, of course, also include your own apartment here in New York, as well as all travel and lodging for shows outside of New York," the woman concluded. "You would be allowed to have a significant other join you on the trips abroad, if that becomes a factor as well."

She was stunned. This was almost everything she'd ever wanted.

"What would be the chances of her bringing her own music to the group?" Charles asked, knowing that it was one of the things that Christie had wanted when they'd talked the other night.

"We would be delighted to look at pieces you've composed," Margaret said. "Each one would be considered on their own, and added to the score on a case by case basis. Richard indicated that you played your own piece when you auditioned for him. He was kind enough to allow me to view that when I asked."

"You listened to my piece?" Christie asked.

"And it was remarkable," the other woman replied. "You truly are a gifted musician, and I am very hopeful that I will get the opportunity to work with you."

"Thank you," was all Christie could say.

"I'll leave you to it," Margaret said as she stood. "So good to see you again, Richard."

"And you," he said, ushering her out the door. He closed it behind her and went back to sit behind his desk. "Well?" he asked.

"That was rather bold," Charles said.

"It's an offer that she didn't want to make unless she was sure she would be heard out," Richard said. "When I told her that I was meeting with you, she said she had to meet you as well."

Christie looked between the men. "She's serious?" she asked.

"Absolutely," Richard replied.

"This is a wonderful opportunity," Charles said.

"But it's more than I'm worth," Christie argued.

"Nonsense," Richard barked. "You're worth that much and more. The problem is, you can't see your own worth. That's not a bad thing, either. It will keep you humble, which will make you all the more valuable."

"You think I should take it," she said. It wasn't really a question, though she wasn't confident in her convictions, either.

"Unless you have an offer that can match it," Richard said. "I say take it as soon as possible and run away with it. I would if it were offered to me."

She sat there, looking between the two men, pondering the offer. It really was a good offer, and it would be awesome to have a bigger place. The opportunity to compose her own music was the tipping point, though, and she smiled.

"There it is," Richard said. "The moment she picked her destiny."

"And we can say we knew her when," Charles chimed in.

"So," she began. "Should I call her? Or are you going to? I don't have a number for her."

Richard picked up his phone and dialed. "She's in," he said after a moment.

"Oh my god," Darci said. "Look at this place."

"I know," Christie replied.

She'd only been in her new place for a week, and already it felt like home. She had a three bedroom with a bath and a half, and an open floor plan. The extra bedrooms had been a must, as she said she needed a place for a friend to stay.

"And you're sure they're okay with us staying here?"

"I told them I had someone who I needed to stay with me,"

she said. "Why would they worry? They said a 'significant other' was allowed."

"But I'm not your significant other," Darci insisted.

"They don't need to know that," Christie insisted. "Besides, you're as close as I'm gonna get for a while."

"What's wrong with Charles?"

"We've had this conversation," she insisted. "I can't go there."

"But he likes you," Darci offered. "You told me yourself. I think you should go for it."

"You are incorrigible," she said.

"I'm amazing," Darci retorted.

Her phone began to ring, so she looked at it, then slid to answer.

"Ms. Schofield," she said.

"I take it you are all moved in," the other woman said.

"I am," Christie replied. "Thank you for checking."

"You should be receiving a package with your music for this next month," she said. "Along with the schedule for when and where you'll be needed. We have three orchestras working in unison, and you are leading one of them. We'll need you at rehearsals starting on Tuesday."

"Thank you," Christie said. "I'll watch for the package, and begin rehearsing at once."

"I'd also like to see the score for the piece you played for Richard," she said. "We might just want to add that to the next set of music we use."

"I will see if I can find a copy of what I wrote," she said. "Again, thank you for this opportunity."

"You deserve my thanks," the older woman said. "I never thought I'd find another one who was as good as our last lead. It was a breath of fresh air to listen to your piece."

"I appreciate your vote of confidence in me," Christie said.

"I'll see you soon," the other woman replied, then disconnected the call.

"Slave driver?" Darci asked.

"The opposite," Christie replied. "She's so nice, it's impossible to not do what she asks."

Darci smiled at her friend. "I'm glad you like her. It would suck for you to work with an ogre."

"Something she definitely isn't," Christie said.

Days turned into weeks, which moved to months. Christie was busy playing and traveling. Just as Charles had told her, she was wanted all around the world, and was beginning to lead a very different type of show, one where her music was front and center, and the orchestra was accompanying her rather than her simply being one of the pieces.

After three years she was back in New York on a month-long break to compose and rest. Darci and her son continued to live with her, sharing the space while she was in town, and enjoying it while she was away.

"Christie," Darci called. "Someone's here to see you."

She came out of her room and turned the corner to see Charles standing in her living room.

"Hey," she said, walking over to him.

"You look amazing," he said, giving her a hug.

They'd kept up conversations over the phone, but hadn't seen each other since her first big tour took off about six months into her contract.

"Back at you," she said.

"Dinner?"

"You cooking?" she asked.

"Or we could go out," he suggested. "You can afford it, right?"

Christie laughed and said, "Absolutely. What do you want?"

"You're paying," he said. "You choose."

Christie grabbed her purse and phone and said, "See you later," to Darci.

"Have fun," Darci replied, giving a little eyebrow wiggle when Charles had turned away.

Christie rolled her eyes, then followed him out. They walked down the street to a deli that was on the corner and stepped in.

"Miss Christie," the manager said as they came in.

"Raul," she replied, giving him a hug.

"Who is our friend?" he asked.

"This is Charles Ward," Christie said. "He's the reason I come here."

"He is bad for you at home?" the manager asked, confused.

"No," she laughed. "He's the one who discovered me."

"Oh," he said, drawing the word out. "I have you to thank for my best customer, when she is in town."

"You have her to thank," Charles said. "She's the talent. I just helped her find a place to shine."

"Thank you, thank you," the other man said. "Your usual?" he asked Christie.

"Please," she said, then made her way to a corner table. "So," she began once they were seated. "How has New York been treating you?"

"I wanted you to be the first one to know," he said. "Richard is retiring, and has asked that I take over his orchestra."

"Seriously?" she squealed.

"Right after the first of the year," he said, smiling.

"I'm so happy for you," she said.

"And I was wondering," he began, then stopped.

"What?" she asked, curious.

"If you would mind doing a special engagement with my orchestra," he said.

"Have you talked with Margaret?" she asked.

"She said she would love it," he said. "But that it was completely up to you."

"When?" she asked. "And what would we play?"

"I know you have a huge tour for Christmas," he began. "But after the first of the year, Margaret said she could spare you for a month. I'd like to do February with you in the lead. And if you wouldn't mind, we could do the piece you played when you auditioned."

She looked at him and smiled. "You're nervous I'll say no," she said. "Why would you think I would say no?"

"You're kind of big time," he said.

"But you are the reason I am," she replied.

"Nah," he began, but she interrupted.

"Seriously," she said. "If it weren't for you, I wouldn't have had the confidence to accept any offer, let alone the one I did. I feel like I owe it to you to help out. I'm in."

He smiled just as the manager came over with a couple of plates.

"For the beautiful lady," he said, placing one in front of her. "And for her charming partner," he said, placing the other plate in front of Charles.

"Oh," Charles said. "We're not..."

"What?" Christie asked when he stopped mid-sentence.

"Well," he said, looking at her.

"What?" she asked again, clearly confused.

"I don't want this to come off as pushy, but," he stopped again, not really finishing his sentences.

"Just come out with it," she said.

"What would you say if I asked you out?" he asked.

"We are out," she countered.

"I mean on a date," he said. "Like a romantic date."

She looked at him and smiled. "I thought you'd never ask," she smiled.

A FRESH START

Chapter 1

Bryan

That's it?" I asked.

"That's all we need," Dr. Robinson said.

"And you'll get the results to me when?"

"Once we have the final results," she said, "you will be informed. It shouldn't take but a couple of days."

"I guess I'll go, then," I said.

"I know this is difficult," she offered. "I'm sorry."

"It's okay," I replied. "I just wish I had an answer as to why it was me who got this."

"That's completely understandable," she said. "In your post visit notes there are names of some counselors that help with processing this type of diagnosis. You should call and make an appointment with one of them. They can help you with ways to tell your family and friends, as well as coping mechanisms for you to handle the next steps in your treatment."

"Honestly," I replied, "I just want to take some time to myself."

"Just be sure you let someone know where you are," she said. "We often see people go into a depression when they get this kind of diagnosis. I want to be sure that you're safe, that you won't lose yourself."

"I'll escape," I said. "But it'll be into my work."

"That can be just as dangerous," she admonished. "Whether it's work or some other vice, you need to be sure that you take care of yourself."

"I will," I promised. "Thank you for taking such good care of me. I look forward to hearing from you when you have the results."

With that, I walked out the door, papers in hand with a list of professionals to take care of the mental side of a diagnosis of cancer. I told the doctor I wondered why it was me, but I already knew. I hadn't taken care of myself very much since Suzie died. She was my world, the center of my universe. I'd put off getting certain tests done.

Honestly, she was more than my wife, she was my everything, and when the drunk driver took her from me, I wanted to do nothing but hide from the world. Fortunately, my work could be done from anywhere. I wasn't tied to a place, just to her. Now that she was ripped from me, I had the ability to go anywhere. The only thing that tied me to this city was the fact that this was where she was laid to rest.

What an odd phrase that is, though. Like, they're not resting. They're just gone. No longer tied to the planet. Not stuck here with the rest of us making a mess of this place. She was free, and yet I was rooted. We'd never had kids, choosing to be child-free, so no reason to not go somewhere else. Somewhere that the memories didn't invade my every moment. A place where I could lose myself in a crowd that didn't know me.

The problem with that concept was that I would always be recognized by my fans. My line of work put me in a place where some people recognized me. And when one did, then a dozen more would find me. This was why we'd decided the small town in the middle of nowhere was the best place to live. But then that monster had stolen her from me, taken the only good thing about this place away.

Oh, sure, I had a nice house, nice car, all the trappings of a successful career. It was worthless, though, without the lighthouse that was my Suzie. She steered me away from the rocks along the shore of this minefield that was my mentality. Kept me safe and guided me into the safe harbor of her love. The tsunami that was the crash took that harbor and made it unsafe, cluttered with the broken pieces that were once perfect, and I had to find my own way in this world without her.

Cancer sucks, sure, but if she'd been here, it would have been bearable. I could have navigated the turbulent waters of this section of the river if she'd been there as the rudder to keep me on track, going the right direction. Now I was alone, adrift amidst a turbulent sea, lost without a guide, without anything to show me where to head, a place that could be safe in this storm that was my life.

Chapter 2

Anna

Hi," I said. "My name is Anna."

"Hi, Anna," the group parroted.

It was almost exactly like you see on TV, the group dynamic. You say your name, what is going on with you, and everyone encourages you for your progress and comforts you with your mistakes. Didn't matter whether it was for an addiction or anything else, the group dynamic was nearly identical.

"I kinda feel lost right now," I continued. "I'd been doing really good with keeping my needs under control, but I had a big scare medically and I felt like I needed the crutch."

"What did you do?" one of the members asked.

"Called my sponsor," I replied. "I know how to do the work, it was just a struggle."

"You did the right thing," another member said.

Honestly, I didn't really want to hear their praise. I wanted to lock myself away from the world and read. Fall into a world that didn't have everything I was dealing with in it. I wanted to escape.

"Thanks." I said what was expected, followed the 'rules' of the group, then shut up and let someone else have their turn.

My addiction had put me in mandatory group therapy like this for a couple of years. I had to get my little book signed by the group leader to prove I was here every week. Not like I had much of anything else to do. Being financially independent without the need for a job had put me into the mess I found myself, but thankfully I didn't blow through the inheritance. I still had the money, so could afford not doing any real work.

Maybe that was the problem. Maybe I needed a job to keep me on track, to give me some sort of purpose in life rather than just existing.

By the time the group finished, I hadn't heard anything anyone else had said. Oh, I contributed, parroting the greeting, nodding and looking sympathetic, but I was a master at being present without really engaging. Learned that from my dad. He was there, just not interested in anything, even though it looked like he was. When he died, I was relieved. I know it sounds bad, but it is what it is. At least he was good for something, even if it wasn't an emotional attachment to his daughter.

As I walked home after group, I passed the town bookstore. There was a sign that said they were hiring. I hadn't held a job in all my life, simply did whatever I wanted and let daddy foot the bill. Unfortunately, that's what got me to where I am now, which was not a good place. I decided that I'd stop in the next morning and fill out an application.

The little town was good for me, away from the bright city lights and away from temptation on every corner. I wanted to figure out who I was, find the real me, and being away from everything I knew was exactly where I had wanted to start. I felt very fortunate to be able to get away from my hometown and find a place where I could recover and recoup, away from the press that had hounded me for so long. They'd probably find me again, eventually, but for now, I was an anonymous nobody in rural upstate New York.

That was another benefit of these groups. No one really knew who you were. I mean, if I were someone really famous, like an actor or something, then sure, they'd all know me. But I wasn't famous like that. I had a rich daddy, and the only reason people knew about my mess was because I was in the city. Once I moved out here, away from the skyscraper that was my family home, I became just another faceless person with a checkered past looking to start over. It was actually refreshing to go into a grocery store or a restaurant and not have someone whispering behind me about all the things they'd read in the weekly tabloid at the check stand.

I climbed the steps to my little cottage and keyed open the door. Closing it behind me, I leaned against it and sighed deeply. Shutting out the world hadn't been the best thing, but making friends was always hard for me. I eased off the door and moved to my bedroom, flicking the light on. Opening my closet, I looked through what I had brought with me when I came, noting that there wasn't much that could be considered business attire, but there were a couple of dresses that would be sufficient to pass muster in this little town and the corner bookstore.

Pulling out a blue patterned one, I laid it across the chair in the bedroom and inspected it to make sure there weren't any stains or anything on it. Finding it suitable, I then pulled out a pair of sensible low heels and set them under the chair. I pulled out everything else I'd need in the morning to look like the professional I knew I wasn't. That was one thing daddy's money had been good for, boarding school. Not only did I learn how to read and write, but also how to present myself as a professional. Of course, it's also where I found my love of sex, and learned that sometimes it could be better than even the best of drugs that the kids brought with them.

Oh, don't get me wrong. I tried most every drug brought into the school. I just found that sex gave me a better high without all of the downfalls that the others had. No one in my support group knew that sex was my addiction, though. They all assumed it was alcohol, just like them. I could play it off as that, and my attorney assured me that no one in the group would know what I used to cope, and that even though it wasn't technically a support group for this, it counted toward my court ordered rehab.

Feeling pretty good about myself, I hopped into the shower to get myself presentable for the next day. I didn't shower in the morning. Actually, I didn't really people in the morning, either. My day usually started at noon at the earliest, and ran until after midnight, pushing two in the morning most days. Tonight, I would brew myself a cup of tea and get to bed early. I wanted to look like I did mornings when I went to the bookstore to apply for the position. First impressions were always important.

Chapter 3
Bryan

You would really be open to doing a reading and signing in our little bookstore?" the gal behind the counter asked.

"I've been out of touch with my readers," I replied. "I want to reconnect with them. I think this would be just the thing to get me over my writer's block."

"I don't understand," she said.

"Reading tends to get my creative juices flowing," I explained. "When I'm stuck, like I am now, if I read something I've written, it tends to get things flowing again."

"That's really interesting," she said. "Let me check our calendar, but I'm sure I can get you in any time you would want."

"Whenever is convenient for you guys is probably fine with me," I replied.

I didn't want to tell her that I just needed something besides a doctor's appointment to get me out of my house. I needed to do something, anything, that wasn't stuck inside with my laptop and the four walls of my study, with no distractions from the loss of my wife, with nothing but my disease to keep me company. The door chimed and a young woman walked in. She was pretty, but she wasn't my Suzie.

"Tell you what," I said to the clerk. "I'll leave you my card and you can email me a time and day that will work. I see you have customers and I don't want to block your sales."

"Thank you," she said, taking my card.

"Have a nice day," the woman said as I passed her.

"You, too," I replied, then stepped into the sunshine.

I walked down the street and stepped into the pharmacy. I hated the meds that the doctor had given me, but I knew that I needed them to stay alive, so I picked up the prescription and walked back out. Next stop was the florist to pick up some forget-me-nots. The cheery blue with the bright yellow centers reminded me of my Suzie, how she would brighten any room she walked into. I paid for those and then continued on my way down the road. Crossing at the streetlight, I passed the grocery store and stepped in to grab a can of soda. Mellow Yellow was Suzie's favorite drink, even though she didn't have it often. I always tried to bring one when I stopped to see her. I never drank it, just left it there at her headstone for her. They were always gone when I came back, so I have no idea if the groundskeeper took them, some kids picked them up, or what exactly happened to them, but it made me feel better bringing it to her.

The gate was open and inviting, even though it was a place filled with death. Virtually anyone who was in there was grieving, whether it was new and fresh or just waves leftover from times before. Mine wasn't exactly new, but it wasn't long lived either. How had six months gone by without her? I wasn't sure I was going to make it through that first day, and yet here we were, six months down the road, and I was still upright, still working, and still living. The world didn't end when her life did, and somehow, I'd figured out how to continue on.

"Hey," I said, though I knew she wouldn't answer. "Brought you your soda. Found these pretty things, too."

I leaned the can against the headstone, then set the flowers into the built-in vase in the ground in front. Convenient that they offered those so folks could leave flowers. Once they had passed their time, they were disposed of without the family having to remember to do it.

"I talked to the Good Book," I said once I'd settled the flowers and sat next to her. "Offered to do a reading and signing. I know you'd want me to move forward, and it's hard, but I'm trying. Doctor said that she thinks it should be a quick surgery to remove the small tumor in my lung, then the chemo will find anything that remains. I've already started with some pills, but they're awful. They haven't scheduled the surgery, yet, though, so we're still waiting on that. I'm hoping I can get the signing in before I go under the knife."

I didn't want everything I talked to her to be bad, but she was my rock, and I needed her during this.

"I think you'd like Dr. Robinson," I continued. "She's a lot like you. No nonsense, but kind as well. She wants me to join a support group or something. You know me and crowds, though. I'm not very open in the best of times, so spilling my guts to a bunch of strangers is completely outside my idea of something good. Maybe I can find someone to talk to one-on-one. I mean, I can talk to you, but you aren't that good at giving advice lately."

I laughed. I couldn't help it. It was morbid and horrible, but she would have found it funny. The laugh caught in my throat as I realized that I was making jokes about her being gone. I didn't want to do that. Didn't want to make light of her not being here when I continued on with my miserable self.

"Thinking of starting a new series," I said. "You know that fantasy thing I was talking about? Wondered if I should make the lead female like you. Strong, yet kind. Brilliant, yet goofy. Absolutely perfect in every way."

I waited. Didn't know if I was waiting for her to answer or just sitting in silence in her company. Either way, it was calming for me. Being with her, even in this morbid way, grounded me. She was always my rock, my lighthouse in the crashing waves, the one guiding me back to the safe shore. God, I missed her. I wonder what she would have thought about me sitting next to her, regaling my day and my first world problems. She'd probably tell me to get over myself and spend some time in the cancer ward at a children's hospital where kids who were toddlers were stuck with all sorts of needles and tests and likely wouldn't even make it to double digits.

"Guess I better get on that fantasy," I said, getting up and brushing my pants. "Not going to write itself."

I paused. This would be the moment she'd tell me that I could do this, that whatever I wanted, it was within me to make it happen. It was as if I could hear her saying these things to me, but it was all in my head. Sniffing, I walked away, only looking back once. The walk home was solemn. All I ever wanted was to spend the rest of my life with her, and I couldn't do that. She was gone, and there was no getting her back.

My desk was dark, so I flicked on the desk lamp. Opening my laptop, the screen came on and it was her, right there, staring at me with that cheeky smile she would give me when she knew I needed to write. I reached out and touched the screen, only to have it flip to the log in state, her face blurring behind the box asking for the password. I entered it and got to work.

Chapter 4

Anna

"H ave a nice day," I said to the man as he was walking out of the store.

"You, too," he replied and went on his way.

He was familiar to me, somehow, but I couldn't quite place him.

"How can I help you?" the gal behind the counter asked.

"I saw your sign in the window," I said, pointing that direction. "Wondering whether you had an application."

"We don't," she replied. "But you could leave your resume."

"See," I began. "I don't really have one. I've kind of never had an actual job."

"Oh," the gal said. "Well..."

I could tell she wasn't sure what to do with that information.

"I've always had someone to support me," I offered. "My dad was wealthy and I didn't have a need to work. But now I find that I have time, and really want to do something worthwhile. I thought this would be a good place to start."

"I mean," the gal said.

"It's okay," I replied. "If you don't have a way for me to do an application, I'll see if I can come up with something for a resume and drop it off later. I just love books, so thought this would be the perfect place to have my first job."

"Hang on," she said, then picked up the phone and dialed.

"I'll just look around," I said and stepped away from the counter so she could have a private conversation with whoever it was she was calling.

Normally I read romance, but for some reason I'd been getting into the science fiction and fantasy realms for my reading. There was something perfect about a world where even the crazy creatures were just as messed up as us humans.

"Miss," the woman said after I'd been browsing the titles along the shelves.

"Yeah," I replied, turning towards her.

"Would you be willing to wait about half an hour for the owner to come in?"

"Sure," I said, a little confused.

"I told him that there was someone who was interested in the job," she continued. "He said he'd come in and have a conversation with you and see if it was a good fit."

"That would be great," I said. "In the meantime, who was that who walked out when I came in? I recognize him, but can't quite find the name."

"Oh," she said. "That was Bryan Walker. He's a local who is also an author. He was asking about coming in and doing a reading and signing."

"I knew he looked familiar," I said. "I love his work."

"Yeah," she said. "He's had a rough year. It'll be nice to see him getting back out again."

"What happened?" I asked.

"Oh," she said, obviously concerned by what she'd said. "It really isn't my place to gossip. Let's just say that he's had a rough go round and we're all hoping that good things come into his life really soon."

I simply shrugged. I knew what it was like to be talked about behind my back, and I certainly didn't want to do that about someone else. "I'll find something to read to pass the time," I said, and began perusing the bookshelves once again.

Perhaps she wasn't prepared for me to drop it like that because she kind of stood there waiting for me to ask more, then realized that I wasn't interested and went back to the counter. After just a few minutes, I found the first in the Officers of the Solstice series that Bryan Walker had written. Pulling it from the shelf, I walked to the counter and set it down, pulling out my wallet.

"You can just read this until Mr. Holmes comes in," she said.

"I actually lost my copy of this," I said. "I think I left it somewhere and would really like to have it anyway. It's really no bother."

"If you're sure," she said hesitantly.

"I am," I replied and pushed the book closer to her.

She punched some buttons on her keyboard and then gave me the total. I handed her my card and she stuck it in the little machine, then punched the total into it so that it would charge me. Once the machine started printing the receipt, she pulled my card out and handed it back to me. Pulling the receipt off the machine, she placed it on the countertop and handed me a pen. I signed the charge slip, then she stuck it into her register, printing out another receipt for me. I put it into the book to use as a bookmark and went to the window seat to read while I waited.

I was just getting to the good part of chapter three when the owner came over and said hello.

"I understand you are interested in the position," he said.

"Yes," I replied, placing the receipt in my book. "Unfortunately, I don't have any experience."

"Tell me this," he began, indicating that I should retake my seat. "What do you love about books?"

"Well," I said, thinking. "Honestly, they've always been my escape. Whether it was in school when I didn't want to do an assignment, or at family gatherings that were boring, I always found a place to hide within my books."

"I feel the same way," he replied. "But, what do you want to do in working here?"

"I've found myself without purpose," I explained. "I don't need to work, per se, but having something to do, in order to make a difference, would be nice."

"So, why don't you volunteer somewhere?"

"I feel like," I began, then paused. "Honestly, I don't think I'd be very good at it. If I didn't have a reason to go, I would probably just forget or decide not to show up."

"What makes you think you would if you had a job?"

"That's something I thought about, too," I said. "But I am very reliable when it is something that is expected of me. My father would roll over in his grave if he thought I was unreliable. And that's not something I could stomach. So, I would do my utmost to be responsible, prompt, and ready to do your bidding."

"You are refreshingly honest," he laughed.

"Yeah," I replied. "Sometimes that doesn't work in my favor."

"Today must be your lucky day," he said. "Let's get some paperwork out of the way and get you on the schedule to train."

"Really?"

I was shocked. He hired me without knowing anything about me. Without even doing any kind of background check or anything. Seriously just had a conversation and hired me.

"I believe that oftentimes the first impression is the best," he said. "My name is Bill. What's yours?"

"It's Anna," I replied, holding out my hand to shake.

341

"Good to meet you," he replied. "Hey, Mal."

"Yeah," the gal behind the counter called back.

"I'd like you to meet your new coworker, Anna," he said. "Anna, this is Malory. She's been with me for, what is it, ten years?"

"Something like that," Mal replied. "So, what shall we do first?"

"Let's get her information and get her the tax forms she has to fill out," he said, stepping behind the counter. "You go find them in the office. I have no idea where they are."

"I'll go print them out," she said. "You have a Social Security card?"

"Probably," I replied. "But not with me. I'll have to call my lawyer and have him get it to me."

"Your lawyer?"

Bill didn't look too pleased about me using that word.

"I had some trouble a while back," I explained. "Nothing serious, I promise. I just have him on retainer, and he holds all of my important paperwork. It keeps me honest, and helps to keep me on track with everything. If you want, I can have him call you."

"Oh, no," he said. "When can you get the card? I know we can't have you start until we get that."

"I can ask him to bring it up tonight," I replied. "It shouldn't be too much of a hassle. He may even send someone from his office with it. Do you need anything else?"

"If you have a passport," Mal said. "That makes things super easy. I've got a list of what documents we need to verify you. I'll be right back."

"So," Bill said after Mal walked back to the office. "Your trouble. Anything I should be concerned about?"

"Absolutely not," I replied. "It was a while ago, and I'm in counseling and going to meetings to help me cope and keep me on track. It wasn't drugs or theft or anything like that, just a little bit too much time and not enough discipline that led me into some dark times."

"As long as I don't have to worry about the cash I keep on hand," he said.

He was still eyeing me pretty suspiciously, but I offered, "I have more money than anyone has a right to have. My dad was Michael Freeman."

"Oh," he said, his eyes growing large. "I guess you don't need to work."

"Yeah," I replied. "I don't have the same last name, just so you know. My dad wanted to make sure that I didn't have anyone causing me problems, so he gave me his mom's maiden name as my last name."

"What happened to your mom?"

"I never knew," I said. "He didn't talk about her. I think she died when I was young, but I couldn't say for sure."

"I don't remember him every being married," he said. "Although I don't know much about the what nots of the rich and famous, so he could have been married to the Queen of England for all I know."

"Now that," I laughed, "was not the case. For sure, he was not married to her."

"Okay," Mal said as she came back up front. "Looks like I only need a passport if you've got one."

"I'll call my attorney and have him send it to me," I said.

"Perfect," she said. "I've got the form you need to fill out here, along with the tax form you need to do in order for us to take your taxes out of your check. I also have this form that we use to set up direct deposit."

"Wow," I said. "I didn't realize there was so much to do in order to work. I guess that's what I get for coming to this game a little later in life."

"It's not too bad," Mal said. "You can take the forms with

you and bring them back tomorrow, or whenever you get your passport."

"I should have it tonight," I said. "I'll stop back in tomorrow morning with the passport and all the forms filled out. I'll have to ask him what I need to do on some of these, especially since I have no idea what I'm doing."

"Great," Bill said. "Once we get that and get everything verified, we'll get you set up with Mal to have her train you."

"Why do you need someone else?" I asked.

"I'm going back to school," Mal replied.

"And I'm too old to learn all this new stuff again," Bill added. "I actually have a couple of other employees."

"My brother is one of them," Mal said.

"Oh," I said. "I think I've only seen you here."

"Because I'm here the most," she said. "Sam is only here on weekends because he's in school still."

"My wife works here, too," Bill said.

"Yeah," Mal said. "You'll love Carol. She's a hoot."

"Looks like this is just the kind of family environment for me to get my feet wet, then," I said.

"We are like a family," Mal said.

"I look forward to joining the family, then," I said.

"See you in the morning," Mal replied as I walked out the door.

I pulled out my phone and hit the number for Lincoln.

"Hey," he said.

"I need my passport," I told him.

"You know you can't travel," he said.

"I'm getting a job," I said. "I need it to show proof of who I am."

"Why are you getting a job?"

"Link," I groused. "I need something to do. I can't just sit around and do nothing, it's what drove me to my craziness in the first place. I have to have a purpose."

"Where are you going to be working?"

I told him the name of the book store.

"You sure you want to do this?"

"I am absolutely sure," I said. "They are super nice, and it already feels like they're family. I need this."

"I'll have someone bring it to the cottage," he said.

"Thanks," I replied.

"And Anna," he continued.

"What?"

"Be careful," he said.

"Now you're sounding like dad," I said.

"Your dad was worried about you," he said. "I am, too."

"I'll be fine," I said. "When will it get here?"

"I'll have someone bring it to you tonight," he sighed.

"Thanks," I said, then hung up and walked home.

Chapter 5

Bryan

"Hello?"

"Is this Mr. Walker?"

"Who is asking?" I asked.

I didn't get many calls on my home office number, so just pretended to be my own secretary. Suzie would usually answer when this phone rang, but she couldn't do that anymore.

"My name is Bill Holmes," the man said. "I own The Good Book. My assistant, Mal, said he stopped in to see about doing a reading and signing in the store."

"Then I am who you're looking for," I said.

"Oh," he replied. "I'm sorry I didn't recognize your voice."

"No problem," I replied. "I never know who is calling on this line, so I just have to be sure. Would you be open to me doing a reading and signing?"

"Absolutely," he replied. "I just hired a new employee, and thought I'd have you work with her. Would that work for you?"

"So," I began. "Someone who's new to the store is going to be in charge of it?"

"Oh, no," he replied. "I'll have Mal set everything up, get the word out and such. She's much more knowledgeable on that front. I meant I'll have her here as your assistant while you're in the store. You know, help with anything you might need. When would be a good time for you to do the signing?"

"I'm pretty open, actually," I said. "Once I get started on the next book, my time tends to get taken up by that. Right now, I'm in between books."

Honestly, I had no idea when I would be starting the next book. I hadn't written a word since Suzie left, and with the cancer diagnosis and impending treatment, I wasn't sure when I'd feel like writing again.

"Honestly," I offered. "The sooner the better. I do have some engagements coming in the next few months that will make it impossible for me to do it after, say, the middle of June. Could we set something up before then?"

"I'm sure Mal can make something happen," he said. "Shall I have her call you? Or would it be better if she emailed you? I don't do that sort of thing, but she's on top if it."

"Email might be better," I suggested. "That way we have it written down and can refer back to it. I look forward to hearing from her."

"We'll be happy to have you in our store," he said, then hung up.

"Well, Suzie," I said, looking at her picture on my desk.

"Looks like I'll be getting out there again. Hope I don't do something stupid."

Pulling up my email, I shot a note to my agent letting her know that I was going to be doing a signing. She sent me a response almost right away, saying she was happy to see that I was getting out there again and asked what she could do to help. I told her I didn't have any details, but once I did, I'd let her know.

I opened a new Word document, pulled one of the hard candies out of my dish, and began typing. It didn't take long before a story started to form, words falling into place. My Suzie had always been my Muse, and I could feel her inspiring me to keep going.

Three hard candies later, I had over ten thousand words and a whole new world building in my document. I could feel the cramping in my hands, and my back was beginning to bark, so I got up and stretched, then decided to see what I could find in the kitchen.

Dr. Robinson told me that once I started with the chemo, my appetite would go away, so I had to be sure that I was stocking up on calories now, and making sure I had high calorie foods available. She said that my foods wouldn't taste the same, and that I may not be able to keep much down, especially at first. I was determined to have the best options available once that time came, because I knew I wouldn't have anyone to keep me on track.

Risotto and a glass of wine were on the menu. The doctor said once I started actively taking chemo, I would have to give up the wine. Once I was done, I could have it again, so I wanted to relish the fact that I could still enjoy it. I thought about turning on the television, but absolutely nothing interesting was on, so I found my way back to my office and plunked back down at the desk.

By the time I felt like I couldn't stay awake, I realized that I had more words down than I had written in one day, pushing twenty-five thousand. My neck was telling me that I had to stop, even though the ideas were still flowing. Instead of continuing, though, I listened to my body and headed off to find a hot shower.

The beating water against my back and neck were just what I needed, and it didn't take long to realize that it had been a very long day. After I'd toweled off, I threw on some lounge pants and climbed into bed. It was so very big, and so very empty, but my weary body kept the demons at bay and I quickly drifted off to sleep.

Chapter 6

Anna

True to his word, Link had one of the underlings in his firm drive all the way up to the cottage and drop off my passport. I have no idea who the kid was, but he was younger than me by a few years and I wasn't even sure if he'd been there when I was last in the office. I guess it didn't matter, though, because he just smiled and handed me the packet with my document inside. I thanked him, offered for him to come in for a drink, but he declined and left almost immediately. Link probably told him not to stay, which was fine. It was already late when he got to the cottage, so I didn't mind that he didn't stick around for long.

I have no idea how I was able to fall asleep so quickly, but knowing I wanted to be at the bookstore first thing in the morning helped to press that issue. I had just three more dresses that would qualify as "work attire" in my closet, so I had laid one out and decided that a shopping trip would be needed after I stopped at my new job.

"Good morning," Mal said as I walked through the door.

"Hi," I replied. "I brought my passport and filled out all the paperwork."

Handing the documents to her, I waited as she perused them.

"Perfect," she said. "I just need to make a copy of the passport and add it to the paperwork. Did Bill tell you when you should come in?"

"He didn't," I replied. "At least I don't remember him telling me."

"Don't worry about it," she said. "Are you good to come in tomorrow morning before we open? I can show you around the store, give you a crash course on the computer system and how to do charges and such."

"I think I can do that," I replied. "By the way. What's the dress code for the store?"

"Honestly," she replied. "As long as you look somewhat professional and aren't wearing anything with vulgarity or conceived rudeness, you should be good."

"Dresses?"

"If you want," she said. "But, look at me. I haven't worn a dress in I can't even remember how long. If you are more comfortable in dresses, sure. But if you want to wear jeans or slacks, that's good, too."

"I have the dress I wore yesterday," I explained. "This one, and a couple more. Other than that, I think all my jeans are those trendy torn ones. And don't get me started on my shirt collection. I think they would likely all fall into that inappropriate category. I planned on going shopping today to get some things, so should I go with some plain or patterned shirts for now?"

"You honestly don't have to buy anything special," she said.

"It's no problem," I replied. "It's daddy's money that he couldn't take with him. Besides, I figure with a new job, I should do something new with my wardrobe."

"I mean," she began. "If you want to."

"I do," I replied.

"I am working with Bryan Walker," she said. "Working to get him a date to come in and do a signing and reading. Would you be interested in being the point person for him while he's here?"

"Sure," I replied. "What exactly would I need to do?"

"Basically, you'd just be his assistant," she said. "Get him water, keep the readers back, help with autographs and such. Typical stuff."

"You say typical," I laughed, "but you have to remember I haven't done anything like this before."

"That's right," she replied. "I forgot you are getting your first job. Well," she stuck her hand out. "Let me be the first to congratulate you."

I took her hand and shook it, smiling.

"So," she said. "Tomorrow morning. Be here at, say, eight?"

"I think I can do that," I replied.

"Perfect," she said. "See you then."

"With bells on," I replied.

I was much lighter in my step than I had been in a long time. This new adventure was just what I needed to get me out of whatever funk I'd been in. I'd called an Uber to come to the store and pick me up to take me shopping. While this little town had a shop, it wasn't quite my style. I directed the driver to the larger town just a few miles away, paid him, then went into the first of many shops to get a whole new wardrobe for my new job.

By two I was starving and had probably spent a small fortune on clothes. They were cute, country, and comfortable, and I couldn't be happier with my selection. I found a small teriyaki shop that looked to be one of those mom and pop places, where it was family run and obviously a labor of love. The menu was full of all my favorite things, but I opted for a chicken bowl. They had a cooler with canned and bottled sodas and the like, and I pulled out a naked juice to add to my order.

When she rang it up, I handed my card and she did the

whole charging thing. I tipped the bill, exactly what the cost was, I added that much as a tip. The woman behind the counter tried to tell me it was too much, but I simply pulled out a hundred-dollar bill and shoved it into the tip jar she had on the counter as well. Her smile was pure joy, and I felt even better about my decision.

There were only a handful of tables in the lobby area, as this was more of a take-out place, but I didn't have anywhere to go, so I sat in the corner, my purchases piled on the end of the table, and waited for her to bring out my food. It didn't take long and she brought me my bowl, but also brought out an order of pot stickers.

"I didn't order these," I said.

"I know," she replied. "On the house."

It was obvious that she was grateful for my tip, and wanted to show her appreciation by giving something in return. I didn't begrudge her, and took the offering, thanking her profusely. Once I'd finished my late lunch, I gathered up my bags and ordered up another Uber to get me home. I had a lot of unpacking to do, and I wanted to be sure to be on time the next morning.

Chapter 7

Bryan

The email said I could pick my day and they would make it work, so I looked at my ever-busy calendar, sarcasm implied, and picked a Saturday about three weeks out. That would give everyone involved plenty of time to get the word out. Mal, the person who was coordinating the signing, told me I should come in a couple of days before and meet the person who would be my helper. Said it would be good for the two of us to chat and get to know each other better so we could work seamlessly. It wasn't a big deal for me to pop in, so I set it up for a week ahead of time.

The two weeks flew by, and I walked into the store on the Saturday before my "event" was set to take place. My publisher had been all over social media, getting the word out that I would be making an appearance. It would be the first one since the accident, and I was a little apprehensive that I may get mourners wanting to bring Suzie up. They all saw what happened, the fans knew that I'd lost her, and that I had been devastated, but I hadn't had any interaction since then.

There were signs up in the window, and a stack of fliers on the counter, all touting that the resident author would be in the store and signing autographs and reading from the most recent book that was out. I hadn't told them what I was going to be reading from, and honestly still hadn't decided, but it was good PR to say it was from my most recent piece.

"Good morning, Mr. Walker," the gal behind the desk said. She was the same one I had given my card to the last time I was in.

"Good morning," I replied. "I'm not sure who I'm supposed to meet with."

"That would be Anna," the woman said. "I'm Mal," she continued, sticking her hand out for me to shake.

I took the offering and replied, "Good to meet you."

"Officially," she added.

"True," I said. "We have met before."

"I'll be right back with Anna," she said, and stepped from behind the counter and walked to a different section of the store.

"Mr. Walker," the woman, who I presumed was Anna, said.

"Please," I corrected. "Just call me Bryan. You must be Anna."

"I am," she replied. "I've always been a fan of your work. It got me through some really tough times. It will be my pleasure to work with you on your big day."

"I look forward to it," I said. "Not sure what all we need to talk about, but shall we?"

"Yes," she said, turning and walking toward a set of chairs near the window.

Following, I realized this was the woman who was in the store when I was here a couple of weeks ago.

"So," she said, after we'd sat down. "Do you have any preference as to how you want to be set up?"

"What would you suggest?" I asked.

"There are a couple of ways we can do this," she offered. "We could set up a table for you to have a stack of your most recent books on, then you could read from behind it. Or we can set up a chair that you can read from, and we can put a smaller table next to it. I'll be there to help run the sales and such, unless you have someone who usually does that for you."

"I think if we did a chair that I could read from," I suggested. "Then, a smaller table next to it would be fine. Do you have copies of the book that we'll sell?"

"We did do an order to get a few extra copies," she said. "But you are welcome to bring your own stock and we can sell those first."

"I'm sure what you have will be fine," I said. "I'll have my publisher send a box so I've got extra if you run out, but we should sell from your stock, first. My goal is to bring in business for the store."

She made some notes on the tablet she'd brought with her, then asked, "We assumed you'd be reading from your most recent book. Is that right?

"I actually thought I'd read a little of the project I'm currently working on," I said. "If you guys don't mind. It's been one of those healing things I've used, and I'd really like to share it."

"That sounds wonderful." She sounded genuinely enthused.

"Great," I said. "Do you need anything else today?"

"I don't think so," she replied, then looked at her tablet. "Let me just go check with Mal and see if she has any other question or needs anything else before I let you get back to your writing."

She got up and went back up to the counter to chat with the woman behind it. Something about Anna was tickling the back of my memory, but I couldn't put my finger on it. It was like I'd met her before, but not really.

"Mal said that she didn't think she needed anything else," Anna said as she came back. "But if there's anything you think of between now and Saturday, please reach out."

She handed me a card from the store and smiled.

"It was really nice to meet you," she said.

"I feel like we've met before," I replied. "Maybe in passing?"

"Well," she said. "I did see you when you were in a couple of weeks ago."

"I think I remember that," I replied. "But it feels like I met you before that. Like we knew each other a few years ago or something."

"I don't believe I've ever met you," she said. "Being that you're one of my favorite authors, I would definitely remember meeting you."

Her smile was big, and she seemed honest.

"Maybe you just remind me of someone," I offered.

"I've been told I have a familiar face," she laughed.

"That could be it," I replied. "At any rate, it was very nice to officially meet you. And I look forward to working with you in about a week."

"It truly was my pleasure," she replied. "I can't wait to hear some of your new piece, too. I love it when authors I love come out with something new."

"This is very different from what I've written in the past," I said. "You may hate it."

"I highly doubt that," she said.

"I hope you like it," I said. "I guess I'll see you in a week."

"See you then," she replied.

I walked out the door and headed home. I had more writing to do, and was hoping that I could get close to the half way point in this new book. It was going remarkably fast, considering I hadn't flexed my writing muscles in months. Maybe it was the thought of not getting the chance to finish it that was pushing me. I had an appointment on Monday to get my port put in for the chemo, and then I'd start the Monday after that. The timing for this reading was perfect, in that it would give me a good idea as to how the new project would be accepted.

I found myself at the cemetery, though I don't remember planning to come here.

"Sorry," I said when I stepped up to her resting place. "I didn't know I was coming, so I didn't bring any flowers."

She wouldn't have minded, though, and I knew it. She never liked me getting all mushy with sentimentality, so why should I try to do it now? No, she was just as happy to get a dandelion from the yard than a bouquet of roses. I didn't have either of them, though.

"I really think this new book is going to be well received," I said. "I'm doing a signing next weekend and I'll read the first chapter and see what folks think. You would have been able to tell me, but I can't ask you now."

I sat in silence for a bit, then said, "I wish I could hold you. Just one more time. Maybe then I'd be fine with letting you go."

It was a lie, though, because one more minute would lead me to wanting another hour, then another day, and before I knew it, I'd want a century, because even that wouldn't be enough time to spend with my Suzie.

"My cave awaits," I said as I stood. "This book isn't going to write itself. I'll stop by after the reading and let you know how it went."

The walk home was uneventful, and by the time I started

back in on the project, it was nearly noon. Suzie would have brought me lunch, but I settled for a cheese sandwich and dove back in.

Chapter 8
Anna

You did really well," Mal said after Bryan left.

"Thanks," I replied. "Do you think he could tell I was nervous? I mean, I didn't stutter or anything, but I was shaking in my boots."

"I couldn't tell you were nervous," she replied. "And I knew you would be. This is your first big thing. You did really well."

"I asked all the right questions, right?"

"Absolutely," she replied with a smile. "You even thought of some things I wouldn't have thought to ask."

"Like what?"

"About sales and such," she said. "Usually we don't even think to ask that type of thing. I guess even I can learn new things."

"What I asked was okay, though, right?"

"You were perfect," she said. "Now, let's get the rest of those books unboxed so we're ready for next Saturday."

The rest of the day was spent unboxing the books we'd purchased for the event, along with shelving the other stock we had that came in. They'd asked if I could come in on Friday night after the store closed to help get everything set up. It was completely optional, they said, but I felt like it would be the right thing to do. Besides, what was I going to be doing on a Friday night?

I'd had two more group meetings since I got the job, and people were very helpful in telling me that they could see a change in my demeaner since I started. Even the early mornings, at least for me, were becoming easier. The week flew by, and before I knew it, Bill, Mal, and I were setting up for the event. Mal said they'd had a lot of feedback on their social media posts about it, and she was hopeful that this meant that we would see a good turnout.

The store usually opened at ten, but they'd put up special hours for this day to be sure that everything would go off without a hitch, so I'd been asked to show up at eight instead of my usual nine start time. When I walked toward the store, I could see that there were several people sitting in their cars in front of the shop. As I keyed my way in, someone asked when we would be open. I told them the store was opening early, but not until nine.

"Do you always have this kind of turn out for events?" I asked Mal when I came in.

"This is the first signing we've done in about a year," she replied. "Mr. Walker usually brings in a few, but it's mostly just folks from town. Looks like his absence in the writing community has brought in people from farther out."

"I saw a plate from Vermont, and another one from New Hampshire," I said. "I didn't know this would be such a big deal."

"When it comes to authors," Mal said. "You never know what you'll get. Some come with a whole bunch of awesome fans who are polite and wait in line. Others have crazy fans that will cause damage to the store. We've learned who to trust and who to keep at arm's length."

"I guess it's the same with any celebrity," I mused. "I'm just glad no one knows I'm here. That could make things a lot more complicated."

"We would make it work," she replied.

"Bryan said he'd be here in about fifteen minutes," Bill said as he came up front from the office. "I told him to come to the back door so we don't have any issues."

I turned to look up front, and even though it was still

almost an hour before we were set to open, some of the people had gotten out of their cars and were now forming a line outside the shop. I could see some of them holding cups with the coffee shop next door's logo on them, so at least there was a boon to other businesses on the street, too.

The phone rang and Bill picked it up.

"Thanks for calling the Good Book," he said. "We've got your next adventure. How can I help you find it?"

We didn't usually answer the phone before we opened or after hours, but today was a special day.

"I'll send Anna back," he said, looking at me.

I headed to the office hung my purse on the hook in there, then went to the back door. I was pretty sure that Bryan was here, so wasn't surprised to see him when I opened the back door.

"Hey, there," he said. "I've got one box of books in the trunk, but I think we'll leave them there until we need them if that's all right with you."

"I'm sure that'll be fine," I replied, holding the door so he could come in.

"I saw there was already a line," he said once I closed the door.

"People came in from out of state," I replied. "I think it will be a good turn out."

"Let's just hope they don't hate my new book," he replied.

"I hardly think that'll happen," I said. "I've loved everything I've read by you, and I'm pretty sure you wouldn't be as successful as you are if you didn't write well."

"You'd be surprised at how fickle readers are," he laughed.

"This way," I said, heading back to the front of the store. "I've got everything set up how we discussed, but wanted you to check and make sure you didn't want to make any changes."

"Wow," he said as we came out from behind a shelf. "They really are coming in droves. I hope you've got enough room for everyone."

"We can make it work," Bill said. "Even if we have to do shifts."

"You guys are great," Bryan replied.

"We really appreciate the business you're going to bring in," Bill said. "It's always nice to have you in the store."

"I feel like it's my home away from home," he said.

We walked over to the set up and he said everything looked great.

"Maybe I should pre-sign a few of the books," he suggested. "Keep me from getting a cramp later on."

"Did you bring more?" Bill asked when he came to check on us.

"There's a box in my trunk," he said. "If we feel like we need it, I can give you my keys and you can get it."

"I can do that," I said.

"You'll be too busy here," Bill replied. "Between Mal and I, I think we'll make it just fine."

"Should I call Brodie in?" Mal asked.

"You know," Bill said, looking out the window. "Might not be a bad idea. Certainly wouldn't hurt."

"I'll give him a call," she said, and went off to do that.

"You've got about five minutes until I was going to open the doors," Bill said.

Bryan looked around and said, "I think we're good. What do you think, Anna?"

"If you're ready," I replied, "then so am I."

"Let's get this party started," Bill said, then went to open the door.

After a few hours, there were still people in the store wanting books or to talk to Bryan. He'd been gracious and considerate, giving of his time to most anyone who asked the questions. I watched him, making sure that he wasn't getting burned out, but he seemed to be in his element. By two, I wasn't sure whether he could take any more.

"I know you are all here to talk to Mr. Walker," I said. "But let's give him a few minutes to collect himself. You will still get time to talk to him," I continued, "and he will continue to sign your books, but I think we should give him a minute to recharge. You all good with that?"

The chorus of "Sure" and "Okay" were unanimous, and Bryan thanked me as he made his way to the back room. I don't know how he did it, just sitting there reading, then answering questions, signing books, and letting folks get their pictures with him.

"Does anyone have any other shopping they want to do before he comes back?" I asked, and the people began to look around the rest of the shop.

"You are a natural," Mal said once there was less of a crowd in the area.

"Really?"

"Yeah," she said. Dad said we've made more in sales today than we usually do in a month or more during the summer. Fall and winter are our busiest seasons, so having this boost in sales in June is just what we needed."

"I'm glad I could help," I replied.

"Me, too," she said. "Did you notice the way he looked at you?"

"What do you mean?" I asked.

"He lost his wife about six months ago," she said. "Horrible car accident. Everyone in town heard about it. I was actually surprised when he came into the shop that day. He's been pretty much a hermit since the accident."

"That's awful," I replied.

"He was looking at you like he did when Suzie was alive," she said.

"That just isn't good," I said, knowing exactly what she was implying.

"Hey," she said. "I'm not telling you to go after him. I'm just saying that if you were interested, he might be receptive to a dinner or something."

"I'm not in a good place for a relationship," I replied. "I'm still trying to find myself."

It was the excuse I'd been using for a couple of years, ever since the incident in my own life. The one that landed me in this little town where no one knew me.

"I'm not pushing," she said, holding her hands up. "Just saying."

"I'd appreciate it if you kept those observations to yourself," I said. "Nothing personal, but it's a sore subject for me."

"Hey," Bryan said as he came back. "You okay?"

"Yeah," I said. "Why?"

"Just look like someone who ate something sour."

Mal had walked off quickly, so must have seen him coming. The fact that she got all these thoughts running through my head, then abandoned me, was a little frustrating.

"Yeah," I said. "No, I'm fine. Just observing all the fans you have. How do you deal with being famous?"

"I'm not that famous," he replied.

"I beg to differ," I said, indicating the many readers still in the store waiting for their chance with him.

"Okay," he said. "Maybe I do have a significant fan base."

"I'd say that's putting it mildly," I laughed.

Before more could be said, some fans started back our way and we were left without being able to talk further. The more time I spent with him, though, the more I realized that Mal may be on to something. I noticed he'd watch me as I talked to customers, but then look away if I turned toward him. It was probably all in my imagination, though.

Chapter 9

Bryan

The day went better than I expected, and by the time the store was ready to close down, they were having to turn people away because they had sold out of every copy of every book I'd ever written, along with the few I'd brought with me.

"I think they missed you," Mal said as she locked the door.

"Apparently," I replied. "It was a much better turn out than I expected."

"Like I said," Mal reiterated. "I think they missed you."

"Anna," I said, turning to the woman who had been by my side throughout the day. "What do you think?"

"I agree with Mal," she said.

"I meant about my new book," I said.

"Oh," she looked surprised. "I'm not sure where you're going to go with it," she finally said. "I mean, it's a good start, but there are so many things that could happen. Is what you read everything you've got done?"

"Not by a long shot," I replied. "This was just the first chapter. There are twenty more at home."

"Wow," she said. "How long did it take you to write that all? I guess that's a stupid question, isn't it?"

"Not stupid at all," I replied as I folded my iPad up. "I started on it in the middle of May. I usually can get a full book done, first draft wise, in about a month, sometimes less."

"That's fast," she said. "I had no idea what the timeline was for writing. So, when you finish the, what did you call it? The first draft, what happens after that?"

"Tell you what," I said. "Why don't you finish up here,

then we can grab a bite for dinner, my treat, and we can talk all about it."

"I mean," she stumbled over the words.

"It would really be great to have a friend to have a conversation with," I said. "I get tired of my imaginary friends sometimes."

"Never thought about them being imaginary friends," she laughed. "But I guess it makes sense."

"Any dietary restrictions?" I asked.

"Nope," she replied.

"What sounds good?"

"So," she began, then said, "never mind."

"No," I replied. "What is it?"

"Well," she hesitated again, chewing her bottom lip. "There's this little mom and pop teriyaki place up in Watertown that I went to a couple of weeks ago. It was super good, and the folks there were really nice. That's probably too far to go, though."

"Maybe for tonight," I said. "But we could take a trip up there another time, if you're interested."

I'm not sure what had come over me, but I felt like there was a connection between us. Something other than what I had with Suzie. Nothing could replace her, but I also know she wouldn't want me to remain lonely.

"There's Joe's Café just down the block," I suggested. "It's not very fancy..."

"I certainly don't need fancy," she laughed.

"If you're good with it," I said, leaving the question unasked.

"Sounds great," she replied.

"Why don't you two go ahead," Bill said. "Both of you worked your tails off today, and I think that a nice quiet evening out is the perfect reward."

"You sure you don't need me to help put things back?"

she asked.

"Mal and Brodie have it covered," he said. "You two go enjoy the evening."

"If you're sure," she asked, clearly hesitant.

"I am," he replied. "You've both worked hard today, and I can't thank you enough, Bryan, for agreeing to come in."

"It was truly my pleasure," I replied. "Made me feel like I was back in the swing."

"Look forward to next time," the shop owner said, reaching his hand out to shake.

I took it, then thanked him again, and ushered Anna toward the back where my car was parked.

"Do we need to drive?" she asked.

"No," I replied. "I just wanted to drop this in the trunk."

I popped the trunk open with my key, then dropped the iPad into my bag there and shut it.

"Shall we?"

I offered her my arm and she slipped her hand into the crook of my elbow. We set out toward the sidewalk and moved to the front of the buildings along the street. She was quiet, so I wasn't sure what was on her mind, but didn't want to speak until we were a little more alone. It only took a couple of minutes to get to Joe's, and we stepped inside to see that the place was pretty full.

"Two?" the hostess asked.

"Yes," I replied. "In a booth toward the back, if you have it."

"Let me see," she said, looking at her map on the podium. "I've got this one," she said, pointing it out on the map.

"What do you think?" I asked Anna.

"Sure," she replied, and was subdued.

"This way," the hostess said as she grabbed a couple of menus and silverware and walked toward the back of the dining area.

We followed along and once we were seated, she let us

know our waitress would be by to ask for drink orders and to let us know what the specials were.

"So," I began, but our waitress showed up with a couple of glasses of water and asked, "Can I get you something to start with?"

"I'm good with water," Anna said.

"Same," I offered.

She told us the specials, and then left us to peruse the menus.

"You were saying?" she asked once the waitress was gone.

"Oh," I replied, having lost my train of thought. "I wanted to see what you thought of the story."

"It was really a good chapter," she said. "I just don't know where you'll go."

"I should have kept my iPad," I said, kicking myself for the oversight. "It has the whole manuscript of what I've got so far. I'd love for you to read it and tell me what you think."

"That seems like it would be a little invasive," she replied. "Like reading your diary or something. I would feel like I was snooping by reading it early."

"Tell me what your favorite book of mine is," I said.

"I really like the first one in the Officers of Solstice series," she replied. "I had to get another copy because I lost the one I had."

"So," I said. "You liked that whole series? Or just the first one?"

"Oh, no," she replied. "I loved the whole series. It's just been a few years since I read it and I didn't know where my copy was, so just picked up another one a few weeks ago. Thinking I need to pick up the rest of them, too."

"I probably have copies," I said.

"It's no problem," she said. "I like supporting the bookstore."

"Don't they pay you?"

"Yeah," she replied. "And I could take a discount on the books I buy, but I have plenty of money and don't work because of that, so I always pay full price."

"I don't know anyone who would pay full price if they didn't have to," I said.

"Have you decided?" the waitress asked, and I realized that we hadn't even taken the time to look at the menu.

"Can I get a chicken Caesar salad?" she asked.

"That sounds good," I remarked. "I'd like the same."

"Dinner size or side size?"

"Dinner size for me," I said.

"Me, too," she offered.

"Great," the waitress said. "I'll bring them out shortly."

Once she was gone, I asked, "How long have you worked at the bookstore?"

"I just started a few weeks ago," she said. "I needed something to keep me busy."

"Do you like it?"

"I love it," she said. "I mean, what's not to love? I get to spend the day around books, helping others find just the right story for them, and watch them fall in love with that story. It's super fun to have someone come back and tell me they loved the book I suggested."

"Sounds like you've found the right fit for yourself," I said.

"I really think I have," she replied, and the smile on her face told me everything I needed to know about that subject.

"Here you go," the waitress said as she set two salads onto the table. "Cracked pepper?"

"No thanks," Anna said.

"None for me, either," I said.

"Enjoy," the waitress said, then went off to help other patrons.

"Salute," I said.

"Slainte," she replied.

We began our meal in companionable silence and I thought up how to ask her to read the rest of my story and tell me what she thought. From everything I'd learned about her today, she seemed like the perfect person to give me honest feedback on my work. I needed someone to do that for me, someone to fill that void Suzie left. I wasn't ready to replace my wife, but there were some things I needed help with. This was one area that I felt Anna could help.

Chapter 10

Anna

Dinner was nice, and not at all what I expected. We talked about his work, how he hadn't had anyone to read his work since his wife died, which, that was a horrible thing to learn. He was actually doing pretty good considering it'd only been half a year since she'd died. I don't know if I'd have been that put together if I'd lost my life partner. Then again, I hadn't found anyone who I wanted to be a life partner, so I guess I couldn't say for sure.

He told me she had been the one to read his work as he was writing it, give him feedback, ask him questions, keep him honest. When he asked if I would be willing to do that for him, I was a little uncomfortable. I mean, we'd just met, basically, and he didn't know me from Adam. Why he thought I would be good at it was beyond me.

But, the more we talked, the more open I became to the idea. I mean, it wasn't like it was dating, it was a work thing. He said he'd pay me to be his beta reader, whatever that was, but I'd declined the money. If he was going to allow me the privilege of reading his work before it was released, that was payment enough.

The walk back to the car was nice, and we exchanged phone numbers and he said he'd be in touch about getting me the manuscript he had. He offered to drive me home, since I didn't have a car, but I told him I preferred to walk. Felt like he had done enough for me today.

By the time I was in my cottage, I could feel the day catching up to me. It had been taxing, mentally, and I was prepared for that. The physical exhaustion, and sore muscles, were something that I wasn't ready for. I started the water in my tub, letting it fill with warmth and the aroma of lavender from the bath bomb I'd dropped in. Undressing, I was glad I had not been scheduled for the next day, and planned to sleep in and just spend the whole day in pajamas reading.

Soaking in the warm water, I let it wash away everything that was on my mind, relaxing and letting it all go. By the time the water began to cool, I was ready to climb into bed and sleep, and I did just that. No alarm, no lights, just the warmth of the bath and the crisp, cool feel of the sheets.

When I woke, I stretched and felt things pop, but nothing uncomfortably. It was sunny this morning, and I looked forward to a hot cup of coffee to begin my day. After taking care of my morning routine in the bathroom, I turned the pot on in the kitchen and grabbed my phone.

Thanks for dinner. Send me your email address and I'll send you this manuscript.

The text was surprising, in that I hadn't expected to get one. Sure, we got along well, and the conversation was nice, but I hadn't really expected him to follow through with a text, especially so soon.

I responded and sent him my email. Then followed it up with another text.

I am not very responsive on emails, though, just so you know. I'll try to read it quickly so you don't have to wait for me.

Pouring my coffee, I pulled out my chocolate creamer from the cupboard and poured some in. I liked mochas, and this was nearly as good, but without the milk to add more calories than I needed. My phone pinged again, then once more.

No rush on the reading. Do it at your leisure. I really look forward to hearing what you think so far, and whether you have any ideas on where you think it will go. Enjoy.

Not only was the text there, but I saw there was an email as well. I went to the table with my coffee and opened my laptop, powering it up and signing in. When everything was booted up, I opened my email and found the one he'd sent. Attached was a PDF that I opened. Just as he'd said, the whole thing was there. I started and realized when I'd reached the end of the document that I'd shut out the entire world. Looking down at the time in the corner of my screen, I realized I'd been sitting there for three hours. I hadn't even taken a drink of my coffee, I was so engrossed in the story.

I hit reply on the email it came in and responded.

I read the whole thing. I didn't intend to, but I got so into it that it couldn't stop. It's wonderful, interesting, and I have a few questions.

I added my questions about the plot points that didn't make sense to me, then thought better of it and decided to just send the first part. I didn't want to make him uncomfortable or make him answer a bunch of questions from some random stranger, so just sent it off with the note that I liked it.

Taking my cup, I stuck it in the microwave and pressed the quick start to let it heat back up. It wouldn't be the best cup of coffee, but I'd had worse. I pulled some bread out of the bread box and stuck a couple of pieces into the toaster, then pulled out some jam and a spoon and set them on the table. The microwave buzzed, and just as I took my first sip the toast popped. I buttered the toast and took it with my cup to the table. There was an email from Bryan and I opened it up.

I'd love to know your questions. Was anything confusing? Did it flow well? These are all things that will make my story better.

Seems like he really did want to know what I thought, so I typed up all my questions, and the few things that I absolutely loved, and sent it off. I was like a school girl with her first crush, waiting for a response to my text. But that couldn't be it. There was an attraction between us, sure, but it was more business than personal. I had to believe that, because if I thought it was personal, then it might lead to sex, and I couldn't let that happen. At least not for quite a while.

Chapter 11
Bryan

It had been three months since I first really met Anna, and in that time, we had grown closer and closer. She hadn't seen me since the signing in the store, all our communication had been either via text, email, or the occasional phone call. I hadn't wanted her to know about the cancer, but she called me and I couldn't hide the fact that I was sick any longer.

"It's cancer," I said.

"Oh, no," she said, and the sadness was clear in her voice. "How long have you known?"

"I found out a couple of months ago," I replied. "I'm taking some meds, and surgery is scheduled for next week."

"Do you have someone to take care of you when you come home?"

"Dr. Robinson didn't think I would need anyone," I lied.

The doctor had said it would be best if I could find someone who could stay with me while I was recovering from the surgery. There would be lifting restrictions and things that I wouldn't be able to do for myself. But I didn't want to put that burden on anyone, so I just figured I'd struggle my way through.

"You should probably have someone with you," she said. "I mean, I can stay, if you want."

The offer was hesitant, but genuine.

"Are you sure?" I asked, though I wasn't sure why I was asking. Was this something I was willing to do? Could I allow this woman into my home, into my life, in such an intimate way?

"I'm sure I can take time off from the bookstore," she said.

"Oh," I began, but she interrupted.

"No," she was firm. "I'll call Mal right now and tell her that I am going to be staying with a friend who is recovering from surgery, that it was unexpected, and to make sure that it would be all right. I'll call you right back."

She disconnected before I could even get a word out. She was a force, that was for sure. I wondered if she'd let them know it was me that she would be staying with. If she did, would I be okay with that? I had to think about it, and finally came to the decision that if they found out, I would live with it.

I turned back to my laptop, trying to figure out where I was in the story when the phone rang again. I answered it without looking.

"Hello," I said.

"Mr. Walker," the woman on the other end said. "I am Penny from Dr. Robinson's office. I wanted to get your pre-op check in taken care of if you have time."

"Sure," I said.

It only took about five minutes to answer all of her questions and get my testing set up for tomorrow morning. There were a few things they had to do before I could have surgery, just to make sure I'd survive, I guess. They were non-invasive, save the blood draw, but that was negligible. By the time I was off with her I had lost my train of thought again and headed to the kitchen to see if I could find something that I could eat on the restrictive diet they'd given me.

Cheese sandwich in hand, I sat back down at my computer and saw that I'd missed a call from Anna. She left a voicemail, so I pushed the play button to listen.

Hey, it's me. I talked to Mal and she said it was fine to take as much time as I needed to help my friend. I didn't tell her it was you, wasn't sure if you wanted that info out. I also had to check in with my lawyer to make sure this was something that was allowed. Don't worry, I don't have a lawyer for anything nefarious, I promise. We can talk about it later. Give me a call when you get a minute.

That was unexpected. I knew she said she didn't have to work, but wasn't sure exactly why she didn't. Now that I knew she had a lawyer, things might be different. How do you ask that question? I mean, do you just come out and ask? Or is there some sort of finesse that is required when asking about the reasoning behind someone having an attorney on retainer? I guess there was only one way I was going to find out, so I picked up the phone and called her back.

"Hello," she answered.

"Hey," I said. "It's Bryan."

"You get my message?"

"Yeah," I said. "I gotta ask..."

"Let's talk about it in person," she said. "It's kind of a long and complicated story. Do you mind if I come over?"

"Why don't I come and get you," I suggested.

"I'll just call an Uber," she said.

"No need for that," I replied.

"It's fine," she said. "I just need the address."

I gave her my address and she said she'd text me when she left so I'd know when to expect her. The town was small enough that she could have walked it, but it was still big enough to make that walk take longer than was practical. I got the text just a few minutes later, and she said she should be here shortly. I finished my sandwich and took the plate into the kitchen just as I heard a car pull up. I opened the door before she had a chance to knock.

"Oh," she said, hand raised.

"Sorry," I replied, opening it wide for her to come in. "I heard the car, so thought I'd open before you got her."

"That driver was a bit off," she said stepping past me. "Most drivers I get are great, but this guy seemed, I don't know, just off."

"This is why I wanted to come get you," I said. "Then you wouldn't have to deal with strange drivers."

"It's fine," she waved the comment off. "I took self defense classes when I was in school, and have kept up with online videos to stay sharp. I think I should be able to take care of myself."

"Didn't think you couldn't," I replied, leading the way to my study. "Just looking out for a friend is all."

"I appreciate it," she said. "Wow!"

Her eyes were wide when we stepped into my office. She took in the space, the bookshelves lined with my own books, but also books of friends, as well as my resource materials.

"I don't think I've seen this many books in one place since I left home," she said. "Even then, though, they weren't this organized and neat. This is amazing."

"Yeah," I replied with a smile. "I am pretty proud of my library. It took a lot of work to get where I am, so I like to show it off if possible."

We sat, me behind the desk and her in a chair in front of it.

"Feels like I'm in a doctor's office," she said.

"Suzie always said she felt like she'd been sent to the

principle's office when she sat there," I said. "Something about it feeling like she was in trouble."

"I never went to the principle's office," I said. "Occupational hazard of having a father who pays a large sum of money to the school."

"Money can change things," I replied.

"You probably want to know why I have a lawyer," she said. It wasn't a question, so I just nodded and allowed her to continue. "I got into some trouble when I was a freshman in college," she continued. "Well, the troubled behavior started before that, but I was always under daddy's roof until I went away to college. Even when I was at boarding school, he was still very active in my life.

"Anyway," she continued, and I could tell she was a bit nervous. "I was caught in a fraternity overnight after a party. I didn't get drunk, didn't do drugs, just wanted to stay with all the boys. By that, I mean I wanted to sleep with them. I know it's a horrible thing, but it was my vice. The one thing I could do that daddy couldn't control. That is, until the dean found out and let my dad know what was up. That was when he decided that I needed some consequences for my actions."

"Was anything you did illegal?"

"Technically, no," she replied. "I mean, staying overnight was against the school rules, as well as against the fraternity's policy, but according to law, no."

"So, then, what was the lawyer for?"

"There was a boy who was at the frat party that got into some really bad something," she said. "Not really sure what it was, but he got hurt, and ended up spilling the beans about my round robin meetings with the boys. The cops thought I was drunk under age and there were some issues of some of the boys there being under the legal limit and drinking. The cops thought it was rape, even though I told them I was there willingly. It was a big deal and my father was worried that I'd end up in real trouble if I kept on going the way I was, so he decided to send me to a rehab place."

"I thought you said you weren't doing drugs," I said.

"It's not that type of rehab," she offered. "Let's just say it was more a convent than an actual rehab facility. Daddy thought it would keep my mind off boys and give me a little more focus on my studies."

"Did it work?"

"Not exactly," she replied. "It kept me away from boys, but my mind still went there."

"Why are you telling me this?" I asked.

"Because I want to be up front with you," she said. "If I'm going to spend time in your home, taking care of you, I need you to know what my struggles are. I wouldn't feel right if you didn't know my history. That's why I wanted to check with my attorney, see if he could see any downside to me staying with you."

"What did he tell you?"

"To do exactly what I'm doing," she said. "Make sure you were aware of my faults and were comfortable with me staying. I'm not planning on trying anything. Won't accost you in your sleep or anything."

"Thanks," I said, a little taken aback. "I guess I appreciate your honesty."

"Kinda awkward, huh?"

"Just a little," I said.

"So," she continued. "Now that we have that ridiculousness out of the way, let's talk logistics."

Just like that, she swung the conversation back to something that we both knew had to happen. My need for someone to stay with me, and her need to help without the extra stuff. Honestly, it wasn't as awkward as I thought it would be.

I told her the day of the surgery, when I would be at the hospital, and when I'd be coming home. She'd told me she didn't have a license, but could definitely offer an Uber or whatever I needed, and would be willing to ride along with me to ensure my safety. All in all, it was a very productive afternoon, and left me feeling like we had this under control.

"Have you written more?" she asked when all the business and logistics were taken care of.

"Unfortunately, no," I replied. "Though, I hadn't expected to."

"Why not?"

"My brain's been fuzzy lately," I explained. "I think that with all the stress leading up to the surgery, it's shut the creative side down and has gone into focus on recovery."

"That's good," she said. "I mean, it sucks that you aren't writing, but at least you're looking beyond the surgery."

"I guess you're right," I agreed. "Hadn't looked at it that way. Just focused on the fact that the words weren't coming."

"They will," she said. "You said this happened after Suzie died, too, right?"

"It did," I replied.

"So," she offered. "Seems to me, when you're in the middle of it, the words stop. But once you're on the other side and on the road to recovery, they come back."

"I definitely need someone like you in my life," I said.

"Really?"

"You are encouraging," I explained. "You know just what to say to push me further, yet comfort me where I am. I appreciate that."

"Glad to be of service," she said. "So, you want me to ride with you to the hospital on Monday?"

"You don't have to do that," I said.

"It's no trouble at all," she replied. "Might make you laugh before you go under the knife. That would be a good thing, right?"

"It would," I said.

"Great," she replied. "What time should I be here?"

We worked times and then she was off, back to her cottage. I booted up the computer and realized that I wanted to write. It had been a while since that feeling came over me, so I set out to do just that.

Chapter 12

Anna

Helping Bryan after his surgery was exactly what I'd really been looking for. I mean, the bookstore job was great, and it got me out there and working, but caring for him, in his home, making his meals and making sure he was comfortable. Getting him to his appointments after the surgery. All of it was what I felt I was meant to do. You always hear about people finding their calling, and that's what this felt like.

I would be lying if I said I wasn't attracted to him. But it was more than anything I'd ever felt towards any other boy. No, Bryan was a man, and he treated me as an equal. Not once was there anything that was outside of the bounds of a normal friendship, and I really appreciated that about him.

"What's for dinner?" he asked.

"Chicken alfredo," I replied. "Unless you want something different."

"That's perfect," he replied.

It had been six weeks since his surgery, and while he didn't really need my help much, the chemo was taking its toll on him and my being here was just as much an emotional help as the physical one had been when he first came home after surgery.

"You see the doctor tomorrow, right?" I asked.

"Yep," he said. "Hoping she'll let me do some lifting."

"You don't need to do that," I argued. "That's what I'm here for.”

“But I don’t want to continue to take advantage of you,” he said.

“I could leave any time I wanted,” I countered. “I’m not a prisoner. Besides, I really like taking care of you. I feel like it’s given me a better purpose for my life.”

“Really?”

“Really,” I replied.

“I thought that’s what the bookstore was supposed to do,” he said.

“It did,” I replied. “It led me to you.”

He looked at me then, and I could see the wheels turning in his head.

“What?” I finally asked after I couldn’t take it any longer.

“That whole ‘you complete me’ phrase is running through my head,” he said.

“Okay,” I said, drawing the word out.

“Not like that,” he corrected. “Well, not exactly.”

“Hang on,” I said, sitting down. This was definitely not a conversation to be had while standing. “Okay,” I continued. “What are you thinking?”

We’d spent a lot of time together, and we’d learned how to communicate with each other really well. One thing we knew was that we had to process thoughts, sometimes out loud, and eventually we’d get to where we were going. Not once had one of these conversations complicated our relationship as friends, but that one phrase made me nervous.

“Suzie,” he began. “She was my everything. We met in college when she showed me up at a reading. I was never the best author in our relationship, and I knew it. But she never wanted to put her work out there where people could criticize it. Our writing relationship was symbiotic, in that she’d read what I wrote and tell me how it could be better. You do the same thing, which is remarkable. To find someone who fills that role in my life once was a miracle. The fact that I found two people who have the same…"

He stopped, unsure of himself. "I get it," I said, letting him off the hook for trying to find the right word. That was one of the things that was so hard to watch with him. Between the surgery and the chemo, his brain wasn't working like it used to, and finding words to express his feelings would frustrate him to no end. As long as I understood the gist of what he was getting at, he let it go.

"Anyway," he continued. "The fact that you have the same eye for detail within the written word is beyond amazing. I know it might sound weird, but would you be interested in actually working for me in that capacity?"

"Like, as your proofreader or something?"

"To begin with, yeah," he said. "I like you, Anna. You are growing on me, and not in a bad way. Spending time with you has been a privilege and I would miss you if you left. Do you think you could see yourself working with me on my projects?"

"Aren't I doing that now?"

"Not in any official capacity," he replied.

"Does it have to be official?" I asked.

"Someone has to be paid for this," he said.

"I don't need the money," I reiterated.

"It's not about that," he continued. "I like you, and you are helping me in ways much bigger than just reading my work. You cook, you clean, you change my bandages. All of those things are easily hired out for. The thing is, you keep me company. You listen to my complaints, then help me get over myself and move on. These last six weeks would have been miserable if you weren't here."

"Anyone could have done that," I argued.

"No," he said. "Because what you've done couldn't be paid for as a service. There isn't enough money in the world to pay for what you've done for me. You brought me out of my funk and inspired me to continue writing."

"You were already doing that," I countered. "I didn't do anything."

"Can you just stop," he said. "I'm trying to compliment you, trying to let you know that you have value in just being yourself. It's something I want around me for a while."

"Just friends, though, right?"

Having borne my soul for him before we started on this journey, I needed to make sure that he knew I wasn't going to go there with him. I couldn't fall into that cycle again.

"Business associates and friends," he said. "What do you say?"

It was a curious thing, this feeling I had. Like I was embarking on becoming an adult. I mean, I was an adult, had been for a decade, but I had never really grown up.

"I can do that," I replied.

He smiled, and it was a beautiful thing. Yeah, I could do this.

An Interview with
CARRIE AVERY MORIARTY

When did you start writing and why?

I have always been a storyteller, from before I can remember. I told stories and spoke a different language (not an Earth bound language) when I was about three. Could be from the shock I received by sticking a bobby pin into an outlet, but maybe not. I was convinced I was from Mars. It's pretty fascinating looking back on it. Storytelling has been my outlet for most of my life. I wrote some short stories in grade school (found those recently, boy was that fun). I also created plays and the like with a neighbor that we would either act out with puppets or record on his home video camera (long ago, big and bulky, definitely not as easy as it is today). My first published short story was in 2014 in an anthology that I applied to get into. From there, I've written several under this pen name. I have also branched out to write some stories under a separate pen name as well.

Which authors or books influenced you the most as a writer?

That's like asking someone who their favorite child is. I began reading at a very young age, and was reading chapter books by kindergarten. I think the early books I read had a great impact on me, as they showed me that there were worlds out there that I could explore if I just allowed my imagination to be free. As I've grown older, I have found that many authors draw me in. I think currently, the authors that give me the most inspiration are those who I know personally. I see the "ugly" side of being an author, the work that goes into it and the theft that takes place from unscrupulous publishers and others. But, I also see the joy that readers get from meeting someone they admire. It's amazing the work ethic that many authors have, and to watch them craft a story from nothing, then create the world it resides in, and watch as others fall in love with their characters and want more, has really been an inspiration for me. I have a close friend who is an author and she has pushed me to go outside my comfort zone and work to create a name for myself with both pen names. I'm very inspired to see where my career goes with respect to writing.

Which authors or books had the biggest impact on you as a person?

Honestly, there are a lot of books that I see that can push a person to be better in what they do and who they are. Really, though, the authors that inspire me are the ones who continue to push through, even when they get criticized and put down. The ones who take nothing for granted and keep pushing, simply because they have stories within themselves that the world needs to hear. Authors who struggle with getting their projects done within deadlines and with many other things going on in their lives, those are the ones I look to in order to keep me inspired to keep on pushing forward.

Which of your original twelve Trinity stories are you most pleased with?

Again, which child is my favorite? I think that March was a fun one to write. I had just found out that I was going to become a grandmother for the first time (we have two older grandkids, but they weren't officially part of our family until June of 2019, but my daughter was pregnant). It was fun to play with a world where the children really were our future, that they were the best of us, and that they could transform a world full of hate and fear into something that was so much more. Something that was filled with love and intelligence and the need to be better.

Which of your original twelve Trinity stories did you find the most difficult to write?

The short that was most difficult for me was the one for June. It came to me and I had a great story that took a tragic and terrible turn. I didn't realize it was going to be so dark until I got there. I tried to add more, tried to find a happy in it, but it simply wasn't there. There's a content warning on the short because it deals with mental health and suicide. Honestly, it is probably the darkest story I have ever written. It was extremely heart wrenching to write, and I wanted to find something positive. I guess the only positive that came out of it was that there are some things that cannot be fixed.

What book on writing do you recommend?

On Writing by Stephen King. It starts as a biography of how he got to where he is, but the back half of the book is invaluable. He explains so many thing so easily, and it makes writing seem simple. It isn't, but it gives you the idea that it can be. There are a *ton* of books on writing out there, and many have great pieces, but as the first one to get, I'd highly suggest this one. I have a whole shelf full of books that I use for writing. Some are on the craft, but most are reference books for specific subjects. If you've never written, or if you aren't sure how to craft a story, then this would be where I would point you, at least to begin with.

What advice would you give an unpublished writer?

Read. Honestly, it's the best way to improve your craft. That, and get someone you trust who is pretty good at the written word and have them read your work. Ask them to be honest about how you can improve your work. If all they say is they love your work, then you need to find someone else. Be prepared to hear that your writing sucks, because it will when you first start. Hell, it will when you've been doing it for years, too. There is nothing wrong with that, because you can improve that with practice. Read and write like crazy, as much as you can. And create a space where you can create. It can be anywhere you feel inspired. Oh, and don't just write when you're inspired. It's work, so treat it that way. If you treat it like a job it will give you what you want in return. You can't be like Hemmingway and only write seven words a day. You will get nowhere if you do that. Treat it as if you were working for someone else. Make your boss (you, the one who pushes yourself) cranky and rude and demanding. Make them push you so that you get more words down than you think you can. Eventually, it will become a habit and you'll be able to give the "boss" the finger and tell them that you're doing fine and to back off. Don't give up, either. When someone says you suck, show them that you are improving. When you get bad reviews (because you will), ignore them, or see what you can glean from them, and put it into practice. Just keep at it.

Do you have a "dream project" as a writer? What would it be?

Ultimately, my dream is to become a writer full time. If I can get my series started with my other pen name, I could see it making me enough to give up my day job. I would love to write all the things and then some, but I don't have as much time as I would like because I am not making enough with my writing to give up that office job. I have wanted to be a storyteller for most of my life, and I've done some things to get there, but it's been in the last decade or so that I've really pushed that side of things. I'm getting my name out there, getting a little bit of royalties, and starting to see advancement in my career, but it's still slow going. My goal for 2021 is to complete the short story projects I have on my calendar, then dive into the full length novels that I have planned. If it's possible, I'd love to be able to move to part time with my office job (if my boss will let me) and put more effort into writing. I'd love to "retire" from office work in the next five years, so I have to write to get there.

The original twelve Trinity stories were written in 2019. In 2020 we all experienced a global pandemic. Did the pandemic impact your writing? How?

The pandemic created chaos in my world, just like everyone else. The other thing it did was remove all my creativity. I saw it in many of my author friends as well. So many people were unprepared for working from home, for losing their jobs (my husband was out of work when it started and still is), and for having family around all day every day. It's a struggle for me to get started, and my family is not yet used to me needing space in order to create. It's gotten better as time has gone on, but it still has its issues. I will often be in the middle of a project and one of my family members will begin talking to me. I am working on making sure that they know when I am creating they need to leave me alone. When I was in the office full time, I would have an hour every day to write. I would use my lunch hour to write, and I don't have that now. I still have my lunch break, but I don't have that quiet space to use in order to get into my zone. I've learned a lot during quarantine about what does and does not work for me. I'm hopeful to be more creative in the months to come, and when the world gets back to some semblance of normal, I hope to be ready to tackle bigger projects and get ahead.

Made in the USA
Middletown, DE
08 June 2023

32297618R00215